The Public Library of Nashville and Davidson County

BUFFALO SOLDIERS

buffalo soldiers

robert o'connor

ALFRED A. KNOPF   NEW YORK   1993

F

For Donna, who takes care . . .

. . . and to the memory of
Jacob Solomon Meshibosh
Jack Marsh
Solly

If you know your history
Then you would know where you're coming from.
Then you wouldn't have to ask me
Who the hell I think I am.

I'm just a buffalo soldier
In the heart of America.
I'm just a buffalo soldier
In the war for America.

—BOB MARLEY

When there is peace, the warlike man attacks himself.

—FRIEDRICH NIETZSCHE

BUFFALO SOLDIERS

1

OUTSIDE MANNHEIM, West Germany, you are stationed with the 57th. It is November, and Novembers in Germany remind you of the sadness and despair of a fallen woman. Let us also say we know of your fondness for heroin. You want to get off, and two men in your squad need to shoot up. This is how you do it:

There are three floors to your barracks. You get your main buddy, Stoney, and the two others, Simmons and Cabot. You go to the top floor where there are storage rooms and broom closets. Generally, this is the kind of place to be avoided. It is too quiet here, too lonely, and if the yams catch you napping they might tear you a new asshole just for the hell of it. But with Stoney to protect you, you're not worried.

To Stoney you hand the key. He has taken the padlock from your wall locker and will shut you in a room with the two men. Stoney will hunker down in the next room until you are done. Then you will bang on the wall twice and he will let you out. There is an advantage to this. Should the new Top, Sgt. Lee, come by on a sudden inspection of the barracks, he will pull the doorknobs of each of the sixteen rooms in succession. Sgt. Lee is after your ass and will look in the rooms that surrender their secrets willingly, but he will not look in your room, because that door is locked and your buddy Stoney is next door with the key.

You choose the room at the end of the hall. At forty degrees with a chill in the air that grips you in its fist, you sit with your men in a deserted third-floor room of your barracks and you listen. Outside, you hear trucks rumbling past to the battalion motor pool and, downstairs, the faint sounds of the men in Bravo Company. But close by, there is nothing. No footfalls, no creaking. Just the sound of your men breathing. You can almost hear their hearts.

"Let's get a move on," Simmons says, his voice shaking because he needs it so bad.

"Shut your hole," you say, turning on the flashlight and pointing it around the room. You resolve to do Simmons second. You do this to make him wait, make him sweat, make him beg. To make him want it more than anything else in the world. To make him understand his place in this world.

The room is full of mattresses and lockers and the metal superstructures of bunk beds. They are piled with typical Army neatness: corners squared to present a broad, flat face to whoever is interested in looking at them. But they do not interest you. Nobody but a freshly minted newbie bunks double anymore.

Satisfied, you take your kit from a small pouch you store on the inside of your pants, pillowed against your scrotum. You take out the Glad bag with the goods and put it to the left, next to your foot. You must remember not to move your foot. You take the spoon from your mess kit. And you take out your gold-plated Varick lighter, which held level with your navel can shoot up a flame that would singe the stubble on your chin.

You crack the bag and tap the small brown granules into the spoon. It is only from the Turk, you know, that you can get base to make scag of this strength and quality. You hand the spoon to Cabot and put down the bag. At the end of this, after everyone has had a taste, you will close the show by taking the Varick and having it melt the ragged ends of the Glad bag. It occurs to you that you could do an ad for this. Seals scag in, keeps moisture out. Household tips for heroin use.

You look at the wolflike face of Simmons. In the near dark, his eyes glow with need. "What kinda ordnance we talking?" you ask.

Simmons pulls out two syringes.

"They good?" you ask.

"Twenty-one gauge," Simmons says.

"What else?" you ask.

Simmons pulls out a liter of distilled water and a small bag of sterilized cotton swabs.

"Looking sharp," you say.

Simmons and Cabot are clerks in the dispensary, and can smuggle things out as long as they don't push too hard and strain the system. So, each time, he and Cabot will use new syringes and then sell them to somebody less fortunate.

You break open one of the syringes and draw the distilled water directly from the liter, then squirt it into the spoon, which Simmons is holding. Next, you spark the Varick and start cooking. When the crystals turn to liquid you drop in one of the cotton swabs to filter. You watch as the brown mixture soaks into the swab. You place the tip of the needle deep into the swab to draw the scag through the cotton. Then you force the air bubbles out, pointing the needle up in the air like a tiny missile. Simmons takes out the adjustable tourniquet with Velcro clasps and begins to tie off.

"Cabot first," you say. The moon face of Cabot lights up, happy about getting bumped to the front of the line.

"The fuck you say," Simmons says, but you know he's weak. You hear it in his voice and you can see it in his arms, which are covered with small angry indentations that might be mistaken for mosquito bites. But it is November, the mosquitoes are long gone, and he is due for an attitude overhaul, which in fact is why you are doing this.

"Cabot first," you say.

"Shit. Hurry up," Simmons says. He rips off the tourniquet and slaps it on Cabot's arm. There is no problem here. Cabot's vein swells immediately. On older addicts the ropes burn out, but Cabot is a recent recruit to the pharmacological front: his veins show nothing but a few freckles of penetration. You do him, and then get back to Simmons, who by now is twitching and sweating. Simmons ties himself off and you make the hit, pressing the plunger partway down, but when you pull back you get nothing.

"Shit," Simmons says, "you missed."

"Nothing left to hit," you say, but you want to raise the flag of blood. Coming up empty means you've missed the vein and hit meat. You pull out, tie off the other arm, and look for fresh territory. Not many landing zones left on the arms of Simmons. You find a space, get in, and pull back the plunger. This time you hoist the flag. This is good. Now you're in business.

"Bull's-eye," Simmons says.

You push the plunger down a little more, giving Simmons a rush. Then you pull it back up, milking blood from the vein and mixing it with the scag in the syringe to make gravy. You wait a moment, letting Simmons get a feel for it. His eyes focus on the bloody mixture in the syringe. It contains everything: Hope, Love, Life, Death. Taking it is like having the greatest pussy in the world, ice-cream-cone soft, customized for your cock. You know you can't give him too long because the fix will cool, clogging the needle. You push the plunger down all the way and send the gravy through his body, giving him a second, better rush. He sinks back, and you finish by taking the syringe out of his arm. You notice the room no longer seems so cold.

Now that you are done with them, you wait a few minutes till they've vomited and their breathing has steadied. Their eyes have pinned and they have that walking-dead look, but they're not dead. It is important that you take this precaution. There was the case of Parsons McCovey, whom you were not careful with. A week ago you brought him to this same room and then left him to do himself because you had other business to attend to. This lack of care had very unfortunate consequences for Parsons McCovey. After you left, something happened to the Parson, although precisely what remains in doubt. There are two possibilities. One, that the Parson, who was afraid of being caught with the works, might have thought he heard the Top coming down the hall, and he decided to go to the roof. It was night, so no one would see him. He stuffed his shit down his pants and then went to the window and opened it. Though you were not present, you know how this is done. You have done it yourself at times. The windows are tall and narrow, and to get out you lean backward, hanging on with your fingertips to the edges of the frame. There would be no light in the room and no light outside save the few pips that appear around the base. In the night, silhouetted only by darkness, it can seem as if you are climbing in the middle of nowhere. The key is to ignore this sensation, gathering your legs underneath you as you slide your fingers along the sides of the window frame while straightening your body. Once standing, it is an easy matter to reach the roof. Your legs fly out from the windowsill, and your combat boots act as a counterweight as you pull up with your arms. That is the simple part. The disadvantage is climbing back down when you've got your head up your ass. If the Parson had been a fireman or had climbed trees as a youth, this might have been natural, and there would have been no trouble. But for Parsons McCovey these things were not natural, and on his way down, when he kicked out to find the windowsill, he just kept going.

That's the first possibility. The second possibility is one you do not like to think about. The second is that someone who did not like Parsons McCovey came upon him. There are many such personnel in the battalion. Whoever it was might have realized that this was a unique opportunity. Whoever it was could have picked up Parsons McCovey and thrown him out the window so that he fell down the three stories and landed on his fucked-up head and died.

"How you guys doing?" you ask.

Simmons is nodding out and cannot lift his head.

Cabot looks up for a moment and then lifts his hand. He jerks his thumb into an aviator's salute. "All systems go," he mumbles.

Satisfied that Simmons and Cabot have hit their stride, you take a dose, but through the nose. You have a feeling you're trying to tell yourself something, though what it is has not become apparent. But if there is one rule you do follow, it is to stay on top of things. Keep your act under control. To give in to the needle means that sooner or later your ticket will get punched. You hope to emerge from this tour in one piece, and so you will stay off the needle, although naturally you will indulge now and again purely for medicinal purposes. So you take yours off your shaving mirror, which is almost as good. You kick your kit as you relax, but everything in it is closed, and nothing is lost.

2

Yꞎour job on the base is battalion clerk. You are directly under the command of Lt. Colonel Berman, and you write memos, reports, requisitions, proposals, as well as the monthly battalion newsletter. You are also in charge of sending a personal note home to the family of each man who dies. For a peacetime ordnance battalion, this happens with a frequency that on your more lucid days can seem alarming.

When you get to your desk at 0810 hours you see a memo from the Criminal Investigation Division stating that Parsons McCovey's body is being shipped home. Tagged and bagged. This is unexpectedly quick work on their part, and that means you have to get on the ball. Colonel Berman will green light the note out and you should get to it immediately, but right now you are flying instruments-only. Heavy brain fog is rolling in, with expected clearing by midmorning.

Until your system purges the shit from last night, you will take care of some of the routine forms in order to warm up. You light up your third Camel of the day and start collating LOGREPS for Colonel Berman's okay. These simple forms are ideal, because this morning you are able to follow only simple instructions. LOGREPS are Logistical Reports from units, which translate into requests for supplies that Colonel Berman must fill. You are not a combat battalion: your mission is to maintain and support both active and reserve forces. Should there be a global alert and war declared, within thirty-six hours there will be reserve forces hustling from the United States to Europe in c-130s. It is your battalion's job to give each of them an m-16 and a box lunch and pack them off to the front.

At 0905 you see Colonel Berman walking across the parking lot and you stub your cigarette out and dump the ashes and butts into the wastepaper basket. From a distance, the Colonel seems young, a freshly starched movie colonel played by Henry Fonda or Gary Cooper, with springy step while the cameras roll. But as he gets closer he seems to age, and when he finally enters the office the movie impression goes by the wayside. In the movie of his life, Colonel Berman is only a character actor.

The Colonel is coming straight from his Breakfast Club meeting. The Breakfast Club consists of sitting with General Lancaster over Danish and coffee in the dining facility and discussing whatever it is the General wants to discuss that day. All the senior officers attend. Getting ahead on the career fast track involves guessing what the General will be eating in order to gain conversational position with a minimum of fuss. From the white powder at the edge of Colonel Berman's mouth, you see that he has gone for the sugar donuts. You guess raspberry filled. The General has a weakness for sugar donuts, so this is a high-percentage move.

"Good morning, Elwood. Open a window, will you. The air's really thick in here." He stares hard at you. The Colonel knows you've been smoking, a habit he detests and has strict orders about, but since you have gotten rid of the evidence there is nothing he can do.

"Good morning, sir," you say, opening a window. "Must be the night-duty guys had a smoke." The air outside is cold and hits you like a slap.

"What do we have here?" Colonel Berman asks, ignoring the lie. He has picked up the mail and radio-traffic transmissions and is rifling through them.

"The Criminal Investigation Division sent a memo about PFC McCovey," you say, returning to your desk. "They're releasing the body to his parents stateside."

"He was my driver for a while, you know," Colonel Berman says. As he begins to read the memo, the lines on his face deepen. "He was about the worst driver in the whole damn Army."

"Yes sir," you say. Parsons McCovey had cracked up Colonel Berman's command jeep twice and his personal vehicle once. The Parson, you reflect, drove much the way he lived.

"It also says here that they're continuing the McCovey investigation," he says. All last week, you remember, the 57th was crawling with CID. They interviewed members of the Parson's platoon, dusted his quarters, and checked angles of fall trajectory. But what you mainly remember was the chalk outline of the Parson's body, which rinsed away in the rain.

"What does that mean, sir?" Actually, the meaning of the memo is absolutely clear to you.

"What this means is they are keeping the file open on McCovey," Colonel Berman says. He purses his lips so the lines of his face pull together into a point. "I think I can see what's coming. What we need to do is initiate a preemptive strike."

"Sir?" you ask.

"We need to hit hard on the memo front as to the accidental nature of the McCovey incident. I want you to get right on the bereavement detail."

"Already on it, sir," you say.

"Outstanding," Colonel Berman says. "When you're

done, buzz in. I want to get it off immediately. This McCovey business has taken a hell of a lot of time and it's bound to use up more."

"Yes sir," you say. From this you understand that Colonel Berman has other festivities planned for Parsons McCovey, whose death is turning into a pain in the ass for all concerned.

Colonel Berman has kept you as his clerk simply because there is nobody better at writing letters of bereavement. Since you came on, he has been sent letters by several congressmen who have heard of his thoughtfulness from constituents.

In your state it takes you an hour and the rest of your pack of Camels to cook up a reasonable draft of the note:

4th Battalion, 57th Division, VII Corps
Mannheim, USAREUR

Dear Mr. and Mrs. McCovey:

I regret the death of your son immensely. He was personally known to me and there was nobody in the battalion I would have trusted more with my life. In him were resplendent the virtues of honor and loyalty to his country and God that are what keep our civilization together. He fell off the rooftop of his barracks while trying to make technical repairs on the antennae that we use to guard against the enemy. He died, though not in combat, still in the line of duty, and he had his country uppermost in his mind.

> My deepest regrets,
> Lt. Colonel William C. Berman, Commanding

All that you have written about Parsons McCovey is, of course, a lie, but writing bereavement letters is an art and art always appeals to the higher orders of truth. The first higher truth is that a top-drawer bereavement letter makes Colonel Berman look good in front of the hometown crowd, and another is that making Colonel Berman look good guarantees you plenty of slack. You type up the note, dump your ashtray, and buzz Colonel Berman on the intercom.

"Talk to me, Elwood," he says.

"I have the first draft of the bereavement letter, sir."

"In here," he says. Colonel Berman is brusque with you—he believes it is important to maintain distance between officers and enlisted men—but in fact he regards you as his right hand.

You go into the office and hand the Colonel the letter. As he reads it, you stand and look around the room. His desk is cleared and a map is spread across it; you recognize the serpentine shape of Vietnam. On the bulletin board are pictures of this same country from the air, and from the air it looks beautiful. In fact, this is what the Top, who was deep in the shit for three tours, has told you. He has told you it was the most beautiful place in the world to blow the fuck out of.

But the map on the desk is not just for decoration. It is research for an article Colonel Berman is writing on Dien Bien Phu. Each month Colonel Berman receives military journals that analyze past battles, current troop administrative strategies, and various nuclear and nonnuclear scenarios. It is part of your job to sift through these journals and maintain them in a library along with any notes he has made. Xeroxes of articles of interest are circulated to the junior officers, and occasionally brought to the attention of General Lancaster during a Breakfast Club pause. Just last week Colonel Berman had you Xerox an intriguing feature comparing the Maginot Line with forward-based US Army strategy, and the week before you copied off a piece on tank repair under the stress of tactical nuclear attack. Until you began to work for Colonel Berman, you had never imagined that war required so much in the way of reading.

"You kept this one a little short, Elwood," Colonel Berman says, picking up a pencil and marking something on the letter.

"It's better not to get lost in details, sir," you say. Since your head is still somewhat foggy from last night, details are not your strong point. To counteract the scag you've taken a Dexedrine and megadoses of coffee, but this has made you tense rather than alert. There is no solution, however, other than simply waiting. You wait for the Glide to kick in, and with it the possibility of an MPC, which is the moment that you live for. An MPC is the Moment of Perfect Clarity that comes when you go from wading in pain to the muddy bank of not caring. When you have an MPC, the world becomes sure; you move in the groove, and for as long as you are in it, the nature of the universe becomes abundantly clear. Until then, you will suffer from what feels like the beginnings of the flu but is in reality a heroin hangover.

"This thing about technical repairs on the rooftop antennae could be just what we're looking for," Colonel Berman says.

"I tried to think what Parsons McCovey might be doing on the roof," you say. You would kill for another cigarette.

"I also like the touch about trusting him with my life. I don't believe we've used that before."

"That's a new wrinkle, sir," you say.

"Hullo, here's something," he says, scratching with his pencil on the paper. "I don't like this word 'resplendent.' It's not the kind of word you use about a soldier. Let's say we replace 'resplendent' with—how about 'contained.' " He writes this down in the margin of the letter and reads through the sentence again. "Yes, that's much better. 'In him were contained the virtues of honor and loyalty,' etc. That's a better read all around."

Colonel Berman always has one objection to each letter or memo you write, if only as a way to keep them under his control.

Reading the letter over again, Colonel Berman pulls at the small fold of flesh under his chin, a characteristic gesture. You have noticed that when the Colonel meets someone for the first time, he presses his tongue against the roof of his mouth in order to correct the sag. He has explained this trick to you and suggested that you employ it in order to grant your chin a more military character. The difficulty, you have discovered, is in trying to speak with your tongue in this position. Somehow Colonel Berman has mastered this, too.

"Yes. Scratch 'resplendent.' Make sure that word doesn't leave this base."

He hands the corrected letter back to you. "As soon as that's done, we can run it by Meyer."

Lt. Meyer is Colonel Berman's version of Grant's captain. According to Army legend, during the Civil War General Grant employed on his staff the simplest son-of-a-bitch he could find. Every order Grant gave he first tried out on this captain; if he could understand it, Grant then knew that no one in the entire Union Army could fail to. "Everyone," Colonel Berman has told you, "needs a Grant's captain in his life." While this sounds like a good idea, you have observed that in Colonel Berman's battalion Lt. Meyer is used in precisely the opposite capacity. Whenever Colonel Berman gives Meyer a memo or report that he readily understands, the Colonel revises it until it is beyond his reach.

"Very good, sir," you say. With a head two sizes too big for your skull, life is a series of holding actions, of escape and evasion, harassment and interdiction. You need to lay down a suppressing fire. One quick snort would do. Hair of the scag that bit you.

"I have something else I want to ask you, Elwood," Colonel Berman says, a hint of pride creeping into his voice.

You know he is referring to the Vietnam article. "What's this one about, sir?"

"Is that supposed to be funny, Elwood?" Colonel Berman asks.

"No sir, not at all." In your pain you have forgotten that Colonel Berman is sensitive to the fact that three of his articles have already been rejected for publication. It is your destiny to somehow in each conversation say the one thing that gets Colonel Berman mad, to find the one word or phrase that strikes a discordant note. It is a kind of hidden talent, one you cannot entirely control.

"It's called 'Dien Bien Phu: Logistics and Defeat,' " Colonel Berman says, his finger tracing the slim waist of Vietnam on the map. "I think the reason those goddamn shitbirds didn't like my last article was because it wasn't a famous battle."

"That could be true, sir," you say, thinking positively. Colonel Berman, you know, is an admirer of positive thinking, especially when a suggestion of his comes under scrutiny.

"Dien Bien Phu, everybody knows what that was," Colonel Berman says, his voice changing to its normal mode of logistical evangelism. "You know what that was, don't you, Elwood?"

"Oh, yes sir," you say. "The French defeat that eventually got us into the war."

"Exactly," Colonel Berman says. "If the fucking French had been able to hold the line, we would've stayed out of Vietnam. That's one of the selling points of my article.

The reason why none of my other Vietnam articles have been published is because who wants to go back and fight Vietnam?"

"Absolutely nobody, sir," you say, but then you remember this is not what the Top has told you. What the Top has told you is that everybody and his brother wants to go back and fight Vietnam. This time, he said, it would be a much better war.

"But if we take it from the French point of view—you know what I discovered?" Colonel Berman asks. Colonel Berman has small hands, which tend to windmill uncontrollably when he gets excited.

"What's that, sir?"

"I found a way the French could win." By now, the hands are in full flight, creating a shadow dance on the map of Vietnam.

"How so, sir?" you ask.

"Look at this." He moves to a card table on the side and pulls off a sheet. In the middle of the table is a big valley surrounded by hills. It reminds you of one of those science projects in grammar school when someone built a volcano and mixed baking soda and water. The baking soda would bubble in a pale imitation of lava, and the class would cheer.

Colonel Berman's hands circle the valley like choppers as he describes the battle. Attacks merge with counterattacks, and are succeeded by more attacks. Your head begins to swim as you remember the pictures from the journals of dead soldiers littering the floor of the valley. In black and white, their bodies looked like bundled leaves.

"By then both sides were fucking exhausted," Colonel Berman says. "And that's where the battle becomes interesting to the goddamned professional soldier."

You have noticed that Colonel Berman coarsens his language when talking to enlisted personnel such as yourself.

This habit began after one of the military journals ran an article about the "Patton Principle." Evidently, a little rough language made the enlisted men believe in the humanity of their commanding officers.

"It was a pure and simple siege after that," Colonel Berman says. "All the French needed were better logistics. They didn't have enough supplies to last. The air force had to drop food and medical goods so they wouldn't be starved out. It was pitiful."

"Yes sir." Cigarettes, you reflect, are one of the world's great civilizing influences. Lack of smoke is the root of much evil.

"It just goes to show the value of good logistics. Without paper to push the war, we'd be in some sorry shit."

You are not surprised that this is Colonel Berman's solution to bungled warfare. Colonel Berman, in fact, has a genius for requisition. During his one tour of duty in Vietnam, the Army recognized this unique talent and put him in charge of logistics for Saigon HQ. Several of his decorations, in fact, issued from this eventful period of ordering supplies. Casualties were low; morale high. It was, you suspect, among the happiest times in his life.

Even now, Colonel Berman's base in Germany is by far the most splendid ordnance base in all of Europe. Its sprawling barracks are laid on poured cement, subcontracted to a top German construction firm through Hermann Dietz, otherwise known as Hermann the German. Hermann is your resident rad, a comrade-in-arms who worships the money you walk on, and is used by your battalion as a community liaison. Through Hermann, the Colonel has either upgraded or rebuilt whole sections of the base, which now boasts two field houses, sixteen bowling lanes, clay and cement tennis courts, a roller-skating rink, a shopping-mall-size Post Exchange, and a duplex movie house—all the Army amenities. There are heavy antiterrorist bunkers on the perimeter, and Colonel Berman has resurfaced the access roads to Mannheim and the surrounding autobahns for swift transportation of the reserve troops to the front. It is his dream someday to be placed in charge of a base in the States, perhaps with his own nuclear silo. There would be improvements there that one can only dream of.

"Want to hear more?" Colonel Berman asks.

"Of course, sir," you say.

As Colonel Berman talks you feel the Glide beginning to kick in, crossing happily into the MPC Zone. It is as if the world has suddenly been set right, perfectly calibrated to your mood and person. Your worry over cigarettes is a thing of the past.

"You see any problems with this article?" Colonel Berman asks, finally drawing to a conclusion. "I want your honest opinion, Elwood."

"No sir," you say. "I think that's a great idea."

"Not even a single quibble?" Colonel Berman says. "Talk to me, Elwood. There's got to be something."

You clear your throat. "Well, there was one thing, sir."

"What's that?"

"I think they might be looking for more on the actual battle."

"Is that so, Elwood," Colonel Berman says softly, and you begin to feel yourself sinking into some deep shit. Even the fact of the Glide doesn't help.

"But I do think the logistical end has never been properly recognized as decisive," you say, summoning up what brain cells you have left and backpedaling as quickly as possible.

"Logistics is the backbone of the Army," Colonel Berman says. "Everyone wants killings, melodrama. That's not where the real war is. The real war is on paper. I've often said that in this man's Army, power comes from the point of your pencil." He picks up the Parsons McCovey letter from his desk and waves it. "Do you read me loud and clear?"

"Yes sir," you say. You decide to adhere to one of the maxims you live by: when in a hole, quit digging.

However, Colonel Berman has begun staring at the Parsons McCovey letter, and seems to require something more.

"I was just thinking that the audience may not have your field experience, sir, that's all," you say. Then you decide to go for a flanking maneuver. "The way you're handling the Parsons McCovey business demonstrates how experienced leadership can make the best of a bad situation."

"About this McCovey thing—I can't get it off my mind," Colonel Berman says, going for the bait. "I have the OERs coming up and there's no way an ongoing investigation will help my chances." The OERs are the annual Officer Efficiency Reports, and Colonel Berman is looking down the barrel on this one. He has been passed over for promotion once already, and a low score on the OERs means that in the up-or-out scheme of the Army he will be out.

"I understand, sir," you say, relieved that you have moved on to Colonel Berman's career prospects, his all-consuming passion. "What do you think we should do?" What you suspect is that Parsons McCovey will not rest in peace until every ounce of public-relations juice has been drained from him.

"I think it's time to open another front," Colonel Berman says, pulling on his chin and staring at the letter. "It's a shooting war now."

"Yes sir," you say. The MPC Zone has long ago been left behind. You're back to escape and evasion, rearguard holding action.

"Here's what we do," Colonel Berman says. "We build the next battalion newsletter around McCovey. A regular memorial. Get some photos, put a collage together for a pullout centerfold. We hustle up some quotes from the other men in his squad and platoon. Get his company commander, platoon leader, and first sergeant in there. I'll contribute the memorial preface. We'll do the whole thing up and send it out to his grieving family."

"That could be a bit difficult, sir," you say.

"Why is that?"

"Well, for one thing, there aren't that many pictures of Private McCovey."

"We have the platoon and company photos, right?" Colonel Berman says. "And we can requisition his Basic Training and Advanced Individual pictures. We blow them up, plus whatever else you can scrounge—maybe he wandered in while somebody else was taking a snapshot—and we have ourselves a first-rate centerfold. That, plus the quotes. Go for the sorrowful stuff—you know, *nostalgic*."

"That might be the other problem, sir," you say. "Private McCovey was not well liked among the men." There was a reason for this. Parsons McCovey was a bully, a prick, a finalist in the Motherfucker all-arounds. It is a comment on the limitations of your social situation that he was also one of your best friends. "Getting the proper kind of quotes from the men could be difficult."

"I know that," Colonel Berman says. "I knew McCovey, remember? But let me tell you something: there's nothing that improves a man's character faster than dying. If you have to, find some personnel who didn't know him well and quote *them*. But I want you to get right on this. Give this top priority. I can hold the fort here."

"Yes sir," you say. You understand that you are free for the rest of the day to pursue leads. The first lead, you decide, is to find Stoney and get your head straightened out.

3

T RACKING STONEY can be problematic. Today Stoney
is pulling guard duty at one of the perimeter posts.
You set out to check the guardhouses, keeping to
the well-traveled areas. Traveling around the base alone is
inadvisable, of course, even during daylight hours. A yam
pack can come upon you, and explain the painful impor-
tance of numerical superiority. Even the officers know to
stay away from certain sections. But you are careful, keeping
out of the shadows, places where a shakedown is likely. If
Stoney was along, you wouldn't have to sweat.

Stoney is your best buddy, and there could be nobody
better. You have discovered that for census purposes the
Army can be divided into two types of people: the Motherfuckers and the Motherfucked. It is your earnest desire
to keep yourself from landing among the latter. You do this
with great charm, extreme caution, and the liberal distri-
bution of pharmaceuticals. These are investments in friend-
ship and loyalty, whose dividend is the good graces of
Motherfuckers like Stoney and, in his time, Parsons Mc-
Covey.

You take a person like Stoney or Parsons McCovey. They
are *the* Motherfuckers of all those presently in the Army.
Motherfuckers are this way because they long ago determined that it was to their advantage not to care. They are
to be treated as a force of nature; and as with any force of

extreme and indiscriminate proportions, provisions must be set aside. Parsons McCovey did not care. Eventually, of course, a Motherfucker like the Parson, because he cannot or will not foresee the consequences of his actions, will end up among the Motherfucked. This is for certain. Your philosophical inquiries have revealed that such a fate is, like old age, an eventuality.

But the Parson is history; Stoney is current events. It is to your advantage to buddy up with as many Motherfuckers as possible. Generally, this is not a difficult task. One of your talents, perhaps the only one, is for tuning people. Considering the situation you find yourself in, we can see how this would have its uses. Searching out a radio station hidden on the FM dial, you keep twisting the knob, coming closer and closer, until you reach the precise frequency they're broadcasting from.

As part of your capacity for tuning in, when necessary you are able to put personnel in touch with others who can transform stolen goods such as stereo equipment, televisions, and clothing into cash and pharmaceuticals. In chemical terms, you are a catalyst: you make things happen. The most important of these items, of course, is the pharmaceuticals. While it may be true that music soothes the savage breast, in your experience a couple grains of high grade can work wonders on the disposition.

There are three things to remember about Stoney: he's black, he's big, and he hates whites. However, he is willing to overlook your whitehood because of your peculiar abilities. For instance, you have done him favors in your capacity as battalion clerk. As it happens, Stoney does not like to march. This is not unusual—no one likes to march—but only you could have written a form detailing his previous leg injury that gives him a special dispensation against marching or standing in formation. There is no previous leg injury, naturally, but because of this, Stoney regards you as a magician. You have taken away the power of the officers with a mere scribble of the pen. No officer, not Colonel Berman or even General Lancaster, can tell Stoney to march unless you were to go on full alert. Motherfuckers, you have learned, are rather simple in their perceptions. This has less to do with the level of their education than with their view of the world, which consists of polar extremes. These extremes are Life and Death. This worldview allows them to be Motherfuckers as long as they are alive, but also leads them inevitably to the moment of their Motherfuckeddom. Just ask the Parson.

Because of all you have done for him, Stoney is your Motherfucker. He reinforces your image as a player and keeps some of the more militant yams off your case. He is also, now that the Parson is gone, the closest thing you have to a friend.

By the time you get to the last checkpoint you are freezing to death, and you have figured out that Stoney has paid someone to take his guard duty and is back in the barracks in a card game. Stoney in a card game is one of the crosses you have to bear. Stoney is hopeless at cards, but like most hopeless players he maintains an infinite optimism. You have explained to him that poker is not a game of chance but of risk management—a concept that escapes Stoney, mostly because it is your money he is risking.

Back at the barracks you hear some chatter from the third floor, and take a moment to light a Camel before going up. For one thing, if Stoney's not up there you could jeopardize yourself by parachuting in on the yams. But Stoney has hidden what you need, and you don't know where to find it. You used to hide the shit in your room or someplace close, but since the Top has been sniffing around, you let Stoney handle security. So he has the key. You could wait for him to come back, but your desire for clearheadedness outweighs your general concern for safety.

On the third floor, you walk past several doors before one opens, and a big yam, Kirchfield, steps out. From a glance you can see he's fucked up and mean.

"We got a problem," he says in a conversational tone. He moves in front of you, and one of his big hands drops on the side of your neck. "Nobody called ahead with your invite." He increases his hold on your neck, and you can feel him cutting into the circulation of your carotid artery.

"Don't go nuclear on me, Kirchfield," you say. You blow smoke directly in his face. "It's Elwood. I've got to talk to Stoney."

"You're the El-man?" Kirchfield says. "Stoney's buddy?" He releases his hold on your neck and pats you twice.

You can feel your flesh heat up, as if he's given you a hickey, but you breathe a sigh of relief that he's not quite as fucked up as you thought. "That's right."

"Stoney's your number one, right?"

"He helps out."

"Parsons McCovey was your number two, am I right?"

"You got something you want to say about the Parson?" you ask. "I'm looking for quotes for the newsletter."

"Sure, I got something to say," Kirchfield says, swaying slightly on the balls of his feet. "Now that the Parson's out of the picture, you got room for someone else? Maybe you could use a guy ain't dead."

Kirchfield, you understand, is not a man easily overcome by sentiment.

"I'm out of that shit," you say. "Operation's folded. Everyone's rotating out." This is true, as far as it goes. There hasn't been a major operation in six weeks, and the word is the Turk has been having some problems of a *Polizei* nature. So the deal is to lay low for a while, wait until things sort themselves. Meanwhile, if you don't re-up, you are scheduled in less than three months for a ticket back to the States. This time you might actually do it—fold your cards and cash your chips—but odds are you'll sign on for another hitch. The Army's for shit, but the world, you have learned, is even worse. At least with the Army you have some things under control. Besides, you're due to make E-5, sergeant's pay, and once you make sergeant, you can corner the market on slack. Slack by the wholesale. But you're still thinking about it. You want to make Colonel Berman worry he'll have to train somebody else to man the memo front. Recruitment levels being what they are, it's hard to find someone to play the skill positions. Unless he gives you some incentives, you might just declare free agency and shop the league.

You take a step to pass him, but Kirchfield moves in front of you again. Nothing can put a crimp in your karma faster than mixing it up with Kirchfield. He is soda-machine solid, built like Stoney but wider. One on one, you're not sure who would have the edge. Your head is pounding from last night, and you think that too much of your life is spent having conversations with people like Kirchfield. He breathes on you and you feel your stomach begin to move.

"That's not what I hear," Kirchfield says. "I hear the show's starting up again. You know, I could take Stoney out, nothing flat."

"Never happen," you say, with more confidence than you feel. "But that's not the way to get ahead. Who're you with, Sgt. Saad?" Sgt. Saad runs the Top Hat, the NCO club on base, and through careful fiscal management and a liberal attitude toward inventory, he is able to make a tidy profit. Kirchfield is his low-level muscle, and occasionally bounces for him at the club. Right now he's keeping the poker game from being raided, a minor precaution, but with the Top on the warpath a necessary one.

"That's right," Kirchfield says. "He's the boss."

"The important thing is to stick with the program," you say. "You get places faster you drive in your own lane."

Kirchfield still doesn't let you pass.

You inhale deeply on your Camel, which warms you slightly, and then come to a decision. "Look, how about something to smooth the wrinkles?" you ask. Now is the time to do a little advance public-relations work. Win hearts and minds. The heart and mind of a carnivore like Kirchfield can always come in handy.

"Could be," Kirchfield says, relaxing a little, and you think you have him. It is time to tune the station on him, adjusting the dial until you hear the tweeters and the woofers.

"I can help," you say.

"How much?" Kirchfield says.

"We can work something out," you say. You've got him loud and clear, no static in the back. "You stick with Saad, your credit's A-1."

"When?" asks Kirchfield, finally stepping aside.

"I'll be in touch," you say.

As you walk down the hallway, you think of why you are going to carry Kirchfield. You do not like him and you do not trust him. The scag, however, is an investment, seed money for the future. At some point in that uncertain future, perhaps Kirchfield won't kill you. The one thing you have discovered about the future is that sooner or later everything comes to pass.

At the last room, you hear a lot of noise. You knock twice and someone calls, "Who is it?"

"Elwood," you say. "Gotta talk to Stoney."

The door opens. The room is dark, filled with smoke, and it takes your eyes a moment to adjust. All the players around the table are black, the kind of thing that normally would make you feel insecure. When you first came to Germany there were a number of instances when, after payday, a bunch of yams approached you for a charitable contribution. Their charity, as you quickly discovered, was for the Ministry of Getting Fucked Up, a noble ministry with a highly motivated clergy. At the time, being inexperienced, you refused to make a contribution. Under the principle of God helps those who help themselves, they held you down, punched the piss out of you, and cleaned out your pay.

However, we know science teaches that for every action there is an equal and opposite reaction. Stoney is your reaction. He is the balancing factor in this equation by virtue of being the largest Motherfucker in this part of the world. After you hooked up with him, you visited each of the former charity workers and explained in terms they would understand the sudden change in your position. One of them you held out a third-floor window by his ankles until he understood the error of his ways. Since then, Stoney's contributions to your peace of mind and physical well-being cannot be overestimated.

Right now, Stoney is sitting with no chips in front of him, looking as if he has been shot in the heart. He has never been able to master the poker face.

Sgt. Saad, who you predict will have raked in his first million by the time he pulls the pin at twenty, is glad to see you. He's got his finger into everything, and is a regular customer at the wholesale level.

"El," he says. "Your man here is down a hundred fifty. You staking him?"

"He's good for it." You nod to Stoney. Predictably, he stays in the hand trying to bluff with a low two pair, fooling nobody and losing seventy-five more. When the hand is over, he throws down his cards and gets up.

"It's a pleasure doing business with you," Sgt. Saad says. "I'll send somebody by later pick up your contribution."

Stoney waves his hand and follows you out of the room. You walk together past Kirchfield, who makes his fingers into a gun to strafe you as you go by.

"What's up?" Stoney's big black face is gray and dull from all the weed smoked. Not that Stoney had any of it. This is just a contact high, which is, you figure, one of the reasons he's such a poker fiend. Stoney is religious about not touching shit because it might ruin him and endanger his amateur standing. The body beautiful. This also makes him the perfect associate to hold your stuff.

"Got to check on inventory for a second," you say as you walk down the stairs.

"Problem with you white guys," Stoney says. "No self-control. A little more attention to the principle of delayed gratification. That's where it's at."

"Save it," you say. It is Stoney's habit to keep you up-to-date on the continuing decline of the white race.

"Once you guys had us by the balls," Stoney says. "But you got weak. Pretty soon, we be putting you up on blocks, checking you teeth. Maybe you grays even make a comeback on the fighting end of things. Years of breeding."

"Can't wait for that day," you say.

"Until then, I'm carrying you," Stoney says.

"Thanks," you say.

Stoney smiles. "So, you need a little pick-me-up. Army C rations?"

"That's the ticket," you say.

"We got to go to the Field House."

"We're not holding close to home anymore?" you ask.

"Heat's turned up," Stoney says. "I saw the Top cruising

your crib last night after you come down. I got to keep you grays educated as to the dangers of the world, El."

"I appreciate it," you say.

"Black man's burden," Stoney says.

The Top, you figure, is getting out of hand and perhaps someone should put him straight. You long for the good old days of your previous first sergeant, who lived off base and was happy not to know from shit. Since he left, the barracks have become a very uncool place to be.

You cross the field, and the air gives you a chill. A formation of A-10 Warthogs passes overhead, buzzing the base, drowning out any conversation. Your whole head is throbbing, but prospects of relief are good.

At the Field House, Stoney leads you into the pool area, which is Olympic size and has separate racing and diving pools. This is one of the few improvements on base not requisitioned during Colonel Berman's command. In preparation for the 1972 Olympics, the Army put in the pools so Mark Spitz could get in his laps, do his flip turns. Nothing came of it, of course, the Olympics being just an excuse dreamed up by a battalion clerk into creative requisition. You admire the guy's memoranda chops, and you know it was one of the first big paydays for Hermann the German, who probably sent his whole rad family through college on the money.

The big number you're working on, which you do not think will pass muster in your lifetime, is the eighteen-hole golf course, situated on base, a little bit of Augusta on the Rhine. Fight off the Red Menace with a nine iron. Occasionally, when you want a favor done, you break out the blueprints of that requisition boondoggle and let Hermann the German salivate. What he'd skim off the landscaping alone would set up his act for early retirement, Swiss-chalet style.

Meanwhile, the pool area stands as a monument to memoranda dreams come true, and who are you to rain on someone's requisition parade. The base has been left with electronically timed starter's blocks, and a diving pool that has two one-meter boards, a three-meter board, and a ten-meter platform, which from below looks as if it presses right against the heating ducts.

The wet tiles are slick as blood, and the heated chlorine air makes your head feel like it's in a box, which starts a coughing fit.

"Jesus Christ, don't fucking die on me," Stoney says.

There are some people there for the midday swim, mostly dependents of the officers. You watch them steam back and forth, their arms pulling at the water. One of them waves to you, and calls. Your name echoes as if underwater. Making eye contact, you realize it is Colonel Berman's wife.

"Shit," you say to Stoney. "This'll be a minute."

"Meet you in the locker room," he says.

You walk over to her lane on the end. She has popped her goggles off and is spitting in them, and then dunks them in the water.

"Yes, Mrs. Berman," you say.

"Hand me a towel," she says. "These things leak." Her eyes are rimmed from the goggles and she looks like a raccoon. Her shit is piled by the side of the pool. Duffel, two towels, pair of sandals. You pick up one of the towels and hand it to her. Nice monogrammed terry cloth, wedding-present material. She's in the Mrs. Colonel mode, you realize, the Command Presence. Lock heels and salute. Officers' wives get that way. It's as if they were commissioned along with their husbands.

"How can I help you?" you ask.

"Where are you off to in such a hurry, Specialist Elwood?" the Mrs. Colonel asks. Just like being in her husband's presence, the Mrs. Colonel makes you wish for a cigarette.

"Did the Colonel tell you about the newsletter?" you ask.

"I was the one who planted the idea with him," she says, and you believe her. The Mrs. Colonel is the brains of the family, the behind-the-scenes strategist. If she ever divorced him, Colonel Berman would sink without a trace.

"Do you have anything you want to say about McCovey that could help us out?" you ask.

Her face is absolutely still as she says, "We are all shocked and dismayed at his tragic ending. When a good man is cut down, we have all taken a blow." This all sounds familiar, and then you realize it is because you wrote it. It is the phrase the Colonel complimented you on the last time he had to express his sincere condolences.

"Thank you," you say. "This will be a big help on the McCovey end."

The Mrs. Colonel examines the backs of her hands, rubbing her fingers together, which have wrinkled from the water. "Did you ever have grubs, Elwood?" the Mrs. Colonel asks.

"Ma'am?"

"Grubs, son. The larvae of insects." The Mrs. Colonel is from the South, and when she is at her most obscure her voice returns to its roots. "One of the greatest embarrassments of my life came when I threw a party at home in South Carolina to show off my gardens. The guests came, and as I was running my hands through the topsoil, a grub appeared. And then more and more, until I realized the entire garden was inhabited by grubs."

You are at the beginning, you understand, of one of the Mrs. Colonel's gardening parables.

"Grubs are insidious creatures, getting into the soil, devouring the nutrients meant for your garden."

Gardening, for the Mrs. Colonel, is a way of expressing her vaulting ambition, and the Mrs. Colonel has a gardening parable for every occasion. She is the *Farmer's Almanac* of the 57th.

"One grub—if you let it get out of hand, there'll be more. Once you see the enemy, you go after it with everything you have."

"This is about Parsons McCovey," you say, finally beginning to grasp the point of the parable.

"The way to eradicate grubs," she says, nodding with pleasure, "is to go in hand to hand. Get down in the dirt and pull them out." Her voice begins to take on a lower tone here, as if she is imagining herself in combat with the grubs at this very moment.

"And Parsons McCovey is a grub," you say, trying to grasp the pattern here. The Mrs. Colonel likes you to translate the parable as she goes along, if only to make sure you're listening.

"Parsons McCovey is only the first of the grubs," she says.

"What are we going to do?"

"I'd like to throw a party for the Division, get everything out in the open, all of the problems we've been having lately, put those grubs to rest. By bringing fresh air and light to bear, we can prevent the problems from obscuring the Colonel's strengths."

"Do you have a guest list?"

"In my locker," she says. She ducks under the lane and walks to the ladder, a ship making steady progress to port. As she emerges from the water, you take her hand and then wrap a towel around her shoulders. It is good policy, you understand, to keep in the Mrs. Colonel's good graces. If Colonel Berman is a sheep in wolf's clothing, the Mrs. Colonel is the real thing. The last battalion clerk got shitcanned for not knowing who wore the silver oak leaves in the family.

"I want a different motif this time," she says. The last party's standard Oktoberfest theme did not go over big with the Army crowd.

"I'll work on it," you say.

"Something martial, I should think," the Mrs. Colonel says.

"Certainly." With the Christmas season coming up, the Mrs. Colonel wants to get her parties on a wartime footing. You walk with her to the locker-room door and she disappears inside. You turn and look around. In the separate diving pool you see a girl making her way up the ladder to the ten-meter platform. You have never seen someone try the ten-meter except on TV. The girl is going slow, making deliberate progress, one rung at a time.

She's now at the edge, looking over, and you realize why she's been going so slowly. As she swings her arms up, you realize that one arm is not whole. It's cut off just below the elbow, a dowel perched on her shoulder. Then she dives, twisting in the air, hanging for a moment of grace before plunging into the water. After she bobs to the surface, she swims sidestroke to the ladder and pulls herself out with the same deliberate care.

Mrs. Berman appears from the locker room with a piece of paper in her hand. "It's sad, isn't it?" the Mrs. Colonel says, looking at the girl.

"Who is she?" you ask.

"I believe she is the daughter of your new first sergeant," the Mrs. Colonel says. "Stunted at the beginning of her growth. Just when she should be beginning to bloom into womanhood."

The Mrs. Colonel hands the paper to you, and you open it to look at the names. The usual list of 57th suspects, as well as some HQ types from Heidelberg. When the Bermans give a party, they plan it like the Normandy invasion. Your job is to make sure it doesn't turn into the Bay of Pigs.

"This shouldn't present a problem," you say, tucking the list into your front pocket. The girl is climbing the ladder again, making her painful progress.

"You will get back to me on the motif," the Mrs. Colonel says, smiling, the Parsons McCovey grub talk already history.

"You bet." You reflect that if the Colonel had the set of brass ones on his wife, he'd be on the Joint Chiefs by now.

The girl is approaching the edge of the platform again. There's a moment of hesitation, a hitch in her stride, and then she dives, her legs piked in front of her as she flips forward two and a half times and hits the water, making a big splash.

"Something else, Specialist Elwood?" Mrs. Berman says, climbing down the ladder into her lane.

You realize you have been dismissed. "No ma'am," you say.

The girl pops up again and she watches you as the Mrs. Colonel turns and pushes off. You fold one of the Mrs. Colonel's towels and put it under your arm as you walk out of the pool area. You feel the girl's eyes on your back as you go through the door.

Stoney is waiting on the other side, shaking his head. "No sale on the Mrs. Berm, huh?"

"You know who that girl is on the platform?" you ask. "The one who was checking me out?"

"All you white folks look the same," Stoney says.

"Get this," you say. "She's the Top's kid."

"Ain't half bad for a chick with one arm," Stoney says.

"Maybe the Top gnawed it off."

"You're a cold one, Elwood," Stoney says. "Totally fucking cold." Coldness, you know, is a quality esteemed by the Motherfucker set.

"How do you like the new acquisition?" you ask, holding up the towel.

"You don't got enough shit happening—you want more," Stoney says.

"Just keeping my hand in."

"Someday, Elwood, somebody chop your hand off too," Stoney says.

You hold up your left hand. "That's why I carry me a spare," you say. "Let's go get the shit."

Stoney checks ahead for anything in stripes and then comes back. "You'll never guess where I got it stashed," he says.

He leads you to the equipment room and takes a key off his neckchain and hands it to you. "This one's yours," he says. "Don't lose it." Part of Stoney's Motherfucker status derives from the fact that he runs the battalion karate and boxing clubs and fights in the monthly smokers. As part of your work as a clerk, you have gotten Colonel Berman to sign authorizations for all types of karate and boxing shit, and Stoney stores it in this room. There are heavy bags, pads, body armor, karate clothing, and mats, even a regulation-size ring.

Stoney turns on the light. "Where you think?"

"Beats me," you say.

"That's the trouble with the white race, Elwood. Lazy, shiftless, rather be doing drugs than taking on challenges. You're going downhill. Only a matter of time."

"I'm in need, man."

"What would you do without me?" Stoney asks, going over to the heavy bag. He puts his hand in a rip in the side and rummages around, finally pulling out a coffee can of drugs, along with some of the stuffing from the bag.

You open the can and pick out the Kodak film container. You do a couple lines off your field shaving mirror. The coke settles you down, takes the edge off the scag shakes.

"Looking solid, El," he says.

You're feeling everything hooking up again. "Going from seventeen to thirty-three and a third."

"You boys do like your music," Stoney says.

You take some money out of your wallet and lay it on Stoney for his gambling. "I got to ask you something," you say.

"What's that?"

"What do you know about Kirchfield? I'm thinking about moving him onto the payroll."

Stoney rests his bulk against the stacked mats. As your brain kicks out of neutral, you consider that with the Parson gone and the Top gearing up, you may need somebody to back your play. This somebody must be already half in the game and of the card-carrying Motherfucker variety. No assembly required. Stoney is one, your main man, and Kirchfield, with some serious grooming, could be your number two. The one thing you have learned from the Parson episode is that it is better not to place all your Motherfuckers in one basket.

"Take the brother on," Stoney says.

"I think we should keep an eye on him, though."

"What for?"

"I don't trust him, and he wants your spot."

"You thinking of giving it to him?" Stoney asks.

"You know better," you say.

"What I know is don't turn my back on you."

"Always a good policy," you say. "All I'm saying is, be careful. I think he might be crazy."

Stoney looks at his callused hands and then around at the queer indoor light of the equipment room. The place reeks of bodies, liniment, and humidity. "Not as crazy as us," he says. "What you looking at for the rest of the day?"

"I'm looking for quotes on Parsons McCovey. Anything you want to say?"

"He was a fuckhead and a scumbag," Stoney says evenly.

"Tell me something I don't know," you say.

4

ENTAL WEATHER REPORT remains partly cloudy,
with a possibility of severe storms. Relative paranoia index very high and climbing. The bad thing
about mixing scag with cocaine is that running yourself
AC/DC sometimes creates thunderclouds in your brain.

As you drive along the autobahn, parked vans wink their
lights. It is a signal, you know, for the weary traveler to stop
and get his ashes hauled. Prostitution is legal in Germany,
and enterprising working girls park their vans alongside the
road and flash their lights at oncoming traffic to indicate
they're willing to jump that commuter trade. They'll stuff
the cash in the glove compartment and then spread it for
you in the back of the van, a rad innovation on the American
drive-thru.

But tonight you're not in the mood for any anonymous
curbside service. You want to go to the Stop 'n' Pop, where
the merchandise is guaranteed and there are Grade A
women at PX prices. You head off the exit ramp and begin
following the usual weekend invasion routes. Traffic lights
in Germany are the same configuration as in the States with
one important variation: instead of only one side going yellow, both sides do, in order to let the stopped traffic know
they are going to have to start up again. That leads, naturally, to drivers playing German chicken by anticipating the
shift from red to yellow to green. When the light turns

yellow, they shoot across the intersection. You avoid this, because the traffic lights have small cameras mounted on them that photograph cars that jump the gun; you then receive a copy of the photograph in the mail along with the ticket. It is a typical rad enforcement policy, you understand. Rather than change their light system, they'd rather start some new surveillance scam, get more people under their thumb.

You finally pull up to the Stop 'n' Pop, which is situated right on the Rhine across the street from the police station. It looks for all the world like a big school building, built in the brownish brick that all the rad community buildings are made of. Here to stay. The building is good-looking, neat in the German way, maybe eight to ten years old, dominating the stucco jobs that surround it. Everything in Germany is either very old or very new, you have noticed, as if the land itself had swallowed the residue of the war. But you know it is the rads themselves who have learned how dangerous it is to cast back, to talk of that time. You suspect this isn't due to embarrassment, anything so ordinary as that, but because if they began talking about it, they would discover something worse: that they miss it.

You lock the car but take everything with you. The Stop 'n' Pop isn't like one of the Combat Zone establishments back home. Once in high school and a couple of times in the Army you tried those out, the requisite punching of your ticket, but those were seedy, illegal affairs. There, you put your wallet in the glove compartment and put your spare money in your shoe before you ungirded your loins and went into battle. Back in the world, the oldest profession, not having kept up with the latest techniques in human resource management, simply does not attract quality personnel. You had the impression you could catch a disease walking in the door. But the Stop 'n' Pop is a classy joint.

All the girls are inspected monthly and before they shift into high gear they flash a blue card, certifying that they've had their shots and inspections.

Dietrich, the rad at the front desk, looks more like a librarian than a motel clerk who orchestrates the musical beds.

"Colonel Berman," he says, shaking your hand.

"At ease," you say to Dietrich, in your best Colonel Berman voice. "Hard day at the battalion this week."

"Well, Colonel," Dietrich says, smiling in his unctuous way, "is there anyone here who interests you?"

The front desk faces out over a room decorated like a Victorian living room. Sumptuous chairs, mirrors, nice wallpaper. There are bookcases along the walls. You can sharpen your mind on the classics while you contemplate getting your tube lubed. Some of the women you recognize from previous excursions, and they smile at you because they know you'll stay overnight, easy pay for an easy lay. But you don't want any of these. The reason isn't only that at Howard Johnson's you don't order vanilla every time, it's that among the many ways to fuck yourself, falling in love with a whore is one of the easiest to see in advance. There aren't any whores with a heart of gold—or perhaps gold is the best unit of measurement, the economic imperative never being far from their minds.

"I'm not in the mood for any of the floor models," you say, fumbling for a cigarette. Dietrich immediately helps out with a light. "Any rookie cards in there?"

Dietrich opens up his card file and begins flipping through. The card catalog contains all the pertinent data on the women in his employ.

Dietrich selects three cards and fans them on the desk. They're all beautiful, which doesn't surprise you. The girls come to Germany, put in two, three years on their backs, save their money, and maybe try to hook up with somebody. A rent-to-own situation.

"Three queens," you say. You pick the one in the middle. "How about her?"

Dietrich picks up the card and scrutinizes it, a jeweler examining a gem for flaws. "You have excellent taste," he says. "Her name is Mireille. The penthouse for overnight, Colonel?"

"That's an affirmative," you say as you place the pile of money on the desk.

You walk through the lobby and then down the carpeted hallway. Single rooms open off the hallway, and most of the doors are ajar, indicating that the girl inside is ready for business. At the end of the hall you go up a stairway to the penthouse, which is really just a private room off the main concourse, luxury boxes for the better paying regulars.

The penthouse is unlocked, and you walk in, taking off your coat as you look around the room. The walls are covered with travel posters: a bullfight in Mexico, the wickedly hooked horns gleaming at the matador's brocade; kickboxers in Thailand, their features an artist's smudge as they leap into each other; a beach in New Zealand; the gardens of the Alhambra; the Wailing Wall of Jerusalem. The idea is to take you out of the state of mind you're in right now—and they do. Girls come from all over the world to end up here with you for a little time, you who have been nowhere and seen nothing, who even when you went to Germany brought your world with you in the form of the Army.

You walk to the window and look out at the boats along the river. The few that you see are already slowing, looking to tie up and rest over, because nothing moves at night. You pull the latch and open the window out, letting in fresh air. You drop your cigarette butt out the window and watch the sparks it throws as it tumbles to the street. You take a deep breath, though what you smell is not the clear November air but the exhaust from the boats and the smell of winter sludge.

There was a time before you came to the Stop 'n' Pop when you believed you had some sort of ass-backward version of the Midas touch: everything you touched turned to shit. There were too many nights waking in some girl's apartment, it didn't matter whether they were pro or amateur, too many nights at CC's on the strip outside the base where you mom-and-popped your scag and at the end of the evening porked the leftover talent. Too many nights when after balling some stranger, you would lie awake, afraid to go to sleep, thinking that you could see all too clearly the many sharp objects in the room and how easily they could penetrate your vitals.

What you have learned is this: every man has a key. This key unlocks some inner sanctum of self that, once penetrated, allows you to understand everything about him. The key is the First Principle, the building block of personality from which all else may be deduced. Once we know this, we can know everything.

The key to Stoney is he has a side kick that would numb a gorilla and a relatively uncluttered idea as to what constitutes a friend.

The key to Colonel Berman is the Mrs. Colonel.

The key to the Parson is that he hasn't got one anymore.

Here is your key: you cannot remember the last time you were unafraid.

Once you have another man's key, you can hold him in the palm of your hand. But once you know your own key, you can never fool yourself for very long. And fooling oneself with practiced regularity, we know, is one essential element of the happy life.

The door opens and a woman steps in, closing it gently behind her. She is wearing a short skirt with a gray jacket, and her dark hair, so wild and loose in the picture, is pulled back into a ponytail.

"You look like a businesswoman," you say.

"I am," she says laughing, and you think you're going to like this one.

"I'm glad you speak English," you say. "What's your name?"

"Mireille," she says. She takes her blue card from her purse and hands it to you. You glance at it and give it back.

"I like your name. Is it a stage name or are you really French?"

"I am French," she says.

"Let's hear it," you say, but you already believe her, even before she begins a demonstration, the words becoming a torrent.

"What did you say?" you ask.

"I asked, what is it you wanted to do?"

"Very businesslike," you say. "I want you to say my name."

"What is it?"

"Colonel Berman," you say. "Now please say it."

"Colonel Berman," she says, elongating the syllables.

"Now I'd like to watch you strip—real slow."

"Okay," she says.

You walk toward her then and take her into your arms, kissing her. She holds back for a moment as you feel the prickly wool under your fingers, but then she gives in, letting your tongue roam with hers. Whores don't like to kiss, you know. They will do anything else with their mouths: blow you and suck you to the edge on the front end of a half 'n' half, stick their tongues up your anus, but they will abstain from the most ordinary of affections. It is as if by keeping one part separate, they can maintain themselves. And what you like to do, naturally, is break that down, and by breaking her down, make her yours, if only for a little while.

You reach behind her neck and slide off the hair tie, and she shakes her dark hair to let it go over her shoulders.

"How is it I can help you, Colonel?" she asks.

"I'd like us to take a shower together. Is that okay?"

She nods and steps back from you and continues getting undressed. You'd pay just for that. You watch her maneuver through the intricacies of buttons as you see sudden flashes of flesh still half-concealed by clothing. She turns from you, draping her jacket over the back of a chair, shedding the blouse, then unzipping the skirt. She leans one foot on the chair as she rolls down the nylons, and you are impressed as always by the unhurried grace of a woman undressing. When she is finished, you strip. Standing on the linoleum scarcely two feet away, you are so close everything feels electric. It seems as if the air between you will suck you forward. Your knees bend, you feel the hair on your chest begin to rise, but you do not touch.

Mireille goes to the bathroom first. You hear her get into the shower, the bleating of water against tile.

"Ready," she calls.

You step in, carefully pushing the plastic liner so that the water will not leak onto the floor of the bathroom, soaking through to the bedroom below. With a woman, even this woman, for a little while you can pretend to be a better person, concerned for the world.

"Can I get around?" you ask. She moves and your bodies just brush, and every part of you is alive. You pick up the shower handle and bring the showerhead close to her skin, massaging her with the water. You prefer the showers in Germany with their hoses and high water pressure. When you come out of a shower in Germany you feel clean.

"Would you like me to piss on you?" she asks politely. "Many men enjoy this."

"It's my whole life," you say. "Go ahead."

You see urine flowing down Mireille's leg, the yellow mingling with the water and swirling around your feet, the distinct animal smell.

She laughs, wiping water from above her eyes and shaking her head so that her hair slaps around. The sound of her laughter soothes you, brings you back into yourself.

"Shampoo?" you ask. She bows her head and you take her in your hands and gently soap her hair, rubbing the creamy fluid into her scalp, moving your hands down the steepness of her neck and onto her shoulders. You rinse her off, and then you soap her back, working your way down the small stirrups of muscle above her buttocks and circling them with your fingers. You work your way down to the bent part of the knee, the cracks in the toes, the heated red soles of her feet.

"Now do me the same," you say.

You feel her educated fingers touring your neck and shoulders, kneading the knots from you, changing the weather report from partly cloudy to a clear and unbroken sky. You are so happy you are almost afraid to breathe.

She works her way down, her hands touching the perimeter of your organs, bringing you alive all over. Every part of you is electric and coming. Your big toe can come, the knobs on your shoulders, your earlobes, the tips of your fingers, your hair.

After you step out of the shower, you dry her hair by hand, pulling the towel through it and then wrapping the towel so she looks like the Queen of Sheba. Her body is slick as a seal.

"Now?" she asks.

"All right," you say.

In the bedroom, you take the Kodak container out of your pants and take a hit of coke. Scag is bad for you—you can't fuck on scag—but things go better with coke. You offer her some, which she accepts, and when she's done you take another hit to get you hard. Then you put the Kodak container right by the bedstand in case you need some middle-inning relief. For perfect pictures, fuck on Kodak.

You begin to touch each other. You explore slowly, discovering each other's bodies. You snake down her body, your tongue circling her nipples, her ribs, and then continuing down until the prickly hairs of her bush are in your mouth. You won't eat her, but you warm her up by finger-fucking her. First one, then two, then three, widening the channel, greasing her up, until you bring her to the edge. Then you stop and reach for the Kodak container again.

"I just need some help down here tonight," you say, feeling your hard-on beginning to soften. You need help down there every night, in fact. The secret of the body is entropy, better sex through chemistry. What you need to do is MIRV your warhead. A dash of coke and it's like renting Superman's cock. Bar of steel.

"Of course," she says. "I will put it on for you."

She drops a few crystals on the tip of your cock and you immediately feel the bloom. She takes the residue and puts it on her tongue and then French-kisses you. You rub against her and your cock comes to life. You've got a hard-on and a half. Like Popeye and his spinach, you and your C ration. The fountain of eternal fucking.

Mireille does not say anything, already gliding with you, and you get your new and improved cock into her, under and in, guiding it up with your hand. Mireille's pussy, you discover, is different from any other woman's. It is as if she has been constructed differently, her body matched to yours. She's low-slung down there, and once you are inside, you

grind her straight up, and then to the side, and then cork-
screw her. And then you can fuck forever. You're so numb
and hard that you feel like this moment could last the rest
of your life.

As you come, your body stiffening in release, you have
another MPC, your mind set straight, target on the cross
hairs. She has your key now, the inevitable and awful knowledge of you.

She is looking away again, out the window, listening to
the riverboats. You want to be able to crawl inside her head.

"Tell me something about yourself," you say. She puts
her hand on your shoulder, and her touch drains off some
of the bad energy, runs it to ground. You begin to feel great
as you both lie naked on the bed, next to each other, staring
up at the ceiling like children. Steam rises from you, a musk.
Now is the time you can think clearly, where you can let
down your guard for that necessary moment. Clarity and
hope are the order of the day.

"When I was a little girl," she says, "I used to think I
was as a bird—do you understand? Build a nest, and when
the season was to end, fly away and never look back. Once
I have visited a place, and I have learned what there is to
learn, I go away."

"Maybe I'll come with you," you say, though you both
know that you're lying. She doesn't say anything to that,
and you like it that she is too polite to tell you that you're
full of shit.

"Is there anyone you love?" you ask.

She touches your face. "Americans," she says. "You have
no past."

"We like it that way," you say. "But I meant any person."

But Mireille doesn't say anything to that, simply looking
away. You light a cigarette and you're at peace, with the
musk rising off you, the whistles from late boats through

the evening stillness. Although you have never said this aloud to anyone, you feel as if you have both been cleansed of the outside world by your shower and lovemaking, as you lie there like an Adam and Eve before the Fall. Everything is new again. And each week you can come back, check out a new Eve.

It is only when you are here in the Stop 'n' Pop that you don't have to be afraid. It is only here, in someone's arms, that you return to some better self, some happier time, when you used to be a real person and had a life recognizable as such.

After Mireille falls asleep, you feel yourself coming down. Relative paranoia index starts climbing, cumulonimbus stacking up. You become afraid again. You reach over and put your hand lightly on her throat, feeling the pulse, the hard windpipe surrounded by lovely muscle. Under your fingers is life, you understand, and you press down lightly, ever so lightly, until the rhythm of her heart is in your hand.

You whisper, "I want to tell you something, Mireille. My real name is Elwood, Ray Elwood."

She stirs and makes a moaning sound. Her hair is damp and hangs together like rope.

"What's my name?" you ask. There is something leaving you, something hollow growing in the pit of your stomach.

"El . . ." she says.

For at least this moment, you have some relief.

5

PORTRAIT OF MEN at war: the infantry is dug deep into the couches and chairs and holds strategic positions on the linoleum. The perimeter has been secured by Sasquatch, while you man the observation post by the windows with Video and Rothfuss. Right now you are on alert status, beverages at port arms.

"See anything?" you ask Sasquatch, a Canadian so dumb he joined the US Army, the only army in the world that can't get enough fights so it goes out and gets into everybody else's. Sasquatch is peering around the door of the dayroom. He stands there for a long moment, then turns.

"All clear," he says, looking at Video, who was the one who called the alert.

"The fuck you want from me?" Video says. "I tawt I taw a puddytat."

You light another Camel and continue holding position by the window, where you can keep an eye out for Sgt. Lee, the puddytat in question. The TV is surrounded, and things are looking very bad for Erica Kane on "All My Children." She is about to climb into the sack with some sleazoid to whom under the best of circumstances she would not give the time of day. The sleazoid, in many ways, reminds you of you. If you were him, you'd cut the drinks-over-dinner crap and get right to the chase, offering her some of your stash. Chemical warfare. Get her disoriented, and she'd give it up in a second. You would have her out of that slinky thing she's wearing and hauling ass to your bunk.

"I don't think nothing's gonna save her now," Video says. Captain Video, who's also a Spec 4, is a TV addict, the commander-in-chief of the television forces. He has even taken classes in German at the base education center so he can watch other channels besides Armed Forces TV. "The woman looks like she's about to hit the sheets."

"Pole into hole," Cabot says, a smile breaking over his great moon face.

"Squash," you say, "I got some good news on the medical front."

Sasquatch comes over, a hopeful look on his ugly face. "You got word from the dick doc?" he asks. Besides being Canadian, Sasquatch's other main feature is that he has a wanger the size of a billy club and it has never been circumcised. Loose, it resembles an enormous pig in a blanket. He frightens the pros at the Stop 'n' Pop, where the joke is that management makes him pay double the meter. This, of course, is untrue. In that establishment one fuck fits all.

"The thing I like about American women," Video says, "the thing I miss—no hair on 'em."

"It's all set up," you say to Sasquatch. "I got the doc, the OR, the anesthesiologist, all lined up. It took a while, though. This is a bigger thing than I thought. I just figured they'd pop you on the table, peel the thing like a banana."

"Check out the pits on Erica Kane," Video says, as she raises an arm to draw the blinds shut in preparation for some lights-out maneuvers with the sleazoid. "Clean as a freaking whistle."

"Squash, you're really gonna go through with it?" Rothfuss asks. Rothfuss is into sportfucking, the horny hobbyist, the Kit Carson of cunt. As such, he maintains a fan's interest in all matters of the male apparatus.

Sasquatch looks somewhat startled that the event he has wished for is actually going to happen. "Can I bum one?" he asks, needing time to think it over.

You pull out a Camel and light it on the end of your own. "Mark it in your date book," you say. "I got you this great doc—he's an obstetrician put himself through school by the ROTC route. The Army's just working him for gynecology and he wants to keep his circumcision arm in shape. He's done a lot of guys."

Eddio, Video's sidekick, clenches his mail in his fist as he comes to the end of the ten-second delay that occurs for any thought in his mind. "I make my woman shave," Eddio says, who has a woman so ugly that you figure she had damn well better shave.

"That's good," Video says. "I say never put up with a woolly woman."

"This dick doc, I bet he never done someone with a rod like the Squash," Rothfuss says thoughtfully.

"Hope you didn't price it by the inch," Cabot says.

"Will it hurt?" Sasquatch asks.

"You just can't fuck till you get the stitches out," you say. "Keep your thing holstered."

"Once he gets his foreskin taken off," Rothfuss says, "the Squash here could become the Babe Ruth of fucking. Go into the history books." Rothfuss, the great singles hitter, has often talked about what he would accomplish on the field of fucking if he carried around a bat like the Squash's.

"What do they do with the foreskin, Elwood?" Cabot asks. "I mean, is it like your tonsils—they put it in a jar?"

"Maybe they'll roll it up, make it into a spare dick," Rothfuss says, "or a flag. Raise that fucker over Washington."

"With the Squash?" you say, blowing smoke in two thin

streams. "The doc is gonna take that thing, mount it above his fucking mantel. I mean, you bag the Squash, he's the twelve-point buck of the dick business."

"How can you smoke these things?" Sasquatch says, coughing on the harsh smoke of the Camel. He remains somewhat dazed over the fate of his massive member.

"Cancer sticks," Rothfuss says. "Coffin nails." He shakes his head and waves away the smoke. "You're killing yourself with them things, El."

"Let's hope so," you say. "And Squash, when you go to the doc, don't forget to bring your dick along."

"On the subject of dicks, remind me of something," Rothfuss says, leaning toward you. "Next time I'm about to get laid, grab me by *my* dick and lead me away."

"This is something I've got to hear," you say to him. You put out your cigarette and think you'll wait till your stomach settles to have another.

"Here is my New Year's resolution which I am starting early," Rothfuss says. "Never again will I take on a woman with a tattoo."

"I hate to hear that," you say. "You're my fucking idol. Talk to you it's like having a wet dream." Fuck it, you think, and tap out another Camel, lighting up. You'll wait till the New Year to start any resolutions.

"Body art," Rothfuss says, shifting uncomfortably on the window ledge. "That's what she called the tattoos."

"What's she cheating on—her fourth husband?" Cabot asks, staring hard at Erica Kane as he goes back to TV. "She must be pretty well cored out by now." Cabot nudges Simmons, who does not take his eyes off the TV screen. Simmons has had his wake-up and his lunchtime, and is now cruising without incident until he gets to his after-dinner shot and then it's good night Irene. Scag, you have noticed, tends to make life regular.

"It's not body art," Rothfuss says to you. "It's a goddamn body billboard that says *This is one fucked-up chick.*"

"I don't see why these shows always got people cheating on their husbands," Sasquatch says, looking nostalgically at his crotch as he moves to the rear door to check for any Sgt. Lee action. "Why can't they just stick to what they've got."

"Because then you got no show," Video says, getting back to TV, the subject of his life. "Or they're all like 'Leave It to Beaver.'"

"I tell you," Cabot says, "I wouldn't mind giving Mrs. Cleaver a pop."

"So we're in the middle of doing it," Rothfuss says to you, "humping and bumping away, and suddenly she stops cold and she says to me, 'You are much too interested in coming.'"

"What did you say then?" you ask.

"I said, 'How about we shut up and get on with the fuck,'" Rothfuss says, "and then she pulls a knife."

"Oh ho, we got liplock," Video says. "Condition hard-on." Erica Kane is into it, tongue-to-tongue combat.

"Go for it!" Eddio shouts out. He flaps his arms around with his mail, nearly hitting you in the head. "Go for it, sucker!"

"Shut the fuck up, Eddio," you say, thinking you have heard enough from Rothfuss. "You're talking about the bimbo I love." Eddio and Sasquatch are your two favorite dumbbells in the Army. They are so dumb they love the Army because it tells them what to do all the time. And when the Army forgets and gives them some free time, you're happy to take up the slack. You have the feeling that if you put your head to their ears, all you would get is a dial tone.

"I'll be honest with you," Rothfuss says, still mulling over his bad experience. You wonder if Rothfuss has ever had a *normal* sexual experience, or if every girl he's met came equipped with whips, thongs, and an assortment of hardware.

"When I saw the blade, my dick shriveled, like a turtle pulling its head in. I don't know if he'll ever come out again. We're talking trauma territory."

"Erica Kane—who needs her," Eddio says. "I got me a good woman of my own."

"A man can dream," you say.

"No he can't," Sasquatch says.

"You in love, Elwood?" Eddio asks with a kind of astonishment, as if he had thought you immune to that particular frailty. You think, for a moment, of Mireille, the deep hollows of her hips where you rested your chin, and the dark hair under her arms that slid so gently into your mouth. A little womanly woolliness, you know, is something you can get used to.

"No," you say, and stub out this cigarette early. Your stomach has seen better days.

"I am," Eddio says. "A man's in love you give him some room. My heart's in my woman."

"Your heart's in your dick like every other fucker in this room," Video says, whose view on life is that it's like TV only not as fulfilling.

Scene switches to some of the old people plotting business maneuvers. You have enough of this shit with Colonel Berman, and so you think about getting some quotes for the Parson.

"Anyone here have anything they want to say about Parsons McCovey?" you ask. "It's for the newsletter."

"Word is, somebody did him," Rothfuss says.

"The word is no shit," you say, trying to ignore the unproductive thinking that comes from dwelling on Possibility

Number Two, the kind of thinking that sends your paranoia levels, already unnaturally high, into the red zone.

"Anything constructive is what I'm asking," you say. "Anybody have pictures?" You decide a little incentive is called for. "I can get three-day passes for pictures. I'll handle the quotes myself."

Eddio and Rothfuss nod and you know Video's holding some photos, so you figure as soon as the official batch arrives, you can make a centerfold spread without much difficulty.

"I'll pick them up later," you say.

"You know what the worst fucking show on TV is?" Video asks. "I'm speaking as a professional here." Video's goal is to be a network broadcaster. He wants to get his break in the Army, become the Walter Cronkite of Armed Forces TV, a dickhead you can trust. One of the things you have noticed about the Army is that except for you, one day everybody is going to be somebody else.

"I give up—what's the worst show on TV?" asks Sasquatch, who's moved away from his post on the Sgt. Lee watch.

"Mission Im-fucking-possible," Video says.

"That hasn't been on in so goddamn long," you say.

"I caught a rerun the other day on a Nazi channel," Video says. "I used to love that show, and now, after serving my nation, I'm convinced it is a total piece of shit."

"That's a great show," Eddio says. "My mother used to watch that show with me all the time." He looks down at his mail and pulls out a card. "Did I tell you she's getting married again? Every time I turn around, she's getting married."

"The problem is realism," Video says. "The other day was just a prime fucking example. The IMF, they go into some South American country, right? Everyone there knows only two words in Spanish—'sí' and 'señor.' The rest of the time they all speak this dubbed-in German. But with a *Spanish* accent."

"He's right," Sasquatch says, the issue of his monumental foreskin having been forced from his brain. "When the man is right, he's right." He's smoked his cigarette down to the nub, and you know he's going to come after you for another.

"Hey El," Eddio says. "You think I can get leave to see my mother get married? Only time I get to see her anymore is when she gets married. Every time she comes to the plate there's a big spread and we have a really good talk. Think you can swing that with the Old Man?"

"Worth a shot," you say. "It's not every day a guy's mom gets married."

Having finished his cigarette, Sasquatch walks over to you from his post by the door. "Hate these things the way they taste," he says, clearing his throat as he drops the butt in your ashtray. "You think I could bum maybe one more?"

"Fuck off," you say, tapping one out and lighting up just for the hell of it. A look of hurt spreads over Sasquatch's big dumb face.

"Last time she got married I was in Basic and couldn't get off," Eddio says. "But I heard about it. She had on this real low-cut long dress—my mom is really put together—and she's dancing away. Somebody gets drunk and steps on her dress accidentally on purpose and—boom—she hits everyone with the high beams. But it don't even faze her. She just yanked it up and kept dancing."

"Now there's a decent mom for you," Video says. "You don't see that shit happening on 'Father Knows Best.' "

"I think the Colonel will go for it," you say. One of the ways you keep personnel in line is to keep the favors coming. There are favors that are easy to do and favors that are hard. Sasquatch's was the latter, requiring nearly a month of investigation to locate a doc who was willing to do the required nip and tuck. Something like this, however, is easy because the Colonel would probably sign off on his own anyway. But you can arrange the leave as well as wangle a free flight on a military aircraft there and back. Eddio and Sasquatch are the kind of personnel you want to owe you favors. After enough favors build up, there will be a payoff. Money in the bank.

"Another thing that happened on the show I saw," Video says, steering back to TV. "And this is just an example of what's going wrong. They got that babe, Lesley Ann Warren, dark hair, you know the one."

You stop thinking of Eddio and put your mind on the more pleasant face of Lesley Ann Warren. In Rothfuss's sportfucking terms, it would be like hauling in a marlin.

"So, she's getting into it with this spic colonel. Again, right, they're talking German with Spanish accents. But the Colonel, he's horny as hell and he's got some information they need. She's supposed to squeeze the information out of him, but without giving it up. Now I ask you, Elwood, as an unbiased observer of the international fucking scene, are you gonna let slip your country's top secrets and you don't get to second base? I ask you this. Maybe it's just me."

"I heard they show that stuff to guys in the CIA," Cabot says.

"No wonder we're so fucked up," Video says. "Reality programming, that's the ticket. Lots of money to be made there."

"Uh-oh," you say, looking at the TV. "We've got some action here."

Erica Kane is back in bed with the sleazoid. Lights are low. The covers are pulled up, and she is leaning her head on the sleazoid's chest. She lifts her head as if she's just coming to. There is some music that lets you know they've done it.

"I wonder if she blew him," Eddio says.

"He has the look of a blown man," Rothfuss says.

"I can tell she's the kind likes to be tied up," Video says. "A couple of square knots and you got a satisfied customer on your hands."

"Never mind the square knots," Rothfuss says. "Two half hitches is your bedpost knot. Doesn't slip, and handles moisture well." Next to Cabot, Simmons gives a start and seems to be coming around.

"I got some bad news for you, El," Video says.

"Just what I need," you say.

"Erica Kane. You've made a big mistake with her."

"Don't tell me—this guy gets his warhead out, she becomes a nun," you say.

"Worse," Video says. "Erica Kane, she's not a chick— she's a dude."

"Maybe she'll enlist," you say. "I'd fuck her anyhow."

"Look at the neck on her. Look close. Late in the show, when the light's a little off, you get a good peek at some first-rate five o'clock shadow."

"Aw shit, I see it. I see it," Eddio says.

"I'm telling you, Video, this is very bad for my morale," you say. You feel serene as you let smoke slowly rise to the surface.

"They're fobbing her off on the American public," Video says, pleased with the reception for his latest line of bullshit, fall collection. The only bigger peddler of bullshit that you know is, of course, yours truly.

"Peter Pan was a broad, you know," Video says. "Lots of people don't know that."

"Really?" Eddio says. "And what was Tinker Bell?"

Sasquatch has gotten up from his post and has his face up close to the TV, studying the situation.

"This is part of the conspiracy. With our hearts hooked on a dude, America quits fucking. We don't reproduce anymore. The Russians, the Cubans, the Chinese, dammit, they're humping their houseboats off. There is no arms race; the race is in sperm. We're losing the sperm race." Video settles back, a smile on his face. One day, you figure, Video will tell a lie so outrageous he'll believe it.

"Holy fucking shit," Eddio says. "I see hair on the upper lip."

The door opens and it is Sgt. Lee. Sasquatch is nowhere near his post, frozen by the TV.

Sgt. Lee doesn't even raise his voice. "All you people get back to your posts," he says softly. "Elwood, you come with me."

You stub out your cigarette on the windowsill before dropping it into the ashtray. This day is going to be a long haul.

"I knew I taw a puddytat," Video whispers in your ear. "I did, I did."

6

IN SILENCE you walk with the Top back to the barracks. When you get to your quarters, two MPs are standing outside your door. Personal morale, you think, is at an all-time low.

"What do you know," you say, "and who says you can't spell wimp without MP."

"Why don't you pick up some new material, Elwood," says one of the MPs, whose name is Rodriguez.

"Open it," Sgt. Lee says.

"This an inspection?" you ask.

"Just open the fucking thing, Elwood," Sgt. Lee says in the same conversational tone, as if everything is under his control.

You unlock the door, grateful that your stash is in hibernation elsewhere. There is nothing to find.

The Top comes in and looks around your room. You watch him from the side. He has one of those dried-out Army faces, deep lines, no fat. It's as if all the juice has been squeezed out. It's in the body, too—straight back but the shoulders just beginning to bend. Someone who has seen his fair share of sin. The Army makes you old quick.

The Top looks at you. "This is pretty impressive," he says. "You really live good." He turns to the MPs. "Now toss it."

The MPs begin going through your stuff as you take a seat on the deluxe sofa bed. "Be careful with my shit," you say to Rodriguez, who is feeling around the mahogany cabinet that contains your state-of-the-art sound system. He overturns and rattles your speakers, which are floor-standing and come up above his waist. The other one is examining your frost-free refrigerator, which you have so you don't have to deal with the mess-hall slop. For cooking you have a programmable microwave as well as a hot plate, toaster oven, and Fry Baby. You also have a bar, fully stocked, on casters with a brass footrail. When he's done with the speakers, Rodriguez puts his efforts toward your TV, using a screwdriver to take off the back of the Sony Trinitron and poking his fingers in, around, and over the printed circuit boards, searching for contraband.

Sgt. Lee looks at you and then around the room. "You're pretty fucking well equipped for a busted-down Specialist-Four," he says.

"I'm thrifty," you say, one of the few Boy Scout virtues you can claim to practice. "I got paper for everything. You want to see it, just say the word. So, is this an inspection? You going to bounce a quarter off my bed or what?" You are not sure whether to push it or not, but you figure you have nothing to lose. Still too much static on the Sgt. Lee line.

The other MP is cleaning out the refrigerator. He hands several packages of meat to Sgt. Lee.

"I see you like the good cuts," Sgt. Lee says. "Keep the fat from clogging those all-important arteries. Have to keep them clear for the real traffic." He makes like he is going to hand the meat to you, but drops it to the floor and puts his heel to it. Blood leaks onto the floor. You do not move.

"Look at this, Sarge," says Rodriguez, who has moved off the TV and is now on your kitchenware. He is holding your Fry Baby, which you use for deep-frying French fries, onion rings, fish sticks.

"See if there's anything inside," Sgt. Lee says.

Rodriguez pours the oil out, the grease and bread crumbs expanding into a lake on your floor.

"Nothing," Rodriguez reports.

"Very bad for the cholesterol, though," Sgt. Lee says. "And the triglycerides I don't even want to think about."

The lake from the Fry Baby has stopped expanding, except for a small finger of oil that continues advancing toward your boot.

The other MP hands Sgt. Lee some German beer from your refrigerator.

"Man, oh man," Sgt. Lee says. "Paulaner. Got to admit, you don't go coach, do you? This shit does not come cheap. Anybody for a brew?"

He yanks the wire top and takes a long pull. Then he pours the rest of the beer onto your mattress. "This Paulaner," he says. "I don't care how expensive it is, it still tastes like motor oil."

You do not look at Sgt. Lee. Right now there is nothing to do. You are outnumbered, outranked, and outmuscled. In the fighting end you are not a mover and a shaker; you are more a quiverer and a trembler, except when the occasion requires. Your time, you know, will come. For every action, an equal and opposite reaction.

"I know what you are, Elwood." Sgt. Lee's voice is low and he gets right in your face, so close the wet beer smell makes you nauseous. "Here's my read of the situation. You think you're the first guy invented this shit. But I seen you before and I'm going to be sitting on you till you make a mistake. You ain't smart enough to take that kind of weight."

You don't say a thing. It is time to lay low, to let this one play itself out. There are a lot of moves you can make, but most of them will come down the line. Sooner or later, if you just listen close enough, the Top will give up the thing that will shut him down.

"Just putting you on notice," the Top says. "I got my eye out. One wrong move and your ass is mine. You read me on this?"

You say nothing, which is the way you decide to deal with the Top for now. Give him a clean read. Zero fucking defects.

The Top, you suspect, has been onto your game from the get-go. He's got the flat eyes—all surface, nothing underneath—that come from looking straight on, no blinders, at the face of God. Some leisure reading in his 201 personnel jacket confirmed this hypothesis. You examine the personnel jackets not only for what is there but also for what is not. Colonel Berman, in explaining this to you, has said that if Christ had kept 201s, he would have spotted Judas on the first day of apostle camp. If someone has top efficiency ratings, all the right levers pulled, righteous postings, training centers, and staff colleges, then you know he is your average Army deadbeat rounding the career track at eight minutes a mile. What you look for is the off-key note, the missing something that makes you prick up your ears. It is your suspicion that the Top took up the life on his last tour and had been into it heavy on and off until he voluntarily detoxed. The detox is not in the jacket, but there is an assignment to Fort Ord, California, where they have the Army narco center. There's nothing specific, just little gaps in time and space. The fitness reports are all high, rating him Grade A Prime Beef, but all that means is that he has a rabbi looking out for him who did not mind filling in the blanks.

For you, as you sit here staring at the mess in your quarters, Sgt. Lee is your worst nightmare: a user who kicked but was in it long enough to know the game. This creates problems in your freedom of action. The first thing you learned about scag was that users know one another on sight. They are like Masons with their secret handshakes and passwords. The bad thing about users is that they reach the point where they are nearly unshittable. They have been shat upon so much that even a principal actor like yourself cannot handle the load required. These are the melancholy facts. The only good news in this whole mess is that he cannot tag your stash.

"You're playing out of your weight here," he says. "You go toe to toe with me you will end up most surely fucked, you goddamned toy soldier."

To be sure, you are afraid of the Top. There is a realness to him, to anyone who has spent time in the shit. Nevertheless, you figure, the Top will eventually have to be handled.

"What are you making this hard for, Top?" you ask. "It doesn't have to play this way."

"I got news for you, Elwood. War is coming back and it's starting personal with you," the Top says, straightening to his full height. "Show me where the stuff is, we'll go amnesty—start over from square one, total amnesia. You're the good citizen turned in the stash. Get yourself a merit badge and remove your name from the shitlist, because right now you're in shit up to your shoulders."

"And if I don't?" you ask.

"Look at it this way, Elwood," Sgt. Lee says. "You're the only war I got."

Rodriguez is pouring barbecue sauce on the floor, taking special pleasure in making figure eights. You take it from the enjoyment he's obviously feeling that there has been a significant downgrade in your status.

"You done here?" you ask.

"This ain't a regulation mattress even," Sgt. Lee says.

"You got a fucking box spring down here. Who in the fucking Army has a goddamn box spring?"

"Health reasons," you say. This day, you figure, is positively shot. No chance for an MPC, no Glide; what you need is a fresh snort to top off your tank and turn your karma control up to medium-high. One quick Camel would hold you over.

The Top takes his knife and slits your mattress, then begins pulling out fistfuls of the stuffing, trying to latch on to something incriminating. "Always wondered what those things looked like on the inside," he says. "The thing about the Army, man, is you get to see the world."

Rodriguez and the other MP are throwing your clothes out of the dresser.

"Open the lockers," the Top says.

"You got a warrant?" you ask.

"This is an inspection, remember, asshole?" the Top says. "Open them both or I'll take them off with the bolt-cutters."

You use your key on the padlocks and shoot the arm on both of them. The Top goes to the lockers and begins rifling through the pockets of your Class A's, shaking out your boots, and tapping the sides of the locker, listening for echoes.

"You got more shit in here than Macy's," Sgt. Lee says. "My fucking daughter don't have this many clothes."

"War is hell," you say.

"First thing we're getting you is a roommate," Sgt. Lee says.

"Smoking or nonsmoking?" you ask.

Sgt. Lee looks at you. His eyes bulge slightly. "You like to watch TV, don't you," he says quietly.

You note that Sgt. Lee is a man who likes to keep things under his control. You do not say anything, but you think you are beginning to get the picture.

He walks over and looks closely at your TV. "Very nice piece of equipment here," he says. "Sony Trinitron, totally solid state. Only moving part the on-off switch. My feeling is you got to go with the Japs. Only way us Americans can compete is drop another A-bomb."

Sgt. Lee turns the TV on. "What channel, Elwood? I see you like them soaps, those slinky-women kind of shows." He punches the line of buttons to go through the channels, finally settling on the picture of an announcer reading the news.

The picture on the Top, you think, is getting clearer by the minute.

"Top," you say, "why don't you send these Multi-Purpose Motherfuckers out to chase some parked cars."

Sgt. Lee nods, and the MPs leave the room.

You wait until the door is closed. A Sgt. Lee, you figure, isn't going to cost much. Guys like him are loss leaders, already figured into your overhead. "Smoke?" you ask. You take out a cigarette and then hand him the pack. He takes one out and you rise from the sofa bed to light his with your Varick. Sgt. Lee is still holding on to the pack, though, letting it rest in his hands.

"What is it you want?" you ask, sitting back down but leaning forward. You are hearing something definite now. It is still not clear, but at least the line isn't dead.

Sgt. Lee sits down on your bed and looks at his boots as he inhales. He puts your pack of Camels in his breast pocket, which you take as a good sign.

"Whatever it is, I can get," you say. "I see you are an admirer of Japanese technology. No problem—the Sony's yours."

Sgt. Lee is still not looking at you. He glances around the room, taking inventory again.

"What I'm saying is, what will it take for us to make nice? I'm very open to negotiations."

Sgt. Lee gets up from the bed, goes to your Sony Trinitron, and punches the toe of his boot through the center of the screen. The Trinitron flies off the stand and drops to the floor. You can see some sparks from the inside and then smoke rising, like a campfire going out.

"You can see what it is I'm saying," Sgt. Lee says.

7

YOU ARE CLEANING UP the mess from the Top's inspection when there is a knock on the door.

"Who?" you ask.

"Hey Elwood," you hear, recognizing the voice. You open the door, and it is CC standing in the doorway.

"The Top—I hear he come by give you some verbal counseling," CC says.

"Word travels," you say.

"You don't know how fast," CC says.

"Cut to the chase," you say. "You buying or selling?"

"I'm mainly here to offer a sympathetic ear," CC says. "Keep up the morale. Make sure the Top didn't get you down." You turn away, indicating a lack of interest, and CC picks up on it. "But since you asked," he says, "how about I go ten bucks on the Sony Trinitron?"

"Thanks for the ear," you say, "but fifty would cheer me like you would not believe. Also, you got anything to smoke?"

"Nasty habit you got yourself," CC says. "We go back to the bar, I can throw in a carton on top of the ten bucks for your set." He sighs as he sits down on the edge of your bunk. Normally that is the kind of thing that would lead to a fight, but CC is the one person around base that it seems everyone likes. No one even knows what nationality he is. He's got kinky red hair and the flat nose of a yam, but his skin is white with freckles. He is a man whose talent it is to fit in; like the blank tile on a Scrabble board, he can be whatever you want him to be.

"Look, I'm doing you a favor," he says. "These Trinitrons, they break down, what, once a century? Will 'em to your grandchildren. I'm just buying yours for parts. Lift out the PC boards and shove them into something else."

You put down the mop and walk over to the set and turn it on. While there is no picture, the Sony powers up and a light comes on in the back. "Takes a licking and keeps on ticking," you say. "Forty-five."

"Like some women I know," CC says. "Fifteen."

"For fifteen I might as well toss it," you say.

"I know you better," CC says.

How you know CC is he graduated first among Army fuck-ups. He is, in fact, a legend. You got to know him because his first MOS established him as clerk-typist, punching out paper next to you in the Orderly Room, and even by the relatively undemanding standards of the Army he couldn't hack it. They moved him to filing, but he and the alphabet weren't on the same wavelength. When they decided CC was not administrative support kind of material, they moved him to the motor pool, where he was canned because he stripped the gears on every truck he tried to drive before it was discovered he couldn't drive a stick. There were a number of other duty stops along the road, each one confirming his incompetence and enlarging his legend.

At each stop, however, he made friends. It wasn't until he moved to Sgt. Saad's platoon and the NCO club that he discovered his true calling in life. CC was a man with a genius for retail. This is a talent you have more and more come to admire. He could sell a bikini to an Eskimo, a hard-on to a whore. In his spare time, and with Sgt. Saad as his silent partner, he has set up a bar right outside the base to service his many friends. This also provides a convenient funnel, of course, for Sgt. Saad to move his NCO club inventory.

You pick up the mop and push the glass shards from under the bed.

"What I suggest," CC says, "is Mop & Glo. I just got a half-dozen gross come in. Pure luck I happened into it. I can get you a discount even off the PX markdown. Give them to you at cost. Guaranteed clean and shine."

"How'd you get a half-dozen gross of Mop & Glo?" you ask.

"Estate sale—what else," CC says, laughing at the joke. The estate sale is bogus, naturally; a few boxes simply took an administrative detour through Sgt. Saad-land to the happy retail hunting ground of CC's Bar & Grill.

"Amazing what people keep around the house," you say. "Forty."

"Nineteen dollars for scrap," CC says. "I hate to break that twenty mark. It's a religious thing."

"You? Religious?" you say. "I'm the religious fucker here. Eight years I went to Catholic grammar school. You're religious, I'm Jesus Christ."

"Then you should understand a man's religious preferences," CC says. "You Catholics, you stay away from the meat on Fridays, Jews they don't eat pork, Moslems always got to figure out which way east is. You know what I worship?"

"Andrew Jackson in three-quarter profile," you say.

"You're a cynical man, Elwood," CC says. "I worship physics. Isaac fucking Newton. I learn all about him at the base education center where I while away my days. We just had a test, I pulled off a ninety-seven and I didn't even hardly cheat. The Army, it sends you away to war and you end up coming home with a free degree. What a world this is. What a fucking world."

"That's a new one on me," you say. The genius of CC, you know, derives from the old bait and switch, a kind of constant attempt at misdirection. By the time you're done talking, you end up so thoroughly confused that you go for whatever deal he's offering. But in this department you are nearly as good as CC, and you are going to take it to the wire, duke this one out with the master.

"Everyone thinks Einstein's the guy, right? But his shit only works in space and what I hear it's cold as a well-digger's ass up there, man," CC says. "Newton, he's still got it covered on earth."

"So what?"

"Cause and effect, my man. Something happens, there's a reason behind it happening. A foot goes through a TV, TV gets busted."

"How'd you ever get thrown out of being a clerk?" you ask.

"Creative incompetence," CC says. "Hanging back behind the power curve. The more you don't know, the less you got to do. Before long, you end up doing nothing, the law of diminishing returns. You should take these college courses, El. Expand your fucking mind."

"Thanks for the tip," you say. "I'll come down to thirty-five."

"I'm losing money here by going against everything I know, but I'll come up to twenty-five."

"You know, when I went to Catholic school, they told me God was on my side," you say. "Thing I learned from the Army—that ain't true."

"You see God, he gets a free moment—send him over," CC says. "I got a source, can tap into those communion wafers, switch over to those whole-wheat jobs. Catholics

start downing those, what with that kind of spiritual rough-
age, you guys'll have the cleanest souls in Europe."

"Cause and effect?" you ask.

"Damn straight," CC says.

"Maybe I'll get out of the shit," you say, "get into some
honest line of work. What do you think of that?"

"You tired of this shit, man?" CC asks.

"To the bone," you say. "Dead and buried."

"I thought that, too, last time I re-upped," CC says. "But
I figured I couldn't handle the cut in pay." He picks a copy
of *People* magazine off the dresser. He looks at it, squinting
his eyes as he bites his lip. "Look at the pictures they got
in this cheap rag. Is it broads throwing you off your game?"
he asks. "I never thought of that with you. Always thought
you were set in that department."

"I read it for the articles," you say. CC has folded the
magazine in half and is looking at a photo of a girl lying
on the beach with her top unstrapped.

"Yeah, this girl makes for very close reading," CC says.
"But look at this shit. You don't even get tit. What kind a
magazine is that? You want to be a degenerate, at least be
a competent fucking degenerate. Get the job done right,
is what I say. This is probably your whole problem.
You're trying to stir your meat with this chick in half a
bathing suit. What're you, hard up? Go take a tour of the
Stop 'n' Pop."

"I'll come down to thirty-two fifty," you say, knowing CC
hates numbers that aren't round. It's the fucking Newtonian
physics.

"Here's the deal," CC says. "Twenty-five and free lend-
ing privileges from the bonepile. As many bone magazines
as you like. It'll be like a library card."

"Jesus, a revolution in porn," you say. "But my religion,
I think it'll get in the way."

"That Catholic shit, I don't believe it," CC says. "You probably never went to a fucking church in your life."

You stand up and lean in close, get in CC's space and tug on your left eyebrow. "See this scar," you say. "Sixth grade, Sister Bibbiana. Our Lady of Perpetual Grace grammar school. We're doing art, and she tells us draw some houses. She's the Michelangelo of grammar school art. I'm working on my house, got this great big mansion, like fifty fucking rooms, but then it comes time to draw the sky. All I had left I hadn't used was purple, so I colored in a purple sky—figured, almost the same thing, right? Sister Bibbiana takes one look and cracks me in the head with her pointer—she carried that thing like a billy club. Took seventeen stitches close this baby up. It was a fight, they would've stopped it in the first round. But Sister Bibbiana, she taught me an important lesson."

"What's that?" CC asks.

"Sky ain't purple," you say.

CC nods thoughtfully.

"You just don't go up against fucking nature," you say. Sister Bibbiana, we know, was one of your most influential teachers. She taught quite explicitly and through example that God, no matter what his press indicated, was solidly in the Motherfucker camp.

"I think that's where Newton would stand," CC says, coming out of his reverie. "I'll tell you what. I'll go to thirty with full bonepile privileges—I even have a collection of Super eight millimeter films that has some shit that is beyond the pale, man, you would not believe."

"Sold," you say. "Maybe we can do a movie night, expand your entertainment potential."

CC nods as he pulls out his wallet and peels off the bills.

"Don't forget the carton of smokes," you say. "You got Camels?"

"How can you smoke that shit?" CC asks. "Don't got no filters, they like to burn out your lungs."

"I hate to miss out," you say. "Let's go to the bonepile and see what you got."

Together you depart your quarters and begin walking through the barracks. In the grim indoor light, you catch glimpses of soldiers playing cards, looking out suspiciously at anybody who walks past. From under several closed doors you smell hash. Why doesn't Sgt. Lee mess with those sons-of-bitches, you think. Outside, the gray sky has turned into a drizzle, and CC starts breathing heavily as he lugs the Trinitron.

"You ain't been around much since Parsons McCovey got took off the roster," CC says.

"Taking a vacation," you say. "Clearing my mind."

"And fucking Kimbrough, too," CC says. "People ain't lucky around you, El."

"Luck has nothing to do with it," you say.

"Yeah, but Kimbrough was a prince."

"I got a question," you say. "There anything you want to say on the Parson? The Old Man wants to make a newsletter out of him."

"He was mean, man," CC says, "but only if you met him." He shifts hands on the Trinitron, trying to keep it turned so water won't get inside.

"You're not helping," you say. "What've you been doing with yourself lately."

"Living the good life," CC says, "Wait till you see the improvements at the bar."

"What?" you ask.

"You'll see," he says.

As you pass the gate toward CC's bar on the strip right outside the base, the raindrops become larger and you smell stale beer. One thing about Germany you have noticed: it rains the same amount every month, like someone planned the weather in advance.

You get to the door of the bar. The parking lot is wet and slick and covered with leaves. Broken glass has been swept to the corners of the lot and the stale-beer smell makes your stomach turn. Sometimes, after a bad night, CC has had to use his mop outside on the parking lot, pushing the blood back into the earth. The picture window has been boarded over and someone has spray-painted obscenities on it, like the joke signing of a cast. CC puts down the TV and takes a big ring of keys out of his pocket.

"What happened to your window?" you ask.

"That's what I was talking about," CC says. "Your friend Garcia tied one on and then got into it the other night— got thrown right through my window."

"He okay?"

"He laid there awhile, but then he got up and walked away, no blood trail, no nothing, so I guess he is. I tell you what, though. Someday somebody's going to kill that poor son-of-a-bitch."

"That's what he's hoping for," you say. Garcia is a buddy who must have incredible karma to have survived against the long odds imposed by his personality. In the pleasure/pain separation, Garcia nearly always chooses pain, and someone big to inflict it, over and over and plenty of it.

"But there's an upside," CC says.

"What's that?"

"I got the glazier to come in. He's going to put in a leaded window with a three-color neon profile of Elvis. The guitar strings, they'll be metal embedded in the glass, connect up to a security-service burglar alarm. We're talking major upgrade."

"How come?" you ask.

"Inventory's piling up," CC says, "and the criminal element around here is getting worse. I tell you—no insult intended, El—but you deal with guys on the fringe, they're not the most trustworthy people. I been broken into twice, and look at the kind of shit they write on the wood. They just don't have the kind of respect you would like. Fortunately, they didn't steal any of my Elvis memorabilia. They don't even know what the fuck to look for."

"Lucky thing," you say.

"I also got myself a line on something else," he says.

The key to CC is there is always some new iron in the fire. You suspect he has deals working with half the personnel at the 57th. His problem is they're all small deals, stuff on the order of bargaining you down on your Trinitron. CC wouldn't know a big score if it leaped right into his pocket.

"This turns out to be legit," CC says. "I could be in Elvis heaven. I got hold of the guy he was the quartermaster got the sheets Elvis slept on when he did his bit in Germany."

"No shit," you say. "He didn't wash them or nothing?" CC, you know, is wild for Elvis, and his fixation on the King is another weak chink in his retail personality.

"I'm going up tomorrow see whether they're for real," CC says.

"How do you tell?"

"I'm telling you, there is an untapped market for Elvis-in-Germany stuff," CC says. "This stuff'd be worth a fortune back home."

Inside CC's you walk past the memorabilia. Elvis on the jukebox, Elvis on clocks on the walls, as well as pictures of

Elvis in concert and in uniform during his Army tour. CC leads you directly to the back room, where he has mountains of inventory. He puts the TV in a corner next to a number of other TVs, and turns to one of the standing footlockers. The footlockers are filled with magazines, porn movies, and photographs. He twists the combo on one of the lockers and takes out an armful of magazines.

"This shit's just in," CC says. "Some of this stuff you would not believe. Pick a couple and take them home."

"Get the smokes," you say, beginning to look through the bonepile. You open up one of the magazines to look at the girls inside, and none of them look like anything but hookers with too much mileage. One of the photo spreads is a date between a guy with two pricks and a woman with two cunts. They're at a table having a candlelight dinner. There's two of everything next to them: two salads, two glasses, two sets of silverware, and two plates. As the pictures go on they strip off their clothes to reveal their true identities. They lie next to each other on the rug, like brother and sister at the beach because you guess that for all the extra plumbing none of it works. You have never seen two people getting ready to fuck looking so dispirited. The man's face is cratered by acne scars, and the woman is fleshy in the middle and one breast is totally flat.

"Bad news on the Camels," CC says. "I'm out. You want something else, maybe? I got Winstons and Marlboros."

"Owe it to me," you say, still looking at the pictures. "Jesus. You got anything normal in the bonepile? You got any regular porn like *Penthouse* or *Playboy* or *Oui?*"

"That's sissy shit," CC says. "Takes a lot to get an Army crowd going. I got one in here of a girl honking a horse."

"I don't know," you say. "Maybe Stoney'll want it."

"Here," CC says, handing you the magazine. "Tell him to eat it up."

"Thanks," you say.

"Can I interest you in a chick and a snake?"

"How does she do it with a snake?"

"It's no sweat," CC says. "Snake does all the work."

"All right, I'll take these," you say. "I want something else for Stoney, too. In basic black, nothing fancy."

CC shakes his head as if in disappointment. "That's how a lot of the brothers are," he says. "They don't know what they're missing." He spreads his arms. "There's a whole world out there waiting to be conquered."

When you come out of CC's you have walked almost back to the barracks before you realize you've forgotten the Mop & Glo. Rather than return to the bar, you take a quick left and go to the PX, where you will invest some of the money from your Sony in household products like a mop, bucket, sponges, and paper towels.

The PX on base is well stocked: aisle upon aisle of groceries, hardware, car-care products. There's a sale on turkeys for Thanksgiving, and already you see aisles being set aside for the Christmas bonanza.

You push your cart along, picking up the items you need, and by the grapes you see the girl with one arm, the Top's daughter. She looks around, doesn't see you, and picks a couple of grapes off the vine, swallowing them quickly as she moves on. Then she's into an aisle that has cassette tapes for sale. You follow her, keeping your distance, not getting too close, simply collecting information. She leans over, picks up a few tapes for close examination. In her cart she's got the fixings for the evening meal: produce for salad, a package of chuck steak, frozen crinkle-cut French fries, French-style string beans, six-pack of American beer. The Top, you figure, is a meat-and-potatoes man, doesn't like to stray far from home. Then you notice her deftly slip the tapes into her jeans. It happens so quickly you almost miss it. Jesus, you think, the whole family is bent.

She's done now, and you trail her through the aisles back to the cash registers, where the enlisted wives usually handle the honors, making some spare change as they give themselves and their families the old five-finger discount. This time of day, the checkout lines are short. The Top's kid gets in the near line, unloads her groceries, and pulls a magazine off the rack. You're right in there behind her. She pages through articles about Liz Taylor's liposuction and Princess Di's boob jobs and how a dwarf couple had twins that now play semipro basketball. But she's not reading, she's just passing time. When the checkout girl, who looks to be pushing forty, turns away to bag the previous customer's groceries, the Top's kid reaches to put the magazine back on the rack and then grabs a pack of cigarettes from the slot and tosses it down the front of her shirt. An impulse snatch with an impressive degree of difficulty. Problem is, the checkout girl turned around just then, and the movement was too quick to be anything else. She's looking at the Top's kid, glancing at the arm, uncertain whether anything has happened but real suspicious, and is about to ask when you grab a pack of Camels for yourself.

"You got matches?" you ask her. "I'm out."

"You can't smoke here," she says.

"Fuck it then," you say, deliberately and slowly, but standing pat with your hand. "Could we move this thing any slower?" Now the checkout girl's so pissed she forgets about the Top's kid and goes back to bagging the groceries. The Top's kid looks at you—grateful, you think, knowing she was about to get nailed.

"You don't have a light, do you?" you ask.

"No," she says.

"Oh shit, I do. Forgot I had my lighter," you say. You

open up your gold-plated Varick, give her a good look at luxury.

"Could I see?" she asks, and you hand it over and she begins turning it around in her hand. She's pretty, with a thin face and strong bones. You see the Top in her, in the angle of the eyes. Oh, yeah.

The checkout girl starts ringing up the Top's kid's groceries. "I said no smoking," she says.

"Nobody's smoking," you say, as the Top's kid flips the lighter open. "We're just keeping warm."

The checkout girl glares as she takes the money from the Top's kid and your stuff slides up next. The Top's kid begins walking off with your lighter, still holding it in her hand, but you let her go, see how far she stretches this thing out. She's moving slow, not a worried muscle in her body, nerves of fucking steel.

"You want two of these they're the same price," the checkout girl says, about your Mop & Glo.

"No," you say. "One's fine."

"We're having a sale," she says, fucking with you now, holding you up by pretending to do you a favor because she thinks you're having a nicotine fit. "You want I can send back."

The Top's kid is already out the door before she turns around and says, "Oh, I forgot this. I'm sorry." And walks it back to you, cool as anything, and drops it into your palm. You feel the heat from her hand. She turns and walks off.

You fork over the cash, and when the checkout girl gives you the change you rip open the pack of cigarettes, tap one out, and light it up, blowing a ring by her. She's standing there pissed but unable to do anything except maybe offer you another sale. "If I were you," you say, "I'd think about taking up a vice."

You turn, expecting the Top's kid to be waiting for you,

but she's already gone, out the door and into the lot, your little escapade having taken up too much time. Outside, you don't see her for a second, and then you see a yellow Montego backing out of a space and turning to go off base. All right, you think. All right.

8

"I'M GLAD he's dead."

"I hated the motherfucker."

"He owed me fifty bucks and I don't think he left a fucking will."

"If I knew who killed the fucker I'd pin a medal on him."

Since these initial reviews of PFC Parsons McCovey's act were not of a laudatory nature, you decide a more profitable activity is to move ahead with the photo requests. You light up and start drafting the letters, but when you look up, the New Guy, Knoll, is standing at attention in front of your desk.

"Private First Class Brian Knoll, reporting for duty, sir," he says. He has a fresh face, all muscle and sinew, some acne, Army reg glasses, uniform that looks like he just stepped into it.

"Stand down," you say, "and can the *sir* crap. I'm not an officer." From where you're sitting you can see that this boy is very cherry. That makes you feel bad, because for him barracks initiation will go badly. The yams protect their own, but one thing you have discovered is whites do not stick together unless they know for sure they are going to win.

You put out the cigarette before buzzing Colonel Berman on the intercom.

"Talk to me, Elwood," Colonel Berman says, coming on the speaker.

You tell the Colonel about the New Guy. Colonel Berman, you know, is busy working on the final version of his Dien Bien Phu article. Once he is done, you will translate his writing from Bermanese into English and type it up.

"Give me ten minutes," Colonel Berman says.

"Yes sir," you say, looking up at Knoll. "They give you the 201 in the Orderly Room?"

"Right here." Knoll pulls his personnel folder from under his arm and hands it to you.

You take it from him and open it on your desk. It is your job to carefully go over each of the 201s, so as to provide background material for Colonel Berman's introductory speech. While it is unusual for a battalion commander to meet with the new men in his command, this is one of Colonel Berman's management tactics. To Knoll he will give a speech, based on the Patton Principle, so loaded with obscenity that it achieves a kind of brutal poetry. He will tell Knoll that his office door is always open, that Knoll is part of an elite ordnance unit, and that the German front is the most important front in the whole damn cold war—which cannot be won, naturally, without the proper supplies.

You notice Knoll is still standing at attention, as if waiting to be questioned on the subject of himself.

"Cop a squat, will you," you say, pointing to the chair at the other side of the office. Once he is seated, you notice he even sits at attention. Knoll's excess energy begins to make you feel old and tired.

According to the 201, Knoll is your TOW trainer, antitank man. In the field the TOW man sights the enemy tank, fires the missile, and then guides it in using the wire.

After his brief stint as driver for Colonel Berman, through your memoranda efforts Parsons McCovey became the

TOW trainer for your squad. As far as you can tell, Knoll could not be any worse than the Parson. During joint maneuvers with German commandos in the Black Forest, McCovey once targeted a civilian summer cottage instead of the simulated tanks. The TOW was nonexplosive, but the impact blew the roof off the cottage, like opening up a shoebox.

"May I ask you a question, Knoll?" you say.

"Yes sir," he says.

"The soldier you're replacing was a good buddy of mine, PFC Parsons McCovey. I wonder if you had anything to say about that?"

"I didn't know the guy, sir," Knoll says.

"But he was a good man and we expect you to live up to his standards." The only standards Parsons McCovey set, of course, were the ones for being a fuck-up and a screw-off. "And stop with the *sir*, goddammit."

"I'll try my best," Knoll says.

"Can I quote you as saying, 'I've got big boots to fill'?"

"I guess so," Knoll says, as you write this down. This is the kind of quote aggressiveness and creativity that Colonel Berman would be pleased with, you think.

You continue to look through the Knoll file. You see that he received marksmanship awards at boot camp. You also discover some university experience.

"Knoll," you say. "It says here you're a college boy."

"That's correct."

"Then how come you're not an officer?" you ask.

"I enlisted. I'm hoping the Colonel will recommend me for Officer Candidate School."

"Never mind the OCS crap. You didn't go the ROTC, weekend-warrior route?"

"No."

"What are you in the Army for then?" you ask. This is

partly out of curiosity. After being in the service this long and seeing all you've seen, you have ascertained that no one joins the Army unless he is absolutely useless at anything else.

"To serve my country," Knoll says.

"Don't tell me you're a fucking patriot."

You would have thought it impossible, but Knoll sits up even more in his chair. "Of course," he says.

You take a deep breath. Either Knoll is more cherry than anyone you have ever met or he has half a ton of brain damage. It's like a kid in diapers walking the dotted on the autobahn. This is bad news, because if he turns out to be terminally stupid, he can bring the shit down.

"Let me clue you in to something, Knoll," you say. "You don't have to believe me, just stick this in your ruck and think about it."

"Yes sir," Knoll says, nodding his head with a fervency that worries you. His Adam's apple boosts up and down. When it comes to rest it sticks out on his throat like a knuckle. You have decided to go this route with Knoll because he looks like somebody who needs handling.

"Today's Army is full of spics, yams, losers, misfits, and world-class fuck-ups. What I'm wondering is where the hell you fit in."

Knoll doesn't say anything—just keeps the gaze straight, as if he's been taking shit so long he's developed a taste for it.

"Look, I'm not trying to fuck with your program or anything," you say, sighing your fake combat-veteran sigh. The Spec 4 with a golden heart. "I'm just trying to give you a read on the situation. You want to keep your head down and watch for ambushes is all I'm saying."

The spin move works on him as well as it does on all the fresh meat. You give him the limp leg and then the shoulder, and next thing you know he's falling all over himself being grateful. Sometimes you think, Jesus, one of them must be able to figure out what you're doing, playing good cop–bad cop all in the same econopackage. Knoll must have learned something at college. But you can see from his face that he is eating this shit up. Another braindicapped recruit.

"How come they assigned you here?" you ask. In your experience, while those who have joined the Army are useless, those sent to Germany are useless even by Army standards.

"I put in for it. My fiancée is here on base and so we tried to arrange a transfer together."

"She's over in the WAC Shack?" you ask.

Knoll nods.

"What's her name?" you ask. "Maybe I know her."

"Margolis, Private First Class," Knoll says.

"You call her by her last name?" you ask. "What do you do, salute in bed?"

"Carol Ann," he says. "We're planning to get married soon. First time we get a furlough together."

Your intercom buzzes. You tap it and Colonel Berman says, "Elwood, in here."

"Yes sir," you answer, gathering Knoll's file with your free hand.

You turn toward Knoll. "Just stay cool," you say, for no other reason than to make him worry. You do not know exactly why, but you have taken an instant dislike to PFC Knoll. It could be, you think, because he practically wears a sign around his neck: LOSER. Then you head into Colonel Berman's office to give him the news about Private Knoll's college education.

When Knoll comes out of the office, Colonel Berman is giving him the ritual pat on the back at the same time he shakes his hand. Big pump, hearty squeeze. Then the patting hand shifts to a shoulder slap. This all started, naturally, after another of the Colonel's military personnel magazines ran an article about the "Touching Commander" as a way of lowering the resistance to authority experienced by the unenlightened enlisted man. Give the masses a little human contact.

Knoll has disengaged himself from the Colonel and is awaiting further instructions.

"If you go to the Orderly Room," you say, "they'll have someone get you fixed up."

There is an awkward silence as Knoll looks at Colonel Berman, who then looks at you. You wonder if Colonel Berman is considering hugging you, too. Why not make it a party?

"Uhm, Elwood. If you'd be kind enough to guide Private—" For a moment, it appears Knoll's name is already lost. But you know what Colonel Berman is doing. His face is pulled to a point of concentration. He's running Knoll's name through his head, trying to link it visually with a key feature he's supposed to have thought up: maybe mole, pole, asshole, who knows. Colonel Berman does this because in one of his management seminars he took the Harry Lorayne memory course, which tells you to link the names in your command with features that allow you to recall them. The problem for Colonel Berman is that he can never remember the key word. "—Knoll!" Colonel Berman nearly shouts with relief. "Elwood, take Private Knoll and guide him to your quarters. He's going to be sharing them with you."

More of Sgt. Lee's fucking with you. It is time, you think, to clear the hell out of Dodge.

You light up a Camel as you walk with Knoll across the parade grounds to the barracks. He's chattering away about AIT, where he was nearly bitten by a copperhead on maneuvers. And then he talks about Carol Ann Margolis, his girlfriend, and all the paperwork he had to fill out, strings he had to pull, asses he had to kiss ("Oh, I'm just kidding, sort of") in order to get assigned to Mannheim, and even to the same base she was on. He's already halfway through the story of how he got lost for two days in processing at the Armed Forces Frankfurt Center, but you cut him off.

"Look," you say, approaching the door to your quarters. For a moment, the torrent of information stops. "I don't guess I give a shit, all right?"

Knoll's glasses are steamed from the sudden change in temperature, but it looks as though he's about to cry.

"You're only here 'cause the fucking Top's on my case," you say. "It's not you, it's him. He keeps this shit up, I'm just going to move out on the economy, leave him to play king of the hill." You drop your cigarette to the floor and grind it out with your boot.

Knoll has taken off his glasses and appears to have composed himself.

"I'm letting you in here and I'm giving you a key until I get this shit straightened out. Until then, I do not want to hear about your fucking girlfriend or your goddamn transportation problems or any fucking thing at all. You roger that?"

You hand Knoll the key and turn around, leaving him to secure his own shit. To calm down, you walk out to the perimeter. Past the south fence, hidden in a blind and impossible to find unless you know exactly where the fuck it is, is one of your principal reasons for living, a Mercedes-Benz 450 SL, your one extravagance. On days like today when karma levels take a nosedive, they can often be restored to acceptable limits by a discreet glance in the direction of your vehicle. She has been bought for cash, virgin pure, right off the factory floor in Mannheim. She is fully loaded, all the options known to man. She is not registered, of course, because someone in the CID's office might wonder how a man who weighs in at a Spec 4 salary rates this kind of machine. There is no easy answer to that, naturally, except that she has been bought with drug money. So you have the necessary papers purchased from Hermann the German, who has all sorts of friends in low places and was willing to give you a discount off the usual criminal rate.

But what you would like to do is go beyond the perimeter of the base, get your Mercedes out of the blind, and take it to the Stop 'n' Pop. You would break your own rule and request Mireille and fuck her till her eyes popped out. But Colonel Berman is still revising the Dien Bien Phu article and has said that he would appreciate it if you could work with him after mess. That was fine with you, of course, since the freedom inherent in your job is dependent on maintaining the good graces of the Colonel.

In the dining facility, you look around for someone to sit with, but none of the usual suspects is available. Stoney has probably skipped dinner in order to stay in the poker game and lose more of your money, and everyone else is probably huddled up in their cribs or smashed beyond repair.

So you grab your chow and sit by yourself. You down some coffee and think about maybe taking an upper to blow through Colonel Berman's instructions, get some perspective. But no, you decide, bad judgment there. Taking Colonel Berman on an upper would be like trying to drive up a mountain in high gear. Just then Sgt. Saad comes over and sits down next to you.

"You get the money you need?" you ask.

"Always," Sgt. Saad says. A ruckus has started over by the chow line, a white and a black squaring off, pushing for space by the applesauce. Sgt. Saad looks over, betraying some minor interest. He has a bald head, the Marvin Hagler do, which gives him an intimidation factor of 9.8. This conceals, however, first-rate businessman's instincts.

"You heard about the newsletter," you say. Sgt. Saad is a man who hears everything and misses nothing. He is connected to everybody and everybody is connected to him. The two men by the chow line are having at it now, and onlookers have arrived. There's a din of cursing and plates crashing as they pump punches into each other and roll on the ground.

"Anything you care to say about the dearly departed?" you ask.

"Better to let sleeping Parsons lie," he says.

Sgt. Saad, in fact, is one of your chief suspects concerning Possibility Number Two, but clarity, you understand, is only an occasional virtue, and this is not the time for it.

The fight has been broken up, contingents from both sides having separated the combatants and pulled them back to their seats. The shirts of both men are soaked, and the white guy is bleeding from the nose.

"So nothing, huh?" you say.

"I do have one thing to say," Sgt. Saad says.

"What's that?"

"Sweet'n Low." He studies you closely for your reaction. Around Sgt. Saad, you know, you have to be careful. Right now Sgt. Saad is happy to have you operate independently, selling high-quality product to him wholesale. The connections you have are outside his reach, but the minute he thought he could achieve a little vertical integration of the business, he'd be on you in a minute.

"What're you saying?" You light a cigarette, taking a long and thoughtful drag.

Meanwhile, a delegation of the blacks has gone over to the whites, and some serious discussion is going on at one of the far tables.

"You got to understand my business," Sgt. Saad says. "It's based on trust. You know you fuck me up, you can trust me to fuck you up worse."

"Age-old American values," you say, blowing smoke through the side of your mouth.

"Like the Kimbrough mess, who's to blame?" Sgt. Saad says. "I know you find an angle, you play it. In the conversion process, you skim off the added weight, then take your cut—I know all about it."

What Sgt. Saad is referring to is the conversion process between morphine base and scag. Because of the difference in molecular weight, after the conversion you end up with more scag than the morphine you started with. One key of morphine base yields 1.2 keys of scag, a hefty profit margin that you hold back from the Turk, in addition to your regular cut.

"And that's okay," Sgt. Saad says. "It don't come out of my pocket, it's none of my business. And I never had no complaints before. You supplied quality shit, I admit."

Things are heating up in the discussion by the tables. More people are gathering around, standing up, taking positions.

"You didn't like what you got last time?" you ask.

"Somebody stepped on it," Sgt. Saad says.

"How hard?" you ask.

"Twice," Sgt. Saad says.

"Twice is greedy," you say. "I wouldn't do that shit to you—I wouldn't do it. I'm making enough as it is. I screw you, I end up with problems long-term. And for what?" For a moment, the battle seems to have been broken off, both sides in retreat, settling back to their respective tables.

"The way it was done, though," Sgt. Saad says, "whoever this individual was, mixed it instead of with milk sugar used Sweet'n Low."

"How do you know?"

"I had to send the fucking thing out, get it tested," Sgt. Saad says. "What, you think you're the only guy with a chemistry set?"

"So you want a refund?" you ask. "Right now I'm low, but soon as the next shipment comes in I'll make it up to you. Rain check."

Sgt. Saad ignores this. "I understand you made an offer to my man Kirchfield," he says.

"Just a little free-lance work, nothing special," you say. "I'm not trying to cut you out."

"The thing of it is, this Sweet'n Low thing, the Parson was the delivery boy. And the Sweet'n Low idea, it's so stupid, only the Parson would think he'd get over."

And it does, you have to admit, have the fingerprints of one of the Parson's off-the-wall schemes, set up a little independent distributorship using his customary persuasive tactics.

"Or . . ." you say.

"Or somebody wanted to make it look stupid. So stupid no one would figure it out."

Sgt. Saad, you have to admit, has a subtle mind. "Why would I want to fuck a good thing up?"

"You're looking at re-upping pretty soon," Sgt. Saad says. "You might be thinking, set up that nest egg, get what you can now, say good-bye, fuck you later, to all your old friends."

"Too late to ask the Parson," you say. "Clear this thing right up."

Sgt. Saad nods his head, exhaling as he bites his upper lip. "That's too bad," he says. "I hate loose ends."

As you're sitting there, Knoll walks over. By the tables, you see the original two combatants nod, as if agreeing on something, then get up at the same time from the tables and move by indirect routes toward the dessert area. In the back pocket of the white guy you see his steak knife.

"This seat taken?" Knoll asks.

"Who's this?" Sgt. Saad asks.

"Knoll," you say, thinking Knoll is going to stay by your side like a fucking hound. "PFC Knoll, Sgt. Saad."

"Pleased to meet you, sir," Knoll says, his plate piled high with the worst shit in the house. He begins digging in enthusiastically.

"We done?" you ask Sgt. Saad.

"We understand each other, that's what's important," Sgt. Saad says. "Keep the communication lines burning." Sgt. Saad, as a rule, never speaks in front of third parties, but he's sized up Knoll immediately as a lame player.

"Your man Stoney has a theory about the decline and fall of the gray race," Sgt. Saad says, referring to Knoll.

Knoll, you consider, is not one of the shining examples. "There's evidence everywhere you look," you say.

"Tell your man Stoney I seen Darnell Moore," Sgt. Saad says.

"Who's he?"

"Good hook, knows how to work inside. Your man's fighting him at the Division Box-Offs."

"So?"

"Maybe your man ought to put in a few extra rounds sparring."

"I'll pass the word," you say.

"You be good now, Elwood," Sgt. Saad says, then gets up and moves away.

"Try my best," you say.

The black guy and white guy are standing by the ice cream now, getting ready to square off.

"This meat loaf sure is great," Knoll says.

"You still here?"

"If you want me to get up and go, I will," Knoll says. "It's just I don't know anyone yet. I didn't want to eat by myself."

"Fuck it," you say, unenthusiastically pushing your food around. Then you see Knoll thinks that means to get up and get the hell out. "No, I mean dig in, stay for the show. You're safer here." The gravy around your food has begun to yield up large fat globules that seem to be advancing on the meat.

"What show?" Knoll asks. Just as Knoll says this, the fight breaks out for a second time. This time, while they're struggling, the white guy whips out his knife and carves into the black guy's leg, right above the knee. The black guy takes an ice-cream scooper and begins smashing the white guy's head. Personnel start swarming over them, and it begins to look like a rugby match.

"Holy moly," Knoll says, watching the melee. He looks like something so fresh and pathetic that you want to tell him to get up and run immediately, that he has no idea what he's in for. You want to tell him he has signed up for a tour of duty in hell. You want to say that it's not even honest like it is in battle, where you look out for the friendlies, shoot the enemy before he shoots you. War, you have been told, isn't so hot, but at least then you have such common interests as staying alive. Here, all the friendlies are enemies, and all the enemies are friendly. The main thing is to keep control of the situation. You keep control of the situation by staying slightly out of control. This is known as Army Zen. The yin and the yang, the yank on the shank.

After the fight's over, all the blood is cleaned up and the two men are hustled off to the infirmary.

"Does this always happen?" Knoll asks. He reminds you of somebody at some time in the past, but you cannot say how long ago that was.

"Welcome to the front," you say.

9

So how, we might ask, did you get into this man's Army? The answer, of course, is ludicrously simple. You volunteered. Not just for Germany but for the whole Army experience. You came in with the True Believers, the Boy Scouts, the tenor section of "God Bless America." You were one of those. There is a reason for this. You have discovered that the Army is like a promiscuous woman. This is a comparison that is both apt and instructive. Like a promiscuous woman, she will fuck any man. But what she truly wants is to be loved, with purity and finality. She does not love draftees, because they give of themselves unwillingly. She loves only her volunteers; and to those who enlist, she will open up the world.

So you enlisted. But not right away. You turned eighteen in 1971, at the bloody tail end of Vietnam, when it seemed as if the war had achieved a momentum and logic all its own and would go on forever, swallowing you as it had so many others. That was the year of your first high school graduation, when you contrived the scheme by which you would save your life and lose your soul.

You were in your senior year of high school, and there were a variety of ways to stay out of the Army. You could try for a Conscientious Objector status, but experience told you that was a hard sell. A religious affiliation would have been helpful in that regard, but you did not have the foresight to get moving on church attendance. As a matter of fact, you were not even particularly opposed to war, though you had sense enough to know that getting killed in one was not your idea of a good time.

You could wait until December 1 and see what number you pulled in the lottery, attending college while you waited. That was a little too chancy for you, however, given your feeling that your number would turn up low. It did, eventually: eleven, very bad field position indeed.

You could truck over the border to Canada, a solution that did not appeal to you on the grounds that there had to be a better way. You considered flunking the medical by taking amphetamines, by gaining weight, by losing weight, by pretending you were deaf or homosexual, by inhaling cigarettes laced with India ink so your X rays would indicate tuberculosis. You heard about pricking your thigh while you gave your urine sample to add a drop of blood, or adding albumin; these were the kinds of ideas floating around. At this point, however, you did not possess the intimate knowledge of evasive tactics that you would eventually master. Other methods of failing the physical extended to mutilation: from obscene tattoos to shooting one's big toe off. The big-toe ploy generally worked, with the disadvantage being that your big toe would never grow back. This method was reserved for the desperate and unimaginative, and there were a surprising number of people who bungled the job and blew off their entire foot. In any case, you liked your big toe.

You thought about feigning insanity, but as friends of yours had discovered, there were so many crazy people in the Army that they simply passed unnoticed. You even investigated the National Guard option, a scam so well known that it had a monster waiting list of volunteers.

None of these methods was foolproof. The problem, you

decided, was that the Army was fully prepared for people who wanted out. You had heard stories of "deaf" people who were asked in a soft voice to close the door as they left the examining room, blowing their cover as they politely complied. One friend abstained from water for twenty-four hours before the exam, then drank a quart of vinegar to turn his urine acidic; all he got was a three-month deferment and a sore stomach. They were like the people who cheated in school by writing the answers on the cuffs of their long-sleeved shirts. The Army was used to them, and disposed of these obvious cheats with bureaucratic good-naturedness.

What you needed was a new ploy. You spent months conjuring, reading all the Army literature you could put your hands on. Then: the loophole that no one had tried. You reveled in the beautiful simplicity that is the hallmark of all great and original ideas. You would go for the defer-ment, but not the college II-S kind, which had lately been shut down. Instead, you would go for the I-S, a high school deferment, which was a lock. The trick was to continue going to high school while remaining in what the Army called "good standing." This meant that you could not fail all your courses but must fail only the courses that were required for graduation. As with most things in life, main-taining a balance between opposite and conflicting positions was the key. If, by the time you turned twenty, the war was still going strong, you could enlist. You would love the Army. When you enlisted, the Army, in the great embrace of its reciprocal love, could refuse you nothing.

There were four months left to your high school career. Your next move in keeping out of the Army called for ex-quisite timing, careful planning, and great discipline. You decided to fail math as your main course and social studies just in case. Fuck math and history, history and math. This was more difficult than it seemed because you had so far been doing well and it would take a determined effort not to pass. With any luck you would stay in high school the rest of your life or until they ran out of war, whichever came first. This was the plan, the loophole. Education was a wonderful thing. Unfortunately, your father—a former police officer, now security consultant, veteran of Patton's Third—heard of your plan from your mother and immediately tossed you out of the house. It was early March, and in Syracuse the snow was still on the ground.

It was time, you decided, to see the world. Since you had no money, travels henceforth had to be done by hitching. The world began on Route 81, flying south with a homosexual painter from Colgate whose watercolor frames poked you uncomfortably in the back. He picked you and your duffel up on a cold sunlit day and took you as far as he could. He naturally asked if you would spend the night, but you had bigger things on your mind and by the next day you were a third of the way across the country. There was a driftiness to the whole thing, as you went from car to car, state to state. You discovered that America was full of people who wanted to tell you the story of the misery of their lives. Their anger at parents and divorces and unfair prison sentences filled the miles. These people did not want you to solve their problems—most of their problems, in fact, had already been solved by the passing of years. What they wanted, instead, was the justice of a hearing, to re-create their sorry pasts as the miles rolled by and you managed to agree now and then.

What you felt as you hitched west was that something was changing. It was in the air, on the move. You started out thinking that everyone was in it together, united by a common cause: antiwar, antiestablishment, prodrugs, tuning the mind to the proper frequencies. But as you got closer and closer to the Pacific, you began to realize that everyone was riding a different wave. By the time you got there, there was no peace, or love, or harmony. You had missed that boat. Things were going haywire. There were bikers and hoodlums and scam artists all working their games. People were hunting each other and preparing for the end. Charlie Manson was king of the beasts. Something had been unleashed, and love had gone to hell. You thought you had left the war behind, that it was going on someplace else, with other people fighting in your place. But in fact, you had left nothing. The war was coming home, from across the ocean, a gathering storm. Hell, it was already here. And the one thing you learned was there were no safe harbors. Pressed for funds, you met Nathan, a refugee from the Haight who introduced you to the efficacy of door-to-door work. You began working for the American Heart Association. A small investment in plastic ID, sportcoat, bright tie, and a lapel button did wonders for your career. In reality you were working not for the American Heart Association but for yourself; the only heart you were helping beat within your own chest. Even so, you developed a great rap in which you explained that you got into this line because someday you hoped to be a cardiologist. Your grandfather, rest his soul, died of a heart attack, and there was no telling about the genetic basis of the disease. As you said this, you strived to have a doomed look on your face. If that went down easily you had a dramatic follow-up about giving him CPR. You described removing his false teeth and whacking him on the chest. This was all delivered with the sorrowful air of a basset hound and was guaranteed to bring down the house and open the wallet. After the first few times, Nathan pronounced you a natural. Should one door be slammed shut, you and Nathan could hustle across the lawn to start your rap over again at the next door.

This type of entrepreneurial work was good because you

only had to hump along between 5:00 and 9:00 P.M. each day. Otherwise people were out at work, and too many door-bells got rung with nobody on the other side. You could pull down between eighty and two hundred a day at this gig, of which your cut was 50 percent. The rest of the day you could be on the beach practicing your sorrowful air and thinking about your Army noncareer.

And your luck held. By this time you were on your own, Nathan having left with his cut and the parting words that the American Heart Association scam had run its course and it was time to get out. Then one day, the day your great luck ran out, a woman answered the door. She was wearing a housedress with faded daisies. Her hair was unraveled, her face swollen. She looked as if she had been beaten.

"I'm Ray Kronquist of the American Heart Association," you said, using your favorite alias. "We're here collecting in the neighborhood, and I wondered if you could spare some money to help us out."

The woman didn't seem to be noticing you. She appeared to be examining a spot somewhere past your left shoulder. Though you wondered if a cop was standing there, you did not turn around. In times of trouble, Nathan had taught you, the best move was to bore ahead with the rap.

The woman then turned her attention to you. "My husband died of a heart attack," she said.

"When?" you asked.

"Last week," she said. "Come on in, the place is a wreck." You walked inside the house.

"My grandfather died of one," you said, moving automatically to the next turn on the rap.

"What was he like?" she asked.

You were going to tell the CPR bit, but that wouldn't come out. Instead, you told her how you bathed him every day. You would pick him up and hold him in your arms like a baby as you carried him to the tub. Once, bending over, you lost your balance and he screamed as you dropped to your knees. As time went on, he became lighter and lighter and you felt like you were carrying one of the pods from *Invasion of the Body Snatchers.*

"That doesn't sound like a heart attack," the woman said, and you suddenly realized that you were in danger of blowing it.

"Cancer and then a heart attack," you said. "Listen, I'd better go."

"I want to give you some money," she said. "Are checks all right?"

"Yes," you said. Checks were not as good as cash, but they still made the grade. Nathan had introduced you to a tame bank teller who was willing to cash these checks for a modest cut of 20 percent.

She wrote out a check and handed it to you. You thanked her without even looking at it. It wasn't until you got outside that you noticed it was for $500, an incredible score.

With the money, you took the plane home in style, first class, and took your final exams. It was nip and tuck all the way, because some of your teachers, with a misplaced sense of charity, knew that by failing the exams you would not be allowed to graduate. They did not know of the grand scheme, and to tell them, of course, was bad policy. But you did the job in math and history, and for an added measure, they tossed in phys ed, which you blew on attendance alone. There was no choice in the matter. You were going to stay in high school and you were not going to get killed. Lack of knowledge was the root of all safety.

The Vietnam War took three more years. You dutifully attended school on occasion, dutifully failed the proper exams, and then took off on your next tour of the country. There was a kind of grandeur to your failure, walking in each term with a secret and opposite agenda. But then one day, when you were on the road, dropping your duffel and waiting for the next ride, it occurred to you that you had seen this stretch of highway and you had seen where it would lead and you had seen where it would end and therefore how you would end. You knew something was waiting for you, around the corner, over the hill, in that great stretch of road in that great stretch of country and you knew exactly what it was.

And all of a sudden, you drew a blank. You couldn't remember your name, what you were supposed to do next, the next thing in the logical progression of days. You sat down and then curled on your side and then went onto your stomach. You have heard from people who have been in the shit that this was what it was like to be wounded—the slow spinning away of the world to the outer edges. You have heard it is like someone shooting out the sun so all the light leaves the room, leaving a coldness that will never get warm. And then a thought came to you that you will forever regret, and you turned around, away from the thing you were heading toward. You stuck out your thumb, hitched back home, and the next day you joined the fucking Army.

You didn't have much trouble with Basic Training. It was a pain in the ass, of course, and it was bullshit, but there was this air to the whole thing like it didn't make any difference. The war was over and now we were going all-volunteer, so we had to be nice to whatever scum we managed to drag in. That was the regulation attitude, at least as far as you saw it.

For some, though, it was tough. There were some Section Eights and people so dumb they could have been the artillery, and there was one guy who reversed his rifle out on the firing range and took the top of his head off like a piece of sod. It was something to see. He had been recycled recently into your squad, but you had never made an effort to talk to him and as he lay there you realized you couldn't even remember his name.

You and another recruit got the duty of carrying his litter to the jeep. He was heavy, as if dying had given him weight and authority. You watched his head, noticing the halo of wetness spreading through his scalp. He was useless now. Meat. As you lugged him, you thought you would never be able to do that to a man, to point a rifle and blow him away. But just as you thought that, you knew it wasn't true—that you could and would, in a second, and that those types of considerations had been left behind and you were not sure when.

The recruit who was handling the feet end of the litter was crying. "The fuck you crying about," the sergeant said when the two of you reached the jeep.

"How come?" the recruit asked.

The sergeant said something in him broke. Those were the words he used. *Something broke.* You imagined that for the Army that was a kind of stock answer, but you began wondering, as you walked back to the rifle range, what that something was. You wondered where it was located, and more important, how to strengthen it against breaking in yourself.

There are three times you have seen somebody die in front of you, and this was the second. The first time had been a year before. You'd been stuck in Galveston, short of cash and unable to get any of your scams operating. To resuscitate finances you'd started a legit stint as a deckhand on a shrimper. You'd been standing on the bow of the shrimper and about ten feet away you'd seen the man go. He had just tied his boat to the mooring, and all of a sudden, no warning, he dropped on the dock. Just straight down, a face-first header right out of the movies. You saw the thing from beginning to end, and from where you were standing, you saw something cross his face—not pain, but a fleeting vision, a word—and then he crumpled, as if someone had yanked the life from him. Later on you heard it was an aneurysm, an extremely thin wall of a blood vessel in the brain, waiting, biding its time before it burst. It had been like a fuse with a surge. Except that what was being turned off was a person. But what you wondered about, even now, was what was it that the man saw, what new word had bubbled to his lips.

Something broke. The sergeant, you thought, held the key. It was something inside, deeper than a blood vessel in the brain, that had failed. Some hidden gear that had worn, an inner spring, some belt that had jumped its track and wound around the heart. *Something broke.* The one thing you were certain of was that you had to guard against this, and monitor the life signs to keep yourself whole.

The Army decided to send you to pharmacy school in Texas for the druggist training program. You had done well in the aptitude tests, and in any case the Army had pretty low quality people to choose from. Once out, with a pharmacist MOS, you could be assigned to a cushy job at a stateside VA hospital to take care of the returning vets. At least that was where the scuttlebutt had it that all the new pharmacists were going. The advantage of this was that instead of having to rise slowly through the pay grades, you would shoot to an E-5, sergeant's pay, by the end of your enlistment, guaranteed. There was some good duty in front of you if only you didn't fuck up.

And of course, fuck up you did. The pharmacist who was training you was named Sgt. Keane. Sgt. Keane, it turned out, was a philosopher. You were there only two weeks before he decided to get you off the sidelines and into the game.

"Come over here," Keane said to you.

You went over to the small bench table where he was sitting. Next to him was something that looked like a diver's tank but was fat and black.

"What do you think?" he asked.

"I don't know," you said.

"Let me ask you a question," he said. "How do you know that you're real?"

"What kind of question is that?" you asked.

"It's the kind of question a person asks who's trying not only to give you the technical skills but educate you. You got a problem with that?"

"I guess not."

"Let's say you were crossing the highway, and just as you were crossing, a big semi eighteen-wheeler comes roaring along and hits you. Would you say that's real?"

"I'd say I'd be dead," you said.

"Who says you were ever alive?" he asked.

"I do," you said.

"Prove it," he said. He waited a moment. "That's the problem. I'll tell you when you were alive: when that eighteen-wheeler was crunching you, you knew you were alive. Let me have your hand." He took your hand firmly in his hands and then struck it against the side of the tank.

"Shit!" you said. "Cut that out."

"Right then, you knew you were alive. It's because you felt it. There are only two times you know you're real—pleasure and pain. The rest is just breathing."

You sucked on your skinned knuckles. "So what?" you asked.

"So the Army, I assure you, it's real. But it only gives you one thing—pain. That's it. That's all. It's made for pain and it's damned good at giving it."

"So what do I do about it?"

"You got to get realer than the Army," Sgt. Keane said.

"How do I do that?"

"I'm glad you asked," he said, beginning to smile. "Let me introduce you to a friend of mine." He tapped his knuckles on the tank.

"What is it?" you asked.

"Ah, my boy," Keane said. "The first step on the road toward happiness."

What it was, of course, was a tank of nitrous oxide, laughing gas. The pharmacy stored it for the dentists.

"The beauty of this—it's all perfectly legal," Keane said. "Not even any long-term side effects."

He showed you how to exhale completely before finally taking the mask, breathing in the gas, letting it flood over you, disconnecting the synapses, pushing aside all manner of thoughts, and sending you into rolling gales of laughter. The high would last a couple of minutes or so, then you could calm down and take another hit.

"I got another for home use," Keane said, still giggling from the last blast. "Bought a canister at a restaurant-supply store. They use it for making whipped cream. The nitrous comes in little bullets called whippets. You just stick one of them little suckers in, suck it up, and you're good for two, three minutes."

Of course, that wasn't all Keane showed you. That was just the test, the first set of moves in the game. If you turned him, it would have looked bad, and maybe he would have been busted down, but he still hadn't done anything court-martial–size. What came next was when he began to show you the chemical processes by which you could distill marijuana into a very potent liquid base. In addition to counting and grinding pills and studying the various properties of ups and downs (the Army had a huge inventory of Dexedrine on hand, which it had been sending to Vietnam for combat ops) you learned the wonders of chemistry and how to purify from nearly any base. You were at this four months before you got caught, when you learned something else about the system.

During that time, however, you had a lot of fun. In addition to your introduction to the pharmaceutical industry, you enjoyed yourself at the base. This particular base, you discovered, had an Officer Candidate School, an eighteen-hole golf course, swimming pools, tennis courts, and three monster officers' clubs. As a matter of fact, you discovered that your base had the highest concentration of officers outside of the Pentagon.

You still didn't have much money, though, still low on the pay scale. Keane, however, your mentor in more ways than one, clued you in to one of the best scams. Every Saturday a new class of officers, second lieutenants, graduated from the school. Their parents and girlfriends came down. The air was filled with ready snatch, although none of it was for you. It was there for the kids who maybe didn't have the chops to get on the real career track at West Point but they had done some college or at least enough for the Army. So graduation day was a big thing for them, something not to be taken lightly.

And there was a tradition to be maintained on Graduation Saturday. Each freshly minted officer that came out of the auditorium, his bars still wet, was dying for an enlisted man to give him his first salute. To the enlisted man who laid the first salute on him, he would give a silver dollar that he had acquired for that very purpose. The scam was to break out the dress uniform and stand by the auditorium door, smoking so as not to look conspicuous. Then, as you heard the new officer approach, his shiny shoes clicking on the asphalt, you would turn and lay a salute on him. It was like collecting a toll. A good Saturday would net you about fifty silver dollars, although they were a pain in the ass to cart around.

How you got caught was simple. It was Keane they were after. He'd been duping the pharmacy logs, sending whole truckloads of amphetamines to the local dealers at bargain prices. You had not even known about this aspect of the operation. With the kind of money this produced, he could have retired in a few years. In retrospect it was clear that Keane had introduced you to the drug end simply so you wouldn't try to cash in too.

So they did not go after you. All the evidence dupes dated from before your arrival on the scene, and the only hand they held was that you hadn't turned Keane when it was clear you must've known what he was doing. The funny thing was, you didn't. You hadn't suspected a thing. You had literally been laughing your ass off the entire time. Keane was given an Article 31: court-martial, with a Punitive Discharge and eight years to think it over in Leavenworth. You just pulled an Article 15: busted down and out of the pharmacy business and sent to Germany.

Sgt. Keane was the first to con you like that, but he was also the one to start you on your path of lifetime learning. You learned that every game has its own natural life span, and the thing was to recognize when it had reached the end and to get out in time. Life is about learning, we know, until you die because you had not learned that one thing. And so here you are now.

But nights when you think about how you got here, you recall not Sgt. Keane but the woman who wrote you the $500 check. As you think of the woman with the dead husband you think also of her careful signature and faded dress.

You felt something there, and that leads you inevitably to a discovery about yourself. It is the kind of discovery that is important to make at one point in your life. It is the kind of information you need to husband against the indignities that have since occurred. You discover that at one point at least, you had a heart.

10

COME NIGHTTIME you are lying in your bunk, never an enviable situation under the best of circumstances. Overhead you hear personnel on the move, heavy hoofbeats that indicate a high probability of yams cruising, looking to put the hurt on. It is in your best interests to stay put, to batten down the hatches and wait out the storm, but you have never been one to take your own advice.

The herd of yams comes pounding down the stairs, a cascade of men. They pound the doors, the walls, rattle the windows, looking for an opening. The door to your quarters, steel-reinforced and bolt-locked, seems to bulge under their blows. It is like being inside a drum. This is standard operating procedure. The idea is to break you down, take you down, put your program on vertical hold and rattle your box. At night, we know, the rules of the game become painfully apparent.

You hear the beginnings of a stampede, a yam avalanche. The yam pack has zeroed on a victim who is now getting a quick introduction to the dynamics of the predator-prey relationship. In the ecology of the barracks the rules remain simple: the smart move is to trade up, and you trade up by getting in with someone like Stoney who is at the top of his food chain. But the four walls are closing in on you, and you have to get going if you hope to make the meet with Kirchfield.

You know where Stoney is—at karate club fine-tuning those Motherfucker skills—and you gauge your chances of making it to the Field House without being taken down. They remain good if you are careful and none of the yams catches you in transit.

You open the door to your quarters and stick your head out. You hear somebody screaming, a body being thrown around, but these are not among your concerns. You could go and help whoever it is, but the probable end result of going in empty-handed would be your ass getting kicked.

You pass other doors, all locked. Your buddies are all hiding out, waiting for the evening storms to pass. Unless you have a buddy like Stoney in your pocket, a king of the hill, a mountain who can make others into molehills, it is an easy thing to cross that thin dividing line between Motherfucker and Motherfucked. Here in Germany it is whites who are in the minority, and no one knows pity.

You run out the side door and into the fresh air, which for a moment causes you to shiver. You are all eyeballs and elbows, stepping into the night, feeling your way through the clear air to the Field House.

First comes the smell. Not the yams but the hash. You press yourself against the side of the building and watch. You make out a bunch joking and toking by the edge of the motor pool, not trying too hard to conceal their action. There's not much to conceal from, in any case. The officers have carpooled home to their little brick shithouses and little brick Army wives and little Army brickbrats, and all that is left on the premises are the MPs and enlisted men. The few officers on watch know enough not to stray and will appear only if things get truly hairy. When the houselights dim, make way for the night feeders.

There is a part of you that wishes to join them, that envies their easy familiarity, rhythms of a life you have left behind.

But to join this group would introduce risks beyond an acceptable level. Even if you know them, even if you have dealt with them before, if they are fucked up enough you may become part of the evening entertainment. You realize you will have to maneuver around this pack, do an end around that will give you a fifty-meter dash through uncharted territory to get to the Field House. You start on this project, creeping around the side of the building and then moving outside the rim of light so that you will not be seen. Surrounding you is the low hum of the base, the traffic on the endless autobahns, the undercurrent of men moving through night. In another time, in another place, if indeed you were somebody else, we might consider this beautiful.

In the woods, past the pack, you pause for breath. Scopes are clear, nothing on radar. You're sweating, but it's not the heat, it's the timidity. You remember coming out during the summer and being stopped cold by hearing somebody sobbing his heart out for whatever reason God only knows. But tonight you are alone.

At the door of the Field House you breathe a sigh of relief. Paranoia index is approaching manageable levels. You go in past the hoops and walk over to Stoney's karate group, where you take a noncombatant seat on the bleachers. Stoney is decked out in his karate duds, the black belt cinched in an awkward square knot around his waist. He sees you and waves one of the yellow foam-rubber hand pads in your direction. Everything on his back comes from your skill at playing the requisition forms; on the other hand your survival is directly attributable to his diligence and considerable ferocity. On the whole, you believe you have gotten the better of the deal. What makes Stoney different is that the capacity for cruelty can be fully realized. Thought is word is deed. Right now Stoney is in the midst of sparring.

It is Stoney's practice as instructor and Chief Motherfucker to take on each of the students, one at a time, all in a row, no rest in between save to bow one out and bow the next one in. Judging from the dilapidation of the students, he is nearly through. He is going at it now with a big white scuzzball MP named Jefferson. Jefferson is actually bigger than Stoney, but he doesn't know how to use it. Stoney crosses one leg behind the other and drives his foot into Jefferson's lower body, propelling him backward. After a few heavy-duty shots to cool Jefferson out, Stoney switches to playing with him, a cat with a beleaguered mouse, stiffening him with the backfist, slapping with a quick kick, a pantomime of pain. Jefferson keeps at it, stepping up to the plate and getting beaned each time as Stoney lobs in kicks and punches. If there is one thing Stoney enjoys, you know, it is giving the white race a taste.

Stoney looks to you as they break, and you tap your wrist, indicating he's running long and to wrap up the show. For Stoney, who in Motherfucker matters is exceedingly prompt, this is as simple as shifting gears. The punches suddenly become sharp and focused. The sheer economy of destruction impresses you. Jefferson freezes, sensing the end, and when Stoney drops him with a body kick, you see him tumble in sections, a tenement crumbling in an old movie.

Stoney picks Jefferson up and dusts him off, giving him a few words of Motherfuckerly advice. There are two types of fighters, you hear him say: those standing up looking down and those lying down looking up, a variation on the essential Motherfucker theme song. One of Stoney's many talents is an ability to cut to the heart of the matter. He looks to you, then turns the group over to an assistant. You stand up and hand him a towel.

"Nice turnout," you say. "You keep beating on them like that they won't come back."

"A little terror never hurt nobody," Stoney says.

"The group gets down to just you it'll be hard to requisition the money," you say.

"I'll make you join," Stoney says, grinning. "Get yourself some people skills." He mops his face, the towel distorting his features for a moment.

"I got you handling the people," you say, which pleases Stoney, "and we have a meet." You tap your wrist again.

"Shower first," Stoney says.

"Whatever," you say. To order Stoney around is both impractical and bad strategy.

"He'll keep," Stoney says, answering a question you haven't asked. "Kirchfield ain't going nowhere without us."

Stoney goes off to shower and you follow. It is best not to stray in situations like this, get yourself involved in a shirts-against-skins game where you could end up stuffed through the hoop. You stand outside the shower and listen to the water beat on his great body. Inside the Field House, basketballs echo over the squeals of sneakers. Stoney comes out with the towel around his waist, pearls of water dotting the coiled hair on his chest. He takes five minutes to get dressed and then you are out in the night air, contrails streaming off his head.

You make your way to the Mercedes by the most direct route possible. When you walk with Stoney no evasive action is required. Personnel part like the Red Sea.

"You don't think you were a little hard on Jefferson?" you ask. After the heat of the Field House, the cold air is a relief.

"Man's got to keep control," Stoney says.

"Keep that terror level up," you say.

"You know something better?" Stoney says.

Terror levels are important elements, you know, in the Stoney philosophy. One maintains terror levels like one keeps a sufficient amount of oil in an automobile engine. To let it get below a certain point means it may seize and bring the shit down. You have known for some time that Stoney's advantage is that he does not believe in anything except himself and his karate-supplemented Motherfucker abilities. He does not subscribe to the hocus-pocus of karate, preferring simply the battle, the fight, the moment of execution. He is also, according to his 201 personnel file, a Category I enlistee, rare in these trying times, posting IQ numbers comfortably within the successful college range. What keeps a guy like Stoney down despite his Motherfucker skills and outsized brain is a diminished capacity for taking shit from the lowly personnel that surround him. He has not yet come to the conclusion that in this life there is some shit you have to take and some shit you don't, and it is this low shit threshold that has landed him in the stockade and, previously, some misdemeanor jail time.

Since he has been with you, however, he has had fewer problems of an administrative nature. You have kept his yin out of the yanger by channeling his Motherfucker energies toward your principal economic endeavor of selling drugs. In this way, you and Stoney and the Parson were an unbeatable combination.

You walk past the guardhouse and onto the road. Garcia, who handles the automotive end of your operation, should have parked the Mercedes just out of sight, around the bend in the road so as not to attract attention.

"Nights like this I miss the Parson," you say.

"Me and him went at it once," Stoney says. "The guy could take a shot."

"Who won?"

Stoney looks at you. "You kidding?"

"You think somebody went and killed him?" you ask.

"How else?" Stoney is, as always, a model of concision, accepting Possibility Number Two as a simple fact of life.

How it worked was you would sit at your table at CC's with the Parson on hand, and interested personnel would approach for discussions of a business nature. The Parson routinely held the shit, which had been divided into dime bags for retail. Wholesale customers like Saad seeking weight made separate appointments. The size and general demeanor of the Parson discouraged would-be entrepreneurs from making a move on your merchandise right there in the bar. On occasion, however, due to the intensely fucked-up nature of the clientele, the mere sight of the Parson would not be enough to impress a customer who might, for instance, have armed himself with a knife or gun. This was where Stoney came in, as strategic reserve. He was usually positioned somewhere close to the door, just outside the light. Once the customer had made his play, the Parson would distract him by bringing up the stuff, and then Stoney would step in and deal with the situation with his customary dispatch. Close, coming up from behind with the element of surprise on his side, Stoney was more dangerous than a gun because he could not be disarmed. There was one occasion, however, when a man tried to take you outside in the parking lot, and after that things were never the same again.

"You know what I miss?" Stoney asks.

"Kimbrough," you say.

"What do you know about it?" he asks.

Garcia, invisible in your Mercedes, flashes his lights at you, blinding you with the brights.

"Fucking asshole," Stoney says.

"At least we know it's him," you say, and Stoney laughs, the tension for a moment relieved.

You reach the Mercedes and climb in. Garcia is sitting in the driver's seat, flicking the halogen headlights he has just installed.

"How do you like that illumination, El?" Garcia asks. He flicks the halogens on again, and they light up the road in front of you. You see eyes reflecting back, the tiny German deer that live around the base frozen by the light.

"Douse the lights," you say.

Garcia leaves them on to annoy you. "Who we waiting on?" he asks.

"Our new security consultant," you say. "He's taking over for the Parson."

"He's late," Stoney says.

"Maybe our new security consultant can't tell time," Garcia says. "But we're not looking for Nobel fucking Prize winners like Stoney here, right El?"

Stoney swivels his head. You see he is considering whether to slug Garcia.

"Cut the shit, Garcia," you say. There is something about Garcia that doesn't like to live. He runs five foot five, 119 pounds after Sunday dinner, and is forced by some inner compulsion to always say the one thing that will result in his ass being stomped.

"You know," Garcia says to Stoney, "we start up I could wrap this car around a tree nothing flat. You here in the death seat, impact lands you right in the hospital."

For Garcia it happens this quick: Stoney fires his left, nailing him just beneath the jaw. Garcia's head bounces off the driver's window, cue ball kissing the eight, a finishing shot.

"Come on," you say.

Stoney shakes Garcia's shoulder gently, just a quick lesson, a Motherfucker Bicentennial minute, and then pushes him with one massive palm to the other side of the car. "Just

so we understand each other." Stoney, besides being con-
cise, does not allow for misinterpretation.

Garcia kneads his jaw. "It hurts," he says. Stoney watches
him, but Garcia is not making any moves.

"Pain is a warning," you say.

"No fucking shit, Elwood," Garcia says.

"I heard you got into it over at CC's the other night," you
say, changing the subject.

"A misunderstanding," Garcia says. "Had to straighten
some chump out." Garcia tests his jaw by moving it from
side to side. When it goes to the right, he has some trouble
moving it back.

"Heard you straightened him out by getting yourself
thrown through a plate-glass window," you say. Stoney
chuckles, always a good sign. "What's your fight record
now?"

"Holding steady at sixty percent winning, fifty percent
losing," Garcia says, as he always does. He moves his jaw
to the left, and then up and down. Except for a slight swelling, it seems to be back in tune. "I give that hundred ten
percent effort." Garcia's life, you understand, reflects the
triumph of the Motherfucked against adversity.

"Turn the lights off," you say, a second time. "We'll flash
them when we see him coming. I don't want the MPs coming down on us, thinking we're terrorists." Security has been
a concern ever since the Baader-Meinhof Gang pulled the
Heidelberg job a few years back, bombing NATO HQ and
wasting a colonel and a couple of enlisted types. Colonel
Berman, of course, has turned even this to his advantage,
invoking the Baader-Meinhof bombing whenever he needs
an expensive construction project, and that is usually
enough to expedite funds from Division.

Garcia flashes the brights once more just for practice and
then turns them off. The woods blacken and in the distance

you see the lights of Mannheim. The dispassionate sky, muscled over with clouds, provides no light.

"How do you like that shit," Garcia says, still talking about the halogen lights. "You flash those at somebody in the oncoming, they'll go right off the road." He giggles with the thought of causing trouble. Garcia's successful violent impulses, you know, are for the most theoretical. In the fighting end Garcia resembles a Volkswagen: always willing but slightly underpowered.

"Here's what pissed me off about CC's," Garcia says, getting back to his plate-glass-window escapade. "That night, CC had just put in that biorhythm machine, you know, type your birthday, it gives a readout of your life line, career, health, energy—shit like that."

"Yeah," you say.

"Mine come out blank," Garcia says. "CC says the pen, it run out of ink but then some cocksucker starts laughing at me. My attitude is, you got to take a stand."

"Get yourself a new attitude," Stoney says, laughing. "Flying through those windows—that can wear a man out."

"I should clean your clock," Garcia says to Stoney, a scenario not in the realm of this reality. It is also evidence that Garcia has ditched his brains somewhere along the learning curve.

There's silence for a while, then Garcia turns to you again. "You heard anything on the transfer yet?" he asks.

"Not a word," you say, "but I wouldn't count on it."

"How come?"

"They're under the impression you're a scumbag," you say. The transfer Garcia is looking for is a shot at the Seventh Cav, where he can be trained as a tanker. For all his difficulties on the human front, Garcia is at home with vehicles. The problem with the Seventh Cav is that Garcia

has been this route before. He was tossed from Tank School
for assaulting one of the training sergeants, after which he
got his ass kicked. For Garcia this is the usual sequence of
events.

"I been keeping in shape, you know," Garcia says.

"How's that?"

"I got a line on an M-1 Abrams," Garcia says. "Going on
some personal maneuvers." Joyriding in tanks is, of course,
strictly verboten, but Garcia knows everybody in Repairs
and can easily borrow one for a spin.

"Just don't go blowing shit up," you say, which would
cause paperwork problems of impressive stature.

"I just got some mail from my folks," Garcia says, keeping
the ball rolling. You don't imagine that in the rest of his
life Garcia gets to speak much before someone tees off on
him. This might be why he's still on your team after all this
time.

"Bad?"

"Worse," Garcia says. "Look at this shit, why don't you."
He turns on the courtesy light and removes a picture from
his wallet.

"What is it?" you ask.

"New family car," Garcia says. "A Pinto, can you believe
it? I think they got the last one alive. I wrote back: 'Buy a
gun and shoot the fucking thing.' " Instead of carrying pictures of a girlfriend or family in his wallet, like most soldiers,
Garcia carries photos of cars he has left behind. In his quarters, by his shaving mirror, is a huge collage of cars that he
calls the parking garage. The wallet contains many pictures
of his current automotive love, an MGB he stores off base.
The key to Garcia, you understand, is that aside from
you, automobiles are the only form of life that will put up
with him.

"My parents, I try to teach them to appreciate the finer things in automotive engineering, but when I go into the service look what happens."

"World's a changing place," you say.

"That ain't all," he says, handing you another picture.

"What's this?" you ask.

"Honda fucking Civic, the cornhole of cars. My sister's. She just bought the damn thing. Friend of her fuckhead husband cut her a deal."

"You got friends like that," you say, slipping into your usual rhythm of agreement with Garcia, "you might as well join the Army and get truly fucked."

"There's a lot of truth to that, El," Garcia says. "Your average Honda Civic, the engine blows while you're steering her out the showroom."

"What are you going to do about it?" you ask.

"What's there to do?" Garcia says, shrugging his shoulders. "It's like you got an idiot born in your family—you do your best and pray."

"Turn off the light," Stoney says, his mind on the business at hand. "I see something." Garcia turns off the courtesy light and flashes the brights.

"There he is," Stoney says, pointing through the windshield.

Kirchfield approaches, shading his eyes against the lights, and peers in through the windshield. You open the back door and, as he settles into his seat, the cold of the air comes with him and you feel the clarity of the night.

"So," Kirchfield says. "It's starting up?"

"Let's get the show on the road," you say to Garcia, intentionally ignoring Kirchfield.

Garcia pulls a U and points you toward the autobahn into Mannheim. The access road is a smooth two-laner. Through heroic memoranda efforts on your part and the construction crew hired by Hermann the German, the little country road has been repaved at US Army expense in order not to buckle under the sixty-ton tank traffic.

"Let me get you acquainted," you say. "Stoney you already know. This here's Garcia, in charge of our motor pool."

"How the fuck are you," Garcia says with his customary grace.

"This is a lot of car you got yourself," Kirchfield says. Kirchfield is bulky and Stoney has his seat all the way back on the tracks, so that Kirchfield is a little cramped. In order to make him yours, you need to make it clear right away who the boss is. To win Kirchfield's heart and mind you must first possess his balls.

You let Kirchfield get a feel for the Mercedes, get him situated on your territory. If there is one thing you've learned in the business, it is how to establish and keep position. Maintain that terrain. You already see some success in this regard. Kirchfield is not coming on like he did in the barracks—he looks like some kid out on a school field trip, face scrubbed, ears washed, Motherfucker tendencies held in check. Black on black against the night, he looks transparent, as if you could open him up and view the heavy machinery of his mind.

"We need some audio back here," you say. "Stoney, hand the man our music library."

Stoney reaches back with the black box and gives it to Kirchfield as Garcia turns on the courtesy light. Kirchfield flips the latch and sees three rows of ten cassettes.

"We got blues, rock 'n' roll, disco, even a classical tape. Mozart for your heart. Make yourself at home. Wait till you hear the kind of sound we can generate," you say. Mood music for Motherfuckers, you think. Get everyone singing in the proper key.

Kirchfield does not say anything, just keeps his eye on the tapes. You have a feeling this is the first look at real transportation Kirchfield has ever had. The key to a guy like Kirchfield is to take him out of his element and put him in yours, where the playbook is unfamiliar. Your Army career has been spent dealing with all varieties of Kirchfields, and you have never seen one who could not be handled.

Garcia slides off the access onto the autobahn and maneuvers into the left lane for maximum speed. He knows the routine, though, so for the moment he holds it down.

"See anything you like?" you ask. "We have a very large selection." Kirchfield simply stares at the box, as if he has opened up a present but can't find the instructions.

"If I may make a suggestion, put on some Billie," you say. "Top left row." Kirchfield pulls out the tape and sees the little knob underneath.

"See that screw at the bottom?" you say. "Give that sucker a yank and then we can take a look at what's behind door number two."

Kirchfield pulls the screw and the cassette tray pops off, revealing the false bottom and the bag you have made up for him.

"That's yours," you say. "You're looking at one O-Z of good faith, cut to retail weight and ready for sale. Stoney, put up Billie."

Stoney slides the tape into the deck. The voice of Billie Holliday fills the car, someone else on the edge, the same old story.

"I got quadrophonic here," you say. "Speakers running front and back, Dolby sound."

Kirchfield is looking intently at the bag, staring at the brown, letting it slide back and forth under the glassine.

"You hear her?" you ask. "You know she used to glom

this shit up. You can tell the way she's singing she's on the string. Ever use on a personal basis?"

"No," Kirchfield says.

"That's good fiscal policy," you say. "But if you deal you have to know how it works. Garcia, hit it."

Garcia hits the halogens and floors the accelerator. He's in third and the rpm's begin building. You open up the bag and scoop out a thumbful and drop it on Kirchfield's wrist.

"Go ahead," you say. "Garcia, ring our Communion bell." Garcia hits the horn, whose noise dissipates into the air.

You take a snootful for yourself as you watch Kirchfield look at the product on his wrist. Garcia has the engine pulling for all it's worth, starting to whine. You keep your eyes on Kirchfield. Motherfuckers, you know, are not by nature good passengers. You are getting him from all sides, the latest in PsyOps technology. Just as you think the Mercedes can't take it anymore, Garcia shifts to fourth and Kirchfield snorts the scag off his wrist. In the back of your own head you begin to feel it work, blossoming, bringing your whole body into tune.

"That's the business," you say. "You're wanting it, wanting it bad, then you take the hit, and it's clear sailing. You can either be snorting or slamming. I advise snorting—that way you stay in charge."

"Yeah," Kirchfield says, a little dazed, his body going through the necessary chemical changes. Here it is, the drug primer: see Dick and Jane get off.

"Put your hand on the seat," you say. Kirchfield touches the seat. Lights flash behind you, and Garcia glances nervously in the rearview mirror.

"Feel anything?" you ask.

"Yeah," he says, and you know from the way he says it that you have him.

"Genuine calfskin," you say. "None of this vinyl shit. I'm talking a 450 SL with a 4.5-liter V8 under the hood. One hundred and eighty horsepower, compression ratio eight to one."

"What the fuck!" Garcia says. The lights behind you are flashing, a car hitting you with the high beams, some German patriot hopping on your rear.

"Here's the deal, Kirchfield," you say, keeping up the full-court press. "I want you in the game. I think you're varsity material, and we got a hole where the Parson was."

"All right, I'm in," Kirchfield says.

"Goddamm it!" Garcia says. "I cannot believe this shit!"

"Crank it," you say, and Garcia steps on the accelerator, shooting forward. You feel Kirchfield tense in his seat as he stares at the speedometer, and you wonder whether he has the brainpower to figure out that it's calibrated in kilometers per hour rather than miles.

"He's still with us!" Garcia shouts. "I can't see with his goddamn brights."

"That's it," you say. You open the door on your side and lean out. You feel the wind against you, filling you like a sail. The high beams of the car behind blind you, as if you were onstage, an audience waiting.

You feel yourself being lifted, being pulled out of the car, about to sail in slow motion over the city of Mannheim, a Superman movie where only your cape is blowing.

"TURN OFF YOUR FUCKING LIGHTS!" you shout, opening your eyes as wide as you can. It's like staring into the sun. The lights suddenly blink down and the rad falls back, switching lanes to get away from you, and you feel higher than before. You feel what God must feel, holding the endless future in the palm of his hand, able to shape it by pure whim. You feel that absolute and perfect sense of control, the Moment of Perfect Clarity that comes when you're at the top of your game, high above it all, playing without a net. And just as you're being lifted up, up, about to fly, you feel something pull you back, and it's the hands of Stoney and Kirchfield who have physically dragged you back into the car and pulled the door shut.

"You're crazy, man," Kirchfield says.

"And don't you fucking forget it," you say.

11

AMONG YOUR DREAMS the most frequent is this: you are in the darkness of the third floor of the barracks, fighting, jabbing, throwing combinations. You cannot see your opponent, but you feel his presence, smell his breath, reel from the heat of his body. When you throw the punches, you hear the slap of your fist on his face, the shock of impact traveling up your arm, but none of them has any effect. You keep swinging while you back up, a Muhammad Ali on spaghetti legs and arms. You keep going until you are against the window. You turn away, but then you see Parsons McCovey hanging by his fingertips. Your opponent inside is still hammering at you, but you ignore the blows, your attention fixed on the Parson. You reach out to help him but at the last minute the helping hand turns into a push, and he begins ever so slowly to fall. Then, from an impossible distance away, he reaches over and pulls you with him. You slip through the window and you too are falling, plummeting toward the earth, which seems to recede as you tumble. You seem to be speeding up, but the earth keeps moving away. You wish you could wake up, but the dream keeps rolling, a movie only in its second reel, and what's worse, there's no way out of the theater.

When you wake, it is Mireille watching you. You have broken your own rule, gone back to the same girl a second time, a victim of your own need.

"What time is it?" you ask.

"Sunday," she says.

"Oh," you say. Saturday has disappeared into the black hole of your life, and you're in for the weekend rate.

"You were dreaming," she says.

"No shit," you say.

She draws back as if you have slapped her.

"I'm glad to be back," you say.

"Come here," she says. She holds your head in her hands, as she would a child, and you press into her shoulder.

"You are sweating," she says.

In fact, your body is slick with fear. "Let's make love," you say.

"Without anything," she says, a question masquerading as a statement. She runs the tip of her tongue along your eyebrows, touching lightly on the bridge of your nose, and then around to your ear. You are aroused but you are afraid you will not be able to get up for the performance.

"Need my vitamins, you know," you say, reaching for your Kodak container. The ultimate weekend warrior.

She pulls back from you. "Let me do something for you," she says, and she pulls her nightshirt off and climbs on top of you. She kisses you, pressing her tongue into your mouth like an old friend, and works her way down your chest. When she gets to your cock, she lifts it by the base, just a light touch, and brushes her lips against it, so light it's like the wind. She opens her mouth and goes down on you, slicking you up and bringing all of you into her mouth, working her tongue around the rim, dipping her head to the root as her fingers rest lightly on the shaft. It's almost enough to get you hard, but your system has been under chemical attack lately and from experience you know you need to fight fire with fire.

"Please," you say, taking her head into your hands.

She looks up. "Not yet," she says, and dips her head down again. While there are signs of life, nothing's thriving.

You wait a minute, Mireille rhythmically pumping away, and then she says, "Come on."

She straightens up, pulling her hair back from the front of her face. Then she adjusts, moving slightly forward, pinning your legs beneath you as she leans the rest of the way. She positions her breasts on either side of your cock, sandwiching it in there. She begins rubbing her breasts up and down along your cock, masturbating you with her tits. It works for you and your reluctant cock like Aladdin and his lamp. You feel it bloom under her, your cock gaining life, the Resurrection, moving with her, your body thrusting up, fucking her chest, and suddenly she turns to the left and scrapes you with the prickly hair of her armpit. This is the honeyfuck of honeyfucks. She has you in her power, your whole life is in her hands and you want to possess her and own her as you drive upward into the soft fold of flesh under her chin. You feel a release that bucks your whole body, because she has taken you to a place you have never been before, and the breath that is coming out of you sounds like a sob. And you bring her gently into your arms and kiss her like Columbus kissing the ground of the New World.

"A QUESTION," Mireille says, bringing you back to the all-consuming present. She has been to the bathroom and back, pulling on a man's silk shirt. Her neck is still wet with water, and one of your hairs has stuck on her by the edge of the V.

"Shoot," you say. You lift the hair off with your fingernail and drop it by the side of the bed.

"This is about words," she says. "What other words in English are there for 'to come'?"

"Oh, Business English," you say, laughing. "How about 'orgasm'?"

"That is a noun, is it not? Is there a verb for 'to come,' or 'coming'?"

"I don't know," you say. "How about 'jism.' That cover it?"

"Can you say, 'I am jisming'?" she asks.

"I guess not," you say. " 'Coming' is one of those all-purpose words." You touch her leg and run your finger over her knee.

"I will make do," she says.

"Whose shirts are these?" you ask.

She looks down at her shirt with the initials on the pocket.

"Oh," she says. Her dark hair falls in front of her face. "They belong to a man which I love," she says. She touches the pocket with her fingers, running her nail along the golden embroidery.

"Who?" you ask, but you don't want to know. Keep it anonymous. Given you a body, taken away her name. Voice in the dark in the confessional.

"My father," she says. "They are his. He gave them to me when I went abroad."

"Oh yeah," you say. It's funny how you think of abroad. You think of her as European, when in fact she's French and psychologically she is farther away from her country than you are from yours.

"Maybe I'll take you someplace," you say, and she shuts down suddenly, a flower closing in elapsed time. "What?" you ask.

"Certainly you will," she says.

"I'm serious," you say.

"Of course." She looks out the window and then back at you. She strokes down your ribs, etching each one with her finger. "Would you like to talk about yourself?"

"What do you want to hear?" you ask.

"Men like to talk," she says. "You have fights, problems, girlfriends, wives."

"Tell me about your first time."

"I have forgotten," she says.

"I want to hear."

"It is boring," she says, closing up again. You can do anything with this woman: she can bring you to the edge, but you cannot gain any part of her, anything to hold on to.

"Want to see something?" you ask.

"Tell me," she says.

You hold out your right hand. "See this dry patch right here?" you say, pointing to a band of skin on the fourth finger. "I used to have a ring there. It was my grandfather's. He was a master sergeant in World War One, fought over in France, got gassed, the whole hero bit."

"It was an heirloom?" she asks.

"We've had it almost twenty-five years."

"That is a very American heirloom," she says, mocking you.

"It's the only heirloom I got."

"And it is the nicest thing about you," she says.

You tell her the true story of your grandfather giving you the ring. He had cancer, and near the end he was so weak he couldn't shave with his old-fashioned straight razor. So every day you took out your electric, which you'd gotten at fourteen to take off the down on your upper lip. You carefully sheared off the white bristles under his chin and above his sunken lips. He would put his teeth in to give you something to press on. When you cleaned the white bristles from your razor they looked like ashes. At the end of one of the shaving sessions he gave you his ring. "Your mother got it for me," he said. "I want you to have this." It was the first time you understood, truly understood, that he was going to die. You kept it with you, but one day you sold the ring to get money for a drug buy. And now you ask yourself what you feel when you remember this. *What do you feel?* The answer is that you don't feel anything. No sadness, no grief. You tell her this and she seems to understand. Your grandfather used to take you on free train rides because he'd been a conductor on the old New York Central for thirty-five years, and he used to take you to his American Legion post, where you played pool and the old-timers told war stories. There were stories of heroes and charges and honor and glory. "It was all bullshit," you say to her. "You understand bullshit, right?" The war stories, you explain to Mireille, didn't prepare you at all for what you are going through now. Now you're in your own war, undeclared, no end in sight. Sgt. York is on the nod. What you're waiting for is the order to stand down. But when you think of your grandfather you remember that feeling you once had. You loved him. This was a fact. It had relevance. Now, you feel nothing. Now he's dead, that's the main fact, turn the page.

"Do you have any brothers or sisters?" Mireille asks, which startles you. You cannot remember the last time you exchanged personal information, talked about yourself.

"Two older brothers," you say. "One fucked up and became a cop. The other one's in medical school."

"A doctor," she says. "He must be rich." She touches her fingers to your face, a healing touch.

"He's not a doctor yet. He has to do a couple years in Mexico. He told me in Mexico all the classes are in Spanish—no English. Well, the joke is he doesn't speak any Spanish. He just sits there trying to figure it out from the textbook. I went and visited him once when I was stationed in Texas. He'd be there, reading the pictures, connecting the dots—so that's where the spleen is. Imagine him working on someone?"

"So you are the bad one?" she asks.

"You kidding?" you say. "I'm their only fucking hope." You rake your fingers through her hair. "I want something from you."

She kisses you, her lips soft on your face. "Here it is," she says. And you understand these rites of concealment, as you have practiced them so long yourself: that to know everything is to know nothing.

"Something else," you say.

"What?" She sits up in the bed and crosses her legs so you can just see the crotch hairs coming out underneath. The shirttail flattens around her.

"Give me something to hang on to," you say. "You know what I mean?"

Mireille shakes her head.

"Tell me something about yourself that you never told anyone before. That's all mine." You are asking her to hand over her key, to give you something different from what you already know. The key to Mireille is that she rents out by the hour to people like you. Knowing this, you need know nothing else. But what you want to know is if there *is* something else, some deeper key.

She touches your head, twisting your hair lightly between her fingers, putting your feathers back in place. "I think you seem to me a very sad man," she says.

"Me too," you say. "But who the fuck cares."

12

ERE IS another dream: you are in Dachau in the rain. A man comes up to you, and his hands are knives. "I will tell you everything," he whispers in your ear. "Everything." He moves closer and his knives chop at you, stabbing you in the hands, the arms, the sides, carving you up bit by bit. You are screeching and then you sink to the ground. There are wounds all over your body, big enough to put your fist through. You have heard that people don't die in their dreams, but you breathe slower and slower and then you are lifted past Dachau's gate, looking up at the tangled web of metal—the stick-figure skeletons in agony. You are carried past the pistol execution fields where the red flowers grow in obscene abundance and then are moved to the side of the building. There are shoes piled in neat rows outside the gas chambers, and everybody walks in their stockings. The dead enjoy their ceremonies. And then you're carried inside to the ovens. The ovens look small, and the doors stand ajar. You have the feeling that they are like the sacramental doors to the altar, and if you looked inside you would see the solution to some great mystery. You reach out with your hand and touch one of the doors, pulling it back, and from where you are standing there appears to be nothing but black. But then you see a small light at the back, a flicker, and you are pushed forward, looking straight down into the old brick.

You see a face suddenly old and familiar, the face you've been waiting for all along.

"It is time, it is time," you hear. "Get yourself awake." You come out of the dream. Your head is pounding and you look to the digital by the bedside. Six twenty-two and you still have to make the 0700 morning formation or Sgt. Lee will have your ass.

"You said that you were awake before," Mireille says. "I have made coffee. Would you care for some?"

"Yeah," you say. Your voice is thick, and you are surprised you have the strength to muster even that much. You are all in favor of chemical intervention of any kind. You have something a little stronger planned for later, a couple of Dexedrines to prop open your lids, gain a little altitude on the day, get that all-important clearance. All you want to do is get through the day. Severe party fallout used to take you one day to recover from, but now you're going into the second, still without having hit the Glide or MPC Zone.

Mireille brings the coffee and you get your feet onto the floor and begin dressing. In the olden days, just a few weeks ago, you didn't have to make morning formation, just get to Battalion HQ shortly before Colonel Berman cruised in from the Breakfast Club meeting with General Lancaster. That would be somewhere around 0900, bankers' hours, but ever since Sgt. Lee took over your platoon, he has required everyone, even headquarters personnel and those with educational duty assignments, to be there for morning formation. You haven't the slightest doubt that Sgt. Lee is doing this to get to you, catching you at a bad moment in the biocycle.

"You do not look very well," Mireille says. "Maybe it is time you should give them a call that you are sick."

Mireille, you understand, labors under the impression that the Army is like a civilian firm except that everyone wears funny uniforms. The enforcement end of the post office, perhaps. Calling in sick is not among your real-world options. You look in the mirror to ascertain the damage. You have definitely been grievously wounded. Battlefield casualty of chemical warfare, brain evacked to parts unknown. You regret that you are very low in the important medical supplies. There's a little bit of stuff left at the base, but not much. On the other hand, you figure that a little break might not be such a bad thing. You've taken so much in the past forty-eight hours that you could have built up a temporary immunity to its wondrous effects. Your eyes are swollen, your face is puffy, you are nauseous and hungry at the same time. There is not a part of your body that doesn't feel as if it has been pierced with a sharp instrument. And in addition to this, you have to take a shit.

You maneuver your body to the toilet, where you drop your drawers and sit down. Every country, you have learned, has different shitting customs. You would think that this is the kind of thing that due to its ubiquitous nature would be standardized. Your Indians squat on their haunches over a hole, your French shit in one pot and scrub in another, assembly-line style, your Spanish have put in bidets to take care of the assholes of the French, and your Italian worries about water pressure. Water pressure is not a problem for the technically advanced German shitter. Your average German shitter, doubtless for scientific reasons, drops it dry onto a porcelain shelf where he can watch it. Get that thing out on the observation deck and eyeball it. The master shit. In the morning this is an especially discouraging sight. The shit you squeeze out is hard, one dry little finger of turd, and it lays there on the shelf, orphaned from the mother shit that you feel you still have growing within you.

Feeling only marginally better, you drink a little coffee as you button your shirt and struggle into your uniform.

"I gotta go," you say.

"You will eat the breakfast?" she asks. You smell the coffee and the German sausage frying, and the warmth of the eggs along with them. They add to your nausea.

"I love you so much," you say, and she strokes your hair with professional courtesy. You don't believe you will ever see her again.

You kiss her good-bye and get outside the building and you blank for a moment on where you put the car. Shit, you think. The part of your brain that contains where you parked your car has been lost. You look at your watch: six thirty-five and the shit is getting deeper as we speak.

You set off in the likeliest direction, trying to think. There's a light layer of snow this morning, just enough to make it slick. There are several moments when you nearly hit the sidewalk. In this part of the world there are too many fucking Mercedes, and you have only twenty-five minutes to get to the base, stash your vehicle, and make the morning formation. If you don't, Sgt. Lee, who is waiting for this opportunity to ream you out, will doubtless confine you to the base. You find the Mercedes, scrape yourself a quick peephole, and pull out.

On the autobahn you drive in the left lane, which hasn't been cleared from the night before. One of the things you love doing, you have to admit, is driving. You're not as good as Garcia, who is a combat kind of driver, but you're good enough. Driving in Germany, when you have something under the hood, is pure. Most Americans don't agree, because at rush hour it doesn't matter if you're cruising at 200 kilometers per hour, there's always some rad asshole on your tail trying to take over your lane. But you've got your righteous machine at your fingertips, and that's what gives you the rush. It's the closest thing to having sex or doing scag that you can engage in legally. The speedometer creeps up as you take the curves, banking into them, one after the next, your accelerator pedal pressing against the floor. On days like today, when your life is slowly kicking in, it's like you were born to this.

You make it to the base with one minute to spare. You hop out, cover the Mercedes with the camouflage tarp, and double-time it to the main gate. You flash your ID, get in, and you're coming around the corner huffing and puffing, your heart feeling like the demands made on it are too much, just as Sgt. Lee is moving along the line of troops.

"Elwood," he says. "Your ass is mine."

Sgt. Lee starts everybody off with laps. You hear the ice crunch under your feet as you set off. The men pass you on either side. You have pains in your ribs, in your head, your back, your knees, your feet. You have to take another shit, and you think back fondly to your German toilet. More men from the platoon pass, until finally you're doing an imitation of someone running in place.

Sgt. Lee comes up next to you. He is strack. If he were a car, he'd be fucking polished chrome. "Are we having fun yet?" he asks.

You feel it start to give. You bend over, and you're coming up with the dry heaves. You feel the taste of quinine in your mouth, migrating to your nose, and you'd give your guts to the Army, but there's nothing to give but wind.

"Hell of a way to start a week, Elwood," Sgt. Lee says, hovering.

You are on your hands and knees, and the spit covering your chin is beginning to freeze in the cold.

"Put yourself on sick call," he says. "I want a full report."

"I'm here," you say. You feel the nausea pass and you get up, a little shakily, to your feet. Sick call can be bad news in this particular climate of opinion. Someone might give you a blood test that would reveal your high octane level, so you'll take your chances in the field.

"Get back in fucking line, Elwood," Sgt. Lee says. "Get ready for push-ups."

Sgt. Lee runs you through the drill for forty-five minutes of Physical Training, then marches you to the armory, where you're issued M-16s. Next stop is the firing range to blow the fuck out of paper targets.

There is a strong wind blowing, pushing snow across the fields, and you are laying down single rounds. Knoll is alongside you, squeezing them out of his 16, one by one. The Top is coming down, inspecting everyone's work. The Top stops at Knoll, squints, and waits until the targets come back.

"Shit," he says, "you can shoot a gnat off a water buffalo."

"Thank you, Sarge," Knoll says.

"You, Elwood," he says, looking at your nearly clean target. There is only one bullethole on it, and with your shooting ability you suspect it's a stray from someone else's rifle. You are happy, in fact, simply to be facing in the proper direction. "You can't shoot for shit," Sgt. Lee finishes.

"Thank you, Sarge," you say, and you realize immediately that provoking Sgt. Lee when your life signs are at their current low levels is a particularly bad move.

"I want you to put in some extra time here in case Headquarters comes under attack," Sgt. Lee says. "Knoll, stay here and show Mr. Fucking Headquarters how to shoot his rifle. Don't come back until I see some passing scores on the targets." The Top laughs, then walks down the line.

When the platoon packs up and takes off, you and Knoll are left together.

"You look like someone was shooting at you last night," Knoll says.

"If they'd hit me," you say, "I'd shitsure be out of my misery."

"You want to do some target shooting?" Knoll, as always, sounds enthusiastic about the dullest things.

"I hate rifles," you say. "They should be outlawed. Particularly in the Army."

"Guns don't kill people," Knoll says, "people kill people."

"With fucking guns," you say.

"You want to know how to shoot, I'll help," he says. "I notice you keep closing one eye. You do that, your depth perception is off. Then you're lucky to hit the target at all."

You keep both eyes open and squeeze out single-shot rounds into the target. Some of them even hit.

"That's better," Knoll says. "Next thing you got to work on is holding your breath. That prevents your body from moving as you shoot."

"That so?" you say.

"The real professionals even try to squeeze off the round between heartbeats," Knoll says.

"Knoll, you're giving me a headache," you say. "Where'd you learn all this shit—in college?"

"My dad," Knoll says. "We used to go target shooting together. Once I knew what I was doing, he took me hunting in the woods. Go ahead, try it."

Sgt. Lee is still hustling the men along, so you lay down another set of rounds, taking your time, holding your breath. You feel a stillness to the world cracked only by the rifleshot, but each one still misses the target.

"It takes a while to get used to," Knoll says. "It's really relaxing after a while. This way, you're one with the target. You can't hit the target unless you are the target."

"Zen and the art of homicide," you say.

"What difference does it make if it works?" Knoll says.

And that, you have to admit, is one of your principles of operation. Maybe you've read Knoll wrong, you think.

"Come on back to the barracks," you say, now that you and Knoll are alone on the firing range. Sgt. Lee has double-timed the men back to the armory.

"Don't you have to get passing scores?" Knoll asks.

"I'll let you in on a secret," you say. "Once I get to our quarters, I'm the best marksman in the 57th."

"We should drop these off at the armory," Knoll says, motioning with his M-16 as he stands up from the prone position.

"You can do that on the way to your duty assignment," you say. "You want something hot? I can cook up some premium ground coffee with vanilla bean while I'm working on my scores. You in the mood?"

"Sure," Knoll says.

Back at your quarters, you rinse out the coffeepot, put in the gold filter, grind down the fresh vanilla bean, and put up the pot.

Knoll obviously hasn't really settled in yet, still keeping his shit in one corner of the room. "This is some setup here," he says. "I was going to ask if I was allowed to use the coffee."

"Help yourself from now on," you say. "Meanwhile let's dip into the armory."

Knoll instinctively reaches for his M-16, but you shake your head and go to the desk and pull out two pencils. You place them in the electric sharpener and bring them to a fine point. "It's important to keep your fucking weapon properly maintained," you say, holding them up and admiring your handiwork. "A properly maintained weapon can save your life."

You walk up to Knoll as you hold out the pair of pencils. "What we have here is a field-stripped number two caliber pencil, sharpened to a military edge. Go ahead," you say, "choose your weapon."

Knoll picks one of the pencils. "Handle it carefully," you say. You sit down on the sofa next to him and pull out one of the targets.

"This is known," you say, "as the M-16 pencil, most powerful piece of ordnance ever developed by the Army." You begin punching bulletholes in the target, getting good tight clusters.

"It looks just like an M-16 bullethole," Knoll says.

"You catch on fast," you say. "The pencil's mightier than the sword. Do some shooting yourself and then we're done. Coffee's up."

You stand up and fix Knoll his coffee, giving him sugar and heavy cream that you have purchased from CC at a great discount from the Sgt. Saad distributorship. He finishes punching in the bulletholes and then you pick up the targets and look them over.

"Nice target spread," you say. "You really have an eye for this kind of detail work."

Knoll puts down the targets and sips the coffee. "This is really nice," he says. "Really, just like home."

"We get by," you say.

"Want to see some pictures of my girlfriend?" Knoll asks.

You nod, the expansive host, the perfect roomie.

Knoll pulls out his wallet and shows you the pictures of the girl.

"Private Margolis?" you ask.

"Carol Ann," he says. The pictures show a woman who is as plain as Knoll. Good honest face that shows no recognition of the danger she has put herself in. There are some people, salts of the earth, pillars of the community, who line up willingly to get fucked. Where would America be without the Motherfucked, you wonder.

"What's this, your senior prom?" you ask, holding up a photo of Knoll and Carol Ann. Knoll nods. In the picture he sports a white tux, black pants with the silk ribbons down the sides. She's wearing a low-cut strapless gown and holding a bouquet of flowers.

"You have any pictures?" Knoll asks.

"No," you say.

"Oh," he says.

You hand the pictures back to him and he carefully inserts them in his wallet. "I've been saving up for a ring."

"That so?" you say.

Knoll pulls a small box out from his shirt pocket and opens it up. "There she blows," he says.

You take the ring out of its velvet slot. It is white gold, one diamond surrounded by small chips. "How much this run you?" you ask.

"Eleven hundred and fifty," he says.

"You have that kind of change?"

"I saved up for a three-hundred-dollar down payment," Knoll says, "and the rest I'm paying off."

You hand the ring back to him. "Big step," you say.

Knoll suddenly looks frightened, as if he had never thought about it before. "Yeah," he says.

"Let's finish up here," you say, picking up another target and blasting away at it with your pencil, a highly accurate weapon for close-in fighting during the memoranda wars. You have spent many an afternoon gunning down targets in your office, keeping the marksmanship profile high for the annual battalion M-16 qualification test. High marksmanship scores in a logistics battalion give evidence of Colonel Berman's strength and leadership capabilities, two categories on the OERs that require constant upkeep.

You think of Knoll getting married as you try to isolate the pain in your head. The way to ward off pain is to put a little circle around it, create a perimeter. Inside is you; outside is the pain. To keep you inside, get that mind occupied.

Knoll is a simple son-of-a-bitch, you think. Someone waves the flag, he'll happily step right up and get shot. The Army needs people like that. The Army, you understand, *is* people like that.

Overhead, you hear the yams on the move again. The rumble of the jungle. Why couldn't Sgt. Lee be assigned to those guys, you think, some of the loose cannons on the Saad Squad. They would eat his ass alive, mail him home Federal Express.

"We're done," you say, finishing up the last target. "We've got to get to our duty assignments anyway."

You unlock the door and walk out of the barracks into the cold with Knoll, him just slightly ahead of you. The sun has appeared from behind the clouds and some of the snow is already beginning to melt, exposing patches of grass beaten into mud.

"I've got to go this way," he says, nodding to the left. Just as he says this, a lit cigarette hits him in the head and bounces onto his shoulder.

Knoll yelps, grabs his neck, and jumps back into the doorway. You look up and in the third-floor window you see the flash of a dark face.

"What's that?" Knoll asks. You kneel down, pick up the smoldering cigarette. A Winston, you observe. Smoked almost down to the filter.

"Winston tastes good like a cigarette should," you say. "First combat injury. Maybe they'll give you a Purple Heart."

Knoll, still rubbing his neck, suddenly turns and runs inside the barracks. "Let's get those sons-of-bitches," he shouts, bounding up the stairs.

"No," you say, not following him, startled that he would

do such a thing. Something like this cigarette, you know, is something to ignore, a random example of the ambient hate filtering down.

"Get back here, Knoll!" you shout, but then you hear shouting, and a body slams into a wall. You hear a scream—Knoll's voice. For a moment you're uncertain as to what to do but royally pissed at Knoll in any case.

Just sit tight, you think, ride it out. Not your fight. But then you tire of this, of always being cautious. It is time, you figure, to assert your authority. The next move, you think, is important. You have to decide whether or not to take the M-16. Taking the rifle means that you've just upped the ante. They've undoubtedly got Knoll's rifle, so going in locked and loaded could mean a shoot-out, and your most accurate shooting occurs only in the confines of your office. But going to a fight, you understand, has some of the same protocols as going to a birthday party: it is best not to arrive empty-handed. If Daniel ventured into the lion's den today, you figure, he would feel a lot better going in packed. So fuck it. You go through the door quietly, trying not to make much noise, keeping the rifle pointed in front of you, safety off. Slowly, you climb the stairs.

As you reach the third-floor landing, you turn out into the hallway, expecting to find the party. But no one is there. You take three steps and you hear a noise, turning slightly to your left. That's when you get hit from behind.

The pain from the impact nearly knocks you down. You stagger across the hall, and someone kicks you in the kidney. Your legs begin to go out on you, but you manage to turn back to the wall and level the rifle. Knoll is in a doorway, being held by two yams while a third is searching his pockets and a fourth is punching the piss out of him. His rifle is in the hands of another yam, and it is pointed at you.

There are seven of them, and you recognize only one, a
yam named Walters. The guy who's holding on you is another newbie, and his rifle, while aimed at the center of
your chest, registers a good deal of movement. It's a Mex-
ican standoff, your rifle aimed at him, his rifle aimed at
you. The first one to shoot dies within a second or so.

"This is the fucking wild West, ain't it," you say.

"Elwood," Walters says, "maybe you should turn around
and get yourself home."

"You got the balls for this, son?" you ask, addressing the
kid with the rifle, working on him. Odds are he's holding
the rifle because he didn't want to get involved in the shit-
kicking. "You ready to go one on one?" The ones punching
Knoll have stopped and are all facing you.

To shoot somebody would be to cross over a line and to
take an irrevocable step that even Colonel Berman with his
great memoranda capability would be unable to change.
But you are already past that point, and you cannot go back
now. You're ready to do it, you realize. You've been ready
and waiting all along.

"They's more of us than you," Walters says, looking at
your rifle. But Walters, you know, is all mouth, and doesn't
have the chops for the dirty thing.

Without looking, you switch the m-16 selector from
single-shot mode to full automatic. You can see that the
yams all register this, too. Your rifle is still on them, not
moving an inch. You feel like picking up one of your targets
to show them how accurate you are. A little piece of ad-
vertising, a selected media event.

You breathe in, exhale, breathe, exhale. Squeeze the trigger slowly. Don't jerk it. Keep the barrel from jumping up.
Your breathing is the only sound in the hallway.

"Now," you say, "I think there's more of me."

The yams back off, unwilling to bring this thing to its logical conclusion. Just as Walters heads down the stairs, he says, "I'll be seeing you, man."

"You bet," you say. There is a part of you that is relieved, but there is also a part of you that was looking forward to the finish.

"Holy shit," Knoll says. "Thanks."

"Let's get out of here," you say. You want to get as far away from Knoll as possible. You walk silently with him to the armory and then go on to the office. Once there, you fix yourself some more coffee and fire up a cigarette. What strikes you, as you pour the brew into the cup and then sip it, is how aware you are of every little thing. The cool grip of the coffee mug, the dry cylinder of the Camel, the bite of the winter morning, the bulging eyes of Walters. You remember all the little details, as if they'd been singed into your memory. As Sgt. Keane, the Saint Paul of pharmaceuticals, liked to say, there is nothing like death to make you feel more alive.

13

YOU SETTLE DOWN after a while, working on what's come in the morning sack, and in due course you have established deep penetration on the genealogy front, one of Colonel Berman's continuing projects. You buzz him.

"Talk to me, Elwood," Colonel Berman says.

"I have a genealogy update for you, sir," you say. "I think we have something here."

"Glad to hear it," he says. "Put the evidence together and then give me a presentation."

"Yes sir," you say.

The genealogy front, like most of Colonel Berman's activities, is about career advancement in the New Army. Career advancement in the peacetime Army is slow and arduous and is accomplished, you have come to understand, by incremental virtues rather than hard charges. It involves not the momentary spark of blind courage but planning, delicate conversations with ranking officers at carefully managed parties, and the willingness to seize the initiative with a well-timed memorandum thrust.

Since your fortunes are very much tied to those of Colonel Berman, you admire his grasp of the essentials of peacetime conquest. Likewise, through your memoranda skills, he appreciates you because you have become the tactical arm for the strategic necessities of advancement. For parties you order the drinks and food, print the invites, arrange the help, and bartend. Through your skills at titration you are able to make a vodka martini that would blow the treads off a tank. In this wonderful symbiosis there is, naturally, a way in which your purposes are also served.

So Colonel Berman is in for the long haul. No charges uphill against a determined enemy. No ambushes, no fire-fights. The only thousand-yard stare he gets is after a long day spent processing hostile paperwork. Heroes are an an-achronism. Colonel Berman has come to terms with the fact that in the New Army it is no use being in the infantry if there is no one to fight. While being a hero hasn't reached the status of being a liability, it has quite simply become beside the point.

Most people would assume that they are stuck with the circumstances of their birth. Colonel Berman, however, with his endless creativity, has found a way to change even that, and before you lie the intimations of a clear-cut tactical victory on the genealogy front. It is here that Colonel Ber-man believes he needs heavy sandbagging; and because it subverts the Army, it is one of the areas in which you are proud to serve.

It is Colonel Berman's goal to prove he is descended from General Francis Marion, who fought in the Revolutionary War and was known as the Swamp Fox. By proving this, he would up the genealogy coefficient and therefore improve his overall career advancement potential index.

For his last post Colonel Berman was stationed in South Carolina, and it was there that the idea began to take shape. Francis Marion fought a guerrilla campaign against the redcoats from the swamps of South Carolina. While reading one of his many military magazines, the Mr. and Mrs. Colo-nel were struck by his uncanny resemblance to the artist's conception of Francis Marion, and so began the search.

When the Colonel Bermans left South Carolina to take over his command in Germany, they commissioned a lawyer to track down courthouse records, correspondence, passenger-ship lists, newspaper morgues, even family Bibles. It is part of Colonel Berman's talent never to let reality become a sticking point but instead to convert it to his own military uses.

Each month the lawyer sends in a report, Xeroxes of raw material that he's discovered, possible ways to link the two up. On their own, the Mr. and Mrs. Colonel have questioned everyone in their families, found the cities in which they lived, and are working back from their end to the inevitable intersection.

It is your job to digest the raw material and keep track of new developments. Right now you have seventy pages of Bermans begetting. A history of holes and hard-ons. At times, when you have read too many pages in a row of Bermans getting it on, you imagine a torrent of heatseeking Berman sperm, searching out Marions wherever they may be.

In the Berman line there were preachers, merchants, thieves, and a lot of military types. The strong suit of the military being documentation, they are the headliners here, with their ranks, battles, and decorations cited in abundant and excruciating detail. "We Bermans have always borne the burden of our country's ambition," Colonel Berman has written in the preface to his genealogy. "It is an article of faith among us that American ambition and Berman fate are inextricably linked."

This is, of course, the truest statement in there. "Having a well-connected set of genes in one's camp never hurt anyone's career," Colonel Berman has said, although you have naturally not included that bit of information in the preface. As a matter of fact, you feel lucky Colonel Berman is going back only as far as the Revolutionary War. You feel certain that if the Colonel heard that Noah had held a commission, you'd be searching ship's manifests back to the Flood.

You look down at the reports and underline the point of convergence in Lynchburg, Virginia. There may have been some begetting going on between the Francis Marion tribe and the Berman horde. It takes you about an hour to highlight the important passages in yellow, paging through the report, double-checking your charts. When you are done, you buzz him again.

"Talk to me, Elwood," Colonel Berman says.

"I have something definite now, sir," you say.

"Bring it in," he says.

"Yes sir." You gather your documentation and go into the office.

"Bring me up to speed," Colonel Berman says.

You lay it out, explaining the Lynchburg convergence, showing him the highlighted areas, and Colonel Berman nods. "Looks like a promising lead. Get that out to the lawyer to focus his energies on that city." He pauses and then sighs. "I just can't get too excited about it, though. Too many other misses. I still haven't gotten over Charleston. Thought we'd nailed a Marion there."

Charleston, South Carolina, was one of the early and big defeats in the genealogy war. The information came from some of the diaries of the ladies who made up the society of Charleston. You had quality documentation, confidence was high. A Berman had moved into town, and it looked as if he or one of his offspring would score with a Marion. All you needed was one debutante to get a little out of hand. But then Berman and company disappeared from the diary accounts and guest lists. It took three months of tracking down court records before it was discovered that this Berman, who had been a manufacturer of patent medicines, had been caught lacing his headache-and-flu formula with tincture of morphine. While morphine was not technically illegal at the time, several of his patients had died from accidental overdoses. He had managed to leave town a step ahead of the law and afterward had shown a certain reticence about the documentation of his whereabouts. Naturally, you feel a certain brotherly sympathy toward a man so far ahead of his time.

"Do you know Pookie Marshall is going around again saying he's descended from George C. Marshall?" Colonel Berman asks. Pookie Marshall is on General Lancaster's staff and as such is Colonel Berman's main competition.

"I doubt Lancaster would be taken in by that old chestnut, sir," you say.

Colonel Berman suddenly freezes, and you wonder if he thinks you're making fun of him.

"At the party we're going to outflank the son-of-a-bitch. We have some preliminary documentation, and we're going to press hard with that."

"Yes sir."

"Oh, and another thing. I want you to arrange for a baby-sitter. We'll go up to three dollars an hour."

At the last party Colonel Berman's baby-sitter sneaked drinks and ended up blowing lunch on the floor of the kids' bedroom.

"I'll find somebody good," you say.

"Is that all, Elwood?"

"I have an idea, sir," you say, which has occurred to you just this moment, in the nature of an MPC.

"Yes?"

"The party motif. Your wife mentioned she wanted something martial."

"What were you thinking?"

"Revolutionary War, sir. The perfect time to announce this possible Lynchburg connection between you and Francis Marion."

Colonel Berman's eyes begin to bulge, but then he extends his hand. "Specialist Elwood," he says. "Ray. I consider you a friend."

Back at your desk, you see the telltale light appear on the phone bank. Conference call to the Mrs. Colonel, the Erwin Rommel of career advancement. The light is on for a while as you prepare the pages, and you imagine them cheering back and forth over the good news. When you look up, however, you see what you were waiting on, and that starts the next phase in the game.

You can see her through the window in the visitors' lot. As you watch, she maneuvers the hood on an old Ford Mercury Montego, all in yellow, an old boat ready to sink. It is the Top's kid, the girl who could do a two and a half in the pike position while flying with one wing and doesn't mind using the other wing to pick up discounts over at the PX. She is, you think, your type of girl.

When she bends over to examine the car, you are up, your coat on, and heading toward the Colonel's personal vehicle, which you have access to for non-Army errands. You drive over, pull alongside, and get out. You see her staring straight down into the guts of the car. But then you stop for a moment. One arm is resting on the car, the other is held against her body. Is it live or is it Memorex.

She turns toward you, looking up. She's just come from swimming, her hair tucked under a knit cap, little wet ends poking out.

"Won't start?" you ask.

"This always happens," she says. "I think maybe the battery."

You're looking at the arm you think is the fake. "How

about I jump you," you say, but she doesn't stiffen, just takes it all in as she nods.

You get the cables out of Colonel Berman's trunk and attach them to the terminals, then have her try to turn over the Montego. It doesn't work, which doesn't surprise you because earlier you told Garcia to take the car out of action. Garcia, with his love for automotive complication, suggested working something with the distributor cap, which he could then repair.

"It may not be the battery at all," you say. You twist off the butterfly nut on the air filter.

"It's my dad's car," she says.

You pick up the air filter and study it. Even your unpracticed eye can see that a tune wouldn't hurt this thing.

"You're the Top's kid, right?"

"Guilty," she says.

"I'm Elwood," you say, extending your hand. "I'm your dad's biggest problem."

"That's 'cause you don't know *me* well enough," she says, taking off her glove to shake your hand, and you know right away that this girl has the potential to be a player. She's not in the game, but she's got the right instincts. She's all suited up on the sidelines, waiting for the word.

"How about this?" you say. "I got a buddy he can fix just about anything. I give him a buzz, he comes over takes a look."

"Sounds decent," she says.

"Want a cuppa coffee while you wait?" you ask.

"Do I," she says.

"Catch pneumonia you stand here long enough," you say, and she comes alongside as you walk back to the office.

Inside, you make the call to Garcia, who has been instructed to take his time. Once off the phone, you get your first good look at her. She's got a long face, really pale, almost pretty. Her nose is red and stuffed, and her eyes are a little bloodshot from the chlorine.

"How come you helped out at the PX?" she asks. "Is this a setup or something?"

"Swim much?" you say.

"That's where," she says. "I saw you take the towel."

"I remember you, too," you say. "Me, I'm afraid to even go up the platform. It'd be like jumping off a goddamn building."

"That's the fun part," she says. "I want to know—why'd you take the towel?"

"You like your coffee how?"

"Black," she says.

"You always do what scares you?" you ask, pouring two cups, one black, one heaped with sugar to get your own carburetor cleaned out.

"I try," she says.

"So do I," you say.

"No you don't. You only take chances you think you can win."

"Maybe," you say.

"Your friend, when's he coming?"

"Already on the way," you say. "You going to tell me your name?"

"Robyn," she says.

"With a 'y,' right?"

"You already knew my name," she says.

You pick up a 201 file. "Did some reading up on you," you say, waving the file.

"What else does it say in there?"

"Everything nobody gives a shit about," you say.

She looks away, out the window, but the Montego is just

sitting there, hood raised in surrender. You think she's getting ready to bolt.

"Let me ask you a question," you say, looking at her arm.

"Okay," she says. "What do you want to know?"

"Everything," you say.

She looks at you. "People don't ask, you know. They just assume it's too painful."

"Is it?"

"Not anymore." She twists the cosmetic arm off and you realize she's done it to shock you, to see if you'd turn away. You hang right in there, staring at the loose sleeve and the nub just peeking out.

"It's a boring story," she says.

"Maybe to someone else, but not to me. You want a cigarette?"

She looks outside and sees Garcia pull up. "There's your friend. Maybe we should go outside so he knows which car it is. Yes, I'd like a cigarette."

"How many yellow Montegos you think there are?" You hand her a cigarette and light it with the Varick.

"Thanks," she says.

"The reason I took the towel," you say.

"Yes."

"I wanted it."

She nods, familiar with the reasoning, sucking in the smoke and blowing it out.

"You're not going to tell me, are you?"

She shakes her head no.

"That's all right," you say. "How about we set something else up?"

"What?"

"Like a party. You like parties?"

"Sure."

"I'm working a party for my CO. How about you come by, baby-sit his brats."

"I don't like that shit," she says.

"Ten dollars an hour," you say, improving somewhat on Colonel Berman's initial offer.

"Really?"

"Officer's kids," you say.

"All right." She stands up, puts down the coffee. "Thanks for the coffee."

"Want to talk some more over dinner?"

"Okay," she says. "What's your name, anyway?"

"Ray," you say.

"With a 'y,' right," she says.

14

Benjamin Franklin Village, where the Top's personal HQ is located, mostly reminds you of welfare apartments back home. Mondo condo. Four-story brown brick, toys and barbecues left out, bicycles with bent frames locked to trees, half-assed kind of playgrounds.

Nonetheless, most of the enlisted personnel who want to live off base, on the economy, try to get in here. There's even a waiting list for that, which the Top, with his General Lancaster connections, must have bypassed.

Crossing the parking lot toward the village, you note the number of American cars. Your Fords, your Chevies, your AMCs. Few of them born in this decade, and the body rot approaches plague proportions. The Army provides transport for cars from stateside, and there's an American dealership just off base, but most of the enlisted personnel can't swing a purchase here. You park your car in the corner of the lot, under a light. You don't want any accidental abrasions, door slams, or envious personnel coming along and ripping you off.

At the door to Sgt. Lee's apartment, you ring the bell and he answers.

"Is your daughter ready yet?" you ask, teen angel in love.

The Top looks you over for a moment, then turns silently and walks in, sitting down in a chair facing the TV, which is on. You follow dutifully. The place is barely furnished:

threadbare rug, card table and folding chairs for eating—
his life is a goddamn poker game and you're getting ready
to raise.

"I like what you've done with the place," you say.

Sgt. Lee turns his dead eyes on you. They've seen everything a man can see, you think, and then some. "You're a
funny guy, Elwood," he says.

"I guess I expected some threats. You know—keep my
spirits up."

"You read up on me, didn't you?" the Top asks, but
doesn't wait for a reply. "You ever heard of stuff called
Haldol?"

"I suppose."

"There's this point you get to in war where you become
it. You go into a bar, someone's standing in your way, you
don't ask the poor bastard to move, you just kill him. Short-
est distance between two points."

Vietnam nostalgia, you think, the real crippler. A tour is
a full year of the Most Perfect Clarity, the especial aliveness
of being soaked in the flame, of finally embracing it. It's
not that war is hell, it's that war is all. MPC city.

"Inside, they gave me Haldol. At first, you get high—
you're not supposed to, but that's how it works. Then you
get on this even keel, smoothed out."

Haldol you have heard of, in fact. Antipsychotic. Another
of the nastier chemical compounds invented to relieve the
stresses of everyday war, make an adjustment on the over-
soul, get your channel tuned to a quieter test pattern.

"All of a sudden, you begin to lose control of your body
parts. Everything gets a mind of its own. First your arm
begins pulling away, all by itself. It stretches out, your elbow
locks and your shoulder locks and then your head begins
to twist."

Regan in *The Exorcist* with nobody to say the prayers,

shake the holy water, handle the crucifix duty. Nothing like a little antipsychotic to send you completely over the edge.

"Do you understand what I'm saying?" Sgt. Lee asks.

Robyn comes through the doorway. "I'm ready," she says. Her face is delicate and gentle in the light, but she's wearing a metal claw instead of her cosmetic arm. The Top gets up and walks you to the door.

"It was a relief," the Top says, standing in the doorway.

"G'night," Robyn says.

"Elwood," the Top says. "Your time—it's at hand."

As you get to the car you notice the Top is still standing in the doorway, watching you.

Robyn looks strangely at the car as you open the door for her. "Isn't this kind of an expensive car?" she asks.

"I got a great deal."

"Did you steal this, too?" she asks.

"Paid for in cash," you say. "I'm hungry, how about you?"

"You said the magic word," she says as you back out of the space and turn out of the lot. In the rearview you see the Top run to his Montego; the lights come up, and the car tears out of the lot.

"Where we going?" she asks.

"Italian place I know."

"They have them?" she asks.

"They're fully equipped out here," you say, as you maneuver slowly through traffic, keeping an eye on what's behind.

"Your father still driving the Montego?" you ask.

"Yes. Why?"

"Your father, he say anything about me?"

She laughs.

"You asked him?"

"He said stay away. That you're an asshole."

"It's good advice."

"I know all about it," she says.

"What else?"

"Said you were a drug dealer."

"He's following us," you say. "Watch." You head for the entrance ramp of the autobahn, and the car behind you keeps up. You switch lanes rapidly, accelerating, and the Montego does the same, zipping along.

"I can't believe it," she says.

"Believe it," you say. You feel strong as you shift through the gears, controlling the car like a woman, playing at being Garcia, taking it to the edge in the autobahn dogfight, gliding in and out of traffic. The Top keeps pace, matching you.

"What are we going to do?" she asks.

"Outrun him," you say, and floor it.

In the left lane you begin to move like you've never moved before. The Top simply doesn't have enough horsepower under the hood. You're flashing the brights at cars in your lane, pushing them out.

Robyn, you can see, is scared but thrilled. She keeps looking out the rear window, a high school vision of *Bonnie and Clyde*.

"Here we go," you say, and punch out the lights, then take a quick right across two lanes of traffic, cutting off two rads and slipping up the exit ramp, no brakes because of the lights, just downshifting, letting gravity and the uphill climb slow the Mercedes down. At the top of the ramp, you see the Top's car roaring past, and you turn on your lights.

"You ever do that before?" she asks.

"Beginner's luck," you say.

Robyn keeps her eye on you, cool as can fucking be. "So when are we going to eat?"

At the restaurant, once you're seated the waiter starts you on bread and wine.

You notice she handles the claw clumsily, a little tentative, but after some work gets a good solid grip on the utensils. There's a kind of dignity in it, just taking her time, getting it right, being precise.

"You want me to help?" you ask.

"It's under control," she says. "I don't go out to eat much."

"You're doing fine," you say, just as the butter knife slips from her metal grasp. You imagine the claw on your back, scratching across.

"How come you don't wear that all the time?" you ask.

"When you first start off, you don't want people to know. But then you get used to it."

"You do?"

"No," she says. "Not really."

"You get phantom pain?"

"Like what?"

"Itches, feeling like the arm, it's still there."

"What do you know about this stuff?"

"Not much."

"Yeah, the phantom pain. I get that."

"How'd it happen?" you ask.

"It's not in those little files you read?"

You shake your head. You want to know because the more you know, the more you have. She is the key to the Top, and you need the key to her. She hesitates again, cuts herself another piece of bread, and this time succeeds with the butter. Then she takes a deep breath, lets it out.

"We were in Texas then. We used to go horseback riding a lot. I got really good, started going bareback, doing tricks, showing off for him. One time my horse threw me—not that big a thing. I'd been thrown before, horse pulling up short, brushing you off in trees. People say horses are stupid, but they're not. Anyway, this time I just landed wrong, broke the arm in two places. I didn't lose consciousness or anything. We made it home and my dad took me to the VA, and the doctor who set it made the cast too tight, cut off the blood flow and gangrene set in. I was complaining about the pain, but he had to go to the base so I just kept taking more pills. It finally got so bad that when he got back, he drove me to the hospital, made them cut off the cast, and there it was. You could see the little black streaks working their way up." She says this tonelessly, all objective, happening to somebody else, a practiced story. "If they didn't take the arm off, they would've lost me. I didn't care, said I'd rather die."

"Where was your father he didn't take you in right away?"

"The base. He had a practice alert. They called him in," she says, but she's closing up on you and you decide to try another tack.

"When'd your mom leave?"

"Year before. Things had been pretty crazy for a while. I stayed with him summers, and her the rest of the school year. But they were talking about getting back together. I guess the arm blew the big reconciliation."

"You know why you're telling me all this?" you ask, tuning her.

"How about you tell me something," she says.

But you're not ready for that yet. The music is the low Italian kind, tinny strings, and the waiter comes over and clears your plates for the next course.

"I know your secret," you say.

"What's that?"

"That you hate his fucking guts."

"Maybe you don't know shit," she says, and you wonder if you've overplayed your hand. The waiter puts the food in front of you, and the steam washes over your face. You dig in, neatly rolling spaghetti—a fork-and-spoon maneuver.

"You know what I spend my days doing?" you ask.

"No." Still pissed, but reachable.

You pick up the butter knife. "Finding out why these things are rounded on the ends."

"Why?" she asks.

"It's for the party at the Bermans," you say. "Conversational tidbits."

"I mean why are the knives round?"

"It's so when people began having meals together, one of the parties didn't end up as the main course. You got so many forks and knives together gives people ideas, so you got to take precautions. Invention of the salad fork was the first step toward disarmament."

"Should I take precautions around you?" she asks, and you think: back on track.

"That's affirmative," you say. "Want some more wine?" Robyn nods, so you pour both of you a little lambrusco, keep your sweet tooth in check.

"This just happened," she says. "I mean, this summer."

"So how come you're not back with your mom?"

"I was," she says. "Started up school. I went in and my mom had already been there, talked me up to the teachers. They all agree they're not going to make a big deal of it, it's like I've got a rip in my stocking or something. So the first day back in English class, the teacher's going around the room asking people what they read over the summer. The usual stuff. I don't even know if some of them can read. She got to me I said, 'Physical therapy books.' The whole class sat like I was pointing a gun at them."

"The reason you hate him," you say, "is it's his fault."

"You don't know," she says. You touch her face across the table, brush her hair back with your fingers and then touch her chin. The next step is to kiss her, but that will come. Her face is long and thin, with good strong bones.

"What happened next?" you ask.

"I just wanted it so someone would say something, so it'd be out in the open. Some acknowledgment. Shit, I mean, *I* knew. But that wasn't why I left. I decide now that everyone's sympathetic, I'd get real social, so I threw this party, get to know everybody. Everyone came with dates, my mother, she cleaned the house for about a week, laying out food and soda. We played spin the bottle, and I just hung back, didn't have anything to do with it, but then the time came for 'seven minutes in heaven.' I drew this kid, Jimmy Garland, the best-looking guy in the school. I had a real crush on him. We went into the storeroom where we kept this spare couch.

"I went to turn off the light, and he said, 'Let's leave it on.' Then he asked me to look at it. I said all right. I only used the cosmetic then. I unwrapped, he shook hands with the arm, all by itself, like a joke."

"What happened?" you ask.

"We did it, you know, right there." She pauses, watching you closely for a reaction, and you wait her out. "But then I looked up, and everybody was watching. I was this show and they'd all gotten their money's worth."

"No you didn't," you say. "You fucked him right there? No you didn't." And you touch her again.

"No, but I did later. So my mother found out I'm doing it with him, doing it with half the kids in school, getting high. She kicks me out, decides it's time for a long vacation. My shrink at the time says I'm having some adjustment problems, I wanted her to catch me. So right then my dad's coming here, a little culture can't hurt, and I go along. So far, the pool and this restaurant are the only culture I've seen. Figures, the only culture I get in Germany is an Italian restaurant. My luck."

"Next time we can eat Japanese."

"I'm sorry I'm unloading this on you. I haven't talked to anybody in like forever, except my dad, who doesn't talk."

Sgt. Lee, you imagine, is an action-oriented individual. "What does your shrink say about shoplifting."

"Classic acting out. Getting back, getting even, you know. What else you want to know?"

"What are you going to be when you grow up?"

"Dead," she says.

"Me too," you say. "But before then."

"Jesus," she says, suddenly suspicious. "Did my dad, like, put you up to this—tell me you're a bad actor so I'd go out with you. Follow us like that, add a little realism?"

"You think he did?"

"He's capable of it."

"Well, he didn't. And I know something else about you."

She now is watching you with full attention.

"You didn't fuck that guy," you say.

"Why would I lie?" she says.

"Pity," you say.

"Fuck you."

"You don't want it, is what I'm saying."

"My dad did set this up," she says.

"They don't see you, they see the arm. Poor girl. So you make 'em look. Like in the PX. Like wearing the claw tonight. It's a test. See if they can bear it."

She's staring at you now, the arm poised in midair, as if she's about to slash you with the butter knife.

"What you want to know about me," you say, "is whatever it is, I can bear it."

"What are you talking about?" she asks.

"I think you know."

"Maybe," she says, "but first let's have dessert."

YOU WANT TO GO someplace close in Mannheim, but instead she tells you to take her back to Benjamin Franklin
Village. You look around the parking lot as you pull in to
see if the Top is there, but you don't see the Montego, still
probably out on the midnight maneuvers looking for you,
checking all the available flophouses.

She opens the door and brings you into the apartment.
On second glance, without the Top hovering, the place has
that Army lived-in look—beat to shit by the hard living of
previous tenants.

"How do we know he won't come home?" you ask.

"We don't," she says, and you realize this is as much a
turn-on for her as you. "What kind of music you like?" she
asks, walking over to the stereo and thumbing through
albums.

"Something with a beat," you say.

Even when he's not there, the place smells of the Top.
Past the living room into the dining area, some of the boxes
are still being unpacked, Sgt. Lee having spent too much
time fucking with you to get his domestic life in order. Books
line walls in makeshift shelves—the usual Army handbooks
and manuals, but also a lot of books on Vietnam.

Robyn has put on some Donna Summer, singe-your-ears
kind of shit, but you nod as she comes over and kisses you.
"How about the grand tour," she says.

"I've seen this part," you say.

"How about upstairs?"

You follow as she takes the steps two at a time, like a
young colt, her ponytail switching over her neck. On the
wall you see the number of mirrors along the walls. Mirrors

everywhere. You can read people's houses, you know, some-times better than you can read their faces. And what you read here is what you read in all the Army houses in Ger-many: this is the place where lost people turn up.

Robyn gets ahead of you and shows you her room, a small alcove with an electric blanket. "You should be honored," she says. "I cleaned up for you." It's draftier than you ex-pected. You can even feel the cold, scraping wind as you stand there.

Robyn picks up a unicorn from the vanity, which has a large tilt mirror surrounded by light bulbs. "I love these unicorns," she says. "I love them stuffed, I have glass ones, I even have a unicorn ranch. You'll like this—half of them I stole from somewhere, too."

"Your shrink must have had a field day with this," you say.

"She says it's typical—to love only a myth. She said I have to get out more and get in touch with the real world."

"And I'm supposed to be the real world?" you ask.

"Why not?"

You touch her hand then, pulling her toward you.

"Hold me," she says. You touch the hair on her good arm, which is thick and dark like a man's, and you feel it rise as you stroke it.

"Show me where your father sleeps," you say.

She moves down the hallway to her father's bedroom—spit and polish all the way. You take her then by the shoul-ders and gently kiss her, and then bring your tongue deep inside her.

"What would he do if he found us up here?" Robyn asks.

"Probably kill us," you say.

"I guess you know him then," she says, and kisses you hard on the lips, pulling you to the bed. She's wearing a leotard, which she slips off quickly. You get your fucking raincoat out, put a Trojan on your warhorse, and then get on top of her; and the thought of it, of fucking his daughter in the Top's own house, gets you going, no chemical assistance necessary. You are aware of the Top, out keeping the American Dream alive while you are home guarding his stuff. She is willing and warm, and she guides you in, your cock alive and well and still motoring without any fuel supplements. You grip the bare cheeks of her ass, and you become aware that she too is listening for the sound of the Top, and it is as if she is fucking him as well as you as the two of you go at it. The whole time you're doing it, plunging away, both of you have your eyes open, neither of you looking at the other, but waiting for the sound of a key in the door, a man returning, the danger you now hold within. When you're done, you lie exhausted on the sheets, your sweat and smell seeping into them. You wonder if the Top, when he lays his head down, will smell the betrayal, know what has occurred. But you take no chances, making sure by taking off the rubber, rolling it neatly and slipping it under the pillow, where it will wait as quietly and patiently and urgently as a land mine.

15

B Y THE TIME you arrive at CC's, most of the folks are already half in the bag. The gang's all here—Video, Eddio, Rothfuss, Simmons, and Cabot—all celebrating the success of Sasquatch's dick surgery. Sasquatch himself has the look of a man who has gotten more than he bargained for.

"How does it feel?" you ask. "Now that your prick is pruned, in no time you'll be ready to rumble."

You pat Sasquatch on his back and offer him a Camel, which he accepts. You light his and then your own before sitting down to stretch your legs. You feel the ache in your balls and the taste of Robyn in your mouth.

"So?" you ask.

"It hurts like hell," Sasquatch says.

"Major short arm surgery," you say. "Hope they didn't whittle you down to nothing."

Sasquatch groans as he sits down at the table. You nod at CC, and he comes out with another liter of draft.

"Hey," Video says, standing by the TV, which is mounted on the corner of the bar. "You think we can turn up the sound?" There is a soccer game on the set, a wide-angle shot of men excitedly running downfield.

"We got entertainment scheduled for tonight," you say to Video. "Right, CC?" Video nods and goes back to watching the soccer game.

"Home-movie night," CC says. "Double feature. Which do you want, El?"

"What do we have?" you ask.

"Two never before released, world premiere features," CC hollers. "*Big Belinda* and *Emphysema Emily: The Sequel*. Which you want to go first?"

"How about we lead with *Big Belinda*?" you say.

"Coming right up." CC moves into the back room to get his movie equipment.

"What's this?" Sasquatch asks, a little bewildered.

"Don't worry about it," you say. "What kind of stuff they give you?" You are, as always, ever on the pharmaceutical offensive.

"Huh?" Sasquatch says.

"For the pain," you say. "They treat you right or am I going to have to prescribe something myself."

"They give me these pills here," Sasquatch says, handing you two vials.

You pick up the first one. "Penicillin," you say. "So's you don't get an infection. Clear up any lingering cases of the clap, too." You put that vial down and pick up the second bottle and look at the label. "Fuck. I can't believe they packed Darvon in your lunchbox."

"It's not working, whatever it is," Sasquatch says, shutting his eyes and moaning.

"Darvon wouldn't cure a dick-ache in a mouse," you say. "The doc, he's cutting corners. All I can say is that's the last time we're throwing our dick business his way."

"You don't think we should go to him anymore?" Eddio asks, looking concerned.

"What's a matter, Eddio?" Rothfuss says. "Your dick need a trim?"

"Oh man," Sasquatch says, moaning as he shifts in his seat.

"Don't worry about it," you say. "How about it, Cabot. You think you can scare up some Demerol?"

"Demerol's good?" Sasquatch says, not a man who keeps up-to-date on his *Physician's Desk Reference*, the bible of the brand-name portion of your industry.

"Guaranteed to put out the lights," you say.

"I don't know," Cabot says. He looks to Simmons, who has the alert and pained face of somebody in need.

"What do you mean you don't know," you say. "Who the hell knows if you don't?"

"It's a bad season now is what he's saying," Simmons says.

"The fuck, we're not talking about lobster here," you say, pissed that the two of them are ganging up on you.

"We're coming up for end-of-the-year inventory," Cabot says. "It's a bad time to start registering losses."

"Don't worry about it," you say. "We've got one more maneuver scheduled."

"Like in REFORGER FTX?" Simmons asks. RE-FORGER FTX is the Army acronym for the Return of Forces to Germany Field Training Exercise, which is the big annual maneuver party the Army throws for the reserve troops in from the United States. It is, in fact, because of the poor logistical showing of his troops in the last RE-FORGER that Colonel Berman is pressing for one more winter FTX before his OERs come up.

"If we're lucky," you say. Inventory losses during ma-neuvers are an accepted phenomenon as long as you stay within statistical loss parameters. The luck you are referring to occurred during REFORGER this August when you pulled your greatest inventory coup and the statistical pa-rameters were thrown out the window. During the simu-lated battle, a treadhead named Sanderson accidentally backed over a diesel pump line while it was in use. Pilot error but you also suspect that Sanderson, the poor chump, was wired to his eyeballs on Army-issue Dexedrine. The diesel blew up, igniting everything. Three men were incinerated, six were badly scorched and had to be medivacked to the burn unit at Wiesbaden. You ended up writing condolence letters for a week.

However, everything feeds into a mysterious center. It was here that you demonstrated both memoranda initiative and the willingness to carpe fucking diem: qualities you learned from your tutelage under Colonel Berman. In the initial confusion you were one of the first logistics people to arrive on the scene. You immediately got buddies to drive off truckloads of supplies under the pretext of removing them from danger. These supplies were taken to a hideout, where they remain should you ever need them. This all occurred, naturally, under Lt. Meyer's signature, so it cannot be traced back to you. From a memo perspective, this was among your proudest moments in the Army. You came, you saw, you wrote it up.

"I'll see what we can do," Simmons says.

"You'd better," you say, just to keep the screws on. Simmons and Cabot, you understand, always have to be reminded that there are thumbs on them, waiting to press down.

"They also give me this," Sasquatch says. He pulls out a small aerosol can.

"Ethyl fucking chloride," you say. "Very decent."

"What is it?" Rothfuss asks.

"Keeps his dick on ice," you say.

"It's a freeze thing," Sasquatch says, "in case I get a hard-on. I get a hard-on my stitches, they all pop out. So I feel one coming on, I take out my can, spray it, and that'll chill it down."

CC by now has set up the Super 8 projector and is fiddling

up front with the legs on the tripod of his mobile screen.

"What does it look like?" Video asks Sasquatch.

"What are you talking about?" Sasquatch says.

"I'm saying, what does your dick look like," Video says. "I'd never let them do something like that to me. What if the doc, he cuts off too much. Just a little slip of the wrist, he happens to look up at the goddamn clock, think of his hot date that night—you never know. You can't tell about these Army doctors. I saw this show once, a lot of times, even good docs, they leave stuff inside you—sponges, bandages. One guy left a retractor hanging on a guy's large intestine, still locked in. Imagine that happening to your dick. You'd never raise your flag again. Always be at half-mast."

"Video," you say, "you could fuck up a wet dream."

"Maybe he won't have wet dreams no more is what I'm saying," Video says.

"Shut up, Video," Eddio says. "I was wondering, El, if maybe this doc, he does other things besides dicks."

"He's a dick specialist," you say. "Which is a lousy job if you ask me."

"But maybe he knows somebody can do a woman right," Eddio persists.

"You want a woman done right," Rothfuss says, "red rover come over."

"What is it you want, Eddio?" you ask. "I'm setting up your fucking trip back home. What exactly are we talking here?"

"It's not for me, you understand," Eddio says. "It's my girl. She wants to have a titectomy."

"A what?" Video asks.

"A titectomy. I think that's its name," Eddio says.

"He wants to have her stuffed," Rothfuss says. "I got to go along with Eddio on this. European chicks, they don't

have the stacking genes American chicks have. Admit it—
it's hard to get yourself a good handful."

"I heard Raquel Welch got reupholstered," Video says.
"But that stuff, you have to be careful. I heard after a few
years it hardens up like a rock. You try and kiss Raquel
Welch on the tits, you wind up with a broken nose."

"That's why I'm asking," Eddio says. "I don't want some
guy out of the phone book."

"You think Raquel Welch let her knockers do the walking?" Video asks.

"I'm gonna marry my woman soon as she gets her attic
insulated," Eddio says.

"An old-fashioned guy," you say to Eddio. "Maybe we
can work something out."

"Jesus, Elwood," Video says. "You're better than Blue
Cross–Blue Shield."

"Maybe I'll put in a dental plan for you guys after you
get out," you say. "The dick doc, he probably has some
colleagues who wouldn't mind a little work off the clock."

"Fucking A!" Eddio says, all excited. "I knew you'd come
through."

"We're ready now," CC says.

"Lights, camera, let's see some action," Video says.

CC looks to you.

"Do it," you say.

Big Belinda is a humongous woman—running 350 plus,
rolls of flesh draping her back and neck, the Michelin tire
woman. She fills the screen as she waddles across it, turning
to look at the camera. Her features are puddled across her
face. The plot of the movie follows Big Belinda's attempts
to find a man to climb aboard. She meets men at work, over
lunch, until finally one skinny dude with a hunk of courage
and a rod on is willing. They go to her apartment, strip,
and start getting ready to fuck.

"I don't think I should be watching this," Sasquatch says.

"Look at the fucking design budget on this," Video says, ever the critic. "They're banging in the same place she went to lunch, just put in bookshelves, took out the tables, threw down a mattress. Jesus." He squints and looks up close at the screen, examining the titles on the shelves. "Looks like she has about twenty years' subscription to Reader's Digest Condensed up there." But what you're thinking of was being inside Robyn, your legs straightened and toes pushing against the sheets. And what you're thinking is it wasn't what you thought it would be. It was more.

"Down in front," you say.

The skinny guy gets on top of Big Belinda and begins tooling away. To see Big Belinda naked is truly an impressive sight. With each thrust, there's a lot of ripple action over the surface of her body, the waves moving up from her groin, swelling along her stomach, cresting at her tits, finally fading into a wiggle by her heavy cheekbones. The skinny guy seems lost on her, a small boat on stormy seas, punching away with his oar. While they're humping, another skinny guy comes in and strips down, and Big Belinda sword-swallows him. When he pulls back, he moves slightly and drops a testicle onto her tongue, where she lets it rest a moment, then draws him into her mouth as the original guy still pounds away, a textbook example of wave action on the coast.

"Where'd that guy come from?" Video asks. "This movie has got big script problems."

"Seems like a perfectly good fuck film to me," Cabot says.

"Sex is in the mind," Video says. "It's got to have a sense of art, not just pile in and drive."

"I think she's coming," Eddio says. Sasquatch's mouth and eyes are perfectly round. The sight of Big Belinda in the throes is truly something to write home about. The wave action heaves up to a tidal wave, a tsunami of fat as she rocks and rolls on the bed.

"You think the earth moved?" Rothfuss says.

"I think the earth couldn't help it," you say.

"Oh man," Sasquatch says. "Oh man." He stands up, fumbling with the belt for his pants.

"Lemon Pledge it," you say.

Sasquatch opens his trousers and pulls out the spray can and begins letting his newly pruned member, wrapped like a mummy and already beginning to rise, have the spray.

"Nothing like the sweet smell of ethyl chloride," you say.

"Cut the film," Sasquatch shouts. A mist is rising from his pants.

"It's almost over," CC says.

Big Belinda finishes off the two skinny guys. When they climb off, her face is red and the sweat makes the pale landscape of her body look like it just got dusted by the morning dew. Fade to white.

"I don't know about you," you say, "but that was pretty fucking disgusting."

"Very bad production values," Video says. "One camera, no close-ups on the money shots, and they got a shit script. But you got to admit, Big Belinda has star power."

Sasquatch is now sitting in his chair with the ethyl chloride poised, looking aggrieved.

"Got something new for you, man," Rothfuss whispers to you.

"Let me concentrate here," you say.

"El, this last weekend the fuck muscle almost had to go into overtime," Rothfuss says.

Sasquatch is peering at his pants, still unbuttoned. "I'm asking you guys," he says. "Don't do the second feature."

"I go to this party in Mannheim," Rothfuss says. "It's not

the usual Army deal—seven guys per chick, and that chick looks pretty well used. This party there is this one great-looking chick there, pushing thirty maybe, but well within attack parameters."

"So she's in your sights."

"Damn fucking straight," Rothfuss says. "And I'm standing across from her—just drinking—and I'm wearing this sailor kind of shirt, V-front, shows off my chest. Suddenly she reaches over, grabs the hair on my chest."

"How about that second feature?" Video calls to CC.

"*Emphysema Emily: The Sequel* coming right up," CC says.

"So she pulls me over to her," Rothfuss says, "and then she starts sticking her hand down my shirt, rubbing all over my chest, my stomach, going under my belt from inside my shirt. So I tell her that it's not fair she can do that to me when I can't do that to her. So I unbutton her blouse and stick my hand down her shirt, and I'm getting into it and we're grooving along, and suddenly she starts saying how she's got this husband and three kids and that she's not sure she wants to follow through on this deal. So I ask her where's your husband and she takes her finger and says, 'Right here,' and points to the guy standing next to her."

"What does Emphysema Emily do in Part One?" Eddio asks.

"She smokes a cigarette with her cunt," Video says.

"What did the husband—his face—look like?" you ask.

"Per-fucking-plexed," Rothfuss says. "So I say, you coulda told me a little sooner, you know, and buttoned up her blouse."

"Rothfuss," you say, "I don't think you're a closer, man."

"Tell me about it," Rothfuss says. "I got a hard-on going up my mouth no place to put it."

"Rothfuss," you ask, "you ever been in love?"

"Every chance I fucking get," he says. The symptoms of love, you think, are something that Rothfuss is immune to.

"Oh shit! Oh shit!" Sasquatch, who has been listening, is now spraying away for all he's worth, a cool mist rising from his pants.

CC is threading the film through the spool of his projection machine. "Ready," he calls.

The lights dim and the projector comes on. Onscreen, the opening shot is of hundreds of cartons of cigarettes. As the camera pans up, you see a woman in a bikini on top of the cartons. She picks up a lighter and strikes a flame, lights a cigarette and stares straight at the camera. You light up another cigarette in sympathy. The music cues, and next is an exterior shot of a high rise.

Then we cut to Emphysema Emily inside the apartment building making herself comfortable. She takes off her top and her bottom and is still smoking, blowing small o's out of both ends, which circle out to frame the credits in a border of smoke.

"Now that," Video says, "is fucking art."

16

U NDER "The Commander's Corner," you wrote the
memorial preface about the Parson:

Every soldier, from private to general, knows
that at some point he may be called upon to make the
ultimate sacrifice. In times of war, the sacrifice is general. Specific actions produce specific losses, body
counts. But in times of war, there is a reason. There
are heroes and medals and survivors to tell the story.
But in times of peace, we assume there should be no
casualties. We let down our guard. But it is in times of
peace that we should prepare the most, and in that
preparation there will be some losses. Private First
Class Parsons McCovey, a soldier's soldier, is one such
casualty. If we consider only the immediate circumstances of his death, we might conclude that he died
uselessly. We might grow bitter at the accidental nature
of his death. We might wish he were less dedicated to
his job than to go up to a barracks rooftop during a
storm. But we would be wrong to do this. The Army
that does not sweat in peace will certainly bleed in
war. We can grieve over Private McCovey, we can remember him with words and photos. But if we consider his death useless, we do him no honor, we learn
no lesson, we will enjoy a short peace. The lessons of

Private McCovey's death are the lessons of accident, ill-luck, and mortality, which are, of course, the lessons of all wars. In the following pages, we honor our fallen comrade by remembering him as he was.

"Some great stuff here," says Colonel Berman, looking at the galleys for the Parsons McCovey newsletter and making final changes before you go to print. "Good general opening, powerful rhythmic climax."

"Thank you, sir," you say, waiting for the suggested changes. You watch Colonel Berman purse his lips as he reads through the piece again.

"I've always wondered what a 'soldier's soldier' is, though," Colonel Berman says.

Someone becomes a soldier's soldier, you think, because no one else would claim him.

"I think we can blue-pencil that," Colonel Berman says. "Clichés have their place, but I don't think we've ever had a man die who wasn't a soldier's soldier. Besides, the sentence reads stronger without that interruption. 'Parsons McCovey is one such casualty.' Comes down hard in the declarative mode. Very fucking powerful."

"I see what you mean, sir," you say.

"Another thing," he says. "You repeat the word 'general' twice in the first two sentences, but with different meanings. That causes some momentary confusion. I'd rather we cut one 'general.' Maybe change the first sentence from 'Every soldier, from private to general,' to 'Every soldier, enlisted and officer,' etc."

"Much clearer, sir," you say.

"And I like these photos," Colonel Berman says. You've managed to scrounge all the official photos, Basic Training, Advanced Individual Training, Bravo Company photos. The Basic and AIT photos you had FedExed to you by a clerk in Washington. Those, plus the informal photos from Video, Eddio, and Co., made enough for a full two-page spread.

"This last one is particularly moving," he adds. This is a photo of the platoon, the men in three rows, looking like freshly scrubbed grammar school kids who just happen to be in possession of automatic weapons. WE'LL MISS YOU BUDDY is the caption underneath.

"Goddamn fucking good," Colonel Berman says. "This is really your best effort, Elwood."

"Thank you, sir," you say. "That means a lot."

"When do we go to press?"

"I'll run it into Mannheim ASAP," you say.

"Use Hermann," Colonel Berman says. "He knows the local ropes better. Tell him I want no expense spared. Four-color printing for the photos and double the usual print run."

"Yes sir." From this you understand that Hermann Dietz is to be given some budgetary latitude as to the greasing of palms. Before you get to Hermann, though, you have to get through the interference run by his secretary, Horst Moetz, also known as Motzi the Nazi. The two of them came with the base, inherited from the last commander, who inherited them from the commander before him. Nearly every American base in Germany has a full complement of German Government Service employees, a shadow staff. Because of the transient nature of American commanders, the rads are, in fact, the one constant of the American military presence in Germany.

You go down the hallway to Hermann the German's office. It is better to burst in and surprise him, prevent the Motz from using his customary evasive tactics. Hermann has his own staff, nearly the size of Colonel Berman's Headquarters staff, and his staff, as could be expected, does all it can to thwart Colonel Berman. So rather than use the telephone, which will guarantee delay, you utilize surprise, the first principle of warfare.

As each new commander comes through, Hermann adds a little more, padding the requisitions with one more sedimentary layer of administration. He is Colonel Berman's equal in memoranda capability, and Motzi the Nazi is his clerical right arm. As a team they can interface anyone off the face of the earth. Hermann has even taken over the corner office, which has a nice view and is slightly larger than Colonel Berman's.

You knock and walk in. The Motz stands up from his desk to shake hands. All the Germans, you know, set great store by pressing the flesh. When you've attended NATO meetings at Heidelberg that included the German command, the first ten minutes of the meeting were set aside for ritual handshaking before everyone got down to the business of screwing each other.

"Specialist Elwood," the Motz says in the lisping way Germans have, "I was just about to telephone you. We have much to discuss." As the Motz sits back, you look down at the paperwork on his desk, where he has evidently been going over the weekend damage reports. Repairing the damage done to Mannheim by American troops is one of Hermann's principal liaison jobs.

"We break your country again?" you ask.

"Ah, Specialist Elwood, it was not a good weekend for the American Army presence," the Motz says. "Herr Dietz would like to schedule a reparations conference tomorrow afternoon with your Colonel. The investigators have just returned from the field and all the reports should be in by then." The layer of administration added during Colonel Berman's tenure is Hermann's own private investigative force. This prevents actions from being handled by Division CID and thus going automatically into a court-martial mode. The men, however, call Hermann the German's two investigators the Gestapo.

"Will do, Motz," you say. "Let me in to see Hermann."

"He is on the telephone at the present time," Motzi the Nazi says in his most unctuous voice, pointing to a light on the phone bank.

"Get him off," you say. "This comes from the Colonel." While you have no authority to say this, the Motz has no authority to stop you, and so you will say it anyway, just to bust his chops.

"He is talking to the *Polizei*, giving them his weekly reminder that SOFA remains in place." SOFA stands for Status-of-Forces Agreement, which means that while the *Polizei* have the right to prosecute American soldiers for crimes committed on German soil, in practice they generally turn them over to the US Army for disciplinary action. It is part of Hermann the German's job to call around the various police departments to rescue soldiers who have been picked up by the locals over the weekend.

"How many of our guys in the jug?" you ask.

"The present total stands at fourteen, but all precincts have not yet reported in," Motzi the Nazi says. "And there are additional problems." The Motz has a prissy air to him. He rearranges some of the papers on his desk but doesn't make a move for the phone.

"What'd we do," you ask, "lose a war while I wasn't looking?" With Hermann you wouldn't play it this far, but the Motz needs reminding now and then who signs the paychecks. Checks and balances.

The Motz clears his throat. "For example, I have here a report on an M-1 Abrams tank. Someone drove it cross-country through the forest, causing considerable damage, and then took it to a car wash just outside of Mannheim, evidently to remove the mud. Unfortunately, the cannon of said tank became stuck in the rotating buffer of the car wash, jamming the machinery and causing the car wash to break down. The tank eventually exited by driving through one of the walls."

Garcia, you dumb cocksucker, you think. "They catch the guy?" you ask.

"Occupants unknown," the Motz says.

"Boys will be boys," you say.

"The owner of the car wash is looking for total replacement costs. You also have liability on the forest. A number of trees were knocked down, and extensive damage was done to an open field."

"Someone owned the forest?" you say. "Jesus." Most reparations conferences involve some enlisted man getting drunk and spinning a couple of 360s on somebody's lawn. The Army issues a formal apology and pays for the resodding job and everyone walks away happy. This tank thing, however, could be fairly serious, a budget buster that might end up at Division.

"Looks like you got us up shit creek without a paddle," you say, but the Motz ignores you because he doesn't understand what the hell you're saying. While both Motzi the Nazi and Hermann the German speak English fluently, everything they learned has come out of books. It is one of your practices to sling the slang at them. You do this, naturally, to fuck up their rhythm, to show them who's boss, to demonstrate that for all they know they still can't hit the curve.

"He's done now," the Motz says. The light's gone off on the phone bank. He leads you in, taking a seat in the chair to the left, slightly out of your line of sight.

As you shake hands, a faint grimace of aristocratic disapproval crosses Hermann the German's face. You know this is caused by the fact that Hermann dealing with you is a breach of protocol. He would prefer everything be handled through the Motz, insulating himself. His distaste, however, is tempered by the fact that it's easier to work with you. In short, you are a man with whom he can do and has done business. Hermann is a heavy man in the German way, not fat but solid, the good burgher of memoranda. On top he's thinning, but the hair is boot black, almost certainly dyed.

"What is it that I may do for you, Specialist Elwood," he says. Hermann, you have noticed, favors an elaborate phrasing. Colonel Berman is convinced that Hermann does it to antagonize him, but you are aware that this may not be the case. Hermann, you suspect, actually does think this way.

You hand over the Parsons McCovey envelope. Hermann pulls the galleys out of the envelope and looks at them without much interest. The profit margins on a print run are not, you imagine, very substantial. "The Colonel wants you to handle this personally," you say. You explain the details. "It's very important. First-class job, you know, the works, no expense spared."

Hermann nods and returns the newsletter to the oversized envelope and places it in the metal Out basket on his desk. The desk is ordered and neat. The Motz, you suspect, will be assigned to take care of this. It's not your problem, you figure.

"Done," Hermann says. "Is that all?"

"You've heard about the M-1 tank that got away," you say.

Hermann nods. "It would seem that the American Army is in for significant liability in this case." That the Army will be forced to pay dearly for a new car wash doesn't exactly displease Hermann; if he takes over the assigning of contracts, there will doubtless be some loot coming his way. The situation is uncertain, however, because something of this magnitude will almost certainly wind up with the CID, thus shutting down the Hermann the German show.

"May I make a suggestion?" you say.

"Your views are always welcome," Hermann says.

"I wouldn't bet the farm on this if I were you." You watch Hermann's face settle as he considers what you mean. He puts it through his mind forward, backward, and sideways, and you wait on it.

"This means?" he asks, giving in.

"Meaning if you're not careful, you can get caught looking," you say. "Liability may not be as clear as you think."

"Why is that?" he asks.

"Did the owner of the car wash collect money to clean the tank?" you ask.

Hermann looks at Motzi the Nazi, who begins fumbling through his investigator's records.

"Yes," the Motz says finally.

"Then there was money exchanged," you say.

"Yes," the Motz repeats. "It is here in the preliminary report."

"I think you ought to tell your man to settle before it goes to CID and Division," you say to Hermann. "Do you understand what I'm saying? You boot the grounder, you blow the double play."

"And that means?" Hermann asks, with an edge in his voice. Starting to sweat here, you think, you sorry son-of-a-bitch.

"A flexible fiscal response is called for in this situation. It goes to Division some CID investigator might conclude that due to the exchange of money the car wash owner entered into an implicit contract. That would make the owner at least partially responsible for the damage, and in any case the damage would not fall under battalion reparations guidelines. You see what I mean?"

"I understand perfectly." Hermann the German can move very rapidly once he's on firm fiscal ground. "We could, of course, explain these difficulties to the owner of the car wash," he says, not wanting to give up a lucrative situation without a struggle.

"How would you do that?" you ask.

"After due consideration," he says, "the owner might remember differently as to whether he charged the tank or not."

"It's your play," you say, "but it's better to go for the easy single rather than the home run ball. Otherwise, you could get called out on strikes."

There is a pause. "I see," Hermann says. "I take it one should not be too greedy in this enterprise."

"I think you can make good on the forest," you say. "Get your gardeners out and they can start planting." Hermann the German has a landscaping firm on retainer.

"You have done me a service here, Specialist Elwood, pointing this error of judgment out to me," he says. "Now what is it I may do for you?"

"You know I'm having a problem with a Sgt. Lee," you say.

"Your First Sergeant," Hermann the German says, "is a very reform-minded individual." It comes as no surprise to you that Hermann is also an avid reader of the 201 files.

"He's trying to reform me out of the fucking Army," you say.

"You understand he was assigned to your unit by direct order of General Lancaster."

"Direct order, huh," you say. "They go back a ways. To Vietnam?"

"Before that, I understand."

"Thanks for the tip," you say.

"Do you believe that this Sgt. Lee will present insuperable difficulties?"

"Just keep your ear to the ground," you say, again ever so slightly flustering Hermann. "You hear anything of interest, get me on the horn."

"That will not present a problem. Now I have occasion to pass some information on to you." It is like Hermann to keep the real information till the end, to protect his hole card.

"Shoot," you say.

"Our mutual Turkish friend has informed me that he has come to an understanding with the *Polizei*. This unfortunate incident has lost him much money, and he would like to start operations again. In fact, our Turkish friend is having guests over Friday at 2100 hours and he would appreciate your inestimable services as to quality control. May I have the honor of informing him you will be present?"

"Does a bear shit in the woods?" you say.

"I have not the slightest interest in that," Hermann the German says, "but I imagine the Turk will be pleased."

17

ON THE THIRD FLOOR, the game is under way. You have taken Knoll to the game and introduced him around. People are knocking back the beers, smoking a little, nothing heavy. You sit next to Knoll, who is studying his cards as if some great secret is about to be revealed. Before the game, you have taken a hit to settle down, smooth out the rough edges.

Video deals, and while you're looking at your cards he stares at his portable TV, which he has brought up specially so he doesn't have to miss any of his shows. Somewhere there is a war in progress with footage of soldiers lying prone in the jungle and returning fire into banks of foliage. Same old shit.

"Video, you're dealing me crap," Rothfuss says. "I'm out." He throws down his cards. "I tell you—I could use a tour of duty in the Stop 'n' Pop. Anyone up for it? How about you, Knoll?"

"Knoll's getting married this weekend," you say, pulling an empty beer bottle over to serve as an ashtray.

"You poor fuck," Rothfuss says. "Anything I can do to talk some sense into you?"

"It's a done deal," you say, answering for Knoll, keeping him on your string.

"Closest I came was living with this one girl," Rothfuss says. "You ever lived with your girl, Knoll?"

"No," Knoll says.

"That's the acid test," Rothfuss says. "Problem was, this girl liked to hide in the apartment. I come home, whole day at work—I'm trying to make a go of it in the world back then—and right when I'm putting my coat away she jumps out at me from the closet. I almost fucking died."

"What's your girl's name?" Eddio asks.

"Carol Ann Margolis," Knoll says.

"Hey, I know her," Video says, glancing away for a moment from the TV and then back again. "Look at the fucking Arabs, man. We should invade and settle their fucking hash, squeeze the oil out their assholes."

"How do you know her?" Knoll asks.

"She's in my college class. AV 340. I think you got yourself a solid woman there. Maybe a little too straight."

"What do you mean?" Knoll asks.

"The instructor, he uses the same tests every year. One year, after he gives the test, he puts it on reserve in the post library so people could figure out what they did wrong. But the fucking guy, it's like he never heard of Xerox machines. Someone Xeroxed the whole damn test, and it gets passed down each class."

"So what does this have to do with Carol Ann?" Knoll asks.

"She won't take the questions," Video says. "It's people like her we need more of. Everyone gets the test, it fucks up the grading curve like you wouldn't believe."

Cabot, who bets wildly until he runs out of money, raises and you check. You used to believe that you could learn things about people's character by playing poker.

"So it kept getting worse," Rothfuss says. "I'd come home, she'd be hiding under the bed or behind the shower curtain in the fucking bathroom. Each time it was like going into ambush."

"You know what?" says Sasquatch, holding his cards in fists, as if at any moment the game might break into a punch-out. "The condemned man needs a bachelor party, don't you think?"

You don't respond, looking down at your hand as you decide it won't get any better. What you discovered about people's character during poker games, however, was that the information could be used only during those same poker games.

"I'm out," you say, when Cabot raises the pot. Sasquatch drops out at the same time, the cards falling from his fists like leaves.

"So this one time I come home, and the place is pitch-black," Rothfuss says. "I mean, no moon, blinds closed, can't see two inches in front of me. I walk in, try to turn on the lights, and the bulbs are gone. The woman's like domestic Vietcong. So I call to her, I say I'm getting the fuck out of here right now if you don't come front and center."

"It's aggression," Video says. "She was aggressing against you. I just took a psychology course. You want to read up on it, I'll lend you the cheat sheets."

"No fucking shit," Rothfuss says. "You think I don't know that? Every time I come home I start to get the shakes walking by the mailboxes. So I say I'm staying right here in the entrance until she comes out."

"Look at the Dow fucking Jones," Video says, focusing on the economic indicators on the TV, jagged lines saying jackshit. "Some days it's up, some days it's down. The bean futures are going wild, you got your pork bellies zooming. You know what the great thing about this fucking country is, El?"

"That we don't live in it anymore," you say.

"It's that no one knows what the fuck is going on," Video says. "No one knows from shit. That's why they got the network news, buddy. You show the shit that's happening, and don't even try to figure out the big picture."

"Did she ever come out?" Knoll asks.

"Who?" Rothfuss says.

"Your girl."

"That's what I'm saying. I couldn't stand there forever. I remembered we had this hurricane lamp in the kitchen. I walked in, I figured open the refrigerator door, get that little interior light working. I open it up, and then I hear this noise. I look up, she's on top of the fucking refrigerator—crouched up there like, I don't know, a goddamn lynx or something."

"What did you do?" Knoll asks.

"Turned around, walked out. Enlisted in the Army the next day. Biggest fucking mistake of my life."

"How's that?" Knoll asks.

"I miss that crazy fucking broad," Rothfuss says. "Hell, with her you didn't know what was coming next."

"Rothfuss, I never said this before," you say, "but I don't think you're a normal human being. I'm embarrassed to be associated with you. Knoll, you go to the Stop 'n' Pop with him tonight, you'll have the sexual adventure of your life. Shit will happen that will curl your crotch hair. You'll get tied up, beaten up, shot—who knows?—but it'll be true love and you'll probably get to come in her mouth."

"Now you're talking," Rothfuss says. "We got to make a run."

"Later," Video says. "Elwood, you know what we're really glad about?"

"What's that?" you ask.

"You ain't brought any of the yams with you tonight. For a while there, we thought you were turning colored. First that guy, what's his name you were friends with—"

"We weren't friends," you say.

"Well, whatever the fuck he was, he was always around. And then there was McCovey, and that fucking maniac Stoney. And what're you into now, that fucking guy Kirch-something? We was worried they were gonna make you an honorary nigger."

"Your mama," you say.

"Get serious," Rothfuss says. "You'd let one go with your sister?"

You don't say anything.

"I'd let one get with his sister," Video says. "Look at the face on Elwood. He's got a damn hog for a sister. She'd be lucky to make it with a fucking mammal."

"I don't have a sister," you say.

"If you did," Video says, "she'd be a hog." Everyone laughs, even you, and then goes back to the cards.

Sasquatch has gotten up and gone to the window, where he is balancing a bottle of beer on the edge, watching it teeter. "Couple of yams eleven o'clock right now," Sasquatch says. "Watch this." He pushes the beer bottle off the windowsill, and you listen to the blank space in the night before it hits. There's a crack on the ground, the titter of shattering glass.

"Man, look at those suckers hustle," Sasquatch says. "Only time you see a yam move that fast it's when you say you got something for them to do."

"Cut the shit," you say.

"That's right, sit down and play," Rothfuss says. "And someone deal Simmons in. I think the only people I can beat are fucked up. I could use a loaner. How about it, Eddio?"

Eddio shakes his head. "No way," he says. "I'm saving my money."

"Oh, that's right," Rothfuss says. "You're saving for your titless girlfriend."

"Almost there," Eddio says. "El's got it set up."

"So what about you, Knoll?" Rothfuss says. "Give me some money."

"I only have enough for myself," Knoll says. He has his open face on, though, and you can tell he's going to give it up.

"Don't do it," you say. "Rothfuss never pays off."

"I always fucking pay off," Rothfuss says. "I ain't welched yet." He sticks his finger in his mouth and then sticks the wet willie in Knoll's ear. "I tell you what. You be my bank tonight and I'll set up a bachelor party for you. It'll be great."

"Lay off," you say.

"I'm not going after him," Rothfuss says. "I'm proposing a merger of our mutual interests. A business proposition."

"I wouldn't mind a bachelor party," Knoll says good-naturedly.

Rothfuss looks at you and then at Knoll. "I got some quality pussy on standby," he says. "I'm talking prime."

"I don't know," Knoll says.

"Besides," you say, "you got nothing but skanks."

"This particular girl—Hilde—she ain't a pro, but she's laid a trail of pipe like you would not believe."

"So what?" Knoll says. He looks at you for guidance, but you don't say anything.

"What I'm saying is, she'll provide dancing and entertainment at a reasonable price."

"You fuck her," Video says, "you get a Combat Infantryman Badge awarded right on the spot. They don't even dress you—they just hang it right on the end of your rod."

"I don't think it's right," Knoll says. "A guy's girl is his girl. That's all there is to it. If she puts out for other people, then she's a whore."

"Look, I'm not asking you to marry her, for Chrissakes,"

Rothfuss says. "I'm just giving her up on a loaner for your party."

"Let's put a ceiling on the bank," you say, "and I'll come in on it."

Rothfuss smiles. "Ah, that's the El-man for you. Always got his mind on the bottom line. Two hundred."

"Fifty," you say. "I seen what she looks like." You have your own reasons for doing this.

"Let Knoll speak for himself," Rothfuss says. "Hundred and fifty."

"I'm his agent," you say. "Fifty from me, fifty from him, and I'll arrange everything else."

"Deal," Rothfuss says. He shakes your hand and then Knoll's. "This bachelor party will go down in unit history."

"I know who he looks like," Video says.

"Who?" you say.

"The condemned man," he says, pointing at Knoll. "Over there."

"What?" you say.

"It's the Beaver," Video says. "Beaver fucking Cleaver."

"Fuck you," Knoll says, but it's an effort. He looks around to see if anyone will help him defend himself.

You look at Knoll. There *is* a certain resemblance, the golly-gee face trying desperately to remember his lines.

"That must make you Wally," Video says.

"Excuse the fuck me," you say.

"Let me be Ward," Cabot says. "While Wally and Beave are at school, I'll be home throwing one into June."

"Private Beave," Video says. "I heard the real Beaver's a DJ in L.A. You're picking up where he left off. Beaver Cleaver, Uncle Sam wants your ass."

"Maybe I'll be Eddie Haskell," Cabot says. "He always wanted a piece of June, man. It's why he was always coming by for the milk and cookies."

"I heard the real Eddie Haskell is a cop," Video says. "It was on the news he got shot a while back."

"He live?" Eddio asks.

"Don't know," Video says. "I'm surprised no one squeezed off a round or two while he was on the show."

"I wonder why they keep putting those old shows on all the time," Eddio says.

"Get your shit together," Video says. "They promote your fucking family values."

Sasquatch is propping another empty beer bottle on the windowsill.

"What are you doing?" Knoll asks.

Video gets up from the game and goes alongside him. "Bombs Away, the sequel," he says. Sasquatch takes his beer bottle and aims it, then gently releases. You hear it shatter on the sidewalk below.

"Not bad," Video says, peering out the window. "That's a fuck of a shot."

"What would happen if you hit somebody?" Knoll asks. Sasquatch is already lining up another.

"Uh-oh, we got something on the scopes," Video says.

"What?" you say.

"Pack of yams ten o'clock."

"What we gonna do about it?" Eddio says.

"Knoll, they messed with you. You wanna get some of this?"

"Yeah," Knoll says. "You bet I do."

"That's what I thought," Video says. You see the yams coming down the path, joking and making a lot of noise.

"This is what I call a target-rich environment," Video says, grabbing his own bottle. "Just grab tight on the neck and then let go, real slow. Let it slip between your fingers and just aim for the center."

"Can't it kill someone?" Knoll asks.

"You kidding me?" Video says. "Them fuckin' yams got heads so solid they don't need helmets. This thing'll just part their hair a little."

"Let's play this cool, all right?" you say, worried maybe Stoney's in the group. In any case, taking on a pack of yams with the men you've got is the next best thing to suicide. "You hit them, they come after us."

"Fuck you, nigger-lover," Video says. "Let them fuckin' get a taste."

"Do it," Rothfuss says. "Now!"

Knoll lets go of the bottle, and you watch it sail quietly into the knot of yams walking past. It hits one of them in the shoulder and drops him, and the rest look up.

"Eat that, you fucks," Knoll shouts out.

You see the yams disappear into the front of the building, and you know they're coming to take you on.

"Shit," you say, "I knew it."

"Everyone get a bottle," Video shouts.

Out in the third-floor hallway you hear the footsteps of the gang pounding up the first-floor stairs and realize you don't have much time. You also realize there's too much light on the third floor, whereas what's required is surprise.

"Get the fucking lights," you say. The lights are all fluorescent tubes, but they're controlled from the CQ's office on the first floor. You throw a bottle, and it smashes two of the three lights. Everyone immediately follows suit, and within seconds the hallway is dark.

You move forward and press yourself into one of the doorways. Knoll moves ahead of you, and so does Eddio. Video, you notice, stays behind. In these situations it's best not to be the first to strike. The first one or two will take the heat, the rest take advantage.

The steps quit at the top of the stairs and you hear heavy breathing. "Let's go," you hear. "Let's get them assholes."

Someone else says, "There's no fucking lights," but still you hear them move cautiously up the steps.

Your heart is beating fast with fear and excitement, and you remember another night when you held a man so close, listening to his breathing until he breathed no more.

They keep coming, moving slowly, waiting for their eyes to adjust to the light. You hear a crack and a bang, and scuffling begins to your left. All the fights are individual now, hand-to-hand. Hugging the wall, you wait until there's a man nearly abreast of you before you swing your bottle, not like a bat; you swing it straight, like a knife, and feel it hit something hard, and there's a scream. Your guy falls back, but there are more screams, more men rolling on the ground.

When you feel another one close by, you swing your bottle again but miss, catching him in the shoulder. He grabs on to you and then you're on the ground, punching and flailing and scratching at each other. He maneuvers to get you by the head and tries to dig his nails into your eyes, but you get an open shot and slam your fist into his balls with everything you've got. He screams and you drive an elbow into his face, then step back as he crawls away.

You're exhausted and your head is pounding, and from the sticky stuff on your hands you're not sure if you're cut or it's blood from one of the bastards you nailed. Whatever, you hear a bunch of people beating a retreat down the steps.

Someone touches you in the dark. You're about to swing when you hear, "Elwood, is that you?"

It's Knoll's voice. He brings his face up close, and in the moonlight you can see he's pretty banged up but all excited. "We fucking killed them, didn't we?"

18

Y OU ARE in the midst of taking a dump when you hear somebody crying in one of the other stalls, the constricted hacking of a chest fighting itself.

"Who's there?" you call out, but there is no reply. You instantly regret saying anything. The best move here is not to get involved. Cut and run.

You finish up, drop your cigarette into the toilet, and yank the handle. You've been on the shitter about half an hour, spending a little quality time.

When you come out of the stall to wash your hands, Knoll comes out of his stall. Knoll, you think, may be bad luck. When he's around, shit comes raining down. If there is one thing you have learned, it is that associating with the Motherfucked rubs off. And Knoll could be poster boy for the Motherfucked.

Knoll glances at you and then runs water onto his hands and splashes it on his face. His face is red and his eyes are swelled up from either being hit or crying.

You punch up one of the thermal hand dryers Colonel Berman just had installed; the heat on your hands is like breath. "What's the good word?" you ask.

Knoll looks at you as if you've slapped him. "You haven't been back yet?"

"Back where?"

"The room."

"You mean our quarters? Try to sound like you're in the Army, Knoll."

"They've just raided our quarters," Knoll says, which sounds like he's getting the hang of it.

SURE ENOUGH, the door is ajar, and a lot of your shit has been tossed around. The place is a mess again, but the only thing they've taken is your new Sony, although they've busted the rest up: punched holes in your speakers, ripped the doors off your bar, sliced the locks on your footlockers, dropped the microwave on the floor.

"What happened?" you ask. Big dark stripes run across the room. It's worse than when Sgt. Lee gave his inspection.

"I left the door open when I came back from lunch," Knoll says. "Four of them, they came in like they owned the place. They began going through your stuff. I told them to cut it out, and they said not to worry about it."

"What'd you do?" you ask. You know what they were doing, and what this means.

"I tried to stop them," Knoll says. "Then one of them saw the Right Guard can and grabbed it."

"And then?"

"He said my spray can was messing up the ozone, that if I fucked with the ozone I was fucking with him. Then he used his lighter to make a flamethrower out of it. The only way to protect that ozone, he said, was burn it off. He made me dance by spraying the Right Guard at my feet. Then the others knocked me around. They took my clothes off and tied me to the bed with my belt while they went through the rest of your stuff. I just got loose."

You tap out a Camel while you consider the situation, figure out the appropriate counter.

"What are we gonna do about it?" Knoll asks.

"Come with me," you say.

You take the precaution of locking the door before you head out of your crib and go up the stairs just short of the third floor. For a moment you listen for anyone who might catch your act and, of course, take advantage of it.

"You didn't see this," you say to Knoll, though you wouldn't have brought him here unless you specifically wanted him to. You undo one of the bolts on the banister post and twist off the metal top. The inside is hollow and you reach down, feeling around the narrow metal shaft for the baggie. You feel something metal taped along the side, the Model #5 John Smith knife, and pull that out first. Then you feel the baggie and pull.

"What's that?" Knoll asks.

"First line of defense," you say. "Distant Early Warning for the troubles of the soul."

You and Stoney have placed a portion of your goods here so you don't have to take the dangerous and attention-gathering trip to the Field House every time you need to get off; moreover, this is a common area, and shit cannot be traced back to you. You take out four pills from the baggie and place them in your pocket, then return the banister post to its original condition.

"Follow me," you say and, once back, safely inside your crib, you take out the small pills shaped like miniature footballs.

"Here. Take one." You drop it into his palm.

"What is it?" he asks.

"Sopor," you explain. You take two for yourself as mood enhancers, downing them with a swallow from a bottle of schnapps you keep stored in your canteen for the inevitable rainy day. Sometimes it rains, sometimes it pours. You can smell the dampness coming on even now. Monsoon season.

"What does it do?" Knoll asks, still turning the pill over in his palm, as if looking for a set of instructions.

"Some light stuff to take the edge off," you say. "It's like Valium but with all the side effects put back in."

He pops it and takes a swallow from the canteen, then sits on the couch and looks around your room. "Some of these people, they're just *niggers*."

You laugh at the force with which this comes out. "Get the terminology right," you say. "We got yams in this man's Army."

"Yams?" Knoll says, frowning as if he's trying to figure out what kind of atom smashing is going on in his head. "You got anything left in that canteen?"

You hand it to him and Knoll chugs some down. "You know," he says, "I hate it here."

"Every day and in every way, it gets more fucked up."

"I'd like to kill the bastards," Knoll says.

You take it from the helpless way Knoll says this that there is little chance of this solution being implemented.

"Three rules," you say. "Rule Number One: buddy up." One distinguishing feature of the Motherfucked is an inability to understand that the strong survive, and the strongest run in packs. Knoll's Adam's apple is in plain view, rubbed raw, as round as a superball.

"Rule Number Two," you say, "learn to roll with the punches." You do not tell him why they did this, because it is so apparent. They did it because they could. Because fresh meat like Knoll would never see it coming until it had already left.

"I hate this place," Knoll says again. "I'm sorry I signed up. I think I'm going to the Colonel and tell him I want out, that I want to go back to the world."

"Have another sopor," you say, handing it over to Knoll,

who downs it without any hesitation. Sgt. Keane, you think, would have found this amusing. The Army, he explained to you, is like any other business except you cannot quit.

"I just want a friend," Knoll says. "You know, someone to talk to, depend on. A buddy."

You do not say anything to this. Let Knoll get in the proper receptive state, tuned to your frequency. He may be the last innocent man left. Or you are.

"If this were a war, we'd be buddies," Knoll says. "We'd be fighting the enemy and depending on each other. My dad still keeps in touch with guys he knew in World War Two. They get together every year for a barbecue. He even has this joke apron with a mushroom cloud that says, 'Thank God for Doomsday.' He was in the Pacific. He told me that without the Bomb he probably would've died fighting in Japan. I never would've been born."

"Real nuclear family," you say.

You can see the sopor taking effect. His face is changing to a relaxed oval of not caring. You can feel the pleasant relaxation in your own brain, the driftiness of it. "So what do I do now?" he asks.

"Rule Number Three: Payback."

"Payback is a motherfucker," Knoll says, repeating the time-honored Army phrase.

"Only if you do it right," you say.

Knoll is phasing out of this world and into a better one—one way to go back. No brain, no pain. He shakes his head and comes to. "It just makes me sorry I missed Vietnam."

"Not me," you say. "Look how hard peace is."

Knoll relaxes on your bunk and curls into a fetal position. For a moment his Adam's apple moves out of sight, sinking into the anonymity of his neck. He puts his boots up on your pillow, but you're not in the mood to pull them off.

Just before you drop off, there is a knock on your door.

"Get out of here," you say.

"It's Walters," you hear. "I hear you're looking for stuff on the Parson."

"Too late," you say.

"But I got something he wanted you to have," Walters says.

"Fuck off, Walters."

"Hey, Elwood, I'm here to let bygones be bygones. Besides, maybe we could talk about some merchandise I understand happened to slip out of your possession."

"What a surprise you know about that," you say.

"I know everything," Walters says. "Come on, I'm all by my lonesome out here. This is an opportunity you don't want to pass up."

"All right." You get up and unlock the door, taking care that only Walters is on the other side. Stoney is not with you, and that can represent a short-term security risk. Lately, with the advent of Sgt. Lee, there have been nothing but security risks. You are, however, well prepared for any eventuality with the Model #5. In the good old days of a few weeks ago, nobody would have dared enter your crib without a fucking engraved invitation. But now, clearly, the climate has changed. You are creeping, ever so slowly, into the land of the Motherfucked. While someone like Walters would know that there would be payback, he might be in a bad way right now and ignore the certainty of cause and effect.

Walters comes into the room and smiles, which looks more like he is baring his yellow teeth. As a matter of fact, all of Walters is looking pretty yellow: his eyes, his skin, even his nails, which are long and curved. You know Walters is a user and has got more tracks than Penn Station. As with most users, the key to Walters is to figure out his angle on the play and then trust him precisely that much.

"Ever thought about doing some housecleaning?" Walters asks. "Place looks like it could use it."

"So what do you know about this?" you ask.

"Maybe I heard something," Walters says. "You in the market for a new television?"

"You keep well informed," you say.

"I stay current," Walters says. "Word is, you're getting out of the game. Maybe somebody ought to take your place can handle this action."

You light up a cigarette and then slowly walk over to the hot plate, where you put a pat of butter on the grill and wait for it to pool. Then you take out a hamburger patty and drop it down. It begins to sizzle. The sound bothers Walters, as you knew it would.

"You don't look too healthy, Walters," you say. "You ever think about shooting vitamins in there?"

"I got some pills I'm taking."

"You get any more yellow they're going to drop you from the Negro race."

Walters laughs, baring his teeth some more as he glances at Knoll. Even Walters's gums seem to have receded.

"I thought you'd like the word on the Parson."

"Where were you when I needed you? No one could think of anything good to say. I had to make that shit up." You blow smoke in Walters's direction.

"You shoulda axed me," Walters says. "I got nothing but good to say about him." He reaches between his feet and pulls a television set forward, hoisting it onto your dresser. "The Parson left me his TV." Walters may or may not have had a hand in the raid on your quarters. It is possible, you think, that he played lookout, the fifth man.

"That's pretty generous of him," you say. "He leave it in his will?" The smell of the hamburger begins creeping through your quarters, the sizzling growing louder as the fat in the meat liquefies.

"The Parson weren't much for writing shit down. He just said one day anything happens to him, this set heads my way."

You can see the smell of the meat is getting to Walters. Someone in his shape doesn't like being around food as it's being cooked. He shifts his stance so he's not directly downwind.

"So here it is," you say. You have only been needling Walters about the will. The Parson was not much for the legal niceties. In fact, the Parson's only acquaintance with the law was on the receiving end as a defendant where the judge offered certain inducements should he elect to join the Army and defend his country. But you are also aware as to how the TV set came into Walters's hands. When the word got out that Parsons McCovey had taken a leave on life, the permanent AWOL, what happened next was a barracks yard sale, where everyone who knew about the unhappy event broke into his quarters and took whatever they could carry. They made off with his stereo, his speakers, and his blues LPs. They took his boots and divvied up his uniforms. They stripped his bed and carted off the linen. They did not leave a crumb. When they were done with the Parson, it was as if he had never existed, just a body, road kill on the autobahn.

"What you think?" As Walters speaks you are aware he is staring at you. You look back at him and he glances away, as if you have caught him in an obscene act. And then you realize something that had never occurred to you before: Walters hates you.

"Not interested," you say. "The Parson's a dead subject."

"Two words," Walters says, "Zee-fucking-nith." He pauses to see the effect. "This sucker's your four-wheel drive of TVs, right out of the PX. Cloud cover's right, I can pick up Armed Forces Network all over Europe. You got an outlet handy?"

"No."

"I got it." Walters unplugs your clock radio and puts in the TV, which you see is pretty much an old-timer with tubes and takes its time warming up.

"This baby has sentimental value and you need that new set."

"Some other time," you say.

"I figure this kind of sentimental value is worth maybe an ounce of scag."

"Maybe you took some before you came over," you say. "All's I'm seeing is a load of green."

"Cash is convertible," Walters says. "No problem."

"I'm talking about the TV," you say. "Everybody's green."

"The pitcher tube," Walters says, squinting his yellow eyes at the set, "it needs a little work. But I got this temporary measure." He whacks the side of the TV with the palm of his hand. The picture shakes, as if the set blinked, and then it comes back in dusty colors of red, blue, and yellow. But the green still seems to be in the background, lurking.

"Look, you heard right. I'm out of the business," you say. "Retired. Full military honors. You know they can slap an Article 31 on you, heavy-duty court-martial for trafficking in stolen goods. I'm talking serious time. But, if you're determined, talk to Sgt. Saad or CC. They're really fixed to move stuff on the retail level."

"I talked to Saad," Walters says. "Said fifteen dollars, and I figured you could go better. Now that you need a TV and all." It is now certain in your mind that Walters was in on the raid on your quarters.

"I'm out of it," you say. "That's gospel."

"I heard Kirchfield just got drafted onto your team."

Kirchfield, the soldier to be named later. "There's some bad information going around," you say. "Try out CC. Give it a few kicks before you show it to him."

"You think that thing's cooked?" Walters asks. The smell of the meat is driving Walters crazy.

"I like mine well done," you say. "And thanks for the tip, but that information ain't worth an ounce."

"I figure you'll go for the ounce," Walters says.

"That's what you figure?"

"That's right. Sentimental reasons. The ounce for the TV and a name."

"Name of what?" you ask.

"I know who eighty-sixed the Parson."

So we know it is Possibility Number Two, the one you don't like to think about, the one that states that it was personnel in your battalion who removed Parsons McCovey from active status to Motherfucker emeritus. "Who?" you ask.

"Cost you an ounce," Walters says.

"One dime," you say. "You could be selling me a sack of shit." You don't trust Walters at all. On one occasion, when you were still new to the game, you employed Walters to drive a quantity of scag to a secure place near the Turk's. Pure delivery boy. He was an hour late for the meet, and when the scag arrived it was the same weight but significantly diluted. You ended up having to make good on it for the Turk, and it nearly wrecked the whole deal. At the time, you did not employ Stoney, nor did you understand that the etiquette of this branch of the pharmaceutical industry expected you to string Walters up by his balls.

"I can't go no lower than half a ounce," Walters says.

When you stare at him, he begins to tremble—not fear but need. The smell of hamburger is oppressing Walters, who is changing from his natural yellow tint to an interesting shade of green.

"It's the TV," he says, giving up a piece. "I'm going past the Parson's crib and I see this individual breaking in, and I figure, maybe something's in there for me. Let the big fish play, then come the minnows. So I hide myself out. And what's he doing—he's searching through the drawers for shit. Doesn't bother with none of the hardware. The Parson had a very decent stereo system. I sold that off to CC and he gave me good dollar value."

"So what?"

"We okay on the deal?"

"Two bags," you say.

"Two bags last me a day and a half," Walters says. "Maybe I take this information to the guy who was looking in the room. Maybe I tell him I told you."

"Maybe you'll end up catching the same disease the Parson had," you say. "You talk to the wrong individual on this matter, they mail you home bulk rate. I'll spring for three bags."

"Four."

"All right, provided it's good."

"I got your word, okay? And we go right from here."

"Can't do it sooner than tonight."

"Now!" Walters says, nearly shouting. Knoll stirs in his sleep, as if suffering from a bad dream.

"Forget it," you say. "Nonnegotiable."

"Now!" Walters says, and for a moment you think he might attack you. A junkie in need becomes a highly motivated individual.

"Eighteen hundred hours," you say. "Take it or leave it."

"Where?" Walters says.

"The softball field," you say. "Visitors' bench. So who?"

Walters leans forward, as if whispering to you. "Kirchfield," he says. "He's the one."

"I'll be seeing you," you say, "but take the TV with you."

Walters bows, which is almost funny, and then departs the room. There are a number of reasons you did not go for the scag immediately. You might go upstairs to collect the scag and be descended upon by the same four individuals who tossed your room. Another possibility comes from the fact that a guy like Walters with a certified jones clearly does not play the game with the proper caution. He may have already gotten jammed up with Sgt. Lee, and turning you may be how he works his way off the shitlist. While you would be going to the third floor for the scag, a number of MPs, aware of your destination, would be able to catch you red-handed. Taking the Zenith would be receipt of stolen property, and even this chickenshit offense would be enough to take you down. But the last reason is the most persuasive: you are certain Walters is lying.

You know Walters is lying because Kirchfield, for all his Motherfucker potential, has not yet killed anybody. Men change after they have killed, though not immediately, and the practiced eye can catch the extra weight—Cain carrying Abel across endless fields of salt.

The move here is to get hold of Stoney and Kirchfield, get the possibilities sorted out, and provide a little payback.

You reach over and shake Knoll, who is still in the half-dreamland of the drugged.

"Knoll," you say. "Get up."

"What?" he asks, barely coming to, and trying to turn away and curl into a ball. "What do you want?"

"Come on," you say. "We're gonna go make some friends."

"I LOVE THE STEAMS," Stoney says, smoothing a towel on the bench. You sit on the edge of the bench, away from the coals. Already you can feel your body begin a wholesale itch, army ants taking a ten miler down your back. Knoll, also naked, is barely conscious. Your overtaxed lungs rebel, and you begin a coughing fit.

"Got to let the air get inside you—don't fight it. You get so hot you're cool." Leaving the towel, Stoney walks naked to the coals and leans over them, taking a deep breath through the nose. "Oh my," he says.

You suspect that one of the reasons Stoney suggests the steams is to parade his body. He has told you that the easiest time to take a guy is when he has his pants down in the toilet, when he is most open, but in fact, when Stoney is naked, it is you who feel weak. You wonder if you should have done a line or two of scag to get yourself idling right, to put the proper perspective on things. The sopor is definitely too lightweight to provide the necessary ambience.

"Used to go once a week," Stoney says. "Saturday night the kid was all right. Come out feeling clean, like anything could be." Stoney's chest and back are puddling with sweat, a tidal pool of water collecting over his brow. Great knots of muscle are smoothing out, moist and shiny. You smell him and you smell yourself and by smelling yourself you know what prey is. You feel the water rising from your skin like a hose has been turned on, and you are ready to scream. You do not remember it being this bad before.

"Sunday we'd drive to the tournaments—everything closed up, dead from the night before. Just us moving. Roll down the windows and smell the quiet," Stoney says. You know that Stoney got his Motherfucker basic training in karate and boxing at a Y, combining the two martial arts in an especially lethal combination. East meets West. Going to tournaments and beating on the citizens, changing their points of view. You imagine what it would be like to come up against somebody like Stoney, fresh out of the blocks.

"What was it like?" you ask. "Winning those tournaments."

Stoney smiles a slow smile that spreads across his face and moves like a ripple over his entire body. "Glorious," he says.

Your breathing settles somewhat, although you are itching all over. You decide a medicinal dose of scag will be required in the future.

"Don't scratch," Stoney says. "You start scratching, everything reds up. Look like you got on the losing end of a catfight."

You nod your head and settle for patting the sweat on your shoulders. It feels sticky, as if you have been sweating blood.

"What you hear about Darnell Moore?" Stoney asks.

This is the man Stoney is going to be fighting in the Division Box-Offs. "I hear the guy knows his shit," you say. "Old school, keeps low, squared away."

"He a hooker?" Stoney asks.

"That's what I hear."

"I hate hookers," Stoney says. "What happened to little brother over there?" He motions to Knoll, who seems to be in a coma. Sweat rolls off him like rain.

"Too much playing Army," you say. "You thought anything about what I said about getting out? Time is right."

"What you know about liquor?" Stoney asks. You have suggested that you both get out, plant your savings in a liquor store and a karate school, and coast for the rest of your natural-born lives.

"You're always in with sin," you say.

"What if somebody comes in, tries to rob your ass?" Stoney asks, exhibiting once again his capacity to cut to the bottom line.

"Not my ass he's robbing," you say. "We get a cop—"

"No cops."

"A vet, then—who gives a shit—and we give him a cannon of his own for job security. That end gets taken care of."

"I saw Muhammad Ali fight in person once—Richard Dunn in Bonn," Stoney says. "Took him in five. On the way out of the ring, just as Ali was going by, I reached out, touched him on the corner of his robe. It was like a shock, like I touched a god."

"That means yes," you say. While you dream of knowing the keys to everybody, the keys to the kingdom, in Stoney's mind it is to physically be all, to move in a ring with absolute freedom.

"That means partners," Stoney says, breaking into a grin. "You run the liquor store, I run the karate school. Same-o, same-o."

"That's what I see," you say, and the deal is set as soon as the Turk gives you morphine base to cook. You are getting out of the Army, and you are getting out soon.

"What we gonna do to be this rich?" Stoney asks.

"The key," you say, "is to be so rich you never do anything at all."

Kirchfield sticks his head in the steam room. "Oh man, it's hot in here," he says.

"You're fucking swift," Stoney says.

"How about it?" you ask. You take out your Smith Model

#5, with a double-edged blade and light Micarta handle. It gleams in the dim light. Stoney eyes it without saying anything. He has seen it before and he knows what it can do. The knife feels as light as a feather.

"Everything's set," Kirchfield says.

"How about him?" Stoney asks, motioning to Knoll.

"Ready as he'll ever be," you say, pushing him in the ribs. Knoll wakes up in a kind of stupefied panic.

"What about our friends and comrades?" you ask.

"Already waiting," Kirchfield says.

You're holding the scag in front of you in a paper bag as you cross the field on your way to meet Walters. Inside, however, is not scag but four bags of pure cane sugar—in case what is in store for you is the official Sgt. Lee option.

Stoney and Kirchfield maneuver around the back, getting position on Walters and whoever else shows his hand. Knoll, whom you have revived enough to hold a rifle outfitted with a sniperscope and flash suppressor, is your ace in the hole, able to provide you with that nuclear threat.

Walters is waiting by the backstop, smoking, all jittery. Four other guys are hanging, waiting with him, not for any kind of takedown, you realize, but because they don't trust Walters either. It is a shitty world you live in, but it's the only one available.

It happens this way. In situations of this sort, the play is helped by the unexpected move, the slight juke that takes them out of their game plan. You're up front handing over the bag to Walters, and when he grabs for it, his eyes hungry, you pull back. The bag rips, and out pop the bags of sugar, which from a distance look like the brown. The others press forward and you immediately swing up the Model #5, slashing Walters in the hand. Walters staggers backward as Stoney and Kirchfield take out the four individuals.

The beating is quick and efficient, and it is at times like this that you envy Stoney: the absolute freedom he employs. When they're done, Stoney and Kirchfield pick up Walters and escort him back to the barracks and take him to the latrine for some underwater exploration.

You have prepared the exploratory field by choosing a toilet with a recent deposit. Stoney and Kirchfield both take one leg each as they dump Walters headfirst into the shitter. Walters struggles around, his puny arms trying to push against the bowl. Small pieces of shit linger on his face each time they bring him up for air. The last time, you bring Knoll over for a look.

"You recognize him?" you ask Walters, then put the point of the knife in Walters's nose, a scene right out of *Chinatown*. Stoney draws back.

Walters sputters. He's banged his eye on the side of the toilet and is having trouble breathing.

"Don't fuck with us ever again." You take the knife away and Kirchfield drops Walters on his head, leaving him sobbing by the toilet. You hear his cries echo as you walk outside the latrine into the night.

19

FRIDAY NIGHT and the indigenous population at the Turk's is not into the niceties. This is where people go when their usual den of iniquity runs dry, which is why you have moved Knoll's bachelor party here for the final laps. Among the survivors, only Rothfuss and Sasquatch are still able to stand. Video remains passed out at CC's in front of his portable TV, the ear clip still attached. But Knoll's still going strong. He is up front, dancing with Hilde, who has one hand down his pants and the other supporting him under the armpit. From where you sit, it looks like true love.

You are sober, which feels unnatural, the world taking on a sharpness and clarity you do not remember. Occasional sobriety, however, works to your advantage. The principal advantage is that it gives you a keen understanding of all the good reasons you have to remain fucked up.

You are seated at a table with Stoney, Kirchfield, and Lt. Louie Leone, otherwise known as Looey-Louie. At the other end of the table is the Turk. Besides the bachelor party, the place is also overrun by Special Forces guys, greenbeanie badasses Looey-Louie knows from Bad Toelz. One of them, a Sgt. Saperstein, is up on stage getting his rocks off on some girl. He and Knoll look like they have rehearsed their act together.

"I always liked this place," you say. "It's got character.

History. It's like the Yankee Stadium of drinking." You light
a cigarette and let this observation seep into the Turk. As
with Hermann the German, with the Turk it's good to keep
up the Americanisms, remind him of his foreign-national
status.

"Thank you," the Turk says sincerely. He likes to hear
his joint has character, even though you would be hard
pressed to define exactly what part of that character it is
possible to admire. The Turk's a little guy, running maybe
five six or seven. Little runty mustache but a good three-
piece suit. He is an inspiring example of the entrepreneurial
spirit. He came across the border to Germany with five keys
of morphine base stuck in his ruck. He had smuggled it
from his family farm in Turkey over land and sea, figuring
that there was a better market than the one his government
provided. That was his stake. He bypassed the perfume
refineries in Marseilles, and his only problem was coming
up with a chemist to transform his morphine base into gold.
The usual alchemy. And that's where you come in.

Knoll has finally gotten into the spirit of things and has
taken most of his clothes off, down to his underwear and
dog tags. Hilde slips one of his dog tags in her mouth and
leads him around the front of the stage.

"Elwood," Stoney says, "what the fuck did you bring
those guys for?"

"Cover," you say. You have been feeling that Sgt. Lee is
closing in, that he has stepped up the surveillance, that you
are under observation at all times. It could also be simply
your routine paranoia. But by bringing the merry men out
on this expedition, you can confuse the opposition. The
essence of this is to increase the background noise until it
reaches epic proportions.

"Some cover," Stoney says.

The Turk sees someone come in and gets up from the

table, excusing himself before he walks to the back of the room. This is impressive in and of itself. You have never actually seen the Turk move once he was situated.

"Who's that?" Stoney asks. Looey-Louie is staring at the girls up on the stage.

"It's Ling and the Chinese delegation," you whisper. You see a thin, dignified Chinese walking through the crowd. Behind him are a number of other Chinese, all of them looking around suspiciously at the maneuvers being performed by the greenbeanies and Knoll.

Up front, Sgt. Sap has taken the cue from Knoll and is now completely naked. His naked peroxide blonde is controlling him by his dick, shifting it around like a gearshift.

"Saperstein really loves a freebie," Looey-Louie says. "And your guy is keeping up, too." Knoll has taken off all his clothes and is now rubbing up and down against Hilde.

"Nothing like a hanging," you say, "to concentrate the mind."

"I had a wife like that once," Looey-Louie says. "Head-on-collision kind of marriage, no survivors. But hell, it's good to see you guys again." Looey-Louie's a little drunk, enjoying himself. "You look as good as ever."

"What did you bring your guys for?" you ask. When you called to invite Looey-Louie, you didn't expect him to come with his army.

"Green Berets," Looey-Louie says. "Don't leave home without 'em."

"You don't look so good, man," Stoney says, nodding at the leg.

Looey-Louie is sporting a cast and has his crutches spread like outriggers, which personnel keep tripping over as they make their way drunkenly to the front to practice takeoffs and landings on the women. Rothfuss has stood up and sat down three times, suddenly defeated by the whole process of locomotion.

"I needed these guys to drive," Looey-Louie says, by way of explanation. "Two places I broke it in. But it was the greatest thing ever happened to me."

"What?" you ask.

"The leg," he says. "Banged it up skiing at the Army Rec Center at Garmisch. Hurt like a mother. Like a fucking motherfucker."

Looey-Louie has been breaking portions of himself as long as you've known him. When whole, he is about six foot five, running 230, 240—but he is an aficionado of calamity. Walking in the shower, he'd slip and fracture his collarbone; pulling at the door of his jeep, he would dislocate his elbow; jumping down from the gate of a supply truck, he would strain the ligaments of his knee. Looey-Louie is a china shop messing around in a bullish world. His worst moment came when throwing live grenades on the firing range. A piece of shrapnel ricocheted wrong and caught him in the tongue. That was when you knew Looey-Louie was not a lucky man.

Nevertheless, Looey-Louie was a man with a dream, chiefly to quit Colonel Berman's ordnance battalion and join the greenbeanies. They are the Army's version of the championship varsity. Every year they list their probable kill ratio as to how many enemy soldiers it takes to knock off one of their own; 7–1 one year, 9–1, the next. This year it shot up to 22–1, so that one greenbeanie armed with a pistachio could take out the starting unit of the Dallas Cowboys. But the Army brass, despite its abiding love for exaggeration, couldn't approve that figure, and punished them down to 3–1.

Finally, Looey-Louie, after numerous requests for transfer, was sent to Bad Toelz to handle greenbeanie ordnance responsibilities. And because you and Colonel Berman handled the paperwork that realized his dream, it is time to call in that marker.

The Turk's is decorated in black. There are black walls, black tables, black tablecloths, and the floor, of course, is black. A certain consistency of imagination is apparent. Without the lights at the front of the stage, and the writhing bodies of Sgt. Saperstein and Knoll dancing in front with their girls, you might lose your bearings.

"Why was it such a good thing," you ask. "I mean, getting the leg broke?"

"Ah, Jesus," Looey-Louie says. "That's how I got to know everybody. That's how I met my fiancée."

"She was your nurse?" you ask.

"No, man, she was skiing, too," Looey-Louie says. "Helped drag me down the mountain. But I also got to know everybody in the unit. Before then, Bad Toelz was this closed society. Couldn't talk to anybody. But now I knew everybody. It was a matter of finding the right flow to go with."

Looey-Louie, you know, is a jock-sniffer. He is one of those guys who loves to sit around and watch the action. Takes no risks, but thrills in the moves. He's not a player, he's a UN Observer.

"You know, Stoney's right," you say. "You do seem different."

"I am," Looey-Louie says. "Want to know the secret?"

You nod.

"I am so fucking happy," Looey-Louie says.

"Swell," Stoney says.

"Any woman here, any woman you want to meet—she's yours," Looey-Louie says. "You too, Stoney. You guys are like fucking family to me."

As evenings go on, you have noticed, the inventory of women becomes severely depleted. You look around the room, finally settling on a blonde with curly hair. "None for me, thanks, but maybe Knoll could use a twofer." You point toward the blonde. "How about her?" Just as you say this, Knoll falls down onstage and lies prone, technical knockout in the final round. Hilde keeps dancing by herself, not particularly disturbed by Knoll's dramatic exit, and several of the greenbeanies lumber forward now that her dance card shows an opening.

"Never mind," you say.

"Oh, except her," Looey-Louie says. "You don't want to get into it with her. She's with Sgt. Sap."

"The guy up front?" you ask. "He brings his girlfriend to this place? He brings her here on a fucking *date?*"

Stoney chuckles, shifting to get a better look at the blonde. "I like her," he says.

"She's a stand-up chick," Looey-Louie says. "Who the fuck knows what goes on these days. Still, you want to meet her?"

Stoney nods.

Looey-Louie grabs one of the greenbeanies going past and says a few words to him.

When the greenbeanie comes back, he's got the girl in tow.

"Hi, my name is Doe." She takes off her jacket and sits down at the table next to Looey-Louie.

This is the perfect name for her. Right away you realize she's one of the missing persons of the drug combat arena, which would be the only way, you understand, somebody could hang out with Sgt. Sap.

"Doe here is like the greatest girl on earth," Looey-Louie says. "Woman like her comes along about once in a lifetime." Which means, of course, she's a punchboard for the greenbeanie A-team, who plant their flags in her regularly. The only thing this makes you feel is tired.

"Are you with Sgt. Sap?" Stoney asks, but she seems uncomprehending. "The guy up front?"

"Right now, yeah," she says. "He's really very sweet."

"And a great dancer, too," you say, but Stoney gives you a warning glance. Up front, Sgt. Sap is grinding hard against the blonde. Knoll has been dragged from the stage by Sasquatch and is now back at the table where they will try to revive him, perform a little triage. Maybe they'll pour some beer on his wounds.

"You want to go somewhere?" she asks Stoney.

"You need me?" Stoney says to you, already getting up from the table.

"Not as much as you need that," you say.

Stoney takes off with Doe, and you turn your attentions to Looey-Louie. "So," you ask, "you think you can do it?"

Looey-Louie nods. "It'll cost, but my men like these security deals."

Since Colonel Berman is coming up for his OERs, he wants the troops of the 57th to stage a mock battle against Colonel Marshall's forces. The plan, which you have suggested to the Colonel and has been approved by the Mrs. Colonel, is for the greenbeanies to come in as ringers, get some heavy hitters in there who know what they're doing and will blow Colonel Marshall's regular Army troops out of the water.

"Where the fuck is she?" you hear, and you turn to see the fucked-up face of Sgt. Sap.

"What are you talking about?" Looey-Louie asks, all innocence. Kirchfield starts to move, but you put your hand on his leg to stay him. While Kirchfield is enthusiastic, he does lack timing and a light touch.

"Sgt. Sap," you say, "you're just the man I want to see."

"Sit down, man," Looey-Louie says, and right away you can see that Looey-Louie, having the disadvantage of being a straight-leg officer, with no jump or real training, is not real to Sgt. Sap. Sgt. Sap is no more his man than you are. Looey-Louie is somebody to put up with, someone to use. If the greenbeanies are the Army's championship varsity, Looey-Louie is the guy who holds the sponge for the real water boy.

Sgt. Saperstein gets right in your face. "You don't tell me where she went," he says, "I'll beat the fucking shit out of you."

Your whole life, you reflect, is being fucked with by sergeants. Kirchfield is starting to stand up from his chair.

"She's out powdering her nose," you say. "But I think you look like a man who's about to get three wishes."

"Sap, this is the guy I was telling you about," Looey-Louie says, putting a big grin on his face. "Elwood. This man here, he can get just about anything done."

"Service is our middle name," you say, sticking out your hand. Sgt. Saperstein picks something out of his teeth before drunkenly putting his meaty hand in yours.

"What's my first fucking wish?" Saperstein asks.

"See that girl that was dancing with my buddy up there?" you ask.

"Yeah," Saperstein says, glancing back at Hilde, who is now dancing with another greenbeanie.

"She's yours tonight," you say, which will require only a quick say-so from Rothfuss—who, judging from his slumped position next to Knoll, would not be inclined to argue.

"Thanks," Saperstein says.

"No charge," you say.

Saperstein sinks down into a chair and looks at you with glassy eyes. He smells pretty bad and without clothes on is a lot hairier than you find necessary.

"So what you have in mind?" he asks. "You want us to fuck somebody up?"

"Sgt. Saperstein," you say. "You've just become my favorite Motherfucker." And now that you've got him tuned properly, you tell Saperstein what it is you need.

A HALF HOUR later you've temporarily stepped away from the festivities and into the back room at the Turk's. You are thinking, however, about the difference between movies and real life. In the movies, checking scag for purity, the evildoer always takes a thumbful and puts it on his tongue, like he's checking the freshness of the chicken salad. Then you see him start, make a face, nod his head. Those miraculous druggie taste buds have told him the whole story. "Good shit," he says, if you're looking at an R rating, "Good stuff," if it's PG-13. Video, you are beginning to think, makes a lot of sense for a nut case. A little reality programming might just be in order.

Here is the reality: if it didn't knock you out completely, a little nip of the pure would disable most of your bargaining unit, and for another, someone who made deals of that weight on the basis of a taste test wouldn't live very long. People would line up to shoot somebody that stupid, put him out of his fucking misery. The key here is to place your faith in the wonders of science.

Sooner or later, science teaches us, things may be brought to a boil. And it is when they are brought to that boil that we learn their true nature. So you have this setup: four flasks filled with mineral oil over gas-stove burners. You measure from random bags small quantities of the scag under consideration. You place this scag into test tubes and locate them in the flasks so that the mineral oil covers the line of the scag and you have a good view of the Celsius thermometers. This is called double boiling and is used in order not to have the flame directly on your sensitive product. Then you light the stove and a cigarette and sit back to watch.

Surrounding you are personnel of the serious Motherfucker variety. There is the Turk, who is seated on one side of the kitchen, while on the other is Ling, who is as thin as the Turk is fat. He is the dignified-looking son-of-a-bitch who has brought the product you are now testing for purity. The drug business, you reflect, necessarily entails a certain lack of trust, which of course provides you with possibilities of employment.

You watch the temperature of the scag begin to rise, waiting for it to hit that magic number. The magic number here is 240 degrees centigrade, which will indicate that the scag is pure, that no one along the great relay race from Southeast Asia has stepped on it.

The temperature keeps rising—now at 180—and the scag is still looking good. Anything over 200 degrees is acceptable, and as you get closer to the 240 mark the wholesale price goes up. You pass 200 and the Turk, as if alerted by some inner signal, gets up from his place and waddles over to look at the thermometers. He gets into your space, patting you on the shoulder as you watch the mercury climb.

Ling remains where he is, in the dark. He is confident that the product is good, giving the kind of body English a man gives when he knows his aces are wired.

"Two thirty," the Turk says with some satisfaction, seeing the mercury rise past that increment and the scag in the test tube beginning to darken. You are approaching the end here. When the scag begins to change color, to go from light brown to caramel to cooked, you've hit its purity level. The scag finally liquefies at 236 degrees, which works out to a purity of 98 percent.

You look at Ling first and then the Turk, who has broken into a smile, which in his case has a distinctly lewd air. "How is it, Elwood?" the Turk asks.

"Weapons grade," you say.

The Turk nods, and Ling walks with his men into the side room for further negotiations. The Turk, however, hangs back a minute, facing you.

"I also have a need to convert some product from morphine base," the Turk says.

"From Ling?" you ask.

"We have reestablished connections with our regular pipeline," the Turk says.

"How much base we talking?" you ask.

"Forty kilos," the Turk says, which would be the biggest single shipment you've done. "I must know if you would be able to handle this quantity."

You pause, looking around the room. Forget the liquor store and karate school; this is retirement city facing you in its sweetest form.

"Is the pope Catholic?" you ask.

20

A PARTY at the Bermans features all lions and no Christians, check your ulterior motives at the door. You are standing with Stoney, who is dressed in a minuteman outfit, blue coat, epaulettes, powdered wig. The two of you are cracking ice into buckets while you are having a nicotine fit. The Colonel and Mrs. Berman have gone upstairs for a last bit of preparation, the preparty pep talk. It is just before 2000 hours, jump-off time. No one has yet arrived.

"My hands are frozen," you say to Stoney, wiping them on the bar rag.

"Shit you on, I'm surprised you feel anything," Stoney says. "You just cannot hold your shit anymore." He has gotten his left epaulette wet from the ice and is wringing it out over the bucket. It took a lot of coaxing to get Stoney to hang by you during this tough time. Motherfuckers, you have learned, are somewhat inflexible when it comes to matters of costume.

"You sure you straight enough to handle this?" Stoney asks. After testing out the precincts of sobriety, you have decided that reality is not your cup of tea. Before you came in, you took a medicinal dose, both nostrils this time.

"I was straight I couldn't handle it," you say.

The Bermans' house has been decorated Revolutionary War–style, all thirteen-star flags and Colonial napkins.

Even the drink cups contain Revolutionary War scenes: Washington crossing the Delaware, Cornwallis giving it up at Yorktown, Valley Forge in deep snow, a few soldiers wandering around looking pissed.

One of the Berman kids comes out of the kitchen. Colonel Berman has two boys and a three-year-old girl. The boys are ages eight and six, with little crew-do's and little straight backs, ROTC kindergartners, already on that long march. They are dressed, like you and Stoney, in minutemen outfits, tricornered hats, and blue costume coats.

The kid looks at Stoney. "You're black," he says.

Stoney, who has wrung out his epaulette, glares.

"Kid's got an eye for detail, you have to admit," you say. You wonder if Stoney would kill an eight-year-old.

"You know, if you lived here during the Revolutionary War," the kid says, "they wouldn't have let you be black."

"You want some seltzer, sonny?" you ask. Stoney keeps up the full-intensity glare on the kid as he busies himself wiping the bar.

"I'll give you some ice cubes and a cherry and you can pretend it's a real drink."

"That would be awesome," the kid says. "Make sure you put a sword in it, okay?" At a Colonel Berman party, even the drinks come well armed.

You try to think of the boy's name as you hand him his seltzer. "That's very good, sir," he says to you. "I need to see my mom and dad right now."

"They're upstairs," you say, pointing. As he turns, you think, Wait a second. "What about?" you ask.

"I have to tell them there's something wrong with that man in the kitchen." He is talking about Simmons, whom you have on reduced rations until the party is over but is already, you suspect, half in the bag.

Even Stoney cracks a smile at this one. "FUBAR, FU-

BAR," he says. What he is saying is that this scene is fucked up beyond all recognition, your usual mode of operation.

"He's probably tired," you say to the kid.

"I think he's dying," the kid says.

"Stoney," you say, "why don't you give this boy a little update on race relations while I go check on the help."

"Can't get good white help anywhere nowadays," Stoney says. You turn and begin walking toward the kitchen, thinking that bringing Simmons into this was yet another mistake. Simmons, despite his great and necessary work at the pharmacy, has lately become a liability. Soon, you decide, you are going to promote his understudy, Cabot, to the big show.

"Does it bother you being black, sir?" you hear the kid ask.

"All the fucking time," you hear Stoney respond.

You light a cigarette as you go into the kitchen and see Simmons slumped over the kitchen table, his tricornered hat overturned next to him. Paul Revere after one too many midnight rides. Cabot, also in a minuteman outfit, is tending to him. They are like two thirds of the Spirit of '76 poster, the fife and drum corps for the chemically dependent.

"He's in a bad way," Cabot says.

"When was he last in a good way?" you ask.

"Needs a little taste get through the party," Cabot says.

"Don't we all," you say. You pick Simmons up by the arm and steer him into the pantry. He is doubled over in pain, sweat all over his face.

You break out your pouch and pour a little scag onto a plate. "Just a snack to get you through," you say.

"Don't shoot till you see the whites of his eyes," Cabot says.

"Jesus," you say.

Simmons snorts clumsily off the plate, doing it all, then

looks at his sad reflection in the plate. The sorrow and the pitiful. He licks his fingers to mop up any stray granules.

When Simmons lurches back into the kitchen, you take a snootful of your own, both nostrils to keep your balance, bringing all karma indicators to within acceptable parameters.

As you walk out of the kitchen, Colonel Berman and his wife are walking down the stairs. The kid is nowhere to be found, and you hope that Stoney has not stowed him in the ice bucket.

"I didn't even want this goddamn party," Colonel Berman is saying. "I hate goddamn parties. I hate the goddamn things."

The Mrs. Colonel looks good, light green dress with plunging neckline, nice tan from catching UV rays overtime under the tanning lamps. At these moments, when the Colonel's nerve begins to falter, she takes over, executive officer of the good ship Berman.

"Have another drink, for Chrissakes," she says.

"I don't want another drink," the Colonel snaps. He turns to you. "Elwood, are you sure the General didn't RSVP?"

"He never RSVPs, sir," you say.

There's a knock on the door, and everyone turns hopefully. When Colonel Berman opens it, you see only the nervous faces of Lt. Meyer and his wife. Colonel Berman's Grant's captain is the only person to arrive on time. Traditionally, he spends most of his time hovering on the edge of conversations and then is the last to leave, one of the extras who can't ever catch his cue.

After shaking Meyer's hand, Colonel Berman makes his hands into fists. "I hate these things," he says to Lt. Meyer, as if it were his fault for causing the party. "Meyer, go get a goddamn drink and start enjoying yourself."

"For God's sakes," the Mrs. Colonel says. The Colonel

and Mrs. Berman are like partners in a business that is steadily losing money.

"If no one comes, it's goddamn Marshall's fault," Colonel Berman says. "I'll get that son-of-a-bitch. I'll remember. I'll land a goddamn ICBM on that fucker's lawn."

But personnel begin arriving, and soon everything is in full swing. By 2100 hours all the essential players are assembled. Introducing, center stage, General Thomas Lancaster. Salt-and-pepper hair, heavy on the chest fruit salad, able to leap tall piles of memoranda in a single bound: this is the man Colonel Berman is banking on. General Lancaster has the kind of connections to go all the way to the Joint Chiefs, Colonel Berman has told you, and as a career handicapper Colonel Berman knows his shit.

Stage left, unfortunately entering into conversation with the General at this very moment, is Lt. Colonel Phil (Pookie) Marshall. Marshall is G3 for the 57th and honcho for Operations and Training, to Colonel Berman's G4 at Logistics. While they are of equivalent rank, Marshall's the comer who is looking to take over as chief of staff for General Lancaster. Colonel Grigson, the current chief, is retiring, and the nod may indeed go to Marshall, despite Colonel Berman's having more time in grade. Colonel Berman has told you that the real choke point for officers occurs not at the star level but between the light colonel and bird slots. As Colonel Berman sees it, if the competition ended today, it would be Marshall by a nose. Hence the party. Come from behind and make up that lost ground, Colonel Berman riding on the rail.

Colonel Berman has counterattacked Marshall by launching into one of his stories, and from where you are in the wings you can see that it's not playing well. The General, Colonel Marshall, and even the Mrs. Colonel are holding themselves in rigid postures, party isometrics for the truly bored. The General looks at his watch and then massages his wrist, as if hoping to hurry the time along. The Colonel's stories are long, you know, and ebb slowly to their finish, just like the tide and about as interesting. He has already discussed the number and varying components of grapeshot, as well as the diet and logistical requirements of Genghis Khan's Mongols, who rode all day and then mixed their mounts' blood with a milk-flour preparation, a kind of Carnation Instant Breakfast for the Motherfucker on the move. He has just launched into an inventory of the baggage trains of British generals in the Boer War, which included dining-room furniture, full settings for tea and meals, and several hundred bottles of champagne and claret should victory unexpectedly catch one in the field. Next up, you know, will be a précis of the dietary requirements of Hannibal's elephants as they made their long march to Rome. All the stories come one after the other, segueing seamlessly, each one a tale of legendary logistical acumen. How you know this is he has rehearsed them on you, and you had the impression that your life was not long enough to make it up another Alp.

As the Hannibal tale winds down, you sidle up with another round of drinks and hand General Lancaster his vodka martini, made for precision bombing.

"Elwood," General Lancaster says, desperate for the interruption. "Bill here says this Revolutionary War stuff was your idea."

"Yes sir," you say, and here the General plays right into the Colonel's gambit. "But it was the Colonel who sparked it. As a matter of fact, we just discovered that the Colonel may be related to General Francis Marion, the old Swamp Fox."

Colonel Marshall coughs on his drink and makes a small,

strangled noise. He looks as if someone has just kicked him in the stomach.

"I guess I'm just surrounded by people related to famous people," General Lancaster says. He turns to Marshall. "Isn't that so, Pook?" Colonel Marshall starts to make his usual claim, offhandedly and as if it made no difference, that he is related, oh, third cousin by a second marriage once removed, to General George C. Marshall, the former Army Chief of Staff. This is as bogus as they come, but so is the Swamp Fox deal.

"I try not to play it up," Colonel Marshall says, a dagger to Colonel Berman's Revolutionary War motif, "but once I discovered I was related to George Marshall I felt as if he were guiding me in spirit, if not in fact." More hokum, of course, but Colonel Marshall didn't get where he is by being shy about flanking attacks.

"To tell you the truth, I hate that lineage shit," General Lancaster says. "I'm not related to anybody very famous, and all that family-line bullshit makes me feel insecure."

According to your astute observation, the two people feeling most insecure at the present time are the Colonels Berman and Marshall.

"It hasn't been proven yet, of course," Colonel Berman says, beating a tactical retreat as he sets about readjusting the genealogy coefficient in his mind.

"As far as General Marshall is concerned," Colonel Marshall says, "I never actually did have the honor of meeting him."

"My belief is, you come from dirt, you fight better 'cause you don't want to go back to dirt," General Lancaster says. "Best fighters in the world—people who got nothing to lose."

"It's the type of dirt that's most important," the Mrs.

Colonel says, drawing the analogy into her own field of expertise and trying to lighten the considerable pall that has come over her husband. "Some men are clay, others are topsoil."

"The connection, if there is one, comes from my wife's side," Colonel Berman says, trying to put whatever additional distance he can between him and the suddenly more elusive Swamp Fox.

The Mrs. Colonel, upon hearing herself being given up like this, suddenly turns to the warpath. "But it is what you put into that topsoil that makes the difference," she says. "The care, the feeding, the pruning, watching for cold snaps—that's where it all comes in."

"You related to anyone famous, Elwood?" General Lancaster asks.

"My grandfather was an engineer on the New York Central," you say. "Worked his way up from fireman."

"Goddammit, that's what I'm talking about!" General Lancaster says. "You're from dirt, right?"

"Pure loam, sir," you say, which causes Colonel Berman to glare at you.

"One of my great-grandparents was arrested for selling patent medicines," Colonel Berman nearly shouts.

"Give me a top sergeant who's willing to break a few rules, kick some butt, get things done," General Lancaster says. "That's where the real power is in the Army—pure power, and no bullshit responsibility. That's where you find initiative, loyalty, and a hefty supply of good old-fashioned guts—those are the kind of people I want in my past."

"My father was a career enlisted man," Colonel Marshall says, seizing the initiative himself here. "He would've made sergeant major easy except he kept getting busted down because he always looked out for his troops. What a hell-raiser he was."

"Of course," General Lancaster says, "my grandfather *was* second-in-command to Pershing in Mexico. I think there is such a thing as an officer gene, a command chromosome if you will. How else do you explain Alexander, Kublai Khan, Robert E. Lee?"

Parts of Colonel Marshall's face have begun to move on their own. Colonel Berman's chin, you notice, has just achieved incredible military character.

"So I would say that to get to that star, a little military background makes you a kind of thoroughbred. Bloodlines are important." You can see why it takes the Colonel hours to recover from his Breakfast Club meetings.

There is a moment's silence, but Colonel Berman is the first to pick up the ball. "I think it's the mix that's essential," he says. His hands are in flight, waving back and forth, choppering the air. "A little bit of dirt, and a little of that military gene—that's what you need."

"General Marshall served under Black Jack Pershing, didn't he?" Colonel Marshall says, a weak return of serve at best.

"Did you ever have your ancestry traced?" Colonel Berman says, seemingly back on firm ground. "I've just had it done, and it's amazing—the kinds of things you uncover. Elwood here is putting it together for me—on his own time, of course—and you really can see the way the past has molded you."

"Who'd waste time doing that?" General Lancaster says, draining his drink. "Elwood, get me another."

Both Colonels Berman and Marshall look like outfielders who have lost a fly ball in the lights. Colonel Berman's choppering hands look to have been shot down, having fluttered to his sides.

"Right away, sir." You take the glass and go back to the bar.

"What's going on over there?" Stoney asks.

"The usual," you say.

"Look who's crashing the party," Stoney says, pointing at the door.

"He's just a taxi," you say. Walking through is none other than the Top, along with his daughter. Robyn is dressed formally, as if for a date. This is all, you know, for you.

"The Colonel'll bounce his ass, he stays around," Stoney says.

"I think we may be looking at General Lancaster's prototype sergeant," you say, watching Colonel Berman maneuver through the crowd. The General, however, follows closely behind. When the Colonel and General get to the door, the General embraces Sgt. Lee.

"You see what I'm seeing?" you ask.

"What's that mean?" Stoney asks.

"Offhand," you suggest, "I'd say we're totally fucked."

The Mrs. Colonel has by now come to the bar and motions you over. "Can you believe what that little shit did?" she asks.

"Things get out of hand," you say. "You know."

The Mrs. Colonel takes a deep swallow of her wine as you see General Lancaster shepherding Sgt. Lee and Robyn through the crowd. You think about escape routes, doing some broken-field running through the assembled guests, but for the moment you are stuck here.

"Very funny on the loam crack," the Mrs. Colonel says.

Drinking, you believe, exaggerates a person's natural disposition, and the look the Mrs. Colonel is sending your way would give a barracuda pause.

"Reap what you sow, Elwood."

"Just trying to keep things rolling."

"You know what was the first thing I noticed when we came to Germany to take over this command?" she asks.

The Mrs. Colonel finishes this drink and motions for another. As the Mrs. Colonel gets more drunk, the separation between her and the command of the battalion becomes smaller.

You shake your head no as you fix her another.

"Hydrangeas," she says.

"Ma'am?"

"That was when I knew we were in trouble," she says.

The Colonel is snaking through the crowd behind General Lancaster, Sgt. Lee, and Robyn. Colonel Marshall, not giving up easily, is matching Colonel Berman step for step, jostling him for conversational position.

General Lancaster arrives at the bar, more excited than he was to see either of the colonels.

"Jim, let me buy you a drink," the General says. "Elwood, get Jim a Johnnie Walker on the rocks. My credit still good?"

"Best in the house, sir," you say. You hand the General his drink first, and then set about making Sgt. Lee's.

"What will your daughter—Robyn, is it?—what will you have?" the General asks.

"Club soda," Sgt. Lee says.

"No. Something else," Robyn says.

"Elwood," Sgt. Lee says, taking the drink from you. "Think you left something at my house the other day."

"My pleasure," you say. "Staying long, Top?"

General Lancaster claps the Top on the back, a sure sign that things are not going as well as they could. "Jim and me, we go back just about forever," General Lancaster says. "I love this son-of-a-bitch, don't you?"

You nod your head. "What is it you want?" you ask Robyn directly.

"Do you have any German beer?" she asks. Her hair is fixed up, glossy in the light.

"No beer," Sgt. Lee says. "You gotta watch the kids."

"Wine then," she says.

"One glass," Sgt. Lee says. "Then you can put the kids to bed."

"Stay awhile, why don't you," General Lancaster says to Sgt. Lee. The General looks over at Colonel Berman. "It's all right with you, isn't it?"

It is hard to imagine anyone agreeing faster than Colonel Berman. "Come on over and I'll introduce you around," Colonel Berman says.

"Let me have a word with my man Elwood here," Sgt. Lee says.

"I've been thinking," you hear Colonel Berman say to General Lancaster, "how good for the troops it would be to have one more Field Training Exercise."

"I think that's a terrific idea," Colonel Marshall says, keeping right up, ready to go *mano a mano* against the opposition.

The General continues walking off, flanked by the competing colonels.

You hand the glass of wine over to Robyn, touching her hand as she takes the glass, feeling the slight shock of static electricity.

"Thanks," she says.

"Don't mention it," you say.

She turns and moves off upstairs with the Mrs. Colonel.

You turn to Sgt. Lee. "Didn't expect to see you here," you say. "Maybe you reconsidered the offer I made. Girl like that Robyn, getting ready for the college experience, broadening her mind—that's got to cost."

"Let me tell you something, Elwood," Sgt. Lee says. "You and me, we're going to come to terms." You have a feeling that those terms would not be in your favor.

"An old-fashioned dad," you say. "You don't see much of that anymore."

"Think of me like your shadow," the Top says. "Close your eyes I don't go away." The Top moves his hands, holds his shoulders, shuffles in place. He is a man in constant motion, a boxer loosening up for a fight. He looks at Stoney. "You two gonna get engaged or what?"

Stoney has come closer to you, staring hard at Sgt. Lee.

"You and me, we can go right now," the Top says. "Save us some time. I'll take you right across this bar, see if I give a shit."

Stoney hesitates, and you realize for the first time how far over the edge you are.

"You poor fucking buffalo soldier," Sgt. Lee says to Stoney. "Dressed up like this. Jesus."

"Customers," you say, pointing to the other end of the bar, thinking it's more dangerous with Stoney here.

"You don't even know what a buffalo soldier is, do you?" the Top asks. He pauses after firing for effect. "That's when we let you guys in?—the black army. You poor bastards fought the peace, took on the Indians after the Civil War. It was a dirty job, you couldn't get a white man to do it. Know what the pay was?—thirteen dollars a fucking month." You know from the military magazines about the buffalo soldiers. Hapless chasing the hopeless—the oldest Army story.

"You know what's changed?" Sgt. Lee asks.

Stoney says nothing.

"Your per diem went up."

"Let's step outside," Stoney says, but the usual Motherfucker confidence isn't there and that is worrisome. He takes off his tricornered hat and places it on the bar.

Sgt. Lee laughs and takes a gulp of his drink, letting it slide down his throat. He is in control and he knows it. "See this stuff," he says. "After I cleaned up my hand you're supposed to lay off the mind-alterings, but Johnnie Walker, he keeps my vision twenty-twenty. Now you think you can take me, and maybe straight up, hand to hand, you got a shot. But all you know is what you got. You ain't got a clue as to what I'm holding. Maybe I'm packing, maybe I wear a blade, maybe I got an M-16 locked and loaded to shove up your ass—you ain't considered that and yet you're willing to throw down. Want to know something? You're not like Elwood here—you got guts."

"Stoney," you say, "I'll take it from here."

"Think carefully about that offer," Stoney says, moving off down the bar.

"I like him," Sgt. Lee says. "Guys like him get all the medals."

"So how long you known the General?" you ask.

"That ain't the question," Sgt. Lee says. "Question you want to ask yourself, Elwood, is how deep you're in it."

"I'll bite," you say. "So?"

"Deep as it gets," Sgt. Lee says. "You ever hear about coconuts?"

"The movie?" you ask.

"You're one funny fucking guy, Elwood," Sgt. Lee says. "I knew Lancaster from Hawaii—the Pineapple Army. Way we used to get coconuts is we'd hire one of the natives, some hardheaded son-of-a-bitch, get that guy climb the fucking tree, shake it out, see what kinda nuts came down."

"Shake all you want," you say. "I'll do some shaking of my own."

The Top nods as he gulps his drink, starts to walk away, but then turns back. "I want you to know I zeroed on you fifteen minutes after hitting post. You're pathetic. You don't think I know, you don't think I see it right now—you're hooked to the fucking gills, troop, and you're going around like no one can see. But I got news for you, I got X-ray eyes."

Sgt. Lee takes a final gulp of his Johnnie Walker and breathes on you, the sweet smell of alcohol breaking like a wave.

"What you are, Elwood, is a buffalo soldier who don't even know it." Sgt. Lee turns and walks over to the crowd surrounding General Lancaster, which parts to let him in.

Stoney comes over, staring meditatively at the Top's back. "What's the man say about our offer?" Stoney asks.

"He said he'd get back to us," you say.

The party drones on, and after things have settled some you walk toward the stairs. Too late, unfortunately, you see Lt. Meyer at ten o'clock on an intercept course. You fake left into a crowd of G2 officers, then cut back against the grain by the sofa, but Lt. Meyer does not go for the jukes and catches you on the salient.

"Elwood," he says, pulling within range. "I have a little question to ask you."

"Yes sir," you say.

"We can relax the military formalities," Lt. Meyer says. He nervously breaks into a giggle, then takes a sip of his drink.

"Enjoying yourself?" you ask.

Meyer looks surprised, as if that had never been one of his expectations, which is, of course, an accurate estimation of a Colonel Berman party.

"I was wondering if I could just speak to you about something. It's actually quite personal, although it is official, too." Lt. Meyer comes close to you, so no one else can hear.

"How about the library," you say. "You ever been in Colonel Berman's library?"

"I imagine he reads quite a bit," Lt. Meyer says. "I find him among the most intellectually responsive commanding officers I have ever had the pleasure to serve." As Meyer says this, he raises his voice slightly, so others around him can hear.

"Let's go," you say, and lead Lt. Meyer to the library, which also contains Colonel Berman's weapons collection. "Ever seen the big display?" You light up a cigarette as you walk over to the shelves.

"I didn't know Colonel Berman had a gun collection," Lt. Meyer says. "This is very, very nice." It does not surprise you that Lt. Meyer is one of the few people on the planet not to have seen Colonel Berman's armory. He picks up a wickedly curved six-inch knife and runs his finger along the edge. "What's this?"

"It's called a kukri," you say. "The British Gurkhas use it."

"Looks dangerous," Lt. Meyer says.

"Thing can tear your heart out," you say. "But this is all leisure reading for the Supplyin' 57th. Lieutenant, can I give you some informal advice?"

"Please," Meyer says, nodding about as vigorously as a man can.

"Get to know your commanding officer. Every junior officer in the battalion has been here for the personal tour except you. You've got to make the Old Man feel that there's some interest here. Drop a few offhand remarks about the M1905 Mannlicher, for instance, you'll be inside here nothing flat. He's got an Argentine model right over here by the encyclopedias in very decent shape."

"I see," Lt. Meyer says, nodding his head. "I'm very grateful for this, Elwood." He pauses. "But what I have to ask you about is rather personal . . ." Meyer looks around, as if the room is bugged.

"The OERs, right?" you say, helping him out a bit.

Meyer nods. "I just want—I have this feeling the evaluations aren't going in my favor this year," Lt. Meyer says.

"You know I can't tell you," you say. "I breach security like that the Colonel'd have my head."

Lt. Meyer folds his hands and walks toward you. "I'm appealing to you," he says. "You have his ear. Perhaps you could provide a little push."

"I'm just not sure you want to know," you say, fucking with him just for the hell of it.

"It's that bad?" Lt. Meyer asks. His face begins to undergo a set of contortions, at war with itself, and you are afraid he is going to burst into tears.

You pause as you shake your head, shifting your weight for dramatic effect. You walk past Meyer and pick up a pistol. "This is a Walther PPK, like James Bond uses," you say, running your fingers along the barrel. "Nazis used to pack this, and a lot of the rad cops still carry it." You put it back and pick up another. "This one here—the SIG-Sauer P225. Any of the rad cops don't have the PPK carry this— 9 millimeter automatic. And here's something you might be interested in." You pick up a pistol mounted near the end, by the *Encyclopædia Britannica*. "Soviet Makarov pistol, standard Soviet sidearm. I got this one through a guy at Division has an East German contact. I traded him even up for a Colt .45. East-West arms deal." You stretch the gun out and take a combat stance in Meyer's direction, closing one eye, and hooking your finger around the trigger. Meyer stands there, unable to move. You replace it, and then go to a glass case and open it up. "This is the flagship of the fleet. Thirty-two caliber Smith and Wesson Long. Produced in the year of our Lord, 1898, two years after they started the model. This is your Model T of handguns. Never been fired. You tried to take a shot with this, the firing pin'd probably disintegrate."

Meyer's face is drained of blood, which makes him look like an owl caught in a searchlight.

"You want to know how to get in with Colonel Berman?" you say to Meyer. "You go out right now and tell him you've been reading and you just came across this: When Lord Wellington was reviewing the enlisted troops before the Battle of Waterloo, he said, 'I do not know if these troops will frighten the enemy, but by God, they frighten me.' I'll give you the citations so you can quote them. Colonel Berman is planning to circulate that article next week. You hit him with the preemptive strike and show him you're on the cutting edge and you're golden. But then—and here's the clincher—you follow up with an offer to do some of the Enlisted Men Introductory Seminars. The Colonel hates doing those and is looking to assign it around. You volunteer and use the Lord Wellington quote to shoehorn yourself in, he'll go crazy. He's likely to kiss you on the goddamn lips, sir."

Lt. Meyer shakes his head, still in despair. "It's too late, though," he says. You decide, suddenly, to take pity on him.

"Sir, I saw the OERs, and I'll give you this: set your mind at ease. You put up some big numbers on them, some of the best in the battalion."

Lt. Meyer turns around, hope written on his face. "All fives?" he asks, which is as high as each individual category can go.

"Fives down the line, sir," you say.

Lt. Meyer bites his lip and nods. He is flushed with victory. "Thank you, Elwood. You are an invaluable help." He turns around and walks out of the room, a man with both a mission and a citation.

You finish your cigarette and then step out of the library, once again trying to make your way up the stairs, but immediately run into the Colonel and the Mrs. Colonel. In his enthusiasm Meyer has just bumped the Mrs. Colonel, causing her to spill her drink all over her dress. By the looks of things he has already served up the Lord Wellington quote, but in the heat of battle has gotten it wrong.

The Mrs. Colonel, by now, is good and drunk. The Colonel is standing beside her, worn the fuck out by his unsuccessful maneuverings. Like a good soldier, Meyer is standing by.

"Elwood," she says. "Have you ever watched a spider at work?"

"No ma'am." You shake your head. Your only ambition is to get out of here, go upstairs.

"This summer, while the Colonel was out on his RE-FORGER exercises, I was working in the garden. Right next to the basement window a moth had flown into a spider's web."

The Colonel has by now finished patting her dry and is staring at Meyer.

"I just saw your gun collection, sir. Very impressive," Meyer says, trying to rescue himself. "Particularly the M1900 Mannlicher. I was struck by that."

"M1905," Colonel Berman says.

"The moth began struggling, trying to get out, beating its wings against the web. But all that happened was it got more and more caught, wrapped into more strands."

"And that Smith and Wesson Colt .45, I bet that's a rare one," Meyer says. "I'd like to fire that one myself."

"It would blow up in your hand," Colonel Berman says.

"The moth was struggling so hard that it began tearing apart the entire web," the Mrs. Colonel says. "This beautiful web that the spider had built. As the spider got closer, it began being buffeted about, beaten by the wings of the moth, unable to get its teeth in."

"Do you have anything on West German arms?" Meyer asks.

"Will you shut the fuck up," Colonel Berman says. Even Lt. Meyer is able to take a hint of that magnitude.

"What happened?" you ask.

"The two of them died together. I watched the battle go on for two hours. The moth died, but the spider was caught in its own web. That can happen, you know."

"You've lost me, Mrs. Berman," you say.

"This—this *genius*," she says, waving her hand at her husband, "just got the General to have one more Field Training Exercise."

"Yes ma'am," you say. "That was the plan."

"Could you excuse us, please," the Mrs. Colonel says to Meyer, who catches his cue for once and scurries off.

"I'm afraid I don't understand the problem," you say.

"You're usually not so thick, Elwood," the Mrs. Colonel says. "The problem is the General wouldn't authorize a full-scale FTX, so our good Colonel here finally talked him into authorizing a small assault on a base under our battalion's control."

"Congratulations, sir," you say, and then realize from the petrified look on Colonel Berman's face that there is not much to be congratulated about.

"What you don't understand," the Mrs. Colonel says, "is that the base to be attacked is *his*." With this, she points to Meyer, who in addition to being Grant's captain runs the nuclear storage facility, and you realize that no amount of greenbeanie ringers in the world will get you out of the shit.

"You're a fucking bitch," Colonel Berman says, turning on his heel and walking off.

"You understand what I'm saying, don't you, Elwood?" the Mrs. Colonel says quietly. "We're dead. I don't see any way around it. We might as well resign our commission right now."

"Don't worry," you say. "We'll think of something."

As you walk past him on the way back to the bar, Meyer hurries up to you. "Was it something I said?" he asks.

The party reaches a drunken stasis, and at the appropriate moment you go upstairs, pausing outside the kids' room. You listen—for what, you don't know—but the only sounds are those of the drunken personnel coming through your feet.

You knock lightly and enter. Robyn is sitting in near darkness, the kids curled in their bunk beds.

"They asleep?" you ask.

"Shhh," she says.

You sit down next to her, nearly at her feet, close enough to feel the heat of her body. The kids are asleep, the three of them on their backs, their arms thrown to the sides as if they surrendered after a long struggle.

"Want me to go," you ask, "or you want someone to talk to?"

"About what?" she asks.

"This," you say, and you reach out and touch her arm again, its very substance surprising you. She doesn't flinch.

In the dark, you feel her staring at you. You touch her face with your fingers, brushing along the contour of her chin.

"Do you feel phantom pain?" you ask.

"You asked me that already," she says.

"I mean when I'm not with you," you say, and you know you have her. Because you know about pain and its palliatives. You are the connoisseur of injury, the handler of hurt. Pain is the world come a'calling. You run your hands down her shoulders, feeling the light bones of her back.

You explore her slowly, hands creeping under her blouse, touching down here and there, finding crevices, the peculiar geography of the body.

"Kiss me," you say, and she does. Her mouth doesn't settle comfortably, keeping moving, staying loose. She breaks off suddenly.

"I hear something," she says. You hear the heavy tread on the stairs, and right then, unaccountably, you get hard, despite all the chemicals you've ingested.

"What if it's my father?" she asks.

Your breathing is rapid, shallow, and you're sweating. Danger is its own aphrodisiac.

The man's heavy tread stops outside the door, pauses for a moment. Robyn stops, and both of you are absolutely still, listening, and then he moves on to the bathroom. You hear the door close, and water begins running.

You slip under her so she is facing you, legs spread on your lap. Your hands run up and down her body.

"I want you," you say.

"Not here," she says. "Please."

"Not what I mean," you say.

You unbutton the sleeve on the false arm and roll it up neatly, gently, almost to the shoulder. She tries to pull away, but you have her. You unwrap the bandage that is holding the arm in place, again slowly. As you do this, you become aware she is holding her breath. For every woman, you understand, there is that secret spot, the key most closely held, that to give away is to give everything.

The arm comes off, the cup making a noise as it pulls away from the flesh. Your fingers touch first, feeling the hot stump, sweaty from being encased so long. You explore the way the stump tapers to a slender point, a large crayon with rounded tip.

You take her into your mouth next, tasting the uneven muscles, the layers of skin, strip-mined and exposed, pressing your tongue against the delicious and forbidden nub, and she nearly cries out from being known.

21

THE MERCEDES is parked off the side of the road as you and Stoney approach. The interior light is on, windows fogged. You knock on the window and Garcia rolls it down.

"Let's go," you say, getting in the backseat with Stoney.

"Just looking at my honey," Garcia says, putting the picture of his MGB back in his wallet. "I was driving her this morning. I don't think I ever been in a car with a suspension like she has. Tightest-turning radius of any vehicle I ever encountered."

"Just drive," you say. "We're late."

Garcia starts the Mercedes and then turns and smiles. "You like how this sounds?" he asks, gunning the engine while it's in neutral. "Put you in for a tune this afternoon. Cleaned your points, replaced the filters, you could eat off the distributor cap."

"Did it need it?" you ask.

"Need it?" Garcia asks. "Way I feel about this vehicle here—I mean it's nothing like my honey, but I consider it a member of the family." He caresses the steering wheel with his right hand. "And you don't deny your family the very best."

"Let's get on with it," says Stoney, who seems distracted.

Garcia gets you on the autobahn headed away from the nuclear depot, staying in the left lane, accelerating quickly to high speed. As you near the first exit Garcia quickly cuts over, hurtles up the ramp, and then takes a left and shoots back on the autobahn going in the opposite direction.

"Anything?" you ask Stoney.

"We're clear," he says.

"Glad to hear it," you say.

"I was with my B all this morning," Garcia sings. "In a state of fucking Bee-ing."

Stoney leans forward and laughs. "Garcia," he says, "you are the weirdest fucking guy on the planet. You're so weird they ought to make you white."

"You think loving a car's weird?" Garcia asks. "Let me tell you something. You own a car, you treat her right, keep her lubed, valves properly maintained, she is there for you. No matter what. It's not even a question. What you put in, you get out. How many people you can say that about? So fuck off, asshole."

Already you can see the conversation has reached the cutoff point.

"I heard you went tanking," you say.

Garcia laughs. "Told you I was going," he says. "You know, those M-1s, they don't handle as advertised. It's like driving a fucking tub."

"Hermann the German's got his Gestapo on this," you say.

"They know about me?" Garcia asks, truly astonished that somebody would interfere with his fun.

"I think we've got it contained," you say. "But the Colonel has to pay repairs out of battalion funds, and they're putting extra security around the tank park. I'm warning you, you go joyriding again, they'll nail you to the wall."

Garcia seems overjoyed at having caused all this trouble. "Well, who knows what may come up," he says. "When I get out of here, you know what I'm going to do?"

"Gas jockey," Stoney says.

"That's funny, big man," Garcia says. "I'm going to buy my own tank, Army surplus. I read about this guy in California, bought a World War Two Sherman, took off the treads so he didn't tear up the street, uses that as a knock-around-town vehicle. Let me tell you something, you see that baby tooling down the road you don't have no problems right-of-way."

"It must get some kind of mileage," you say.

Garcia laughs again. "He was running about two gallons a mile diesel with half the armor removed. Even taking off the cannon didn't do much good."

"Right here," Stoney says, and Garcia brakes fast, almost missing the unmarked turnoff for the base.

Garcia parks in the grass outside the security gate.

"Brings back a lot of memories," you say, looking at the perimeter wire.

"No good ones," Stoney says.

You hand Stoney the paperwork on the ordnance with Colonel Berman's signature. "See what Meyer's up to, why don't you."

Stoney gets out and walks to the gate. No cars are allowed inside the perimeter, and in any case to go inside would risk further exposure. If by chance there is somebody waiting and Stoney gets nailed with the goods, you can avail yourself of one of the many routes out. If they wait to take him until he gets outside the base, with Garcia at the wheel, you have at least a fighting chance of getting away.

The base is small and inconspicuous, restricted access, because this is the depot for the tactical nuke warheads, which are kept in six of the eight bunkers across the way.

"How long it was you were here?" Garcia asks.

"Three months before I could get myself reassigned," you say. "Got Stoney out two weeks later."

"Wasn't there some other guy, too? What the fuck was his name?"

"Kimbrough," you say. "What a fuck-up."

"They sure beef up the security," Garcia says. Besides the MP company there are three rows of razor wire, electronic sensors, geese and dogs. Of these the geese were the worst, constantly shitting and honking, and if you got too close, they'd try to tear off a piece with their hard little beaks, souvenir your ass. Communication lines run between the guardhouses and sometimes, when you got bored, the drill was to call up your buddy across the way, shout "Incoming" into the phone, and then squeeze a round off while your buddy hit the deck and plotted a return call—the kind of thing one can do only when totally fucked up. Therefore, this MP company—on high-security stakeout, fighting the dull fight—remains among your best customers. This is also why, of course, the Colonel is in such deep shit with the FTX happening here.

"This place gives me the creeps," Garcia says. "Maybe you get used to it after a while."

"You don't," you say.

You were assigned here when you first came to the 57th, handling the personnel and records duty for the MP company and then back to the 57th to sleep at night. This is also how you met Stoney and Kimbrough, who were MP buddies in this backwater of the peacetime war, hot nuclear items in cold storage with limited access but an easy in. When the depot blew during REFORGER and you made your logistical windfall, this is where you stowed all the ordnance you carted off.

Now you are bringing it over to give to the Turk in trade for Ling, who will be happy to receive these big-ticket items. Ling has been engaged in an all-out battle with two rival Chinese gangs in Amsterdam, and his alliance with the

Turk could be good news for all. From the pharmaceutical point of view, Amsterdam is a five-star city, total free fire zone. The Minister of Health's son even announces fluctuating marijuana prices over the radio, a kind of drugger's Dow Jones.

"Where they keep the nuclear shit?" Garcia asks.

"In the bunkers," you say. "Let me tell you, you work at this place too long you end up glowing in the dark."

"They don't leak or nothing, do they?" Garcia asks.

"Take a look at the bunkers," you say, pointing through the windshield. "Notice anything?"

Garcia stares through the windshield. "Look the same to me."

"Look again," you say. "You see two with no snow? Number one and number four bunkers."

Garcia nods his head.

"Put it together," you say.

"The fuckers leak, you're saying," Garcia says.

At first this surprised you, but now, like everything else, you have become accustomed to Army priorities. On a training march to check the perimeter, three soldiers and a specially trained MP guard dog were overcome with heat exhaustion. It was the dog who was medivacked out. Since you had to fill out the paperwork on all this, you found that the Army's financial stake in the dog ran to $50,000, while your regular multi-purpose soldiers, hardly trained at all, were expendable. Another line item in the newsletter. So, a little radiation dosing the men is nothing to be concerned about. Like all armies, you just change the troops when they wear out.

Garcia is still staring at bunkers one and four, all that dead grass and hot mud.

"Radiation, man, it scares the shit out of me," he says. "Stuff kills you, you can't even see it. I don't go for that shit. I don't even like the fucking sunlight, man. I go to the beach, I put on three types of lotion, I got a towel over the legs, sunglasses, umbrella for the UV overhead. I look like the goddamned Abominable Snowman on vacation."

"When Stoney and me were here they kept calling these alerts. You got the guys on duty, and you got the guys in the Command Post—that was where I was, working the office. When the alert goes down all of us in the Command Post, we had to grab our rifles, run out, and secure the tops of the bunkers. Capture the high ground. You know how all the new guys hustle it up and the old guys take their time? Here it's the opposite. The old guys, they're out in a flash, hunkered down on all the good bunkers. The new guys, they don't know any better, you end up having to secure one of the hot ones. First time I was aboard bunker four, it was like laying on an electric blanket."

You see Stoney walk out from the Command Post in the company of Lt. Meyer, who is the acting commanding officer of this MP company. You watch them go across the empty fields to one of the nonnuclear bunkers. Meyer has the OpOrd from Colonel Berman authorizing him to release the equipment for transport. Meyer has access to the key and the electronic entrance codes. Once Meyer unlocks the outside entrance he has thirty seconds to punch in the access code on the electronic panel or the doors will shut, an alarm will go off, and a roll of barbed wire will come down from the ceiling to enmesh the perpetrators. Barbed wire often figures into the Army's sense of humor.

"What's going on?" Garcia asks. A detail is walking across the field. "We in trouble here?"

You see Stoney walking across the field, and wait until he gets to the car. "Meyer wants to talk to you," he says.

"What about?" you ask.

"He won't release a driver for the truck unless that's part of the orders."

"Jesus," you say. "Come on, Garcia."

"What for?" he asks.

"Who do you think is going to drive the fucking thing?" you ask.

As you get to Meyer, the detail is already stacking the weapons. You have not only M-16s and M-60s but also M-79 grenade launchers, flamethrowers, even some Dragon TOWs, should Ling happen to come up against a tank in Amsterdam.

"Sorry about this, Elwood," Meyer says, "but it would reduce my ready force to send out a driver."

"That's okay," you say. "Colonel Berman appreciates your diligence."

"He said that?" Meyer asks, a note of enthusiasm sounding in his voice.

"I trust everything's here," you say.

"I inventoried it myself earlier," Meyer says. "Would you like to check, though?"

You shake your head. "I have something to tell you," you say, looking away from the work detail. Meyer steps up next to you, and you begin walking toward the Command Post. Garcia passes you, backing the supply truck to the front of the bunker.

"This is strictly hush-hush," you say. "It does not, understand, come at all from the Colonel."

Meyer nods solemnly with his round owl face. "He didn't tell you this?" he asks.

You sigh at having to deal with Meyer. "He did tell me, and I am unofficially passing the information on to you. Do you understand?"

Meyer seems to be getting it.

"You're going to get hit," you say. "Week from today."

"Terrorists?" Meyer asks, his eyes beginning to grow wide.

You can't help but laugh. "Colonel Marshall," you say. "It's a practice strike, check out our security arrangements. Everyone's going to be outfitted with the MILES, but they weren't going to tell you until the night it went down." The MILES is the practice laser weapons system that outfits onto regular carbines and allows personnel to record hits during drills.

"Why me?" Meyer asks, beginning to whine.

"LT, you're looking at this the wrong way," you say. "You hold off Marshall's assholes for one night you'll make Colonel Berman look so good your name will move right to the top of the promotion lists."

Meyer straightens up and claps you on the shoulder. "Tell the Colonel we'll hold the line," he says.

"He has great confidence in you," you say, although Colonel Berman is confident only that Meyer will fuck up whatever task is set before him. The greenbeanie ringers have their work cut out for them.

"What should I do?" Meyer asks.

"We're going to send out extra personnel, get this area a little more secure," you say. "I'll be out, and the Colonel will visit himself."

Meyer is standing, nearly ready to salute you. "Tell the Colonel I want to thank him for this opportunity."

"You can do it yourself," you say. "Now let's get this ordnance loaded."

ONCE YOU DELIVER the ordnance you drop off Stoney and Garcia. Then it is time to take a ride out to where the Top lives, wait in the parking lot. It is important, you understand, not to get caught by the Top. You see a shade come up and then pull down, and a few minutes later Robyn appears, but then she begins walking in the opposite direction.

You worry that she's missed the Mercedes, so you get out to pursue her, but she waves you off and you get back in the car. A few minutes later she climbs in and kisses you.

"We'd better get out of here," she says.

"I missed you," you say. You know that it is true as soon as you say it.

"I mean now," she says, and you think you see the Top peering from the second-floor window.

You get on the autobahn and then pull off on a woodsy road, get along the side and make love in the backseat. When you get to the point of release, you suddenly say, "I love you," and you wonder if this could be true. When you're done, she lies there, her body wet from yours, staring up at the roof of the car.

"What'd your father say about me?" you ask.

"You don't want to know," she says.

"Sure I do," you say.

"Okay," she says. "He said you're just doing this to get back at him. That he's going to get you for dealing drugs."

You sit there in silence. In the forest, you hear things creeping about.

"Is it true?" she asks.

"Do you trust me?" you ask.

She looks down at the seat and then up at you again, straight into your eyes.

"Yes," she says.

"Your father," you say. "He's right about everything."

"You're using me?" she asks, her voice quiet and low.

"Yeah," you say, "at first. But not now." You touch her, just lightly under the chin. "I'm sorry."

"I think," she says, "I think the problem is, I don't care."

"No, the problem is, I fell in love with you," you say, and now that you've said it, word becomes fact.

"How do I know?" she asks.

"You already do," you say.

She thinks for a moment, looking outside. The naked trees whisper. "I want to see everything," she says.

"That's my girl," you say, as you hold her tight.

When you get to the *pension* where Simmons and Cabot live, you pull into a parking space.

"Make sure you lock up," you say. "You can't trust anybody around here."

"What's here?" Robyn asks, getting out of the car.

"You'll see," you say.

You climb the stairs to the second floor and then ring the bell. You hear music pulsing from behind the door. Cabot pulls it open. His face lights up when he sees you.

"We didn't think you were coming," Cabot says. "But you're just the man we want to see. Who's this?"

"Robyn Lee," you say. "My new assistant."

"She okay?" Cabot asks, nodding to her, thinking he's being slick.

"At what?" you ask, gaining control, which is your principal object here. "We coming or going?"

"Coming," Cabot says, and steps aside so you can get into the apartment.

Once you get inside, Cabot says, "You carryin'?"

"Nope," you say. "I'm light tonight."

"What?" Cabot says. "Look, man, Simmons is in a bad way. You better go back and get something. He's climbing the walls in there."

"Hold your water," you say. "I'm just shitting you. Cavalry's here." You can't help it in your dealings with Cabot and Simmons: there is something in them that always bites on the inside curve.

Cabot breathes a sigh of relief. "I knew you were," he says, and for a moment you hate him for being so weak. But it's over in a moment, like swimming in the piss-warm Med and suddenly stroking through a band of cold.

"You want something to drink while El and me tend to business?" Cabot asks Robyn.

"She wants to see it," you say. "She wants to get in the game." You turn to Robyn. "That right?"

She nods.

"That a good idea?" Cabot asks.

"It's my idea," you say.

Cabot nods and scratches hard at his head. "I guess it's all right," he says. Cabot, you know, is not in a position to give you any recommendations.

You and Robyn follow him down the hallway to the bedroom, and he pauses at the door. "Take it easy on Simmons. Don't fuck with his head, all right?" There's a tender tone in Cabot's voice, and that, in its own way, is astonishing. You wonder if anyone would do that for you should the need arise.

You step into the room. At first, in the darkness, you don't see Simmons, but you can smell the flop-sweat. You turn on the light by the door and can see him huddled in the corner, eyes bright with hunger. Jesus, you think, Simmons has really hit the wall this time. He's dropped weight and his head seems heavy, larger than it ought to be for his body. You break out your kit, depending on Cabot for the syringe.

You turn to Robyn. "You really want to see this?"

She nods her head. Her eyes are bright, pupils dilated, taking it all in.

"You stay, you got to work. Help Cabot tie him off and track down a vein."

Simmons moves out of the corner and comes closer. The

smell reminds you of lint and cum. Out of the corner of your eye, you see Robyn standing as still as a deer on the roadside, knowing the danger but loving the light.

"Let's get down to business," you say. Robyn goes over to Simmons. She's hesitant at first, watching Cabot tie Simmons off with the Velcro tourniquet, as if she's afraid to touch Simmons. But there is a part of her that is pulled in, and you can see it's in the genes that she's a user. There are users, you know, who have never taken a shot, done a down, supped an up, but they're hooked as soon as they take their first. They're addicts just waiting for an addiction, a chamber inside their hearts expecting that key to be turned.

Cabot plinks his index finger against Simmons's arm, trying to raise anything.

You heat the scag and draw it up into the syringe. "Well," you say to Robyn, "how do you like the show so far?"

She doesn't reply, but Cabot looks at you. "I can't get any traction."

"Try the other arm," you say.

"Already tried that," Cabot says. "Can't catch nothing."

You examine Simmons's arms. Nothing is coming up. All the veins are dead, and both his arms are covered with red craters from the digging he's done on his own.

"I could skin-pop you," you say. "Be like farmers. Leave one field fallow and grow stuff in the rest."

"Nothing doing," Simmons says, suddenly speaking up. It seems to take all his energy to talk. He unstraps his belt and begins to pull down his pants.

"The fuck you doing?" you ask. "Don't pull that shit in front of my lady."

"It's okay," Robyn says, and you think this woman has got the balls of her dad.

"Hit me in the femoral," Simmons says. "I been doing that the last couple times."

"No way," you say. "I've got some limits."

"Since when?" Cabot asks.

"New policy," you say. "No way I'm gonna shoot you holding your balls to one side." The fix, you know, is starting to cool. Cool and clog. Botch and bog.

"All right, all right," Simmons says. His voice is shaking even more than he is. "Do me in the carotid. We got some virgin territory right here." He tilts his chin up, and you can see the clean area in the light. There is a sheen of sweat on his chin, and all the bones and tendons seem to be rising to the surface. He is like a concentration camp victim, with the same wide flat eyes of the people in the photographs, the certain look of people who know exactly where they are headed.

"You're talking some precision archery here," you say.

"Oh Christ, I can't watch," Cabot says. But Robyn is up close, right in there. You feel her presence, her breath in the air, the electricity of a body just coming alive, a fish out of water who just for a minute feels the delicious light taste of air.

"Hold his hands," you tell Cabot.

"Okay," Cabot says.

"And you steady him from behind," you tell Robyn. "I don't want him jumping around on me." She reaches out and puts her good arm behind Simmons's neck, and he leans back into her almost reflexively. You notice she doesn't flinch, despite the fact that Simmons is not the easiest guy in the world to stomach.

"He's so light," she says.

"Best diet in the world," you say, "if you don't mind a few side effects."

"Let's do it," Simmons says. You have a feeling that in his state Simmons would kill you for what you have in your hands. Cabot shifts position but doesn't get up. He wants to watch, you decide, in order to see the future.

You try to push the plunger on the syringe.

"Shit, we're fucked here," you say.

"What?" Simmons says.

"Needle's clogged. Give me a minute," you say. You take out your Varick and run the flame along the stem of the needle, blackening it.

"Fuck-damn-fuck-damn-fuck-damn-fuck-damn-fuck-damn-fuck-damn," Simmons says, the soldier's mantra, battle hymn of the Motherfucked.

You press the plunger and this time there's some play back in the syringe. "Boys and girls," you say, looking at Robyn and smiling, "don't try this one at home."

You lift Simmons's chin so as to get a clear shot. There is some danger here. If you dig too deep you can nail the windpipe, punching a hole that would suck blood from the carotid. You know that carotid men are on their last laps and you suddenly feel helpless. You want to do something for Simmons, get him out of it, but you think to yourself, Be real. You plunge it in, harpooning the carotid perfectly, it's Captain Scag and Moby Dick, your experienced hand guiding it home. Because of the clog factor, you don't mess with milking it, draining it instead in one shot.

"Ohh yessss," Simmons says. "Thaasss right. Thasss right."

Cabot, you can see, is looking pretty green around the gills. He is staring at the little knob of blood on Simmons's neck. Robyn, however, is steady, still holding the patient. This is some kind of stand-up chick, you think.

"Will he be all right?" Robyn asks.

"Simmons will be right back after the following messages," you say. Simmons doubles over and vomits into a garbage pail, then leans back onto the floor.

"How about you," you say to Cabot.

Cabot nods and extends his arm.

"You think you can handle this?" you ask her.

"Yes," she says. She ties him off, plinks his arm, and you get in with no problem.

"Now it's just you and me," you say. "What do you think?"

"I don't know," she says.

"This is what I do," you say.

"I want to do it," she says.

"No you don't," you say.

"Yeah," she says, "I do."

You touch her, waiting for a jump under your hand, but none comes. "Look, sometimes it gets started, you can't control it. Like him." You look to Simmons. "See the kind of service stripes he's got."

"You can control it," she says.

"I'm careful," you say.

"I'll do it," she says. "Once won't hurt."

"If I shoot you," you say, "nobody gets hurt."

"Okay," she says.

"You're sure?" you ask.

"I'm sure," she says. "What do I do first?"

"Roll up your sleeve," you say.

"You'll have to do that," she says. You nod and roll it up, exposing her bare arm. You use both hands on her arm, running them along the inside. How soft it is, you think, the muscles and nerves and veins making ridges under your fingers. You notice the brown peppering of freckles up the fish-white inside. "It must've hurt so much," you say. "What did it feel like?"

"I don't remember," she says.

"Sure you do," you say.

"Don't ask me that," she says.

"One day you'll tell me," you say. "Close your eyes."

You measure out the scag and start cooking while you look at Robyn. Her eyes are shut tight and she's holding her breath. You are reminded suddenly of your grandfather. The past, we know, is always there, waiting. Just open the cover, like a book, and it lives again. After he died you went through his things and found a picture of him as a young man, marching onto a troopship, on his way to World War I. His face, like all the other soldiers', was blank; the same quiet look on all of them, willing to go to their deaths without making a fuss. People are really sheep, you think, and here is another member of your flock. And then you think of the sheep you have slaughtered.

Robyn opens her eyes and looks at you. "Are you ready yet?"

You do her fast, slipping the needle just under the skin, pulling back to make sure you're just in the meat end—no vein—then drop the load.

As you take the needle out, you cannot help but feel the power under your thumb, the absolute control you have. As you watch her lean back, still holding her arm, you feel as if it is happening to you, too. You are making love through her arm. There is nothing more sensual.

She pitches forward and you pick her up under the arms. She vomits into the garbage pail and then you lay her down in the corner on a pillow. You revel in your relative strength and experience in this matter. You feel all-powerful, full of love. In this world, God is Drugs. Scag is His Son. God has sent His Son to earth to spread the Word. The Word is that Scag is good. Scag is our shepherd. We shall always want. You and the other apostles are spreading the Word to the uninitiated like Robyn, who is now, whether she knows it or not, in the fold.

22

THE BANGING on the door to your quarters seems as if it is busting through your skull.

"Get up! Get up! Get out of the rack, now!"

You get out of bed and open the door. Sgt. Lee is banging on doors, shouting. He turns and walks back to you.

"What's up?" you ask.

"You are," he says. "Get into your BDUs and report to the parade ground in five minutes."

"Five minutes?" you ask, still somewhat groggy.

He holds up a hand with his fingers splayed. "Count 'em," he says.

You get into your Battle Dress Uniform, lace up your boots, and you are out on the parade ground along with the rest of the platoon, everyone looking somewhat groggy. Dawn begins to creep over the horizon. Knoll, the newly married man, is looking somewhat the worse for wear.

"What the fuck is this?" you say to Knoll, as Sgt. Lee walks by, straightening the rows of troops. Sporting two monstrous hickeys on either side of his neck, Knoll seems to be sleeping as he's standing up.

Sgt. Lee hears you, as you intended, and he turns and comes up into your face. "This is about you," he says. "Now straighten up. Pretend you're a soldier." And then Sgt. Lee turns on his heel.

Once assembled, you march to the armory, where you check out your weapons and are each issued two clips of thirty bullets. Then Sgt. Lee marches you through the gate and starts a cross-country trek.

"Elwood," he says, "you take point with me. Everyone else, watch your spacing."

You walk up front and move alongside. There is an unmistakable air of happiness about Sgt. Lee. Dawn by now has come and gone. The bushes and the trees are all underlit by the rising sun. The ground retains its morning frost, and you hear the crunch of men's feet.

Sgt. Lee motions for another man to come up. He is carrying the M-60.

"Hand me your rifle," Sgt. Lee says to you.

You turn over your M-16.

"I want you to pack the M-60," he says.

"I'm not qualified on it," you say.

"Elwood," Sgt. Lee says, clapping you in his mock-friendly way on the back, "for everything there is a time. You're going to learn in the heat of battle."

"The 60," you say doubtfully, "is a heavy mother."

"So am I," Sgt. Lee says.

You hoist the M-60 across your shoulders, preparing for a long hike. You have no idea why the Top is doing this, but the general idea, of course, remains the same. Fuck you up and fuck you over, again and again.

"How long you been in the Army, Elwood?" he asks.

"Too long," you say.

"You're a fucking smart one, ain't you," Sgt. Lee says, keeping the pace, listening to the musical crunch of frozen leaves from men pounding ground.

You swing the muzzle of the M-60 toward him. "Top," you ask, "you're not worried I drop this thing maybe shoot somebody?"

Sgt. Lee looks at you. "You saying something to me, troop?" he asks.

Sgt. Lee, you understand, is the type to stay in to the end of the hand. You keep soldiering along, trying to get a steady rhythm to your pace. You have a feeling this is not going to be a good day.

"Ever been to Turkey?" Sgt. Lee asks.

"Nope," you say.

"Ass end of the Army," Sgt. Lee says. "They hate Americans there. Used to be this one sheep farmer right outside the base, every time we came out he'd throw stones at us —big fucking rocks, about yea big." He gestures with his hands, indicating the size of a softball. "So this is going on for a while, then one day he spots the commanding general in his personal vehicle driving his wife, and he chucks a couple. That's what broke it. The guy had a fucking arm on him, too. Always threw strikes."

"This is so interesting," you say.

"We'll find something hold your attention," Sgt. Lee says. "I always keep my men in mind." As you walk, you realize you're getting dangerously close to where the Mercedes is parked in the blind.

"So one day my company commander gives me a mission. If you were writing one of your HQ memos, you'd probably say the objective was to suppress sniper activity and provide extensive collateral damage."

"That's pretty good," you say. "Maybe one day they'll promote you to clerk."

"You have no idea what a good mood I'm in, Elwood," Sgt. Lee says.

You harbor grave worries as to why this is so. On the karmic seesaw, when the Top is up, you can be sure you're going down: physics for the Motherfucked.

"I was only a staff sergeant then, so the company commander had to sign out the M-60. We wanted to have some firepower on our side. Me and him, we went on the mission, showing admirable cooperation between officers and enlisted men."

You are at a clearing across the way from your Mercedes, which remains hidden. But what you see is a terrible thing. You see two sets of footprints that have broken the morning frost, going in and coming out. They are not yours, you know, and therefore are signs, most likely, of an early-morning reconnaissance mission.

Sgt. Lee holds up a fist, which stops the line of troops. "Fan out across the field, watch for booby traps," he calls out.

"Now in this story I forgot to tell you something about sheep. Sheep, they're hungry little fuckers. Eat the grass right down the roots. You got to keep moving 'em around, took us forever to find them."

"But you found 'em," you say.

"The thing about an M-60, you can lay on that steady firepower. You know that a round from an M-60, it can go through a car, front to back, bumper, grill, engine block, seats, spare tire even, perforate the jack, come out and still kill some poor son-of-a-bitch hiding on the other side? Halt!"

The men all freeze, spread across the field about thirty yards from the blind, all standing with weapons at the ready.

He turns back to you. "We took that M-60 and leveled those fucking sheep, they went down like goddamn tenpins. Whole valley had wall-to-wall sheep carpet."

"They give you a medal for that, Top?"

"I want you to understand something," Sgt. Lee says. "You're responsible for what you do, Elwood. Everyone is. You think you're different, but you're not. I've come today to collect."

"I'm asking you, Sarge—" you start, but in reality you know it is too late to call a cease-fire. Things have already gone too far. Sgt. Lee scratches his face in embarrassment, finding you a suddenly unworthy opponent. He turns away and walks in front of the troops. "I direct your attention to that spot over there that has been marked with an X." One of the MPs is marking the outside of the camouflage tarp with red tape in the shape of an X.

"We are faced here with the prototype of a new Russian tank." Sgt. Lee says. "We are here to test the vulnerability of said tank to sustained fire from an infantry rifle platoon."

Sgt. Lee looks at you and then swivels his head to face the troops. "You have authorization to lock and load," he shouts.

You hear the metallic clicks of clips going into rifles.

"You too, Elwood," Sgt. Lee says.

You load the belt into the M-60 while Sgt. Lee waits patiently. Then he helps position the M-60 in firing position.

"Set to automatic. You will fire on my command at the red X!"

You see the men aiming their M-16s, some standing, some crouching, some prone. A firing squad for your personal vehicle.

"Direct fire! Fire at will!" Sgt. Lee shouts.

You open fire with the M-60, and everyone else does, too. You imagine the Mercedes taking the bullets, the grillwork disintegrating, the windshield splintering like morning ice, the tires deflating. The bullets rip the seats, puncture the hood, bounce around inside the car. The tarp begins to slip a little as pieces of metal fly up in the air, and then you see the first evidence of flames licking the morning sky. The men have shot their first clips, and throw them down and punch in the second, opening fire again. In a few seconds, there is an explosion, smaller than you would have thought, and then a fireball leaps into the air.

The shooting dies down after everyone has fired off his ammo. The black smoke from the fire hangs in the air, drifting out toward the men in the field.

"Those Russian tanks," Sgt. Lee says, laughing, "they sure don't make 'em like they used to."

He comes up and claps you hard on the back. "You know something, Elwood. You can talk till you're blue in the face, but there's nothing gets a man's attention like a well-organized firing squad. And Elwood," he adds, "I want you to know this is just the beginning."

DURING TIMES OF TROUBLE, you have discovered, movement is curative. Get on the trail and start humping, change the landscape, move the scenery around, get another act under way once the old one starts to wear. And so here you are taking the show on tour. You are standing with Robyn at Dachau, the German concentration camp, in front of the ovens. The ovens are the ovens of your dreams, cracked open to invite a look, but none of the tourists whom you were reduced to taking the bus with makes the move to get in close. Instead, they huddle around you in your uniform, touching a shoulder, brushing against your sleeve. You've been here once before, and it was the same thing, the herd recognizing a threat when they see one.

"Jesus," Robyn says, and begins to tremble.

"That's not the half of it," you say. Dachau, you think, is the ultimate monument to the Motherfucked. The tourists, as they got off the bus, fell silent, except for the few who remarked on how small it seemed. They had expected something larger—the theme park concentration camp, with greeters and guides, refreshments, T-shirts, wheelchair accessible. What they got instead was tidy little buildings of functional brown brick and concrete. The rads built their concentration camps like they built their libraries or post offices or cathouses. Everything made to last.

On this particular cultural tour you are standing in front of the ovens, long since fallen into disuse but still smelling of death.

"This is some place you picked," Robyn says. "What was it you wanted to say to me?"

The strange thing is that this is one place where you feel an odd kind of comfort. No ambiguity, no gray areas. Here it is in the purest sense. It is like arriving at the edge of the earth, stepping over the horizon and seeing precisely what's on the other side.

Inside the ovens is the mystery at the heart of things, the answer to all your dreams. Around you and your uniform orbit the tourists. Although they have cameras around their necks, for the moment none of them is taking pictures. But that'll pass. If you stand around long enough, death becomes routine. Check the light meter, get the f-stops secured, snap a few rounds for the slide show in the family den.

"Let's get out of here," Robyn says, burying her face in your shoulder.

"Can't you see it?" you ask.

"See what?"

"When you look," you say, "you have to be able to see it all. The whole thing."

"I'm leaving," she says, and takes off. You follow. What you and she need right now is a hit. A little permafrost for the nerves. You rush headlong into the air, but still you feel no clearing. Dachau has been converted into a kind of bitter monument, an angry finger reminding the Germans, who

never visit, that there are things from the past worth remembering. For the rads, however, you are certain this is
old news.

"I know a place," you say, catching up to her. Your immediate move is to search out some privacy and get your
shit secured. Scag has, as part of its wondrous effects, the
distinct ability to allow you to ease back on the throttle.

You walk past the tourists, who once again instinctively
drift toward you, Nikons swinging, box lunches hanging,
stunned by the glimpse of the other side. It's like a *Night
of the Living Dead* deal. They're looking for some of your
official karma, US Army variety; the laying on of hands,
splinter of the true Cross. The dead, however, give no
autographs.

You keep going until you get to the pistol execution fields,
which during the heavy summer tourist season are land-
scaped with flowers that have now withered. For Robyn, all
karma levels are reaching absolute zero.

"I need something," she says.

"I know you do," you say.

You hide behind a small bush and take out your Kodak
film container. There's coke in one, scag in the other, so if
necessary you can run AC/DC. Coke, however, would push
Robyn's paranoia indicators to their breaking point. What
you need to do is dial her down, give her some of that long-
range perspective that scag provides. Then things will be
under your control.

You provide shelter from the wind as she snorts the scag,
and then you take a sizable noseful yourself. Both of you
squat, waiting for the nausea to pass. The world closes in
for a suffocating moment—that pause as you change gears,
lifting out of this world and into the next—but gradually
you come back out of it. You feel good, and so does Robyn,

everything taped down, playing life with the safety net. Once again, by this act of God, the two of you have been made whole. And one.

"I used to wonder why they didn't do something, like fight back, revolt," Robyn says.

"Do you know why now?" you ask.

"No," she says. "I mean, if there was no hope, why not take a chance?"

You move toward her, holding her tight. "They had hope," you say. "It was the hope that killed them."

"This doesn't bother you?" she asks.

"No," you say.

"It makes me sick," she says. You get in closer, put your nose up against hers. Her nose is cold, a little wet on the end like a puppy's, but inside, the chemical fire has been turned up.

"Tell me what it felt like?" you ask, touching her arm, searching for her key. "Tell me."

"It felt . . ." she says, and you see she's beginning to cry. "It didn't feel like anything—like it was still there, and then one day I knew it wasn't."

"I know," you say. And you are ready to give it up, give her the key to you, which is Kimbrough, the thing that unlocks the deepest recesses that for the life of you cannot be ignored. And you tell her the story of you and Kimbrough and Stoney. The story is about how once you got out of the nuclear depot and brought Kimbrough and Stoney with you, you opened up your business at CC's. And things went along smoothly until one day Kimbrough, who was a user, decided to take you down in the parking lot outside.

"I know that name," Robyn says. "My father mentioned that name."

You tell her about how you had thrown Kimbrough off the team because he was using more than he was selling, but that one night, as you walked out of CC's he made his move, came out of the darkness, determined to get back his share. He was armed with a knife, the Smith Model #5 that you now own, but Stoney, who could play mongoose to anyone's cobra, easily took him out, disarming him without a scratch. Scag has a way of making you desperate and therefore dangerous, but up against someone like Stoney, Kimbrough was out of his weight.

You tell her how you picked up the knife and walked over to Kimbrough, whom Stoney was holding in a reverse hammerlock, his eyes still gleaming with need.

There was no reason for it, no reason at all. You hadn't thought about doing it, and to this day you wonder what it was that made you take that next step. But as you got within range, you felt a need yourself, as pure as the striving toward an MPC, as impossible to resist as the urge that once turned you around on that highway and made you head toward the Army and Germany. You glided toward Kimbrough, unaware as to what you intended next, but of course absolutely sure. And you brought the knife, which was light as a feather and had become part of your arm, directly up and then across. You stepped into him, yanking the knife, propping his body against you as Stoney fell back, as though he were the one you had stabbed. And in that moment, as the fire went out, you saw relief in Kimbrough's eyes. You also saw in Stoney's eyes that things had changed, that in killing Kimbrough you had killed a piece of him. But what you waited for, what you had hoped for, would not come: you waited for understanding. There should be some change, an MPC, the key to all things, once you had crossed this final boundary. But there was nothing. You were the same after you had killed as before. It took you weeks to understand that everything *had* changed, that the thing was growing inside you, and that at the very moment of your permanent installation as Motherfucker you had also become a charter member of the Motherfucked. And now this has become the key to yourself that will not go away.

"I'm afraid," Robyn says.

"I know," you say.

"What do we do?" she asks, and you have her.

"Listen," you say. "We're going to have to make some moves."

"What do you mean?"

"I'm saying, I'm getting out of the Army, going back home. It's here. It's this place. Once we leave this, everything will change."

"Good-bye," she says, and looks away. Snow is beginning to come down, a light swirl that lands on her face and shoulders. You brush it off.

"No," you say. "I want you to come."

"Are you crazy?" she asks. She begins to laugh. "You bring me here, ask me this. This is how you ask me? This place?"

"Where else?" you ask. Robyn bites her lip, looking down at her hand.

"Don't say no," you say. You hold up the Kodak container with the scag. "You may need this, but I need you." Contained in the Kodak container is hope, as well as its opposite. You want to tell her that if she doesn't come with you, you'll be lost.

And then you tell her.

"What am I going to do?" she asks.

"Save me," you say. And you don't think you've ever believed anything more strongly in your life.

"No," she says. Then, "Yes."

23

THAT EVENING, back at the base, your team is assembled to provide conventional support while the nuclear forces are engaged elsewhere. You are here to watch Stoney take on Darnell Moore in the Division Box-Offs. Most of the base and a good part of the Division has packed into the Field House. The winner of this match goes to the Army Championships at Fort Bragg. And while you are waiting, being watched closely by the Top and his MPs, Robyn will be driving the morphine base right through the main gate in the trunk of her Mercury Montego.

The air in the Field House is stuffy, smoke hanging in clouds over the ring. There's a tingliness to the whole thing, a certain tension in your groin as if a part of you is up there, about to get busted up.

You are seated with your buddies in the bleachers, the cheap seats, and smoking like crazy. The gang's all here. Video is watching the Stoney and Moore Show through your binoculars, and Moore is getting shelled hard. From where you're sitting, you can see the Top has you in his sights, eyeballing you, letting you know he's on your tail. The key to operations like this is misdirection. Sleight of hand. Keep their eyes on the obvious while you wiggle the rabbit out of the hat. Right now Robyn should be at the Turk's, where he will be loading the shit into the trunk.

The first round was easy for Stoney, your man feeling

Moore out. Stoney likes to check out his opponent's reactions against the obvious ploys, the basic jab, the hook, the right lead, see what kind of surprises Moore has in store. The second round begins, and Stoney comes out seeking to establish a pace, lay down a rhythm that eventually will become all his. Moore fights crablike, muscling in with the jab, throwing piston shots to the body, thick arms taking Stoney's punches and then trying to get underneath.

"What do you think?" you ask CC, who is sitting next to you and has taken most of the betting action on the fight.

"Moore's an arm puncher in a world full of arm punchers," CC says. "I don't think he's got the chops to take Stoney. What do you think?"

"I don't know yet," you say. You wonder if Robyn is on the road yet, picking up speed in the acceleration lane of the autobahn. "I just don't like it is all. Too close."

"That's why they make 'em lace up the gloves. This is the longest he's gone in a while," CC says, showing an appreciation of previous box-offs. Usually, Stoney's rhythms have by now become apparent, your eye staying on him. But you keep drifting to Moore, an unknown quantity who is rapidly making his presence felt. He digs in, hooking to Stoney's ribs, burying it deep in the liver, then rising to the head. He's better than you thought, a little harder hitting, willing to stay in and trade with your man.

"I hate these things," Video says, handing the binoculars back to you and turning to the portable battery-operated TV on his left knee. He's been watching the TV on and off since the lighter weights fought, but now he is tuned to "Dynasty" and a conversation between Linda Evans and Joan Collins. Video keeps going from fight to TV, TV to fight. The Good, the Bad, and the Horny.

"What are they saying?" Sasquatch asks, who is also watching Video's left knee.

"They're getting huffy all right," Video says, twisting his earplug in tighter.

"No shit?" Eddio says, suddenly leaning on Video's shoulder.

"May start duking soon," Video says. "More exciting than the real fights."

"Didn't they have a girl fight last season?" Eddio asks.

"I seen that one," Sasquatch says. "The blonde took the dark one out."

First Moore and then Stoney buckles slightly, exchanging good hits. From where you sit, even with the binoculars the punches seem light, unspectacular, odd notes that hang in the air. Robyn by now should be on the autobahn, cruising quietly in the right lane, mild-mannered Polly Purebred muling shit cross-country.

"What was the action like?" you ask CC.

"Stoney started two for one, then Darnell Moore money began coming in," CC says. "Ended up even, maybe a little edge for the new guy."

"You know, you catch a fight on TV, you see everything," Video says. "The grand strategy. Close-ups of heavy-duty whacks. But you show up live, it's a disappointment." Moore crowds Stoney into the ropes, windmilling wildly. The ring tilts slightly as Stoney bends and dips, absorbing shots that singe the air. Suddenly, for no apparent reason, Stoney drops to his knees.

"Oh shit," you say.

"Take it easy," CC says. "Man's cold, no sweat on him, he can get hit like that. Besides that, we already beat the under and over." After she gets off the autobahn, Robyn will drive right through the main gate, but then go past the regular parking lot to the dispensary.

"What the fuck's going on, anyway?" Sasquatch says, but he's looking at the TV. Stoney is up on his feet, having shaken it off, but he's been surprised, the legs still too stiff, the bounce not quite back in his knees, and for the first time you see Stoney beginning to move backward, play the angles, Motherfucker status on the serious wane.

"How much did Saad bet on Moore?" you ask CC.

"Can't say," CC says. "Professional ethics."

"A bookie's got ethics?" you ask.

"You got money on this one, Elwood?" asks Rothfuss, who is seated directly behind you. Stoney's jab is back, his rhythm is returning, and you breathe a sigh of relief. The last time Stoney fought, it was a haymaker derby, the men swinging from the toes, weaving from shots like trees in a strong wind.

The bell rings, and Stoney and Moore go with relief to their corners. "What's with the shades?" CC asks Rothfuss.

Rothfuss pulls them down. His left eye is discolored, the lid fat and red. "I got popped," he says. "You wouldn't believe how this happened."

"Try me," CC says.

"Last night, I'm all alone, I figure cruise by the autobahn and look for some quick action."

"What'd she do, hit you with her wallet?" CC asks.

"I wish," Rothfuss says. "I see the van parked along the side, I got a feeling about it. My problem was, the lights I thought she was flashing, she was just turning them off. This rad lady, right, she had a flat, she blew the fucking tire on a pothole."

"I think they're getting ready for a rematch," Video says, staring intently at the TV. The women are getting into each other's faces, eyeball to eyeball, mouths working overtime, all in extreme close-up. Video has put his finger in the other ear to shut out the din of the crowd.

"Ten bucks on the blonde," CC says.

"No way I'm taking that action," Sasquatch says. "The blonde, she don't look it maybe, but the bitch can hit."

"I'll go for it," Eddio says. The bell has rung for the third round, and Moore comes out charging, Stoney still circling, wary.

"So I get out," Rothfuss says, "open the passenger door, and slide in next to her to ask how much, figure maybe a military discount, a quick pop for democracy. She pulls this tire iron from under the seat."

"Bell has rung," Video says. On TV, Joan Collins has Linda Evans in a headlock and they're rolling across the bed, knocking over an end table, a lamp, and then spilling onto the floor.

"Looking bad for the blonde," Eddio says.

In the ring, Moore has got Stoney cornered again and is driving his punches hard. He keeps pitching, and then Stoney clinches, blowing hard, the two of them locked together.

"I think he butted him," CC says. Stoney pulls back, and he is pawing at his eye, blinking hard.

"There blood?" Eddio asks.

"They took out the screen door now," Video says. "Heading west for the pool, outdoor arena."

"Five bucks says they're in the water inside thirty seconds," CC says, then looks up at the fight in the ring.

"You're on," Eddio says.

Now Evans and Collins are pitching lawn furniture at each other, then some potted plants, topsoil flying, ferns waving.

"That Alexis," Video says, "she's got a decent arm on her."

"What are they fighting over, anyway?" Sasquatch asks.

"Who cares," Video says. "Five seconds left on the thirty, CC."

Even from where you're sitting you can see Stoney's eye is getting worse. Moore fires overhand rights, and they're catching Stoney, the spray from his head exploding into the air. You wince as each of the punches hits.

"Did you see that?" Video shouts. "Just over the time." Alexis and Krystle, locked together, have fallen into the water, where they continue struggling.

"Maybe they're fighting over Blake," Sasquatch says.

"Who's he?" Eddio asks.

"Krystle's husband, Alexis's ex-hub. He's the guy does the voice on 'Charlie's Angels.' "

"Man, that guy knows some rough women," Sasquatch says.

Moore's crowding again, trying to finish Stoney off, but then the Stoneman, as you have expected, comes alive, firing a couple of short lefts under Moore's chin. You see Moore's head bob up as he takes a kind of half-step to the left, but then he crunches Stoney, a hard left underneath and then a hook to the temple. You cry out involuntarily when your man goes down, as if you were the one who was struck. Stoney's leg is bent under him, a hurdler's split while his chest moves up and down, his eyes staring up at the gym lights.

"Saad bet on Darnell Moore," CC says. "Fucking guy knows his horses."

"Shut the fuck up," you say.

"No need to get touchy," CC says.

"But anyway, the chick in the car, she doesn't understand what the fuck I'm asking," Rothfuss says, "so I take out my wallet and peel off some bills. And then she gets hot. Takes the tire iron, whacks me a good one on the eye, so I fly back and the door opens on me and I go flying out on the pavement. Rolled halfway down the embankment, got mud all over my uniform. It was a fucking disaster."

"So the upshot was you didn't do her," CC says.

"The upshot?" Rothfuss says. "The upshot was I got my ass kicked."

"I think we got a decision here," Video says. On TV, Krystle is holding Alexis's head underwater, bubbles and splashing going on all around. Krystle lets her go, and Alexis crawls to the side of the pool, where she lies in the gutter, breathing hard. Krystle takes the ladder out, her dress clinging to her as she stalks inside. In the ring, they have Stoney on his stool and the trainer is waving his towel at him, sending some oxygen his way. When he stands up to stumble out of the ring, another set of fighters enters, purposely looking away.

"Man, this show beats 'Mission Impossible' by a mile," Video says. "You know what they should do—get more girl fights on TV. Put in title fights, weight divisions, everything. How about this: Donna Reed versus June Cleaver. Put Cabot in June's corner as cut man and make sure Donna Reed doesn't load up her gloves with crockery."

"Lucy Ricardo," Rothfuss says, "versus Alice Kramden."

"Alice'd clean Lucy's clock," Video says. "Her husband's a bus driver, handles that shit all the time. It would be a fucking massacre."

"Bullshit, man," Eddio says. "Lucy's got some real spunk. What I'd like to see—the girls on 'Gilligan's Island' getting it on, fighting over the Professor, just wearing those ferns."

"That guy's a wimp," Eddio says. "Nobody'd fight over him."

"Maybe Mrs. Howell can referee," CC says.

"TV, it's already had these intramural battles," says Video, the tycoon of the tube, historian for the heartland. "When I was a kid, Batman and Robin were gonna take on the Green Hornet and Kato in a big two-parter, duke it out and see who's the baddest crimefighter. The whole school was betting on it."

"What kind of childhood did you have, Video?" you ask. Maybe Robyn's already there, you think, unloading the shit to Cabot in the dispensary.

"Made me the asshole I am today," Video says. "I spent days thinking about it. Couldn't sleep at night. It was like Ali-Frazier for little kids. And for the life of me, I couldn't see how Batman and Robin could do shit. I mean, maybe the Hornet was a little soft around the middle, but Kato was fucking Bruce Lee—the real fucking thing. And who's Batman got? His ward, Dick Grayson. Big fucking deal. Let me tell you—I was always a little suspicious about those two, sliding up and down the Batpole."

"Holy shit, you're right," Sasquatch says. "You're so fucking right." Now Video is off and running, the bullshit steaming right along.

"You see where I'm at, Elwood," Video says, smiling because he knows he's got everyone in tow except you. "So I'm going around school and I'm giving predictions, even taking a little action here and there. I convince everybody—everyone except my best friend, Charlie Dumas. Charlie fucking Dumas. I couldn't budge the son-of-a-bitch. We bet on it, and then I ask him how come he's so sure. And Charlie Dumas, he says, 'It's Batman and Robin's show.' It was right then I began to realize the whole fucking world was a fix."

"Shit, he's right," Sasquatch says. "You are so fucking right."

You have to get out of here, you think.

"Changed my whole fucking life," Video says. "But I still think this is a good idea. We get the right girls, we can really have a show."

"How about the two on 'WKRP in Cincinnati'?" Eddio

says. "Loni Anderson and the Bailey one. Bailey'd give Jennifer a run for her money."

"Are you kidding?" Video says. "Look at the racks on them. They start in, they'd never get close enough do any damage. Now here is the match. This is for the heavyweight girl fighting championship. Stefanie Powers on 'The Girl From U.N.C.L.E.' versus Diana Rigg from 'The Avengers.' What do you say, Elwood?"

"Emma Peel all the fucking way," you say.

STONEY in the equipment room is silent, his breath snorkeling through his crushed nose. He's in the dark, off by himself, a beat-up Buddha. There is a damp smell in the air and a bandage over his damaged eye.

"Who's that?" he calls.

"Me," you say.

"El," he says. "How'd you like it?"

"What can I do?" you ask.

Stoney exhales through the mouth and stretches. "I hurt," he says.

"Let me get you something," you say.

"No way," he says.

"Not that," you say. "How about a tour of the Stop 'n' Pop. I'll buy you a French massage." A little logistics for the soul, get him tuned right back in.

"I'm gonna take a steam," Stoney says. "Think it through. Maybe I'm getting old, guy gets in on me like that. Couldn't get off tonight. It was like I was watching myself in a movie—he'd start to move, and I'd think, hit him, but by then I'd be taking the shot."

So outside himself he could not get back in. The language of the body failing, the mind trying to compensate.

"How bad you hurting?" you ask. You walk over and put

your hand on his shoulder. His shoulders and arms are knotted from the shots he's taken.

"Like death," he says. And that is what you want to know. What it is like to come so close. The inarguable position. At a certain point, reality becomes whatever you imagine it to be.

"So what's it gonna be?" Stoney asks.

"What?" you ask. "What's *what* gonna be?"

"CC didn't tell you?" Stoney asks.

"No," you say.

"I put some money on the fight down direct with Saad," Stoney says. "Some big numbers. He'll be coming for it."

"I'll cover it," you say.

Stoney drops his head and then looks up, breaking into a smile that you realize is an odd joy, and that's when you realize that being a Motherfucker all your life is lonely fucking work.

"I'll be talking to you," he says.

24

AT CC's, the mood is distinctly upbeat. It's dark when you enter, the neon Elvis equipment the only thing that's gleaming except for the movie up front on the projection screen.

"Movie night," Video calls to you. "Grab a table."

"We waited forever," CC says, "but we figured you weren't coming. Did you see this?"

He points, and you turn to your right. Next to Knoll is a wax mannequin of Elvis dressed in full BDUs—camouflage hat, web gear, carbine slung over his left shoulder.

"Hey, I didn't see you at the fight," you say to Knoll.

"I was over at Carol Ann's," Knoll says, a grin coming over his face.

"How's married life treating you?" you ask.

"Can't complain," Knoll says.

"That comes later," Rothfuss says.

"So you like?" CC asks. "The guy I got this off of said it was headed for Graceland, but he robbed it first. First person he thought of was me."

"Long live the King," you say.

"I still can't get over the detail on this fucker," CC says. "Any second I keep expecting him to move."

"So what's the movie about?" you ask.

"Some Jap fuck film," Video says.

"What's going on?"

"The Japs, I think they're fucking."

"I can see that. What's it got subtitles for?"

"I know, I hate them subtitle things," Eddio says. "I like to either—you either read or you watch a movie. You got to do both, that's a pain in the ass."

"We're rolling back the frontiers of cinema here," Video says. *Last Tango in Tokyo.*"

"This film was banned in 1976 from the New York Film Festival," CC says, his voice filling with pride. "I just got hold of the print."

"Even their fucking fuck films are better than ours," Video says.

"Now what's going on?" you ask.

"She's beating the shit out of him."

"What for?"

"So he knows she loves him."

"Jesus," Eddio says. "I woulda took her word for it."

"Here's the plot so far," Video says. "So far, he's fucked her straight, in the ass, in the mouth, come in the mouth, pissed in her, wait—they got married first, then he pisses in her, but then he fucked her again and all the other wives—"

"All those women, they were wives?" Sasquatch asks.

"That's right. The other wives, they gang up on this new wife, I don't know where the hell she came from—this thing has got major story continuity problems—and they fuck her with a celery stick or rutabaga or something and then they go fuck each other. That's why they were all laying there in a heap for a while."

"I wondered about that," Eddio says. "Must be great having more than one wife."

"I knew a guy had that," Rothfuss says. "It was out in Utah, you know the Mormons, they still got that shit going on."

"What was it like?" Eddio asks.

"You ever do two women at once?" Rothfuss asks, getting to the real purpose of his story, the duke of dick on tour. "I'm going along once, Atlantic City, the Boardwalk. I see this woman, she's staring at me, so I go over, figure, talk to her. We're talking, getting along, and suddenly we bump into this other girl, looks exactly like her—they're identical—and what's even better, they're cousins."

"Fucking Patty Duke Show," Video says.

"Patty loves her rock 'n' roll," Cabot sings. "You can lose your mind."

"Patty and Cathy, I woulda loved get those two in bed together," Eddio says. "If I didn't have my honey."

"They were the same person, you fucking moron," Video says.

"So we go back to their room, and I get into it with them, just balled me the fuck away, and then they start in on each other," Rothfuss says. "Greatest afternoon of my life."

"I told you, it would be great," Eddio says. "Imagine if you were married, that kinda shit going on all the time. I wish my honey had a sister or cousin or something."

"But no, getting back to that. The guy I knew, he was married," Rothfuss says. "He hated it. The wives, they get together, they end up, it's like they're in a union. He's got to work like a fucking slave support the whole brood. It's a bad deal you ask me. The thing is, in and out, just an afternoon and a memory, that's the way to go."

"Glad to hear you finally got laid in one of your stories," you say. "Every time I talk to you someone's pulling a knife or clubbing you or saying here's my fucking Hercules husband I'd like to introduce you."

"Geez, I'm having a bad run," Rothfuss says. "It's like I'm in a fucking slump."

"Get married," Knoll says. "Get it regular."

"No thank you, sir," Rothfuss says. "There's nothing that ruins a relationship faster than making it permanent. Right El?"

"Who the fuck knows," you say.

"What's she doing now?" Eddio asks, looking up at the screen.

"She's threatening cut off his dick."

"Ouch," Sasquatch says. He stands up and paces by the edge of the room. "Oh man, that's nasty shit."

"The guy, he says go ahead. She's got the knife right there, he says be my guest."

"Wouldn't be my first reaction."

"You know these Jap fuck films, they got more than their fair share of dicks in them," Video says. "Your average American fuck film keeps the dickwork down."

"Plus they're little dicks up there. Think the Japanese, they got littler dicks?" Rothfuss asks.

"Thing probably wore itself down," Video says. "All the fucking he's doing, thing *eroded*."

"Why doesn't she want him sleeping with his regular wife?"

"Says she's going to cut him up he does that."

"Oh man," Sasquatch says, squirming in place. "I know what the fuck that means. That is bad news. Bad news in the dick department."

"That's the thing—American movies, the guy's always got a dong bigger than the Squash here. They got, like, height requirement for dicks. This guy, what's he got? Makes you feel like you got a shot here."

"Let me tell you," Rothfuss says, "somebody pulls a blade on your dick, it's time to reassess the relationship."

"Probably one of those Ginsu things, too," Cabot says, "cuts what, eleven different ways?"

"How come I don't meet any nice girls like that?" you ask.

"That's 'cause you're banging the one-armed bandit," Rothfuss says.

And it happens this quick, without you even understanding it. You're on Rothfuss in a second, trying to get in a punch, driving into him. It's like there's another you, and he's going over backward in his chair with you around his neck.

It takes a moment for everyone to react and haul you off. You're in the midst of it, feeling a kind of freedom for a change, losing control as you swing away. When Knoll grabs you by the neck, one of your punches glances off Sasquatch's damaged dick and he lurches back, doubling over. Rothfuss's nose is bleeding. You wish it was from you, but you suspect it came from people pulling you apart.

"Son-of-a-bitch," Rothfuss says, bleeding into his handkerchief. "What the fuck is wrong with you?"

Just as suddenly, the anger goes out of you, like it was never there, a summer squall.

"Pinch your fucking nostrils and tilt your head back before you bleed to death," you say.

"You fucking lunatic," Rothfuss says. "I thought you were doin' her, get back at the Top. How was I s'posed to know?"

Just as suddenly, you move to hit him again, but everyone holds you back, jostling into the Squash, who lets out a large groan.

"Jesus Christ," Rothfuss says. "What the fuck is wrong with you. Get a grip, for Chrissakes."

A grip is something you sorely need, you figure.

"Oh man," Sasquatch says, looking down at his pants. "I think I busted a stitch."

"That's lousy American workmanship," Video says. "They should put a recall on that dick."

"Oh mother of Christ," Sasquatch says. But Sasquatch isn't referring to his damaged apparatus. The door has opened and a dozen black guys, a yam patrol, makes its way in, taking positions around the edges of the bar. Entering last, in his element, is Sgt. Saad, commander of the Saad Squad, who no doubt has come to collect on Stoney's bet and decided it was more convincing to bring along a few friends, help him carry the money back.

He walks over to your table, his shadow darkening the movie screen for a moment. "Elwood," he says.

Saad is followed by two large members of the Saad Squad. You see Kirchfield standing by the door. If it comes down to it, you wonder which side Kirchfield will land on. Then you realize this has already been decided. And Kirchfield, you think, has made the smart move.

"CC, this thing looks for real," Saad says, settling in next to you as he looks at Private Elvis.

"Just how he looked when he did his stint in Germany," CC says. "It's the pride of my collection."

Two yams go into the back and begin rummaging through CC's stuff. "Hey," CC says, "watch what the fuck you're doing." He walks into the back room.

Kirchfield and another one of the brethren take seats next to you, turning the chairs around so the backs face their chests.

"Good to see all these familiar faces," you say to Kirchfield.

"You said it, El. Go places faster don't switch lanes," Kirchfield says.

"Getting mighty close here," you say.

"Give the El some room," Saad says, waiting while Kirchfield pulls back his chair.

"Thanks," you say.

"We aim to please," Saad says. "Now let's talk. You and me ain't had a good talk in a while."

"What do we want to talk about?" you ask.

"That was some fight, you know," Saad says, "but that Darnell Moore, you can see that kid is going places."

"To Fort Bragg," you say. "Too bad about Stoney."

"Bad night for him," Saad says. One by one, you can see the folks you know—Rothfuss, Captain Video, Eddio, and the Squash—heading toward the door after receiving some meaningful looks from the yams in attendance. The only one hanging in is Knoll. Except for him, you have no friends. You are outnumbered, outgunned, and the current has turned against you.

"Go back to your Carol Ann," you say.

"I'm staying," he says, standing up, and it is clear he is ready to fight despite everything. You have underestimated Knoll, you think. He's got the heart of a Motherfucker even if he's lacking some of the essential skills.

"Let him stay," you say. "He's all right."

"In the back room." Saad motions, and two of the yams grab Knoll, get his arm behind his back, and pull him into the storeroom.

"I'm shy is all," Saad says.

"What is it you want?" you ask. From the back room, you hear a few grunts, and then silence. Knoll, despite his best intentions, is no match.

"And Stoney, he owes all that money, how's he gonna pay that off?"

"I'll back him," you say.

"Don't worry about it," Saad says. He pulls a piece of paper from his pocket, unfolds it, then dramatically rips it in half. "Stoney, he's even."

"I always like talking to you," you say. "Now what is it you want?"

"Investment advice," Saad says.

"On what?"

"On how much you think you're going to make on the shipment you got coming in?"

"It should tide me over."

Saad smiles at you, but Saad's smile, you understand, has never contained much mirth. "Do you know how much the security on that'll cost you?" Saad asks.

"I guess you're here, give me a price quote," you say.

"The thing I like about you, Elwood," Saad says, "is it don't take long for you to figure out the play."

"I'm a quick study," you say. "But maybe you ought to look at this."

The four yams who were in the back appear, led by CC. One of them is wearing a white Elvis concert cape, but looking bewildered. Knoll suddenly comes out, and he's holding an M-16 leveled on one of the men, just as you did for him. The difference is, however, the guys he's drawing down on won't back off.

Sgt. Saad is looking like you've never seen him. He's genuinely astonished—and, for the first time, frightened—that somebody of Knoll's evident Motherfucked nature could get the drop on his men. Holy shit, you think. But already you can see the move beginning. Saad stands up from his table while Kirchfield and two others fan out, begin flanking maneuvers on Knoll.

"Hey," you say, "this isn't what you're here for. Something happens, we all go down. There's money enough for all of us."

But nobody's paying any attention. "Get the hell out of here," Knoll's saying. "And don't come back." You want to tell him that he's just dropped into the wrong movie.

The first move is always a distraction. One of the guys throws a glass against the wall, and Knoll turns, leveling the M-16 at him. Knoll, in the end, might be good at paper targets but is not willing to squeeze off at the real ones, and the yam in the Elvis cape tackles him, brings him to the ground. When they get up, Knoll is bleeding from the mouth and his rifle is in someone else's hands. Kirchfield is holding a .45 pistol at Knoll's head.

"Jesus Christ," Saad says. "This is why I envy you, Elwood. You're getting out of this fucking Army. I'm a lifer. I got to put up with this shit rest of my life."

"Don't hurt him," you say.

"Fuck," Saad says. "Hurt him. Hurt what? Hand me that fucking thing." Kirchfield hands over the pistol.

Saad looks at the pistol, balancing it in his hands.

"Shame, you know. I don't know what the fuck gets into people. CC, what the fuck you let this happen for? This is your bar. What the fuck is this kind of artillery doing back there? Everything is out of hand."

CC, you see, is cringing by the front of the bar. Saad holds up the gun, points it at Knoll, then wheels and blows the wax Elvis away.

" 'Don't be cruel' is my motto," Saad says, "unless absolutely necessary." He turns to you. "Now, where were we?"

"We were just talking about your cut," you say.

"I don't get a cut," Saad says. "I'm your partner."

You have noticed how streamlined decision making becomes when you have no choice. "Okay," you say.

25

DAWN. Good morning, Mr. Phelps. You are driving with Garcia and Colonel Berman, out patrolling the perimeter of the nuclear base. You've pulled the switch of personnel, inserting the greenbeanie ringers for sentry duty and allowed them to modify the security arrangements, bring them up to code.

"Marshall, he's out there waiting for me, the fucker," Colonel Berman says. "I can feel it."

Garcia takes a left at slightly too high a speed, and the Colonel leans hard into your shoulder. Garcia is wearing night-vision goggles to drive, as is the Colonel, but you're riding blind, like being in the middle of an amusement park ride.

"What did they do to the trees around here?" Colonel Berman asks.

"Cut the branches," you say. "Sgt. Saperstein said it was too easy have them creeping up on us."

"How much did this cost?" Colonel Berman asks.

"Nothing," you say. "He shot 'em off."

"No shit?" Colonel Berman says, surprised. "Well, I'll be damned. I like his style."

Garcia takes another turn, again a little too fast, but that's the way these things are supposed to be played, not allowing you to become sniperbait.

"Pull over," Colonel Berman says.

"You see something?" you ask, pulling on your goggles.

"I got to relieve myself," the Colonel says.

Garcia pulls over and turns around. "I just want to say, Colonel," he says, "how much I appreciate this opportunity."

"You're doing a fine job, son," Colonel Berman says, clambering out the back. "Maybe when this thing is over, I'll make you my regular driver."

"It would be an honor, sir," Garcia says.

You watch the Colonel go off into the bushes.

"Fucking guy," Garcia says. "Stopping to take a leak."

"He's got a nervous bladder," you say. "These simulated battles get him shook up."

"When's this thing supposed to start?" Garcia asks. He picks up his M-16 with a MILES protector attached to the barrel. It shoots out a laser beam that strikes the enemy on either a head detector or a chest detector, which you and Garcia and the Colonel are wearing. If struck, you will begin to emit a beeping signal that can be turned off only by taking the key from your MILES M-16 rifle and plugging it into your chest protector, thus rendering your rifle inoperable and you KIA.

The Colonel comes walking back, zipping his pants, and climbs into the backseat. The light has changed to gray, and the darkness of the world is being lifted.

"I don't think he's coming for us tonight, Elwood," Colonel Berman says. "I think he took one look at our security arrangements, decided to stay the fuck away. With the new troops and all that television equipment we hooked up, we got him by the fucking balls."

"I don't know," you say. "Marshall, he's gung ho. He may be laying for us somehow."

"I don't see any sign of it," Colonel Berman says. "We've been all over the area. We've got our own patrols out, we've got men in the trees, and we've got some of your guys dug into the ground. Let's get back to the depot. I want to give my wife a call, tell her how things went. She's waiting up. She had a bad feeling about this whole thing."

"We should wait till dawn," you say.

"Garcia, turn around," Colonel Berman says in his most authoritative voice. His hands have begun to roam. "By the time we get back to the gate, it'll be daylight. I tell you, I have Marshall's number. He figures let us wait up all night, get our shift exhausted, he hits us the next night or the night after. He wants to wait till we're worn down, used up all our supplies, had a few false alerts."

Colonel Marshall's preoccupations do not generally fit into the supply end of the Army, you understand. Colonel Marshall, for all his name-dropping and posturing, is a throwback, a cowboy, an infantry Motherfucker. When the attack comes, whenever and wherever it will be, he will be in the thick of the operation. At one party he compared himself to Alexander, who always charged directly into the most dangerous part of the enemy line.

By now you are tooling through the small access road that cuts through the forest.

"I'd like you to give me a minute," Garcia says to Colonel Berman.

"Garcia," you say warningly.

"What is it, son?" Colonel Berman says.

"I don't want to bother you, sir, but I'd like to say that my real ambition is to drive a tank for the Seventh Cavalry. Elwood here has tried to put it through, but each time it's been turned down."

"Well, I can't see why not," Colonel Berman says. "I still have some friends at Fort Hood, perhaps I could help you out."

"Thank you, sir," Garcia says.

"Elwood," Colonel Berman says, "you should bring these things to my attention. I think an enlisted man should be allowed to get into the midst of fighting if he wants."

"Yes sir," you say. Privately, you think you ought to kill Garcia. But the fact remains there are so many others waiting in line.

You round the turn. The woods are pretty in the dawn, the cold from the night still hanging in the air. You turn up the road for the entrance gate, and two trucks fall in behind you.

"Who're they?" you ask.

Colonel Berman turns around and stares at them. "They're ours," he says. "I decided to have fresh coffee and donuts brought in, eggs, flapjacks, hash browns. There's nothing too good for my men. Also, I thought the General would be here, see how the action went."

You come up to the gate, and Lt. Meyer, manning the gate himself, is of course in the wrong spot. He waves you in, and you take a right toward the HQ building and park. One of the supply trucks is stuck by the gate, and then you hear the sound of MILES rifle fire, the light pop-pop-pop. Lt. Meyer is hit, and so are the greenbeanies at the gate. But down the road you hear the worst sound of all. It is the sound of M-1 tanks tooling down the road at fifty miles per. They are moving, and the supply truck in the gate is holding it open for them. The other supply truck pulls directly behind you. Out jumps Colonel Marshall in cammies. He has his M-16 MILES trained on you and shoots you and Colonel Berman. The din of your MILES chest protectors begins sounding in the dawn as the M-1 tanks rumble through the gate and begin blasting their MILES beams at the greenbeanies in the towers.

Colonel Marshall comes up to you and Colonel Berman, a big smile on his camouflage-painted face. "Bang," he says, "you're dead."

AFTER YOU and Colonel Berman go KIA, the battle doesn't last very long. Because nobody at the nuclear base thought the enemy might come with tanks, there are no simulated TOWs available and so the tanks pick off the guard posts one by one, at their leisure. The reinforcements that arrive from the 57th are equipped to go up against light infantry, not tanks, and they too are easily slaughtered. The dead unplug their m-16s and put the keys into their chest protectors, and then walk off to stand in line.

"Son-of-a-*bitch*," Colonel Berman says. "Jesus H. fucking Christ."

You have stayed with him as he watched the battle unfold, the entire base being taken apart inside half an hour. The nuclear bunkers are overrun, their electronic codes bypassed by Marshall's technicians. The battle has been a rout.

"Let's go," Colonel Berman says. He walks in front of you to the casualty registration center, then turns, clearly bewildered. "Are we in the right place?"

You look to one of the greenbeanie ringers. "Is this the line for the dead?" you ask.

"Huh?" the sergeant says, but then seeing Colonel Berman's insignia, straightens up automatically. "Oh no, sir. I mean, we're already dead here. This is for transportation back to the base. Casualty registration is on the other side." You turn and walk with Colonel Berman. You see the line for the dead backed up and winding around the building. "It's pretty crowded," you say, which makes Colonel Berman wince. "How about I get you a cup of coffee?"

Colonel Berman, however, is alert and looking at the main gate again. The lines of his face have come together in a point, and he looks like he has just recognized his own firing squad. "General Lancaster just pulled in," he says. "I'd better go see him first." The Colonel suddenly seems old to you, a relative who is surprised to find himself ancient and down on his luck.

He takes a step away, and then turns back. "You could do me a favor," he says.

"Anything, sir," you say.

"Call my wife," he says. "She'll want to know."

There is nothing you dread more. The Mrs. Colonel holds grudges against the bearers of bad tidings. "Sure thing, sir," you say.

The Colonel walks slowly toward General Lancaster, who is standing and laughing with Colonel Marshall, now that the battle has been declared over by the umpires.

You go in the side door of HQ and use one of the phone lines. "Mrs. Berman?" you say.

"Yes," she says. "Who is this?"

"It's Elwood," you say.

"Did he get killed again?" the Mrs. Colonel asks.

"Worse," you say.

"How bad?" she asks, and you have to admire the Mrs. Colonel for that. There's steel in her.

"The base got overrun."

There is a pause while the Mrs. Colonel thinks through the possibilities.

"How long did it take?"

"The official time was something like twenty-eight minutes," you say.

"Jesus!" Another pause. "What kind of casualties did we take?"

"Somewhere around ninety percent. They're still registering people, but they got everybody inside the defense perimeter."

You hear a long sigh, and you realize the Mrs. Colonel, the tireless career warrior, is edging toward despair. "What kind of casualties did we inflict?"

"I don't think we got any," you say.

"None!" she shouts, your ear ringing from the tinny sound. "What kind of fucking battle was this!"

"A bad one, ma'am," you say. "Marshall served us up in love sets."

"You stupid fucker!" she shouts into the phone. "It's your fucking fault, Elwood."

"Probably," you say, then you hear a commotion and you hang up the phone.

Outside, Marshall's men are on the move and one of the M-1 tanks is wheeling around, heading straight toward the entrance gate. An umpire is waving. "You're dead! You're dead!" he shouts, but at the last minute he understands the tank isn't going to stop and bails out. It is Garcia, you realize, who has commandeered the tank, now tooling down the road into the sunrise.

You turn around and walk back to the HQ building, where you come upon Colonel Berman sitting by himself. He's gasping for air, and you are worried that he's choking on something. His face is red, and it's clear he's been crying.

"Sir, can I get you anything?"

The Colonel mops his face with his handkerchief. "A new command," he says.

You stand stiffly, unsure whether to sit down next to him or to leave him be. You had never considered him human before.

"You know what being killed this time means?" the Colonel asks.

"I think so, sir," you say.

He gives a short laugh. "When I was at the Academy, President Kennedy came by to give the graduation address. You know, in the pictures you can't really see it, but up close, in person, he just had this kind of heartbreaking charisma. . . . *Incompetent*—that's what he called me. I hoped never to hear that word in reference to me. *Incompetent.* That's what I am, too. He's right. He's so fucking right."

"The General said that, sir?" you ask. "He's going to include this in the OERs?"

"It's not just that. It's the other stuff—the McCovey incident, the race fights. There's been some sort of investigation going on."

"What?" you say.

"They've been after me," Colonel Berman says. "As of this minute, the General is relieving me of my command. Marshall said his executive officer could take over."

"I'm sorry for that, sir. You were the best commanding officer I've ever had." Oddly enough, you mean this. You wish you could offer the Colonel a little something to take the edge off, but you fear the gesture would be misinterpreted.

"You know, I graduated second in my class. Robert E. Lee graduated second. Salutatorian. I shook the President's hand. I felt his strength and I thought I could do anything I set my mind to. But I couldn't. Can't. I thought I'd be running my own show by now. One of the guys I graduated with is a major general. Another one commands the forces in Korea. Me, I'm incompetent. I'm getting the hell out."

"Maybe you should think it over, sir. Perhaps the General will change his mind."

Colonel Berman shakes his head. "Here's the ironic thing, Elwood."

"What's that, sir?"

"I'm getting out of the Army before you do. That's a kick, ain't it."

Just when you were feeling kindly toward the Colonel, he goes and spoils it. "I'll see you back at the base, sir," you say.

As you get in line to register for the dead, you think you have much to do before you sleep.

26

THE DISPENSARY has been tricked out by Simmons and Cabot to accommodate the massive cooking session. You've never cooked this much before, and the problem with cooking scag is that it is a little like preparing Thanksgiving dinner when one of the ingredients is a grenade.

"Ventilators working?" you ask Cabot, who is plugging one of the electrical extension cords into an outlet.

"We're okay," he says. This is a smelly business, and if the place isn't ventilated properly it can finish off the individuals doing the cooking. Naturally you cannot simply blow the shit out the window, where its natural and distinctive smell would be noticed by all who are left on the base. Drug dogs for miles around would pick up the scent. This is why the dispensary is perfect. The hood ventilators take the air to a filter that captures the poisons, makes the air palatable.

Knoll walks in with Robyn, bringing the last of the groceries. "Got it?" you ask, and he nods, laboring under the burden.

"What's she doing here?" Simmons asks. Already, you see, Simmons is fucked up, which is bad news as far as the weekend is concerned. If he gets too fucked up and falls asleep, he could blow up the stash and himself, and that would be the end of your career plans.

"Don't be an asshole," you say, putting Simmons in his rightful spot.

After your KIA was processed, you stopped at the PX with Robyn and loaded up on supplies. When cooking, it is absolutely essential to keep everybody's belly full. Full as in pop the belt two notches full. To that end you've stocked the icebox in your quarters with cold cuts, sausages, cheese, and bread and plenty of milk and ice cream. You've also brought out dinners for everybody on the cooking detail. On a good cooking weekend you might gain five to ten pounds, just from the quantity of food you consume. Otherwise, if your stomach is not kept full and coated, the scag can get into your system and fuck you up worse.

What this is all about is understanding the laws of cause and effect. These laws dictate that something as lucrative as cooking will present unforeseen and complex problems, so it is best to take care of the obvious before they come up. The most obvious problem is how not to get killed.

"So how does it look?" Cabot asks. You walk around the basement, and from the look of things Simmons and Cabot have set you up well. Your inventory in the laboratory consists of the balloon flasks, the glass tubing, Bunsen burners connected to gas lines, suction pumps, recalibrated scales, and thermometers.

"Just like old times," Cabot says.

"Just like," you say. You are keeping your eye on Simmons, who is looking a little pasty. You are thinking that he has had too much of the right stuff to make it through the weekend, and you are glad you brought Knoll in on this. It is Knoll's job to keep a lid on Simmons, make sure he's flying right, doesn't nod off in the middle. Knoll is a true buddy, and truth anywhere is hard to find.

"Is he going to be all right?" you ask.

"He'll be okay," Cabot says. "He's been cutting back on product."

"You know what to do," you say to Knoll, who has been briefed in advance.

"Doing fine," Simmons says, the words coming out slow and a little slurred, not the kind of response that provides reassurance.

"You don't look on top of your game here," you say, but Simmons has wandered off to the other end of the room to check again on the ventilators.

"I don't want him using while this is going on," you say to Cabot and Knoll. "No one uses."

"No sweat," Cabot says.

You decide to let this one go. If you start a war before you even get into cooking it'll sap your energy and you'll be the one off his game. At any rate, Knoll is the built-in safety factor that should prevent misfortune.

Cabot and Simmons are officially on duty at the dispensary, so you shouldn't be interrupted. There's an officer in charge, but he hibernates with his family for the weekend and relies on Cabot and Simmons to give him a call should anything unusual happen. The only unusual situation you can predict is that you stand to make a lot of money, enough to stay in the black for the rest of your life. Sgt. Saad is providing security for his cut, making doubly sure that no one interferes. This is not such a bad thing in the end. With the Saad Squad providing backup, no one will fuck with you, and there is still plenty of loot to go around.

You begin walking Robyn around to show her how to keep things in order. The ventilators are the first stop, and you turn each one on, listening to the steady hum that will keep the air clear. That will work for only a few hours at most, anyhow; sooner or later, the system gets overloaded with the shit. They're most important at the end of the weekend, when you have to allow enough time for the air to clear. Cooking too much can kill you—this much you know. For a while you were cooking ten keys of base a month, and for three or four days afterward you had to keep snorting decreasing quantities of scag in order to dial yourself down and not go into heavy-duty withdrawal. You still experienced cramps, sweats, chills—the works. Going into withdrawal is to be avoided at all costs. Keeping your stomach topped off and rotating you and Robyn with Simmons and Cabot and Knoll, you should be able to keep this party from blowing itself up.

Cooking, as you learned from Sgt. Keane, your rabbi in the drug industry, is not in itself a difficult task. In fact, many people do it with varying degrees of success, and the tricky part has nothing to do with the chemicals used or complex processes. No, the difficulty in cooking has to do with surviving the process. To lose control here is to lose your life.

"Are we ready?" you ask, and everyone gathers around.

First, you take out the morphine base and weigh it on your scale. It's important to do this in order to calculate exactly how much you can slough off the top. From a ten-key batch, you're looking at a key and a half cream. Free and clear. This is what you bank.

You put on your apron, your doctor's mask, and your gloves, helping Robyn and Knoll on with theirs. These are all essential. If you get fucked up and nod out, you might die pleasantly, but you will most certainly make a noise.

The first and most treacherous step is acetylation. To do this, you mix one part morphine base with two parts acetic anhydride, which is the pure form of acetic acid. Purity is the watchword in all endeavors of this nature. As you open the acetic anhydride, the smell hits you. It is like dipping your face in vinegar and inhaling through your nostrils, but vinegar is only 6 percent acetic acid; this is 100. You steady yourself for a few moments and finally your nose, burned out already, adjusts.

You take the balloon flasks and mix in two keys of morphine with four keys of acetic anhydride. Each flask is a spherical ball of glass with a short stubby neck. You top it with serpentine glass tubing so that the vapors can be condensed rather than dissipated, much the same as alcohol is distilled for whiskey. You could make whiskey just as easily, but the profit margin would be considerably less.

Then you start the double-boiling. You immerse the balloon flasks in metal garbage cans filled with water and then light the Bunsen burners underneath them. Each stoppered flask contains the tubing and the thermometer.

"How's it going?" Robyn asks. She strokes your shoulder with her only hand. Knoll is standing there, attentive.

"This is the tricky bit," you say. "You got to keep this as close as possible to eighty-five degrees centigrade."

"What if you don't?" she asks, always looking for the fuck-up, a woman after your own heart.

"You've got a five-degree leeway on either side," you say. "We go below eighty, the reaction stops; we go over ninety, the morphine is destroyed."

You consult your watch. "Mark it now," you say. "This goes on for six hours."

You tell her and Knoll of the further problem, which is why you are worried about Simmons. If whoever is watching the reaction gets fucked up from the considerable contact high and the temperature rises enough until the mixture boils, it will explode with impressive force, killing you and whoever else happens to be in the room. This requires close attention, which is difficult to do on the nod. The wild card, however, you don't tell her about, because there is essentially nothing you can do about it. The wild card is that the parameters are unpredictable. The initial mixture of the morphine base, which contains impurities from the long trail it has followed, can change its boiling point. But in this, as in war, there are agreeable risks and acceptable casualties.

"WE'RE GOING TO get some rest," you say to Simmons and Cabot. "Just fucking be careful, all right?"

"Don't worry about it," Cabot says.

"All I do is worry," you say. "You and Simmons, you stay together."

"I'll keep an eye on things," Knoll says.

"Robyn and me'll be back for the second shift," you say.

You've learned from experience to keep the personnel rotating, not let anyone get tired. Simmons is such a liability, however, he cannot be put on by himself. Right now, however, you are exhausted from being killed so early in the morning and what you want to do is take Robyn home and climb into bed and heal up, prepare for the rest of your life together.

"What are you thinking?" she asks as you walk out the door past two of Saad's hoodlums.

"I'm thinking I hope that bastard doesn't fix. If he does, we'll be fuck out of luck. What are you thinking?"

"I'm thinking," she says, "about how nice it would be to take a swim."

IN THE DARKNESS she could be nobody else. She is standing at the edge of the ten-meter platform, silhouetted against the water. No claw on now. From up here, the water is a deeper blue than you could have anticipated, the blue of dreams, of movies, of thick parts of sky.

"Come here," she says, and she's in control here.

"You're kidding me," you say. You pull on your cigarette and with the other hand grasp the chrome bars.

"I won't push you," she says.

"No way," you say.

But somehow a minute later you are standing at the edge of the platform. The water seems small, the diving pool impossibly tiny.

She takes your hand. "Just step off," she says.

"No fucking way," you say.

"Are you scared?"

"You bet." You're afraid she's going to pull you off.

"Sit down then," she says, as if she can read your discomfort. "Get used to it."

You take her advice and sit on the hard stubble of the platform. She doesn't sit down yet, remaining standing.

"It doesn't seem different up here to you?" she asks.

"Higher," you say. You would need something twice the size of the regular pool to even think about jumping.

"What would it take to make you jump?" she asks.

"A parachute," you say. Then you think that isn't enough. "How about a medical team in Wiesbaden on full alert. Maybe you get used to it after a while."

"No," she says. "That's the point of it, really. Not to get used to it." She sits down across from you, stretching her feet so they touch yours.

From up here it feels as if you are always on the verge of being discovered, someone finding you. The pool is closed, of course, but as with so many other things, you have a key.

"When I was on the swim team we used to play a game

called shark," Robyn says. "Someone sat in the water, everyone else got in a line and dove off the three-meter— we didn't have a platform like this, just a three-meter, and two one-meters. As each person got tagged, they had to help the one who tagged him. I was the last one, everyone else was sitting there, waiting for me. There was no way out."

You nod and dig your toes into hers.

"But then I jumped off the three-meter onto the one-meter, and then bounced back up. It was dangerous, but I knew I could do it this one time, just get away with it this once. And I did. Some things feel right."

"It sounds like falling in love," you say.

"Don't be afraid," she says, as if just like that, you could be cured. She leans forward and kisses you on the lips. She stands up and pulls off her suit, strips it down to her waist and steps out of it. The cheeks of her ass wiggle as she places her feet on the platform. And then quietly as could be, she steps off the platform into the air and disappears.

You hold your breath as she goes down, counting the seconds—one, two, three, before the splash, and there she is, bobbing on the surface, foam spewing beneath her.

You drop your cigarette first, which traces arcs and litters bright ash as it tumbles. Shit, you notice, it lands right in the gutter, not having those good human aerodynamics. Forget taking off the fucking suit. You need all the protection you can get, you think. And then you step off.

You go feetfirst, plunging through space—your body leaning slightly forward, just out of control, the wind pushing against your chest—afraid you'll tip forward and land flat. It is both terrifying and relaxing, flying through a dream. It is, you think, what the Parson must have felt, a moment of pure joy.

You hit the surface hard, the water opening to swallow you, taking your breath, pain stinging your legs and chest.

Once you're under, you forget for a moment to swim. You are simply too caught up in being alive, in having survived, crossing through the boundary of fear and coming through to the eerie underlighting of the water. The tightness in your lungs causes you to stroke to the surface.

"Here I am," Robyn says. You lean your elbows on the corner of the pool, locking your feet on the ladder, and kiss, coming close, her body rubbery against yours. You're dialed in here: into the moment. Everything, you have learned, is real, it's just too painful to keep remembering most times. You push against her, your cock coming alive on its own.

You stack blankets and make love on the stretcher on the side of the pool, no chemical assistance, no strangeness. The two of you are traveling to some remote place, a place you have heard about but never visited, meshing not like gears but like human beings, and words you've never uttered are hot inside, rising to the surface.

27

YOU WAKE UP next to Robyn, who is lying in your bed, asleep and exhausted. The barracks have that creaking sound they have just before daybreak. You are late, you know, for your shift, and soon Knoll will be coming by to get you.

You look at Robyn and lean in close, breathe her smell. She lies facing away, her tapered arm tucked under the covers, hidden even in sleep. After this long time, you feel the hunger within you has disappeared. It was there one minute, gone the next. You realize, with the flash of an MPC, that you are, quite suddenly, happy. It is a strange feeling, like being granted grace, or being told you were going to live forever. Karma filled to the brim. You kiss her on the neck. You could get used to this, you think. Welcome to the human race.

You hear the outside door open and someone come in. You hear steps coming down the clean floor, and then you hear the metal tittering of lockers as Knoll runs his hand along them. The footsteps stop at your door and there's a knock.

"Who is it?" you call.

"Knoll," you hear. "Come on, I got to get back."

"Just a second, man," you say. You get up, open the door, and there is Knoll.

"How's it going?" you ask.

Knoll looks back, past the doorway, and says in a voice that has somehow changed, "Yeah, she's here."

Sgt. Lee appears in the doorway, and you realize you have made a terrible mistake.

"Hi," you say, and the Top punches you in the face.

You stagger back and smash into the bed, waking Robyn. The Top picks you up and hits you again, this time in the ear. A ringing starts in your head, a schoolbell being rung. The Top kicks you in the back of the knee and then drives an elbow straight into your nose. You feel it collapse, and colors explode before your eyes. He keeps hitting you, one shot following another, each one straight into the body, stomach, ribs. Kill the body and the head dies. You attempt to defend yourself, trying to use some of the people skills Stoney has, but you've got nothing and finally you simply cower on the ground, curled up, waiting for the end. You think of the Smith Model #5, gone back into hiding in the banister upstairs, no help to you now. The Top means, you understand, to beat you to death. This comes to you in yet another MPC, hovering on the brink.

The assault stops. Robyn, by this time, is pulling at the Top, getting him off of you. You stagger to the bed and collapse, bleeding from several wounds. Robyn is screaming at her father, and Knoll grabs her.

"Take her outside, sir," the Top says, and it is right then you realize how truly fucked you are.

Robyn's screams and your breathing are breaking the morning quiet. You hope somebody might be coming along, help you out soon, because right now you're not going to make it on your own.

The Top sits down across from you on the sofa bed. "Wanted to have a word with you, Elwood."

"What are you going to do about Robyn?" you ask.

"Don't worry about her," he says. You open your eyes

and look at the Top. He suddenly looks like a defeated man, like any father who has lost his daughter and finally knows it. And at this moment you realize she's yours and that she is something you want. It comes to you, just like that. She is your hope, and it is the hope, you know, that has finished you.

"Okay, let's talk," you say. "Give me a hand, will you." You stagger up, nearly falling into the Top's arms. He supports you under the shoulders out to the bathroom, where you notice there are personnel watching. He helps you all the way to the stalls. You heave twice: the first coming up dry, the second starts the ball rolling. It comes up in chunks, a parade in reverse. First liquids, then vile chunks of the stuff you've been packing in during the cooking process. Each time, you hunch your shoulders and heave and the noise is horrible. When you're done you wipe your face with toilet paper and then go to the sink to rinse your mouth out.

"Feel better?" he asks.

"No," you say.

"That's the ticket," he says. "Come on, let's just talk private. Get to know each other better."

He walks you back to your quarters. Along the way you become aware that a number of people have gathered for the final show. Walters is standing there by your doorway.

"Good to see you, Elwood," Walters says as the Top leads you inside the room, closing the door. Walters, like everyone else, is here for payback. Payback *is* a Motherfucker, and you are about to have your number retired, become a permanent member of the Motherfucked, the thing you've been waiting for all along.

You and the Top sit across from each other. You are fairly certain that, barring outside intervention relatively soon, you are dead meat.

"You know what the difference between you and me is?" Sgt. Lee asks.

You don't respond.

"I work inside the company, you work outside. But the job, it's really the same."

Blood is collecting in your mouth and you have to keep swallowing. "What about Knoll?" you ask.

"PFC Knoll," Sgt. Lee says. "Our officer in the hole. The fucking guy's a second lieutenant, just out of the Inspector General's office. Someone as stupid as you, Elwood, deserves to go down. We got fucking everybody.

"I started out, this was just a fucking job. I been on to you from the beginning. It actually surprised me, how stupid you fucking people are. I even argued with Lancaster against coming, figured you'd look at my 201, know I was hard-core infantry, what the fuck would I be doing in this chickenshit outfit? But Lancaster wanted Berman investigated—the Kimbrough thing, he must've known about that. Turns out Berman's just stupid, doesn't know a fucking thing."

"Look, Top," you say.

"You look and then you listen and then maybe you learn something," Sgt. Lee says. "Want to hear the secret of Vietnam?"

"What's that?" you say, clearing your throat. You were so close, you think. You were ready to pack up and leave, go back to the world, take your money and live off the fat forever and ever and forget Germany, forget this place, forget that this world ever existed.

"The secret of Vietnam's simple. I loved it. Everyone else would too if we'd won. But I remember what it was like. I'm honest with myself. I fucking well loved it."

"I believe you," you say.

"Some people say it was unjust. Never saw a more just

thing on earth. You sucked—you ended up a KIA. You were good—you had a chance. Ain't nothing more just than that. It's about the best odds the world gives."

"Why are you telling me all this?" you ask.

"Who else?" the Top asks, and then you realize that there's no tuning him. He's simply enjoying himself, giving you a preview of the morning agenda. There's a pause as you study the dried-out body, the hairy hands.

"So you been putting it to my daughter and you think that's making war?" The Top snorts, looking closely at you and then into the distance again. "War, you dumb fuck, is playing for keeps."

"It's not like that," you say, and for once in your life you're trying to be honest. "I mean, it was like that in the beginning, but not now." How to explain this. The conversion process from morphine base to scag allows you to come out ahead, and so, you realize, does the conversion process of love. But how to explain. Who to tell. Who would believe.

The Top stares at you, but his eyes are far away. "Let me tell you something, Elwood. You see her different from what I see. You see some broad, she's all fucked up, maybe you like to have some fun with her, get back at me. You fucking snake."

"You got it wrong, Top," you say.

"When the thing happened—her arm—we got over it. And we'll get over you."

The Top's lips are pale and rubbery. You've been out of your league all along, playing by a set of rules nobody else was using.

He turns his head toward the window. "Ah, here we go. Listen."

You hear automatic fire and you realize Saad's troops are under assault at the dispensary.

"We're taking down your whole operation," Sgt. Lee says.

A part of you starts to be relieved, begins working the next angle, figuring the next play. Sgt. Lee isn't going to kill you, you think. It's all fucking legit. You may end up in jail the rest of your life, but it's better than the alternative.

You cough, and as you cough, you see bright spots in front of your eyes. "So, go ahead, take me in," you say. "Only thing is, I want a regular lawyer, no Army assholes."

The Top has something to tell you, you know, some final grace note. You are in pain, but it is odd how objective you feel, like it is happening to somebody else. Movie night at the 57th, where you're the audience. The one advantage of being an audience, we know, is that they always come out alive.

Sgt. Lee smiles. "When I was in Vietnam, my second tour six months in I got this new second lieutenant, Cransdorf, fresh off the Point. First week in country he tries to report me to the colonel for Honor Code violations. Well, he finds out that shit don't float and so he puts me up for night guard and hopes I pay someone off so he can catch me and bust me down with an Article 15. By now I'm doing all sorts of shit, everything you're doing and more, but this guy was too dumb to see that, picks the one thing I can't fuck up. I'm too broke from drinking and drugging to pay off somebody take my guard duty, so I decide take the shift my ownself. I'm out there and I hear some thrashing around, and I call out, 'Halt, who goes there?' but nothing. There's more crashing and I figure it is either the F Troop version of the VC or our beardless leader. So I call out again, ask for the password, still don't hear shit. Finally, I figure, fuck it, and I lay down a clip. After that, it was pretty damn well quiet. By that time the whole camp is up and they send out a patrol and who's it on the ground but our new second looey. They found him out of uniform. No face. Blew his face clean off whatever your face is stuck to."

"You did the Parson, didn't you?" you ask, realizing for the first time that it is both Possibility Number One and Number Two, the answer in front of you all along. Sgt. Lee who had walked down that corridor and Sgt. Lee being the only one who walked back.

"That is affirmative, troop." Sgt. Lee says, his eyes clear with the recollection. "And the thing about killing is it's everything you expect it to be."

"So where are we now?" you ask.

"Killing's easy when somebody gives you a reason," the Top says. "Elwood." He begins laughing. "You are one dumb fucking GI."

There is no escape, you know. It is that simple. You've got to play your only card.

"I love her, you know," you say.

"So do I," the Top says, looking down at his hands and then up at you again. "I thought what I'd do, release you into the custody of Walters." You see the Top's face change for a moment, suddenly become tight and hard, and he swings a punch straight from the shoulder right into your jaw. And then you black out.

When you wake up you're on the floor. It's dusty, and you're surrounded by yams. The familiar third floor. Walters leans into you. The game is over.

"Hoist him up," Walters says.

Two of the yams pick you up and hold you under the shoulders. You feel like your insides have been ripped apart, and you keep swallowing blood from your broken nose.

"I think you know everybody," Walters says, "and they all sure know you, Elwood. Now, put him in."

Another yam grabs you by the feet and they swing you into a metal locker. You realize what they're about to do, and you struggle, trying to get out, but you don't have enough strength and they handle you like a child, closing the door on you.

For a moment you are in darkness, the darkness of your dreams, of the ovens of Dachau, of entrances with no exits. They pick up the locker and carry you toward the window. You bounce around inside, coathooks stabbing your back, the metal closing in like a coffin. You smell sweat and old fatigues and worn leather.

"Son-of-a-bitch," you hear one of them say. "We coulda put the locker a little closer to the window."

You can barely see through the air vent, and just as they put you down by the window you hear an explosion. The scag in the dispensary, you think. And then there are other explosions, the scag setting off other chemicals, blowing whatever's there. The door to the third-floor room crashes open, and through your vent you can make out Stoney. He has a mop, and his first move is to jab Walters in the face, flattening him as the other yams come forward to take him on.

"Get him out! Throw him!" you hear Walters shouting through his crushed mouth, and you feel yourself being lifted, borne high, the blaze of light coming through your vent, and then you are on the edge of the windowsill, balanced on the edge. You feel yourself tipping toward the open window, and your head bangs against the top of the locker. You feel the metal beginning to give. There is screaming and suddenly you recognize your own voice, echoing in the darkness. You pick up speed, the hard wood of the windowsill gliding underneath you, and then you are in free fall, moving toward the ultimate MPC. You begin to fantasize that you are back on the roof, in the clear air, heating up a spoonful of scag for yourself. You tie off, raise the vein, double pump it in, and feel the world outside smooth into a final serenity. Your head is banging against the locker as you fly end over end, barrel riding over the falls, moving toward a new edge, a new dream.

As you are falling, in that great long instant, we know that you have learned. Here is what you have learned:

You have learned that for the Army, peace is a continuation of war by other means.

You have learned that love is the key, but that having the key is not enough.

You have learned that death is a constant, but that at any time the constant may be renegotiated by introducing it, in its most moral and liquid form, into the various channels of your bloodstream.

And you have learned that some things cannot be negotiated, and as the wind sings its mournful tune, you hope, hope, hope.